PENGUI

The LAST DANCE

Fiona McIntosh is an internationally bestselling author of books for adults and children. She co-founded an award-winning travel magazine with her husband, which they ran for fifteen years while raising their twin sons before she became a full-time author. Fiona roams the world researching and drawing inspiration for her novels, and runs a series of highly respected fiction masterclasses. She calls South Australia home.

fionamcintosh.com

PRAISE FOR FIONA McINTOSH'S BESTSELLERS

'A blockbuster of a book that you won't want to put down.'
BRYCE COURTENAY

'McIntosh's narrative races across oceans and dances through ballrooms.'
SUN HERALD

'A big, sprawling saga . . . sure to appeal to Bryce Courtenay fans.'
AUSTRALIAN WOMEN'S WEEKLY

'This poignant, romantic read also packs a surprising hit of action.'
INSTYLE

'Spellbinding. . . [Stella is] reminiscent of our favourite literary heroines of the era, only feistier, sexier and more independent.'
BETTER READING

'A fine read . . . The moral ambiguity McIntosh builds into the novel gives it a depth that takes it beyond a sweeping wartime romantic thriller.'
SUNDAY HERALD SUN

'A captivating saga of love, loss, and the triumph of the human spirit . . . McIntosh is an extraordinary storyteller.'
BOOK'D OUT

'A perfect blend of romance, action, mystery and intrigue.'
NOOSA TODAY

'Sure to appeal to lovers of period romantic dramas like *Downton Abbey*.'
WOMAN'S DAY

'This book is fast-paced, beautifully haunting and filled with the excruciating pain of war.'

WEST AUSTRALIAN

'Written with zest and a talent for description that draws you into the world of the novel and its characters.'

THE AGE

'Everything I want in a curl-up-on-the-sofa read . . . an exquisite story that just bursts from the pages and leaps into your heart.'

WRITE NOTE REVIEWS

'A book for readers who enjoy a fairytale romance.'

BOOKS+PUBLISHING

'Dreamily romantic and historically fascinating, this is McIntosh at her best.'

BRISBANE NEWS

'An epic story . . . sensitive, poetically powerful and as gentle as the breath from a fluttering of wings.'

AUSTRALIAN WOMEN ONLINE

'*The Perfumer's Secret* is a romance for the senses. In her signature style, McIntosh weaves together history and fiction, transporting us to wartime France with her vivid descriptions of the scents that shape her heroine's life, for better or for worse.'

BETTER READING

'McIntosh writes a beautiful, engaging and vivid story about women finding strength through difficult times.'

GOOD READS

OTHER BOOKS BY FIONA McINTOSH

AVAILABLE FROM PENGUIN RANDOM HOUSE

Fields of Gold
The Lavender Keeper
The French Promise
Nightingale
The Tailor's Girl
The Last Dance
The Perfumer's Secret
The Chocolate Tin
The Tea Gardens
The Pearl Thief

In the DCI Jack Hawksworth series:
Bye Bye Baby
Beautiful Death

FIONA McINTOSH

The LAST DANCE

PENGUIN BOOKS

PENGUIN BOOKS

UK | USA | Canada | Ireland | Australia
India | New Zealand | South Africa | China

Penguin Books is part of the Penguin Random House group of companies
whose addresses can be found at global.penguinrandomhouse.com.

First published by Penguin Group (Australia), 2015
This edition published by Penguin Group (Australia), 2016

Cover design by Laura Thomas © Penguin Group (Australia)
Text design by Samantha Jayaweera © Penguin Group (Australia)
Cover photographs: woman © Eve North/Trevillion Images, background image: Alamy, dress: Eduardo Jose Bernadino/Getty Images
Typeset in Sabon by Samantha Jayaweera, (Penguin Group Australia)
Colour separation by Splitting Image Colour Studio, Clayton, Victoria
Printed and bound in Australia by Griffin Press, an accredited ISO AS/NZS 14001 Environmental Management Systems printer.

National Library of Australia
Cataloguing-in-Publication data:

McIntosh, Fiona, 1960- author.
The last dance / by Fiona McIntosh.
ISBN 9780143573821 (paperback)

A823.4

penguin.com.au

This is for Pip and Michael Klimentou.
They began dancing lessons as I began to write this story.

PROLOGUE

London – January 1933

Her tears had subsided but left their telltale traces of swollen eyes and numb cheeks that she couldn't blame a frosty winter morning for. Stella hoped the act of burial might give her some respite from the grim tension of the previous fortnight that had conquered her ability to think clearly; a sense of weightlessness, perhaps, as the burden of finally being allowed to bury her parents lifted.

Instead, as the mourners drifted away she felt the loss more keenly, standing at the lip of the grave clutching the shoulders of her brother and sister. She swallowed, reached to dip into the jar they'd brought and tossed her handful of sand over the coffins. Rory and Carys followed suit and they listened in frigid silence as it landed with a light percussion against the side-by-side caskets to scatter eagerly across the shiny varnish like a million miniature marbles.

She had found the jar of sand in Rory's room. It seemed to have trapped the spirit of their happy family weekend beneath its lid; held it captive for this moment of release. Perhaps the ancient shore had known the Myles children would need the reminder of Brighton beach to embrace them, vivid with its sensory memory of laughter and sunshine, picnic sandwiches and ice-cream. Stella closed her eyes and could still conjure the crunch of the pebbles sliding against each other beneath their bare feet. From a distance the beach was a neutral colour, but up close its shingle was a palette of greys and charcoals, fawns and creamy whites – almost all of them worn smooth by the roiling of waves to the foaming water that delivered them ashore. She wasn't ready to let it go yet, so reached further, and could smell the cloying peppermint sweetness of the baton of seaside rock her father had handed her brother and sister. She recalled the sticky, neon-pink residue that clung to their grins like clown's lipstick. That holiday was only last year. Now two of their 'wolfpack' as her father called his family were dead: the two elders, the leaders, the wise ones. How much wisdom had they shown in taking their lives so suddenly?

'Stella?' It was Carys, lisping on her big sister's name in that charming, infantile way. 'What do we do now?'

That was the question she too was casting out into the universe, begging the cosmos to deliver an answer, because she was lost for any idea that may offer this family a bridge from a terrible darkness back into the light.

What do we do now? she repeated silently as her grip on the two youngsters intensified to pull them even closer. She was now the eldest, the one required to lead, the person who must make all the decisions that had previously been the realm of her father.

'Go with Aunty Dil,' she said, catching the tentative wave from where her relatives' car awaited.

'What about you?' Rory wondered. He'd been silent throughout the service, for the entire half hour of formality graveside and his voice sounded as gritty as the Brighton sand that had sketched its pattern of memory across their parents.

'I'm coming. Go on, Rory, take your sister,' she urged.

Reluctantly he moved, taking Carys's hand and guiding her to where they were met with an affectionate hug from their remaining kin. Stella blinked her gaze back to the frozen earth that was now eager to accept the people she loved. Its sinister depth mocked her; asking if she'd like to join them. She took a deep breath and thought she tasted leaf litter at the back of her throat. She didn't want to contemplate that this may be an old grave and that she was tasting the decomposition of someone else's parent.

Rallying, she tilted her head to the sky that was presently a vast smudge of dull grey. Its bleakness felt appropriate.

While she understood her father's pain, his sense of guilt so crushing, Stella's grief was hardening to anger for her mother.

'How could you?' she'd wept repeatedly to her mother's corpse at the funeral parlour. 'You'd leave us for the love of a man?' It was a harsh view to take but when she boiled it down, this was precisely what her mother had done, so unable was she to consider life without the man she adored. And so she had preferred to die with him than find the strength to stay alongside her children.

Stella could not wrap her thoughts around such blind passion. She had never known a connection of that purity; couldn't imagine losing herself so completely in the life of another. She saw it as a weakness rather than the power it represented in her mother's life.

'I'll never allow myself to belong so wholly to anyone or need anyone as you two,' she whispered to them. 'Love like yours can only end in heartbreak.' She put gloved hands to lips that were moist again from fresh tears before turning those kissed fingers to face the coffins in a final farewell. 'I want to say I hate you but I can't, and I already miss you so much I feel like part of me is being buried alive alongside you. For all that love, though, I won't forgive you for leaving us.' She hated herself for sounding so wretched when the moment demanded the compassion of forgiveness. Maybe, despite her words, it would come in time.

A sob escaped and Stella forced herself to turn and walk towards the living, to find a way to create a new life for them all.

I

April 1933

Stella smoothed her palms down the sides of the soft wool crepe of her dress and was reminded that the last time she had worn it was to the funeral. The burial was fourteen weeks ago but it felt like a fresh wound that reminded her of its aching presence in the oddest of ways, from recalling her last conversation with her mother to looking at a pair of old shoes standing forlornly at the back door awaiting her father who was never going to step into them again. Even the smell of the bathroom or the coalscuttle drew buried memories that hurt like separate bruises.

The 'life goes on' comment was muttered to her in so many variations that she'd become immune to it. But, damn it, her life wasn't going on; her life had been halted as though an invisible policeman had just blown his whistle, held up his hand and forbidden her to move on. Instead, he'd pointed her in a new direction and no matter how much she protested, he insisted she take the diversion.

She glanced down at her outfit. The simplicity of her only fully formal garment made it adaptable, fortunately, and so tonight she had disguised the funereal palate with a cream handbag and gloves, before adding a touch of whimsy with her silk voile scarf. Outwardly, she knew she looked the part for a night of dance but inside she felt anything but jolly. Her life's trajectory had swerved with a bottle of pills and a bottle of whisky, neither of them hers, and yet all of the aftershock of the bombshell of her parents' suicide was hers to bear and continued reverberating through her world.

The initial numbing disbelief of sudden death had altered and over the last few weeks it had distorted to a simmering rage that she sensed would also pass and likely end in despair as she returned to the same unanswerable questions. *How could they be so selfish?* No, cruel. Why leave her to face the tearful, enquiring expressions of her two young siblings? How were the little ones to face growing up without parents, without a family and its love to nurture them?

She felt her friend Madge's elbow connect with her rib and return her consciousness to the glittering ballroom of the Berkeley Hotel. The warmth from people dancing, smoking and laughing had chased away the chill of it still being wintry and there was no denying the music from the thirty-strong orchestra was hot enough to make everyone but her want to hit the floor.

'If you tell me he's looking this way again, I'm going to deliberately step on your toes,' she replied, throwing a soft scowl that was ignored.

'No, he's not looking,' Madge confirmed. 'He's staring. Even tipsy, that stare makes me feel weak.'

'Well, I hope he asks you to dance, then. You can swoon for him and really make his evening.'

'He's not interested in me.' Madge gave her a look of dry amusement.

'I'm not in the mood.'

'Well, get in the mood,' she replied in a tart tone. 'You have responsibilities. We're doing this for you.' Madge dug her again. 'Uh-oh, he's making his move. Here he comes with his friend. Looks like you'll earn double.'

It was Madge's inspiration to come to one of the hottest dance spots in the city. She'd heard about the secret that girls were charging to dance and had been persuasive about the opportunity to earn potentially a few shillings and have fun as well.

'Madge, are you sure about this? What if we get —'

'We're not the first. I've told you, plenty of girls are topping up their wages with this. The organisers turn a blind eye so long as we don't make it obvious or too regular.'

'My mother would be so ashamed of me.'

'You're doing this to put food on the table.'

'And yet I feel like a pros—'

'Don't say it. We're dancing, nothing more.' Madge's lips pursed as she tried to speak without moving them. 'Now, be quiet, and smile!'

They watched as the pair of well-tailored gents breezed around the fringe of the dance floor, dodging the swish of silk from women's dresses or the flick of men's heels. She said no more, not wishing to make Madge cross as it was true that her friend was only trying to help ease what could become a dire situation. She knew the very least she could do was be grateful and go along with the plan. Those shillings could make a significant difference to her grocery bill this week.

With the image in mind of her brother and sister licking their lips at the smell of roast chicken scenting the kitchen, she noticed that the gentleman whom Madge had referred to was hanging back slightly. He was the taller of the two, the untidier as well with one of the buttons on his white dress waistcoat undone and his bow tie crooked with a smile to match, but even at this distance she could tell he reeked as much of money as he likely did gin.

'Hello, girls.' His friend beamed from a round face, flushed from alcohol. He lost control of the monocle balanced at the top of his podgy cheek. 'Fancy shaking a leg?'

Madge giggled. 'Sixpence a dance,' she whispered. 'But not here.'

'Oh yes, yes, of course.' He tapped his red nose. 'Mum's the word, what?' He chortled, patting his waistcoat's change pocket.

'I'm Basil, by the way, and this is my friend, Montgomery.' He wasn't slurring yet but he was just on the edge. 'Monty here has had eyes only for you,' he said, looking blurrily past Madge to where Stella stood, who suddenly wanted to be anywhere else but here. Basil grinned lopsidedly again. 'How about a couple of bob for a twirl around the floor with the loveliest pair of girls in the Berkeley tonight?'

She noted that Madge didn't show any embarrassment. 'I'm Margaret,' she said, and took Basil's arm. 'If I decide I like you, I'll let you call me Madge as my friends do,' she added and they drifted away, chuckling.

Stella breathed deliberately before she returned her gaze to him. His intense stare hadn't wavered, she noticed, and it was as though he was looking right at her internal chaos.

'And you are?' he asked, his tone polite, expression open.

'Bored,' she cut back. The word was out before she could halt it.

He didn't look offended. If anything she sensed it amused him, for his crooked grin made a return. 'That makes both of us. Shall we?' He opened his hand in invitation.

'You've paid too much for it already,' she said, shrugging, and immediately regretted how hostile she sounded.

'Basil paid. You can refuse me and dance with him if you prefer.'

She gave a small shake of her head in apology and stepped forward when he gestured for her to go first. As they reached the dance floor, the bandmaster gave a flick of his baton and the music calmed from a foxtrot to a slow waltz. They stepped onto the boards and she felt the grit of the chalk beneath her soles and the warmth of his hand that he placed with only the softest pressure in the curve of her back. She was obliged to look up and wished she'd worn higher heels now to feel more equal.

'Can I know who I'm dancing with?'

She wasn't expecting the tender note in his voice.

'Stella.' No surnames were necessary and he gave a wink before their bodies moved as one as the band played a song about the girl of someone's dreams. It was a favourite of her father's – he used to hum it frequently as he shaved or waited for his tea to brew or stirred the morning pot of porridge for the family. She pushed that image away by opening a conversation.

'You're a good dancer.' She hoped it didn't sound condescending.

'I suppose I do have to be light on my feet.'

'In your work, you mean?'

She presumed he probably hadn't heard her over the music because he didn't answer. 'Tell me about you, Stella,' he said instead. 'Why don't you want to be here?'

She lifted one shoulder slightly as a way of avoiding anything churlish being said again.

'Are you unhappy because you're taxi dancing or taxi dancing because you're unhappy?'

She wanted to smile but it wouldn't come. Instead, she sighed. 'Both, I suppose. Is that what I am? A taxi dancer?'

'It's an American expression. They have regular taxi dances in the States.' He gave a shrug. 'Men will always gladly buy tickets to dance with a pretty woman.'

She wasn't sure whether to feel complimented or offended and realised too late that her face had become blank as she stared back at him.

He politely filled the awkward silence. 'What could possibly make someone so young and possessing of an unfair slice of the world's beauty so melancholy as music plays and people dance?'

Stella's Nanny Popkin, dead for a decade now, had taught her granddaughter that false modesty was more conceited than none at all. People had been mentioning Stella's fine looks for a decade since the plump of childhood fell away and her face had hollowed from roundish to a high-cheeked elfin structure. Plaits had disappeared and the darkest of hair that glinted warmly when the sun fell on it contrasted strongly with her now lightly blushed complexion that was traditionally pale. But it was Stella's eyes that were apparently what caught people's attention first with their glacier-blue brightness. 'Accept their compliments with grace, for it is true,' Nanny had said. 'No need to be coy.' So Stella had learned to be gracious, but in this instance she wasn't ready for what sounded like an accusation accompanying the compliment.

Once again her response was out before she could censor herself. 'Are you hinting that I have no right to feel sorrows?' She didn't let him answer and the real pain rushed out. 'My parents took their own lives and delivered up their suicide as a new year present, leaving me with a ten- and eight-year-old to care for, and lots of debt.'

Amusement drained from his expression and his gaze narrowed as her mouth formed a circle of surprise.

'My outburst is unforgivable,' she admitted, instantly distraught at how raw she sounded. Yes, just over a month is too soon to be publicly socialising. 'I didn't mean . . . I'm sorry. I should leave.' She dropped her hand from his but he reclaimed it immediately.

He looked confounded but his voice was gentle. 'Don't go. I was being patronising. Of course you have a right to feel forlorn.' She liked the way he seemed to choose his words with the same care she might use to select a single chocolate from a box having been told she could only have one. 'Now I'm miserable for you, Stella. I won't ask about your parents, I sense you'd rather not discuss it.'

'It only earns pity and that's the last sentiment I want to receive from others.'

'Nevertheless, it's a burden of monstrous proportion for shoulders even as gorgeously wide and angular as yours.'

Those shoulders relaxed slightly and she let out a breath. 'The dancing is a distraction, I'll admit, but I'm angry with my parents that these extra pennies make such a difference now and I'm obliged to dance for that shilling or two. It was Madge's idea.'

'Basil tells me quite a few girls are supplementing their income in this way. I rather admire the industry of it.'

'Most wouldn't view it as much above selling myself.'

'We're all selling something, Stella. At least you're earning an honest, harmless shilling that I for one would be happy to exchange for a dance with a beautiful woman.'

There was no denying his charm. Madge had impressed that the key to more dances from the same fellow – especially if he was a good dancer and not 'handsy' as Madge described it – was to make pleasant conversation. 'Um, Madge and I work together at Bourne & Hollingsworth, a department store. Do you know it?'

'Who doesn't, sprawling across an entire block of Oxford Street as it does? The architects did a fine job with the redesign; it's a most handsome building and must be a pleasure to work in.'

'I've been there since I left school. Nearly a decade.' Her expression must have told him she had not recently counted the years and their sum was a surprise to her. 'Anyway, Madge works in ladies' millinery and perfume but I'm in the offices now. I've been working in various areas on the floor but now I'm training as a buyer. It's not my dream, though.'

'No?'

She found a small smile for him and shook her head. He regarded her intently. 'Is it a secret?'

'Are you good at keeping them?'

'More than you can possibly imagine,' he answered and his smile felt like a private one, just for her – as though two hundred others were not in this ballroom. 'To the grave, I promise.' His hand briefly left hers to cover his heart in an odd gesture of sincerity.

Stella laughed, taken aback that she could be amused and felt a trill of pleasure when his large hand cupped hers again. 'All right, you're a stranger, so it can't hurt. My dream is to have my own tea-rooms.'

'Truly?' He looked disconcerted. 'I'd never have thought it.'

'Why's that?'

'You're so . . . well, I'd have thought girls dream of different, more glamorous things to do with themselves.'

She nodded, smiling. 'Ah, but my teashop would be glamorous. I'd serve dainty cakes on exquisite china and the range of tea would be remarkable. Black, green, white, scented, herbal, floral, spicy . . . I would teach people about tea in all of its incarnations and they would sip from porcelain so translucent they could see daylight through their cups.'

His eyes glimmered with a misty pleasure as though he was becoming happily entangled in the images she described.

'Ladies especially would come from far and wide to meet and gossip in my tearooms,' she continued. 'Waitresses would be impeccably attired in neat black outfits.'

'Where would you open these tearooms?'

'Oh, in a spa town, it has to be. People visiting for therapeutic reasons and complete relaxation. Stella's Tea Emporium would be the most popular place to be seen by day.'

'Somewhere terribly fashionable for the wealthy, then,' he said, joining in the dream. 'Kent?'

'I was thinking north. Buxton; perhaps Harrogate, or even Bath.' They both grinned at the vision. 'It shall have to remain a dream. Right now I have a sister and brother to raise, educate, provide for.' She deliberately stopped herself sighing and packed away the dream. 'How about you? What do you do?'

'Oh, I work in the city like most of the men here,' he said briefly but while the practised smile smoothed the slightly offhand tone she heard him deftly avoid her question. Years in a vast, busy store in the liveliest shopping precinct of London and being part of a big team had exposed Stella to all sorts of people, backgrounds and attitudes. She'd developed a keen perception for traits. Instinctively Stella knew her companion was being evasive. If he had been important to her, she might have pursued his line of work, or the fact that while he had acted tipsy earlier she was now convinced that the smell of liquor was coming off his black dinner jacket, not his breath . . . but he was simply a paying dance partner and they were leagues apart in a social sense. Stella couldn't imagine they'd see one another again even in passing.

The music stopped and the restless twirl of dancers sighed to a halt. People clapped, some began drifting to the sides of the ballroom to cool off, to light up, others back to the glow of lamplit tables, or to find friends, and order more champagne that seemed to be flowing with frenzy this evening. Wasn't the world supposed to be in economic crisis? Hadn't her father taken his life and her mother's with him over the financial crash? Apparently no one in this ballroom cared too much about the state of the world's economy. All that mattered was that the Great War was behind them and even the sinister, invisible Spanish flu that had killed more than the war could, had also burned itself out.

Around her women slanted conspicuous gazes at other women's outfits but Stella suspected no one would use hers as a benchmark. Nor did she care – she was happy to move through them like a blackbird in the shadows of peacocks. Black was her shade still. Black was her mood despite the twinkling of fairy lights and the dazzle of chandeliers reflecting sparkles of colour.

'Well, thank you,' she murmured, immediately parting and pretending to look for Madge, but knowing something gracious needed to be exchanged. 'It's a treat to dance with someone who doesn't tread on my toes.'

He straightened his white bow tie. 'Speaking of tea, do you fancy a pot?'

She had to meet his gaze square on now – no more dodging it. In the lower light of the dance hall his eyes looked black and shone like the patent leather of his formal wingtip shoes. A whisper of the scent of coconut oil ghosted past her as he leaned forward to impress that there was no guile to his invitation. He waited for her answer as she searched her memory and recognised the smell of Murray's Hair-Glo, a pomade from America that wealthy men preferred for its sleek effect. She had watched the paperwork for countless tins of the hair cream pass through the office. Englishmen of less extravagance – like her father – used the locally made Brylcreem.

'Why?' she finally said.

'Why not? You obviously enjoy tea?' he challenged with a soft shrug. He guided her away from the floor.

'Mr . . . ?'

'Monty,' he assured.

She frowned. Why did she not trust that name? 'Well . . . Monty, it's kind of you but I'm not that sort —'

'Nor I that sort of man,' he finished. 'I'm thirsty, Stella, and you've just told me you don't wish to be here and that you rather like tea. So,' he said, straightening with an airy sigh, 'share a pot of it with me in the hotel's salon and I will put you in a taxi to your home – alone or with Madge, which I shall pay for. If you'd prefer not, that's fine but you look like you need to talk, not dance.'

'Why?'

His grin widened. 'Which bit?'

'Why do you want to share my sorrows?'

'Because I'm tired of examining my own; I'm a good listener and something about you intrigues me and I too am bored of all this,' he said, giving a small sweep of a slightly bronzed hand as though he'd been out in the sun longer than most. 'Now, I'm guessing you have your siblings to get home to.' He reached for the gold fob watch, whose chain glinted as he lifted the dial towards him. 'It's not even nine yet and it gives you a perfect excuse to flee the dance floor early.'

She smiled sadly. 'I must admit I'm thirsty too.'

'Let's go,' he said, and offered an elbow.

2

Madge had given Stella a look of such arch amusement when her friend had murmured that she'd meet her in the lobby in half an hour that Stella felt a flush of embarrassment flood her body. Nevertheless her cheeks had cooled by the time they were seated in a quiet nook near one of the large picture windows. Stella and her dance partner were hidden by alabaster pillars and the quiet level of their voices lifted to the high ceiling, far enough to be lost. Several other couples and groups were enjoying a similarly private break from the liveliness in the ballroom, which made her feel immediately less conspicuous.

'I might have a coffee, actually,' he said to the waiter before he glanced towards Stella who gave him a mocking glare. 'But my guest may prefer a pot of tea . . . ?' She nodded and let her companion order.

He sat back and smiled briefly in reassurance so she caught only a glimpse of teeth gleaming ivory like the starched brightness of his waistcoat. 'I'm really very sorry to hear about your family troubles, Stella. Why would parents do such a thing, or is that too inquisitive of me?'

She took an audible breath and shook her head. 'It's the logical question. My father was an accountant and money advisor – a good one; he really cared for the people who trusted him with their money. The financial crisis, cost of the war . . . it took it all, everything we had that he'd invested for our future and on behalf of other families.'

He looked down and gave a muttering groan. 'You don't need to say more. She looked up at him from her hands. 'The time we live in says enough. Did he really think his brutal actions would solve anything?'

'I suppose it solved a problem for him in not having to face the failure and its repercussions. He'd survived the war, kept us safe from Spanish flu and other troubles, but he couldn't protect us from the outside forces of the Depression. And Mum was a gentle soul. She's French . . . was French,' she corrected herself. 'She adored my father and obviously preferred not to face life without him.'

'So gentle that she'd leave her three children?' He tried to cover his dismay but Stella heard it nonetheless echoing between them as he cleared his throat and looked down. 'Forgive me, that's none of my business.'

'It's not,' she agreed, 'but it's also complicated to explain and I'd have to know you better to want to try. All I will say is my mother faced enough emotional challenge in her early life and as Dad was the rock she built her life upon, she chose the more permanent solution than feel that rock crumble away from her.' He held her gaze for a fraction longer than she thought polite and his silence forced her into an uncharacteristic hurry to fill it. 'Nevertheless, in their cowardice they left me with a raft of new problems that go beyond money.'

'Such as your brother and sister?'

'Rory and Carys . . .' She shook her head. 'They're so young. I'm effectively their mother now and I don't feel equipped.'

'Then don't try.'

'What do you mean?'

'I mean don't try to be their mother. Remain authentic and do the very best you can as their big sister. Children are surprisingly perceptive. They'll know how hard you're trying.' She nodded at sage words cutting through the blur of anxiety. 'Control what you can, Stella. The rest, work it out as you go along. They'll never lack for love, I suspect, and perhaps right now it's your affection that counts more than anything.'

'Oh, they're very easy to love. They're even easy to raise. They don't complain, they don't give me cheek, they're doing their damndest to help. Dear little Rory puts on our father's boots and clomps out to the coalscuttle, telling me he's the man of the house now and has to think like Dad would.' She forbade the tears that were threatening. 'It breaks my heart that he's already worked it out and the saddest part of all is that I'm relying on him to take out the rubbish, to take Carys to school when I can't, to remember to tick off lots of little chores that a lad of his age probably shouldn't be concerned with.'

'He'll be a better man for it.'

'But I don't want him to grow up too fast. I want him to have the childhood he deserves. I don't want Carys crying herself to sleep because she wants our mother to sing the French lullaby that she sang to each of us at Carys's age. I don't have the French accent!'

The corner of his eyes wrinkled again with amusement but one that told her it was filled with sympathy. 'You can't turn back time, Stella, but if you're strong, make sound decisions for your family, you can navigate the path.'

She gave a low sigh. 'My life had . . .'

'What?' he asked tenderly.

'Trajectory,' she shrugged. 'I knew what I wanted, I knew how to get there. I've been knocked off course.'

'Get back on course,' he replied rather obviously.

Her eyes welled and she reached quickly into her bag for a handkerchief but he was quicker, flicking out the perfectly ironed white square linen from his outside pocket.

'Please,' he urged when she hesitated, but unlike most he offered a thought beyond the obvious. 'Self-pity delivers no answers.'

She felt the sting of rebuke but knew he was right. He continued speaking as he glanced over a shoulder searching for the waiter before returning his attention swiftly. 'Do something else for a while that gives you a chance to stand back from your problem and study it. You've heard the saying about ways to skin a cat, no doubt.'

She nodded.

'So, approach your dream from a different direction. It's perspective, Stella. And who knows, you may discover something wonderful along the way; you may think entirely differently about matters; you may meet interesting folk you otherwise would never have met . . .'

'Like whom?'

'Like me,' he grinned and she smiled sadly, feeling her eyes water helplessly at his kindness.

The waiter arrived with a pot of coffee, another of tea and began laying out the cups, jugs and sugar bowl. She dabbed her eyes surreptitiously and blew as if fighting a mild cold. As she did so she smelled the liquor again, this time from the handkerchief, and once again it didn't add up, especially now as he spoke so lucidly.

'We can pour,' he said to the waiter and tipped him to go away. 'Are you all right, Stella?'

'Yes, yes. I didn't think I had any more tears left. I'm sorry. You've been kind, thank you.' She sniffed as they waited for the tea to draw. 'Do you have family?'

He nodded. 'I'm married, yes.' At her raised eyebrows, he smiled. 'I'm simply keeping a friend company. I'm not in the habit of trawling dance halls and paying girls to waltz with me.'

'I'll bet you don't,' she snapped.

'Damn, that came out wrong. I meant no offence, just wanted to assure that I have no intention of making any improper advance.

I don't even want to be here. Oh, bloody hell, I'm digging a deeper hole, aren't I?'

Stella laughed at how visibly mortified he looked. 'No offence taken.' She held up a hand to reassure. 'Truly.' She nodded to say that the conversation was complete. 'So . . . family?'

'My parents have passed on, and unlike you I have no siblings to care for.' He trotted out the details without emotion.

'Where is home?'

'Good question.' He sighed and began pouring her tea. It looked strong, as she liked it. 'I'll leave you to add your preferences.' He smiled and she couldn't fault his obvious attractiveness. She was aware of women turning in their direction, stealing surreptitious and admiring glances at the dashing stranger she was taking tea with.

'So, Stella, I'm certain you know a sixpence or two isn't the solution,' he continued, cutting deeply to the core of her fear.

'I do,' she said. 'But I've recently buried both my parents and I need some time to think without panicking. I know I have to sell the house; we may even have to move away from where we've all been raised. My head spins with worry. But despite my tears, I am much stronger than I appear.'

'I can imagine.' He blew on the black coffee he'd poured and sipped.

She liked the sweep of his expressive lips that were neither full nor narrow; in fact all of his features were like that – so clearly defined she could draw them – and yet hard to describe because they were the idealised shape of eyes, nose, mouth. And like a chorus of individuals suddenly singing together they formed a whole song of beauty. She had to look away but not before noticing that he hadn't bothered to shave this evening, which the stubble around his jaw attested to. There was something exciting about this fellow and his slightly mysterious, definitely non-establishment ways – both of which she was sure he was hiding.

'Can you?'

'What?' he said, swallowing his coffee but she caught the bounce of his Adam's apple as though he knew he'd been caught in a lie.

'Can you really imagine my situation? I suspect you're not short of a penny and you certainly can't be short of dance partners, so why you have to pay for it is anyone's guess. That aside, how can a wealthy man possibly understand my situation? You are rich, aren't you?'

'I suppose.'

She gave a murmur of disdain. 'You suppose,' she said softly. 'There you go again.'

He looked at her quizzically. 'What am I doing again?'

Stella added a cube of sugar and a splash of milk to her tea. She stirred gently with the silver spoon and focused on the whirlpool of bronze liquid. It felt dangerous to bait him but she was feeling in a careless frame of mind, knew the anger of self-pity was behind it and frustrated that he'd managed to unleash it again by encouraging her to talk about her situation.

'You're lying,' she said, fixing him with an accusatory stare.

'Pardon?'

'Monty – if that's even your real name – let's just share that I think you'd make a fine conjuror.' He smiled uncertainly and she knew she'd hit a nerve. 'You're adept at finding out about me but you clearly don't believe I'm owed your respect of telling the truth. I've been honest with you – too honest, I suspect – and while we don't come from the same social backgrounds I don't deserve your scorn. I'm nothing to you, I know that; a girl in a dance hall with dreams of making something of herself, who thinks sixpence is worth humiliating herself for.' As she said it she knew she would never sell herself cheaply again. She could see his jaw grinding at her quietly spoken but heartfelt tirade as the steam from their drinks mingled, curling and twisting around each other from barely touched china. 'Thank you for the tea but I'll leave you to enjoy your coffee alone. Perhaps if you see Madge, you could let her know I found my way home.'

He sat forward, about to say something.

'No, please, really. I don't need your money or a taxi. Goodnight . . .' Her voice trailed off as she shook her head, hoping in that final gesture he picked up that she already regretted her attack.

'You're right,' he said, and then murmured something to her back that she didn't catch.

She turned. 'Sorry?'

'I said it's not Monty . . . at least not the name I prefer.'

Stella stared at him, waiting.

'My name,' he continued, 'the one that people who loved me once called me by is Rafe.'

Rafe. Now, that did sound like it belonged to him. Simple, elegant and as straightforward as his suddenly open expression appeared and her shoulders relaxed in apology to see a hint of horror in it.

'I appreciate your telling me – wasn't that hard, was it?' She frowned. 'What's wrong?'

'Very few people know it. I'm frankly surprised I shared it.'

'Why is your name a secret?'

'It's not,' he said, standing, and she was aware – as surely were most of those envious women staring – again at how well the dress suit hung off his shoulders and hips. 'It's just . . . private.' He took her arm. 'Come on, I'll see you into that taxi or I'll hate myself forever.' He signalled to the waiter and signed for their refreshments.

'Do you have an account here?' she said as they walked to the main entrance.

He laughed. 'No, but Fruity does.' He helped her on with her coat. 'I hope you have gloves?'

She pulled the small leather pair from her coat pockets with a smile of triumph. 'Fruity?'

'Sorry. Basil. His surname is Peach, can you believe it? Poor fellow. School must have been hard for him.' Stella chuckled, relieved that they would not part on her harsh words. He must have heard her thoughts. 'I'm glad we could say farewell with a smile, Stella. I do regret making you feel anything but valued. If it's any consolation, I loathe events like this,' he said, jabbing a thumb in the direction of the ballroom. 'My mood is always slightly off when I'm forced into my penguin suit.'

He paused at the cloakroom and handed in a ticket. Moments later he shrugged into an overcoat but pulled his bow tie looser and undid the top button. She looked away, suddenly shyly aware of how dashing he appeared. There was no doubt he wore his 'penguin suit' with an effortlessness suaveness, but that gesture of undressing made her blush and she hadn't felt the full weight of his attraction steal up and tap on her shoulder until this moment.

Stella cleared her throat and glanced towards the concierge, who opened the door so they could step out to wait at the top of the three shallow steps at the entrance to the Berkeley and into a bone-shakingly cold spring evening.

'Cab, Sir?' the man asked, breath swirling in a fog around him.

'Please,' Rafe replied, clapping his now gloved hands together.

'Where to, Sir?'

'Er . . .' he glanced at Stella.

'Just off Clapham Common,' she said to the man and the concierge touched his cap.

'Right away.' He smiled and moved away to blow into a whistle as she hugged herself to conserve warmth. Her toes already felt like Jack Frost was gnawing on them.

She began to move from foot to foot. 'Why come to these dances if you loathe them?' she asked.

'Fruity enjoys them. I'm sure it didn't escape you that he likes a drink or two; he also likes women and is starved of female companionship, I suspect . . . of the young and extremely pretty kind. Poor old Fruity is caring for his invalid mother.'

'And you don't drink, do you?' she queried, sensing a jigsaw piece fitting into its rightful place.

'Not much. I kept tipping the champagne and gins into pot plants, even onto myself.'

She laughed. It was her first genuine sound of delight since she'd walked into her parents' bedroom and found them in one another's arms and dead for hours. 'I could smell you yards away – I fell for it, but only briefly.'

He grinned. 'Thank you for not saying anything. It makes Fruity feel better if I'm looking as intoxicated as he's feeling. Listen, have my coat? I can't bear to see you shivering like that. My suit has to be a whole lot warmer than your dress and coat together.'

She stopped him taking his thick coat off but she felt warmed by the gallant offer. 'No need. Look, the taxi's here,' she said as an Austin High Lot took a wide turn into the hotel's forecourt. She normally took buses or the underground. Stella had hoped this would be a night she could put behind her and forget, but a ride in the handsome taxi with the moonlight bouncing off its shining black exterior would deny her that. What a treat.

The concierge opened the door and gestured for her to enter a world she had not previously experienced. She could smell the polish on the leather seats as she admired all the gleaming metal of the vehicle. Best of all the heater was turned up and she could detect the remnants of a previous client's perfume that had been warmed enough to linger. She was aware of Rafe muttering to the concierge with a slight frown.

'Good evening, Miss,' the driver said, touching his hat. 'Cold one.'

'Good evening.' She smiled. 'Deliciously warm in here, though,' she replied as she clambered onto her higher positioned seat to the cabbie as gracefully as she could.

Rafe leaned in and she could clearly see the flesh bared from undoing his tie and collar earlier. It was only in this moment of seeing his skin, unexpectedly dark in that triangle with pale flesh either side, that she realised his teeth appeared so white because his face was tanned. What a lazy life he must lead, she thought, as she regarded his squarish face. Other men must hate him.

'Stella, would it be awkward of me to ask if I might ride with you back to Clapham? The concierge tells me there are few taxis available tonight and a high demand. I could be waiting a long time for the next one.'

'Er, yes, of course.' She could hardly refuse as he was paying and she was eager to get the door closed. 'Um, but where are you staying?'

He hopped up easily next to her, thanked the concierge and tapped on the glass separating them. 'Thank you, driver, we're heading to Clapham Common and then back to Mayfair, please.'

'Right you are, Sir.'

They lurched off and the looming golden presence of the Berkeley was left behind as they merged into the careening night traffic of Piccadilly.

'You're going to have to cross the river twice,' she said in a tone suggesting only a madman might.

'I do odd things on full moon nights,' he quipped and gave a grin full of mischief. 'But I promise I shall deliver you safely to your door and then you will never have to put up with my irritating presence again.'

'You're not irritating. I'm just not comfortable with insincerity.'

'Well, you can be sure I am most sincere in my apology.'

'I misjudged your intentions, so I'm the one who is sorry. You were being a good friend.'

'Friend? I don't know about that. Basil is a colleague.'

'You both looked friendly enough.'

He gave a small shrug.

'But it doesn't explain why you protect your name. Not even Basil knows, obviously.'

'Which if we follow that theory surely makes *you* my friend, Stella, because I have told you.' His smile was disarming. How many women in his past had fallen for it? How many women continued to fall for it?

'Why keep it hidden, though?'

'I go by many names, actually. Don't you know my type has about three Christian names?' His tone was self-mocking and she couldn't help but like him more for the dry observation.

'Like royalty, you mean.' She smiled.

'Exactly. Rafe – well, Rufus, actually – is one of them. It's the name my mother and sister called me by.'

'Sister? You said you didn't have siblings.'

'They're dead,' he said, matter-of-factly. 'All my family is. It's why I say I don't have a sister because I don't like explaining. It was a boating tragedy. The only reason I survived is because I was on my way back from school and supposed to meet them on the Isle of Wight.'

'I'm so sorry.'

He shrugged as though he didn't allow himself to get upset over it. She was the one caught out now and was glad of the dark interior of the taxi as she reached quickly to lighten the conversation. 'So what did your father call you by?'

'My third name!' he said archly, eyes widening in mock horror. 'Because it is a family name he wanted me to be known by. It's the official name that every eldest male is called as a matter of course.

Now, the name most people know me by, Montgomery – the one that I was introduced to you by – is my grandfather's name on my mother's side and as my first name is a silent family name, Montgomery comes next in the tiresome trio – without brackets,' he added in a tone loaded with irony, 'so it's the one they used at school, on formal paperwork and so on. Complicated, isn't it?'

She gave a mock expression of dizziness but the gesture had an edge of truth to it for her companion had been leaning closer during his conversation about his various names and at one point their heads almost touched. Stella was sure she could feel the wispiness of a few licks of his mid-brown hair just touching her own. He was also close enough that she could feel his breath caress her cheek and she could smell the rich roast of coffee on it. On her old boyfriend, Harry, nicotine and coffee smelled old. On Rafe it smelled enticing. How could that be?

Stella cleared her throat. 'Is your home in Mayfair?'

'No, my club is,' he said, leaning away as if suddenly uninterested. 'The family home is south, quietly rural, you could say.'

He was being careful again, she noted.

'How is it that you are what . . . twenty-four?'

'Twenty-six,' she corrected.

'But your brother and sister are so young.'

She nodded with a sad smile. Maybe she didn't need to know him better to open up; it suddenly felt easy to explain. 'My mother had me out of wedlock – and far too early in her life.' She watched his expression shift. It was slight but it was there, the inevitable judgement of her mother, a lovely, shy, fragile woman. The explanation hurried with the desire to be shared as if someone else was in control of her will in that moment. 'You see, she was attacked by a group of youths when she was barely into her teens. She was —' She stopped; the details didn't matter. 'I am the mistake, not my brother and sister. I was conceived in shame and horror, birthed in despair, no doubt. My little darlings were made with nothing but love.' She watched him swallow but he stared back at her unblinking and she was glad to see his expression didn't reflect pity. 'My grandparents were brave to send my mother, Dianna – she was known as Didi – to family in Wales; she was even braver to demand that her child be allowed to live. I was not quite two when she met Evan Myles and fell instantly in love with a young, brash, ambitious Welshman who would become the only father I've known and someone who cherished me as he did my mother. If they had cross words, I never heard them.' She shook her head. 'They made a perfect bond. But they couldn't make a child for a long time together.' She lifted a shoulder. 'My mother was badly hurt in the attack,' she explained. 'And then a beautiful pair of gifts arrived. My brother came along when I was sixteen, my sister two years later. I didn't resent them, I adored them and had already enjoyed so many years as a beloved only child.' She looked away and out of the window to where they moved through Whitehall, passing the Houses of Parliament in silence as the taxi gained speed heading towards the newly redesigned Lambeth Bridge. She recalled its opening by the King the previous year and how its odd red painted colour scheme was a reflection of the leather on the bench seats in the House of Lords.

He finally spoke. 'When did you learn the truth?'

'On my twelfth birthday. We all cried, but I think for them it was tears of relief to unburden the truth.'

'And for you?'

'Oh, as you would expect. Shock, grief. We never spoke of it again but from thereon it lived with us, like an extra person we didn't set a place for at the table.'

'What do you mean?'

She took a breath and let it out. 'My real father. Invisible but present, casting a shadow.' She gave him a cheer-up smile. 'I learned to live with it. I loved my parents deeply and never felt anything but love in return but I did feel changed from that day.'

'Changed? In what way?' He was leaning forward again and she could feel the warmth of his body; moonlight and street light conspired to show her that triangle of skin beneath his throat that she suddenly wanted to touch. Forbidden flesh. She looked away quickly as the taxi passed Lambeth Palace and she saw the familiar crenellated gatehouse that she passed daily on her way home in the bus from work.

'It wasn't that I didn't belong, it's just that I felt suddenly responsible for her fragility – why she relied on my father for every decision, leaned on him . . . I didn't want to be like that – I'm not like that . . . I'm independent, even rebellious at times . . . perhaps more like the man whose blood I share.'

She cut a hand through the warm air that had built in the taxi and breathed out. 'Anyway, enough of all that and the reason for her cowardice. Now you know my other secret, which I suspect I can trust you with, but I note you remain a mystery,' she said with an accusatory smile to lighten the tension that had also formed itself around them.

'Listen, Stella. Can I offer some help for your situation?'

'No,' she said with bright alarm in her tone. 'Absolutely not. I do not want charity from —'

'I'm not talking about charity,' he insisted, grabbing her arm gently to stop her next outburst. His hand was large and closed around her thin wrist, encompassing it like a manacle. She was surprised by the roughness of the texture of his flesh against hers. Caught unawares by his touch, she did stop talking.

'I'm suggesting a different line of work – just to tide you over.'

She frowned. 'I earn a decent wage at the store.' She sighed. 'Although I'm suddenly called trainee again, now that I'm learning to be a buyer.'

'I happen to know you can earn more in the short term.'

Alarm bells sounded in her mind now as dawning occurred. She twitched her wrist out of his grasp. 'Gosh, what do you think I am?' she growled in a murmur only for his ears. She glanced at the taxi driver who was making a wide turn and was heedless of his passengers' conversation.

'No, you're getting me wrong again,' Rafe appealed, as he put his hands up in defence. 'Just listen to me. There are wealthy families up and down the country who would pay you a very good wage to help them with their children.'

'A governess?'

'Yes, I suppose you could describe it that way.'

'How thoroughly Victorian,' she remarked.

'Not really. Wealthy families hire in help for all sorts of reasons. You said your mother was French. Are you fluent?'

She nodded. 'Yes, of course.'

'Music?'

Stella lifted a shoulder. 'Piano, flute.'

'You can read it?'

'Read it and write it. I had a very good education; my parents saw to that but I've got my own brother and sister to look out for.'

'Well, this is how you can do it. I know families who would likely pay twice as much as you probably earn now, plus board and lodging, if you were prepared to teach their children at home beyond the three 'Rs', but definitely refining their reading, writing, arithmetic. Most of their daughters may never have to reckon figures if they marry into similar money but society is changing and the war, the Depression too, is putting formerly unheard of pressures on grander homes . . . especially on the women who make a lot of the household decisions. It's important the next generation of women, now they have their right to vote, can back up their new freedoms with financial know-how. Women need to be independent, capable of not just running a house but understanding all of the financial implications as well as having an admiration of culture. You have the skills to help with that.'

She nodded. 'I'm impressed. I didn't expect you to be so liberal,' and in the close confines of the taxi she tried not to be dazzled by the slightly mocking delight in his grin.

'By my attitude or by my suggestion? Here, let me write down the name of an agency. The woman who runs it is a friend of Fruity – and she's very good at placement, from what I hear. I mention her only because I met her recently in passing. You never know – the work, change of scenery and mindset could suit you for a short time until you get clear about . . .' he shrugged, 'the way ahead and all that.'

She watched him pull a fountain pen and tiny blank white card from his inside pocket, and with the intuitive balance of a circus performer, he seemed to be able to write effortlessly despite the bounce of their vehicle and the twists and bumps that came without warning.

'There,' he said, handing it to her. 'That's her agency. I don't know the exact address but I know it's almost directly opposite Victoria Station.'

She couldn't read it in the dark but she placed the card in her handbag. 'Thank you. I'll think about it.'

'Do more than that. I'm urging that you go and see her. At least find out more.' Half of his face was in shadow now and this image of him seemed appropriately mysterious. She was convinced that Rafe possessed secrets he shared with no one, not even his family.

'I promise you I will seriously consider your suggestion,' she replied and felt a sensation of warmth sizzle through her as he squeezed her wrist with a glad smile.

'Good.' He bent slightly to stare out of the window and get a fix on where they were. 'Clapham already,' he murmured, spying the Common, and she wondered if she were reading far too much into what sounded like disappointment in his tone.

'If you take a left up here, please,' she said to the driver. 'And then the second right – it's number twenty-six. Thank you.'

Soon enough they were both standing on the pavement outside the elegant row of Victorian houses that clustered around a pretty green. The taxi purred loudly as she returned her gaze to him and he took a breath to speak.

'So this is where you live, Stella?' he said, regarding the Gothic-style house that suddenly felt far too large for her and her siblings, and yet she knew must seem tiny to him.

'This is where I was raised.' *Where my parents died*, she thought, and pushed it away. 'Where my brother, Rory, and my sister, Carys, were born.'

'Who looks after them?'

'My aunt moved in for a while. She's my father's sister and they were close growing up in Wales. The arrangement can't last, though. She has her own family – they live in St Albans, always threatening to move back to northern Wales.'

He reached for her gloved hand. She thought he was going to shake it but he simply held it loosely, staring at it silently for a few heartbeats. 'Please, go and see the agency. I will contact the owner and leave your name, just in case you do. And I'll be asking her to ensure you are given the best possible placement and not too far away from London so you can visit your brother and sister regularly.'

'What do you propose I do with them, while I'm looking after someone else's children?'

'Send them to St Albans with your aunt. I say this respectfully when I suggest that she's surely better equipped to raise youngsters while you raise funds. Take a sabbatical from work and earn some good money and get some distance from grief. A change of scenery and new responsibilities will help you see life through fresh eyes.'

He was standing in a halo of yellow light beneath the sodium street lamp, which washed out his colour and flattened his features but couldn't erase the earnest expression. Stella stared at him, unsure of how to end this discussion. She didn't want to commit yet, but she didn't want to disappoint him either.

Rafe ended her dilemma of how to respond by unexpectedly raising her hand to his lips and kissing the back of her gloved hand. She was unsure precisely what he was communicating, other than he felt some sort of deeper connection than their cursory hour or so together might suggest.

'Goodnight, Stella. I hope we meet again.'

He didn't wait for her response but hopped nimbly back into the taxi. She raised a hand as she heard him say: 'Thank you, driver, back over the river, please.' But he didn't look back at her and she was still staring at the empty space where the taxi had parked well after its departure, her hand remaining lifted in farewell.

Finally Stella turned, deep in her thoughts as she closed the small gate behind her and walked up the short pathway to her house. Aunt Dil had left the porch light on for her but as she dug into her bag for her front door key, all she could feel was the warm memory of his kiss that had melted through the cotton of her glove and lingered now against her skin, marking her with his tender touch.

3

Theirs was a traditional Victorian upstairs-downstairs, semi-detached house with four bedrooms, a slate roof and minimal decoration; traditional in every sense other than her mother's passion for colour, which stretched to painting the exterior. The rest of their row was conventional red brick but the Myles family of Clapham had opted for the notoriety of painting their house a pale yellow, like the Breton cream of memory from her mother's childhood.

'We like colour in France,' Didi had explained with a soft outward sigh of disdain. She was plucking home-grown thyme leaves into her Sunday special of simmering chicken casserole at the time. 'And cream is hardly, how you say . . . brave.'

'This is England, dear,' her father had soothed, looking over the top of his newspaper, pipe billowing its sweet-scented tobacco smoke from the corner of his mouth. 'Bold colours are not in our blood. We're essentially grey to our marrow,' he'd winked, and yet he'd been the one to hire the painters and give them their brief, ignoring the raised eyebrows.

Happier days, Stella mused as she sipped a mug of tea, seated in the bench window of the kitchen and overlooking the garden where sparrows scrabbled over a small knuckle of bread she'd tossed out moments ago. It was mild but drizzling – the worst combination, she thought, because it made her hair feel wretched and frizzy. She touched her soft dark curls and considered what to wear. It felt important to get her outfit right.

Aunt Dil yawned, bustling into the kitchen in her dressing-gown. It was Sunday morning and church had been passed up in favour of having a sleep-in. Stella believed after last month's mind service – many weeks later than it should have been, because neither she nor the children could face it – was more than enough attention from the congregation. The gossip-mongers would be working hard at spreading the news around the neighbourhood of how her parents had died.

'Penny for your thoughts, love?'

Stella smiled at how much Dil was like her father. He had used that expression regularly too but it was more than that; something about the way they said it, the shapes of their heads, even her aunt's smile that flattened her lips and dipped her eyelids was reminiscent of her brother's.

'Just thinking about tomorrow,' she replied, 'you know, whether this is the right decision. I didn't pour you one because I wasn't sure —'

Her aunt waved a hand to assure her it was not of any consequence and busied herself making a cup of tea from the big brown pot beneath the knitted cosy; she remembered when her father had knitted it how her mother had laughed at him. 'I like knitting,' he'd replied to the snickering. 'Good skills for the trenches, too.'

She'd missed what her aunt had been saying about today's dilemma. '. . . and it's a brave decision, Stella, that's for sure. But they say fortune favours the brave, don't they? And if what your friend says is right, then maybe you can get yourself on your feet fast.'

Friend? She didn't even know Rafe's last name.

'I spoke to Uncle Bryn and he thinks you're wonderful, by the way – but then he always did – and he said you're not to worry about Rory and Carys.' She came over and squeezed Stella's shoulder. 'You know we love them like our own, darling. We're all in this together. While I still feel as shocked as I did the day we learned of their terrible end, I think if we don't help you to make changes, don't help you to take a step forward, then we all risk being trapped by the grief. You're an adult, you can reason it out, but we have to show Rory and Carys that a good life is ahead of them and that they're safe and loved. If you think doing this might make all the difference, then we're right behind you.'

'What if it's too much of a change for them?'

'Change never hurt anyone and they love our house, our garden. Rory can bring his bicycle – he'll have fun riding the country lanes, he can fish in the river nearby and I'll make an extra effort with Carys, I promise. I'll teach her how to sew and I'll make up that pattern she's talking about – we can do it together.'

It sounded like a perfect shift of scene from Clapham and her aunt was surely right – it couldn't hurt them. If anything, the shift could help them to look past the constant sorrow that pressed on their young shoulders. 'What if they forget me?'

'Rory, forget you? Don't be ridiculous, girl. He worships you! And Carys wants to *be* you. No, we'll make it like a holiday for them. We'll talk to the school and I'm sure they'll understand and support this plan. You're doing it for them, after all. But more than anything, Stella, you need some time to get your head together. I'm not worried about your brother and sister, I'm worried about you. You haven't grieved properly and it's all bottled up in there,' she said, pointing towards Stella's heart. 'You're having to be so stoic for the children that you're forgetting you need to find a way out of the bleakness too. Maybe going away from this house for a while will give you a chance to take a break from the memories crowding in all the time.'

Stella nodded glumly at the truth of her aunt's words.

'I feel like they're still here,' Dil continued with a sigh. 'I can still smell your father's tobacco, your mother's perfume around the house, but we're all moving so silently around it as though we don't want to disturb the ghosts. We all need to leave here – and them – for a while.'

'You're right.'

'I am. And when we come back to the house we'll all feel a bit differently about it and we'll have what your uncle Bryn likes to call "perspective".'

'I'll go for the interview, then,' Stella agreed, feeling the decision settle into place snugly.

'Go and listen. See what this woman can offer you. You said your traineeship should be safe . . . any more word on that?'

Stella put down her mug of half finished, cooled tea and nodded. 'One piece of luck; apparently my timing couldn't be better. My supervisor is going to be in America for a number of months on a special buying trip as we broaden our range of products. Management is quite glad that I've broached the subject of time away. The manager of our department said he could view it as compassionate leave and that I could take an extended holiday.'

'Oh, Stella. I think it's meant to be, don't you?' Dil said.

She nodded. 'I'll meet her tomorrow, then.'

Twenty-four hours later Stella was seated across a wood, chrome and glass desk from a blonde, glamorously attired woman who smoked using a cocktail-length cigarette holder and wore a chic black-and-white satin dress that tied at the hip. Suzanne stared at Stella with liquid eyes that were the colour of chartreuse. They were seated in a large office of a Victorian building, spring light filtering its way through an overcast Monday and the crowded buildings around Victoria Station. Both of the bulbous wall sconces were switched on, throwing a muted glow from their opal glass, and the tall desk lamp added its yellowy highlight to the surface that was free of clutter and inlaid with gilded leather. Stella's thoughts were already reaching to the fact that she would be heading home from this appointment in the rain.

'Do you want one?' the woman suddenly said, her voice as smoky as the tobacco residue she exhaled as she spoke.

Stella regarded the box of pastel-coloured Sobranie cigarettes. It was surely no accident that Suzanne Farnsworth had chosen to smoke the pale yellow that echoed the waxen quality of her flawless make-up. Stella knew all about make-up from her days on the department-store floor and she was sure the woman was using a colour called gardenia. She wore Jean Patou's Moment Suprême perfume too, Stella was sure, for despite the cigarette smoke, the room still held warm notes of rose and clove, and even the spicy geranium she remembered from the perfume counter days was echoed close up.

'I won't, thank you,' she replied.

'It's just that you look anxious.'

'Do I? I'm simply unfamiliar with how this all works. But they're very pretty,' she admitted, admiring the gleaming gold tips of the remaining cigarettes in the box.

'They're like lovely jewels. I prefer to smoke Black Russians at night, though, especially with a flute of champagne.'

And Stella could well imagine this elegant woman in a flowing gown at the theatre, clasping an opera-length cigarette holder and a sinful black cigarette with gleaming gold tip smouldering at its end, while she draped herself in the dress circle. Stella had served enough of those wealthy customers in her time.

Suzanne lifted the holder to the corner of her peach-frosted lips that contrasted with shocking black nail varnish and lazily inhaled from her cigarette again. She apparently had no qualms about studying Stella so obviously, head cocked this time with interest, before blowing out the smoke high.

'So, Stella, let me explain. My client wishes to secure the services of an educated woman with a "refined demeanour" who can live-in and improve her charge's French in particular, but also encourage her student to read widely and have a greater appreciation of art and culture.'

Stella nodded and let out a silent breath. Did she really want to do this? 'Um, may I ask how old the child is?'

Suzanne consulted some notes on a sheet of paper. 'It says here that Georgina is around sixteen.' She glanced up and the look in those intelligent green eyes echoed Stella's sinking feeling.

'That's a tricky age,' Stella remarked.

'It is, I won't deny it. But you and I have both been there and I always think the key to teenagers is remembering that we were likely all fractious and self-centred in our teens. I would suggest you think of it as Georgina's rite of passage if you take the role on. But this is a very wealthy family and everything will be done for you. Your role is simply to be a guide and tutor to Georgina; other household staff will take care of all your domestic needs such as meals, laundering, ironing and so on. You will have a driver at your disposal if you and Georgina wish to take an excursion and of course all expenses, outside of private ones, will be catered to.'

Stella blinked, uncertain; it sounded too good to be true. 'So just one child?'

'There is another daughter but far younger. Her name is Grace. She's um . . .' Suzanne scanned her page. 'Ah yes, Grace is nine.' She lifted an eyebrow. 'Quite a gap, I agree. But your role for Grace is again French, perhaps some music – you play piano, don't you?'

Stella nodded.

'Good. And keeping up her reading, spelling. Nothing too wearying.'

'What about school?'

'They both go to a fine ladies' college – I'll furnish you with the details if we proceed. So the good news is that you are essentially free during the day of the school term, although you will be responsible for ensuring their delivery and pick up from the college daily. During evenings you supervise Georgina's homework. On weekends you will work around Georgina's schedule to ensure she has an hour of French over the days and an artistic excursion once a month. During school holidays is when it becomes more intensive – and as you might know, the girls' private school holidays can extend longer than your brother's and sister's school holidays. As such, you are required to work out a holiday program that steps up your tutoring while still allowing Georgina to enjoy her term breaks.'

'Where is the family based?'

Suzanne picked up her cigarette from the ashtray. The flakes of burned tobacco dropped off silently. She inhaled slowly and Stella guessed the woman was considering whether this was information she should share at this point. 'The family resides not far from Tunbridge Wells,' she finally said.

'Oh, that's good to know. It's easy to get back to London.'

'Yes. Straight down the line, no train change necessary from the nearest station.'

'Which is?'

Suzanne smiled softly. 'I'll get to that. Now, Miss Myles, thank you for all the information you gave me,' she said, briefly waving another page in the air that Stella recognised her own handwriting on as being details of her music exams. 'I should let you know that your French test was flawless too.'

Stella didn't want to mention that she knew her French was colloquially flawless but that Miss Farnsworth's test was not, with errors typical of those made by the British who acquire French. The agent continued. 'I will check your references, of course, but certainly from what you've told me you are impressively qualified for this role. Do you care to tell me why you're applying, though – I mean, you are obviously set on a career path in retailing and you've clearly battled to be accepted into the traineeship as a buyer . . . no small feat. Why change that course now?'

There was no point in hiding the truth but she kept the explanation succinct. Suzanne Farnsworth didn't touch her cigarette throughout, her green gaze never leaving Stella's face and she was so still it was almost as if she'd stopped breathing. When Stella shrugged and said, 'I can't change anything. I can only try and make our lives better,' she watched that piercing stare soften.

'And so you will, if you accept this position.'

'You're offering it to me?'

Suzanne nodded, removed the cigarette butt and squashed it in the ashtray. 'There's something about you, Stella. I'm sensing a courage and steadfastness I find attractive. I like the girls I place to be reliable and I also appreciate strength of will when I recognise it. You have it.'

She began packing up her file, speaking distractedly as though thinking aloud. 'It's all very well us women getting the vote and finding new freedoms, but have we the tenacity to make the most of it, I wonder? I suspect an educated, ambitious woman such as yourself is a good role model to all younger women, irrespective of their social status.'

Stella was reminded of Rafe; he shared a view that wasn't dissimilar. And although Aunt Dil and even Suzanne thought she was here because of the tragedy of her parents, the truth was that he was the reason she was pursuing this work. He had seemed so determined that she come along to the interview that she would have felt she'd let him down not to present herself.

'I have to tell you, Stella, this family is prepared to pay an inordinate wage for the right person. And I have seen half-a-dozen girls and none of them until today have struck me as ideal.'

'I'm encouraged,' she replied carefully.

Suzanne gave a soft, throaty chuckle. 'Oh, that was truly the right answer. So diplomatic and yet nothing servile about it.'

'I wouldn't see myself as a servant, Miss Farnsworth.'

'But you would serve, Stella. You would serve the family, you would certainly be serving Georgina's education and, to a lesser extent, Grace's. But happily, I think you would agree you would be serving yourself when you hear the wage is seven pounds per week.'

'Seven!'

Suzanne grinned lazily again. 'Shocking! A slip of a thing like you earning so much; what do they pay you at the store? Two pounds per week?'

'Two pounds ten,' she confirmed with only a hint of offence. 'Three-ten when I complete my training, but seven pounds wouldn't enter my dreams . . . really? Per week?'

'Really. Twice the average wage, in fact. I can't say I don't share your surprise, but that's my brief. And that wage is outside of all other expenses, including full board – I've mentioned that will be covered separately. The family tells me that the amount reflects the quality of the governess they're expecting. I was specifically asked to find someone over twenty-five but under thirty.'

'That is specific.'

Miss Farnsworth's assistant arrived with a tray and two cups of steaming tea. 'Yes, I won't even bother with sending them the shortlist. You're perfect. Over here, Tiggy, please.' She pointed to the young woman. 'I took the liberty of ordering a second. Will you join me?'

'Yes, thank you. May I ask why the brief is so explicit?'

'No doubt identifying with Georgina's needs. Someone too young would not have the mettle and someone older may be too distant from their teens, or potentially overbearing for Georgina.'

'I see. So may I ask what the family is like?'

'Utterly delightful, from what I hear. You would be well looked after and you would have one day per month to visit your family. I have made provision for that, as you requested.'

Stella took a draught of her tea. It was lightly flavoured. 'Lovely, thank you. Orange pekoe?'

'I'm impressed.'

It was Stella's turn to shrug. 'My training at the department store has been long and varied. I did a course on tea during my late teens. Um, how long is the employment for?' She had already calculated that if she saved almost every penny from this job, she could keep up the payments on the house . . . maybe even buy it outright. Or sell it, pay off what had to be settled, add her savings to what might be left and maybe the tearooms in the spa town didn't have to remain the dream . . . She wanted to laugh aloud but Suzanne Farnsworth was clearly not jesting with her.

'Ah yes, shall we say a six-month placement? I'm afraid I couldn't offer less because you understand that it's an upheaval for everyone and we want no chopping and changing, should you agree.'

Stella nodded.

'But I won't lock you into longer until we know everyone's happy with the arrangement, yourself included.'

'Yes, that sounds wise. I've been given up to one year away from the department store.' Stella could hear she sounded in control and yet inside she was churning with excitement. Yesterday she hadn't thought she could ever feel excited again about anything.

'That's generous of your superiors,' Suzanne commented.

'It suits the management right now.'

'So, what do you think, Stella? I would like to ring the family later today and confirm an appointment.'

Stella put her cup and saucer down quietly, using the time to draw a silent breath. The honest answer was that she wasn't thinking about anything but survival; her mind still felt blanketed by grief and confusion. Rafe had surely done her a kindness in obliging her to come to this agency. Plus the money! It would empower her and the family to go forward.

'I think I should say yes, Miss Farnsworth,' she said, looking up from her hands, knowing the decision was sound.

Her companion's bright gaze narrowed from the wide smile. 'Good girl, Stella. I'm thrilled for you and for the family. I feel sure your life is about to change.'

The words felt darkly prophetic but Stella smiled. 'May I know their names?'

'Indeed you may. Douglas and Beatrice Ainsworth. They live at Harp's End, which is a sprawling property not far from Tunbridge Wells on the edge of the Weald. Quite beautiful it is too. I've attended a function on the lawns.'

'What does Mr Ainsworth do?'

'Oh, he's a financier or something in the city. Mrs Ainsworth is involved in various charitable projects and the girls attend Benenden, not far from Cranbrook.'

'When would I start?'

Suzanne closed the folder. 'As soon as possible, Stella. I would be urging you to leave this week.' She must have gauged Stella's response to that recommendation simply through body language because she followed up quickly. 'All right, it's the 8th now, so how about May 22nd? Kent is gorgeous in spring. I'll arrange monies for your train ticket and travel expenses. Take a suitcase of clothes only because the family will organise to send for any other personal items you may like around you.'

'Like what?'

'Oh, you know, a favourite piece of bedroom furniture or your bicycle or whatever,' Suzanne said airily, waving a dismissive hand, black polish catching the glow from the desk light.

'No, there's nothing special, some books, clothes, just essentials.'

'Even easier,' the woman replied. 'Right.' She glanced out of the window. 'More of those May showers threatening. Will you be all right for getting home?'

'Yes, thank you, the Tube gets me near enough door to door.' Stella dug into her bag and pulled out the new Underground map that London was so proud of. 'Finally, it all makes simple sense,' she admitted.

'Oh yes, I'd heard about that – I'm afraid I don't use the Underground.'

Stella could well understand how a cocktail cigarette holder might attract attention in the honeycomb of public transport tunnels. 'When it's raining and the traffic gets so crowded, it's faster and more reliable beneath the streets,' she explained unnecessarily but it bridged an awkward moment that surely highlighted their different backgrounds. Stella stood. 'I'm grateful to you for this opportunity.'

Suzanne Farnsworth followed, becoming upright in a languid movement and held out her long-fingered hand. 'A pleasure, Stella. I'm pleased to know this unrivalled wage is going to someone so deserving. I hope it makes the difference you need to your sister and brother. Between you and me, I've not hired a governess at such a wage before so I'm imagining this to be a very special placement. I know you'll make me proud.' They shook hands. 'I'll have all the paperwork delivered to your address, but shall we plan for your arrival next weekend in Kent?'

Stella nodded, smiling. 'I don't know whether to be excited or nervous.'

'Bit of both never hurts. You've got the goods, Stella. You'll make an impression, I'm certain of it,' Suzanne said, smiling and moving to the office door and opening it.

'Thank you again.'

Stella felt the spring drizzle land on her skin and a ripple of anticipation travelled through her like a current of awakening. Rafe, wherever he was, had been right to insist. The change of scenery and lifestyle was going to be an island in the sea of grief that she could rest on for a while. Six months would fly and she wouldn't miss either of her youngsters' birthdays, she realised. In fact she could even plan a family Christmas in a new house somewhere if she could ask Uncle Bryn to help with the sale of the Clapham home. It felt as though everything was falling neatly into position to give her a glimpse into a new chapter in her life.

She unfolded her umbrella and hurried across the damp streets towards London Victoria Station. People were huddling beneath the awning on the concourse as they emerged into the open air and scrambled for their brollies or to pull on mackintoshes. It wasn't raining properly yet but it would; the sky was looking interminably grumpy with pockets of heavy grey clouds glowering with intent. The dampness intensified the smell of metal and tarmac but the aroma of chips frying somewhere made her belly grumble. She'd not eaten today and she was looking forward to the shepherd's pie that Aunt Dil had promised tonight. Stella was glad to skip down the steps to the Underground entrance, where the second-hand breath of smokers made sure a fog hovered above the hurrying commuters. Her gaze moved briskly past the familiar series of etiquette posters that asked commuters to let people off the trains first before boarding.

Stella pulled the three-penny bit she'd readied in her pocket to pay for her ticket and moved with the fast-flowing stream of commuters deeper into the catacombs, hardly daring to imagine that she would soon be leaving this life behind for the hills and meadows of Kent. She wished she could tell the friendly stranger she knew as Rafe that she had taken his advice, but as the train arrived with its blast of warm air that dragged her dark waved hair away from her face she decided it was perhaps best he didn't know, not that she'd know how to find him anyway. She let herself believe that the handsome man had been sent into her life like a messenger to bring change and that seeing him again might stir up feelings she didn't need to disturb, especially with a married man.

4

Stella was determined to see her brother and sister off to school this morning – her last for a while in London. Carys held her hand tightly through mittens and Stella tried not to think about how to say goodbye.

Ahead she watched Rory, whose spirits had mercifully improved with the arrival of his new bicycle and the news of the move to live with his aunt and uncle. Rory possessed the trait that gave him a sense of measure. While he was deeply and understandably morose at the loss of his mother and father, he was feeding off Stella's stoicism and able to consider that there was brightness ahead.

Already he was excited about taking his new bicycle to their aunt and uncle's house where small lanes afforded all-day safe riding. She saw him twist the handlebars with dexterity to turn the bike so he could double back.

'Stella?'

'Yes?' she enquired, ensuring her tone was cheerful.

'Will Uncle Bryn take me fishing, do you think?'

'Of course! He can't wait. He's already planning to cut down a rod so it's better for your height.'

'Really?' His eyes shone with eagerness.

She made a mental note to ask Uncle Bryn to do just that. 'Yes, he's so looking forward to teaching you. Dad used to love to fish,

Aunty Dil said, and he was good at it. Maybe you will be too.'

'I'll catch enough to feed us all,' Rory swaggered, riding slowly and standing up in his saddle to show off new skills.

Stella's heart swelled at the thought of her brother being allowed to run a little wild; it was something their mother had always hoped for, but living in London had meant too much brick and concrete for the country childhood she'd enjoyed in Brittany.

'What about me, Stella?' Carys wondered, lisping in a sad tone.

'Well, let's just get Rory off to his class before I tell you about all the excitement coming your way, darling,' Stella soothed, knowing her sister would not be persuaded as easily. They'd arrived at the junior school gate. Already children were trooping in, mittens dangling from overcoat sleeves, balls being kicked against scuffed shoes and bright voices breathing steam with their enthusiasm to get a few minutes of play in before the school bell was rung.

'You ready, Rory?' Stella adjusted his cap that was slanting rakishly.

He nodded. She wanted to stroke his soft cheek, stung pink by the cold, but Danny Nichols arrived to punch his arm instead.

Danny whistled. 'Better kiss your sister, Rory,' he taunted, making smooching sounds.

'Shut up, Danny,' Rory replied over his shoulder but Stella could see the colour had darkened in his cheeks.

'Well, how about a hug for your big sis instead.'

Rory was embarrassed by his friend but not enough to deny Stella the embrace she craved.

'Ooooh,' she groaned softly. 'I'm going to miss you, Rory. I need you to be the man of our family now.' He nodded as he pulled away. She was relieved to see his eyes were dry although hers were misting. 'Be good for your aunt and uncle, all right? Back soon, I promise.'

'One month, you said.'

'I did. And then I'll take you bowling.'

'And to the funfair at —'

'I know, I know. I won't forget.' She grinned and he returned it with a gap-toothed smile that was so reminiscent of her mother that the hurt caught in her throat. It made her desperate to keep holding him but she let him go. 'Danny's waiting,' she nodded behind him but couldn't resist any longer. Stella knocked off his school cap to ruffle his dark hair, knowing her aunt would take the scissors to it as soon as she got him under her roof. He surprised her with another hug – a fierce one this time – to melt her heart and then he grabbed his cap and was trundling his bike into the school playground.

She blew him a kiss when he looked around but he didn't blow one back because the other boys had gathered and were nudging each other. Stella didn't feel bad. She knew Rory would be fine and that he'd think of something amusing to say that would crack them up; he was mature beyond his years and this buoyed her.

Carys was different, of course. She'd begun crying the previous evening and now Stella could hear sniffles again as she doggedly pressed on, to walk around to the primary section of the school.

'Stella, I still don't understand why you have to go?'

Stella remained patient and explained once again in the simplest manner she could, finishing with: '. . . and as I told you we'll get a weekend together in just a few weeks' time. Remember how we marked up the Scenes of the Continent calendar last night?' Carys nodded with a sniff. Stella recalled with a heavy heart how she'd taken down the calendar and shown Carys. 'You see, here's today, darling. And here is when I shall be back with you.'

'Forever?'

'Not forever . . . But we'll do some fun things, just you and I, I promise.'

Carys stopped walking. 'Four weeks feels like forever. Mum and Dad have gone and now you're going.' Stella felt the baby of their family trembling with fresh tears that burst into new sobs and she quickly dropped to her haunches so she could look into the huge blue eyes not unlike her own. These were wet with sorrow while Stella was forcing hers to remain dry.

'Please don't be worried, Carys. I'm not leaving you altogether. If you count the days – and this afternoon you can go home and tick off two already!'

Carys halted her bleating and blinked. 'Two?' she hiccuped.

Stella grinned and nodded. 'We didn't tick off yesterday yet, and you can also tick off today. I'll be home before you know it.' She dug into a pocket and found a hanky. 'Here, blow, darling I need you to be a big girl for me.' Her sister blew noisily into the cotton square and they both laughed at the sound. 'Take care of Rory and be good for Aunty Dil. Do you know she's so excited to be having you both stay for a little while, and I just know she's going to spoil you terribly.'

'How long is a little while?'

Stella knew Carys couldn't grasp what the period would feel like so she tried again with the calendar. 'Just one of those calendar pages. And the time will pass so fast you won't believe it. I shall be back for good by the end of autumn and we can plan a wonderful Christmas. I'm hoping we can be in our new home by the time we celebrate the new year of 1934 and you can choose your own bedroom wallpaper. How's that?'

Damp eyes shone back at her. 'I can?'

Stella nodded, meaning it with all her heart. 'Now, I don't want to leave you feeling sad – at least you have Rory and our aunt and uncle. I shall have no one to cuddle. Will you give me a smile and big kiss to carry away with me and a promise to write?'

Carys responded with a hard kiss to Stella's cheek and then fell into her big sister's arms and wept a little more, but not as hard. Practice told Stella that these tears would dry up soon.

'I'll write as soon as I get back from school because I shall be missing you by then,' Carys moaned.

'I know, darling,' she whispered, silently cursing her parents' cowardice once again. Surely they knew how much their deaths would hurt the very people they loved the most?

The parting when it came wasn't as painful as she'd dreaded. It was Carys who saved them.

'Perhaps we should say "See you again" like Mummy always told us. She hated goodbyes didn't she?'

Clearly not enough. Stella couldn't help the uncharitable thought and wished she could drag her mother alongside to witness all this bravery from her children that she had so lacked. 'Good idea. *Á bientôt, ma cherie*,' she whispered, hugging her sister, inhaling the faintly soapy smell still on her skin.

'*Á bientôt*, Stella. Hurry home.'

Mrs Walker, the third-form teacher on duty in the playground had already anticipated the tears and had generously agreed to meet them at the gate when Stella had told her of the family's situation. She nodded with understanding at Stella. 'Morning, Carys. Gosh, do you know what I just heard?' Carys looked up with enquiry. 'Apparently we're going on an excursion to London Zoo tomorrow.' Carys gasped. Stella had known about it, and planned for this surprise to be landed on her sister at this tense moment of farewell. 'I know, it's so exciting and we're gathering a list of the children who are able to come. I was hoping you might like to be one of the leaders of the group going – you'll have a special list of important duties.'

Stella watched her sister's eyes shine with pleasure. 'Really? Me?'

'Oh, golly gosh, yes. You were the first person I thought of to wear the special badge of leader. So come on, I have to get you to agree formally to that important position and I have to give you a badge and your armband. I'm putting you in charge of the green group of your year – along with Nancy Bell.'

'Nancy and I are best friends, Miss Walker.'

'Oh, well, yes, I thought you two would make the perfect pair. Nancy's already here – shall we go and find her?'

Carys turned back to Stella, tears dried, new energy beaming from her eyes instead. 'I have to go, Stella, did you hear?'

'I did. Hurry off, Carys, sounds like you have important things to do.' Her sister fell into her arms once more but there was no trembling now. Stella kissed her nose, as she always did to make Carys giggle. 'Let's both plan to write tonight so our letters kiss on the way to each other.'

Carys laughed now. 'Bye, Stella.'

'Back soon, darling.' She blew her a kiss too but Carys was already gushing in conversation with her teacher and it was Miss Walker who caught the kiss and nodded.

She breathed deeply, her glance skimming across the school playground where she must now leave her heart and turn away from the lives she loved to the new life beckoning.

It had been tempting to drift into a doze on the journey south from London's Charing Cross Station, especially after the early-morning journey into central London. Uncle Bryn had come down with his car and driven Stella and her aunt for their teary goodbye on the concourse of the ornate French Renaissance-style building that fronted The Strand.

'Don't come in with me,' Stella quavered, hugging her aunt fiercely and swallowing back tears that had wanted to fall since she'd walked her brother and sister to school an hour earlier. Instead they parted to look at each other, still embracing. 'It only makes it harder.'

Her aunt nodded, pulling off her glove to dab at her eyes with an embroidered handkerchief. 'I shall miss you, darling, but I promise the children will want for nothing.'

'I know.' She had to run away. This was feeling even harder than she'd imagined. 'Kiss Uncle Bryn for me and thank him again for driving me in.'

'Leave,' her aunt said, 'or I may not let you go!' They swapped a teary laugh. 'You've got your purse? We'll see you in four weeks, then.'

'I promise,' Stella replied, and after a final swift hug she left her aunt's arms. Moving away, she looked back once more and mouthed 'Bye,' before turning and hurrying into one of the many darkened entrance arches that led her into the station proper. Stella sniffed back any further tears as she queued to buy her ticket, promising herself she would not shed another.

'Monthly return third-class to Tunbridge Wells, please,' she said to the man behind the counter, retrieving the ten-shilling note that Miss Farnsworth had made sure was enclosed for Stella's travel expenses with all of her paperwork.

He appeared weary. 'That's London to Hastings via Tunbridge Wells,' he murmured to himself, looking up the cost in his prices book. 'That will be six shilling and sixpence,' he mumbled, nodding as her note was placed in the depression of the brass plate between them. 'And sixpence back, makes it seven shillings and eight,' he said, dropping a shilling on top of the sixpence. He reached into his drawer and found another coin, adding a florin to her change. 'And two more makes ten, Miss.' Checking first the bottom of his rubber stamp before dabbing it on the inkpad he looked to where neat racks of the small cardboard tickets were stacked and selected the correct one. He carefully pressed it against the back of Stella's ticket to date the start of the season ticket before he found a small pincer-like tool that was hung from his desk on a piece of string. He used it to clip a tiny triangle shape from the ticket's top to show it had been properly purchased. She watched all of these processes in fascination as he next selected another stamp – a single large-lettered one – and this he briskly punched against a red inkpad. He blinked, looking up over his glasses. 'Er, this season ticket is for you, isn't it, Miss?'

'Yes.' She wasn't sure why he had checked that.

He nodded his thanks, banged the stamp down on the front of the ticket with purpose and she saw a bold red W appear.

'Oh? What does that mean?'

The man looked up tiredly. 'We mark all tickets of female travellers, Miss.'

'Good grief, really?'

'I don't make the rules, Miss. I'm sure it is meant as a courtesy.' He placed the soft green card ticket beneath the coins. 'Show this at the ticket barrier.'

She wanted to say *Just in case I need to prove I'm a female traveller?* Instead she muttered thanks, adding: 'May I ask, is the next train at twenty-five to eleven?'

He consulted a large book by his side. 'Yes, on Southern Railways, but it would pay you to check on the departure board. There can be delays this time of year.'

'Thank you and which —'

'Platform five.'

She gave him a bright smile of thanks; it never hurt, and he looked surprised by the gesture.

'Thank you, Miss. Safe travels.'

Stella left the ticket office and joined the herd of people fixated on the departure board; people were instantly in frantic motion around her as the man on the tannoy announced the Brighton train. It had obviously been delayed. Stella felt caught in a maelstrom and stood still, clutching her hand luggage as a fast-moving river of people flowed around her for several seconds. Then just as suddenly they were all gone, scampering towards the platform and the train that would rush them off to the popular seaside town she remembered spending one of her happiest childhood summers at.

It was a quarter-past ten so she had some time before she needed to head through the gate. She used the distraction of the newsagency kiosk of WH Smith & Son to kill off a few more minutes and keep her mind occupied. She queued to buy a newspaper she was sure she would not read – although the headline of another sighting of the Loch Ness monster was intriguing – and some sweets. She handed over another sixpence as she overheard talk around her concerning the cricket series that was underway, with England feeling confident apparently.

Stella walked with purpose towards the ticket barrier at the gate to platform five without giving herself an opportunity to reconsider. The ticket inspector looked smart in his dark three-piece suit and gold Southern Railways emblem on his lapel. She handed him her ticket.

'Cheer up, Miss. It might never happen,' he joked.

She smiled weakly as he punched a second hole through it, a slightly different shape this time.

'There you go, Miss. Enjoy your journey.'

She watched the guard blow his whistle and wave his flag. Obediently the Hastings-bound train grunted, jerked and then with a soft squeal eased with a gentle shunt out of Charing Cross Station, smoke billowing around them.

Immediately they crossed the Thames and Stella worked out they were on the Hungerford Bridge. Now with her attention engaged she gazed out of the windows for a distant sighting of Big Ben and the Houses of Parliament.

Goodbye, London, she thought and was surprised to feel no angst. She thought she might experience a wave of regret but in this moment the intense grief of the last month was fading, as familiar sights of London were left behind.

Stella smiled to herself; suddenly the decision to work away from London felt right. It seemed like a pathway was opening and with it a fresh mindset for a new life.

The train's soothing rhythm appeared to be encouraging two people in the carriage to have a snooze already, but Stella had remained alert from nervous sucking on a penny's worth of rainbow drops she'd thrown into her bag. The carriage wasn't crowded but she looked away from the lacquered wood and small framed posters in the compartment urging her to take a Nightboat Train to France. It sounded mysterious and the perfect escape from her troubles but travelling the continent seemed well beyond her reach. Right now Kent was her destination and given that she'd spent most of her life in London, this journey could be considered exotic, surely?

Looking out at the increasingly rural landscape, she ignored her newspaper and eased another sweet into her mouth. Yesterday she'd also bought a block of Cadbury's Milk for Georgina, some tiny jellies for Grace and a box of Black Magic for their parents. The latter, by Rowntrees of York, had set her back the frightening amount of nearly two shillings, but given the generosity of the Ainsworths, she felt it important not to arrive empty-handed. Her gaze tried to lock onto one image but colours blurred as clarity dimmed and the familiar world she knew began to shimmer and hint at its new shape.

The land had changed from the grimy, built-up areas of London to more park-like lands beyond Bankside Coal Power Station. The train stopped briefly at London Bridge Station and then it really was farewell to the city as Stella gazed sentimentally at Tower Bridge and the retreating Tower of London. The train began to accelerate, it too beginning to feel free of the big city pull, and it commenced its long and steady climb through suburban London. Stella noticed that regular travellers in her compartment were already lost to books or newspapers, while she was still leaning forward and entranced by the cityscape giving way to less crowded streets.

She watched trams grinding along, while cars like shiny beetles manoeuvred around them and the old guard of horse-drawn carts continued to move at their slow pace within an ever-increasing mechanised world. She'd heard about the new-fangled electric trains servicing outer London and wondered if she would glimpse one from this higher vantage.

Her train was gathering more speed and the man reading the newspaper was now only pretending. She could see his jaw relax as he drifted to sleep but she was still alert as they sped through stations without stopping. The names of Hither Green, Grove Park and Elmstead Woods moved by her gaze.

Stella had to admit her shoulders were beginning to relax and she sensed she was secretly escaping her duty to grieve.

'It will be worth the tears,' she promised in a whisper to the glass she stared through, watching her breath condense against the cold pane. Sitting back, she was glad that the fellow opposite in his tawny, checked three-piece suit was fast asleep, his newspaper sprawled against his belly. He looked like a squire from the *Country Life* magazines she'd seen.

At Orpington the guard on board announced that passengers were required to close their windows to prevent smoke getting in as they were about to enter a long cutting with two tunnels. Stella wondered if she should obey the instructions as she was seated next to the window but one of the men in her compartment nodded to her that he would take care of this and gallantly ensured all the windows were sealed.

The world outside her carriage suddenly went dark as the train was gobbled up by a tunnel and Stella could see herself reflected in the window as dull black walls imprisoned them and black smoke presumably billowed between her and the scorched bricks. Suddenly all the sounds of the steam-belching snake that carried them from city to city were magnified and the dull light of the train made reading more difficult. Her fellow passengers seemed to rouse from their books or slumber, going by the change of mood, and Stella was struck, as she returned to stare at her reflection, by how changed she appeared in this strange low light. She couldn't pinpoint why, but she just knew she looked different – sadder, somehow – despite the fresh feeling of being unburdened.

There was the briefest of respites, a few glorious moments of release as they were belched out of the first part of the cutting before they were plunged into darkness again as the second tunnel – longer this time – swallowed them.

By the time they emerged a minute later the light drizzle had miraculously stopped and achingly bright sunshine caused Stella to flinch at the sharpness. It was as though they had all just crossed some magical threshold and on this side the world was warm and painted from a sparkling palette. Even her tweedy companion opposite felt the sudden change in temperature as clouds parted and welcomed them into the area known as the garden of England, and he snorted himself awake.

The scenery had changed to verdant, with London's tapestry of grey replaced by a brilliant green with flashes of spring flowers and yellow tractors. The guard was announcing that they would now be making stops at stations with charming names like Knockholt and Sevenoaks.

One more tunnel and they were descending joyfully through countryside so lush that Stella was sure she had forgotten just how green rural England was after so long moving through London's drab streets. She noticed they were crossing another bridge and presumed this was to move across the River Medway that she had read about.

She eventually felt the train slow to a gentle pace as its rhythmic puffing sound lengthened and deepened. They were making their approach into Tunbridge Wells. A whistle blew distantly and a long sigh of steam was expelled as the carriage groaned and wheezed to a halt.

Doors began to open up and down the train that was painted the colour of rich brown-sage with glossy black frames and wheels. Stella nodded a silent smiling farewell at her tweedy friend who had eased down the window to push his arm through and open the door from the outside. He gestured for Stella to go first and as she stepped onto the Royal Tunbridge Wells platform one, she was engulfed by the hiss and billow of steam while the stationmaster and his team of men moved up and down the train helping people off, removing sacks of mail, special parcels and reloading whatever had to go onto Hastings.

Stella was immediately struck by the freshness of the air, entirely convinced she could smell grass, the scent of freesia . . . even taste the ocean that reminded her of visiting Cornwall once with her family. It felt instantly intoxicating. She was anticipating being met and scanned the entrance to the station. No one looked likely, but she wasn't worried. Right now it felt so empowering to have left London far behind. Stella took a moment to breathe in that bright air as she regarded the beauty of the station building with its even red-brick façade and cream paintwork around the many small-paned windows. Its dignified appearance attested to the Georgian influences in Tunbridge Wells that she'd heard about from subsequent conversations with Suzanne Farnsworth.

'Miss Myles?'

She hadn't seen the man, probably only a few years younger than her father, step forward from the shadows of the station. He was not wearing a uniform but instead was dressed in a neat suit from what she could see beneath a driving coat. 'Oh yes, hello?'

'I'm John Potter.' She recognised the name and smiled. 'Welcome to Kent, Miss Myles. The Ainsworths have sent me to pick you up and take you to Harp's End, which is not too far from Tunbridge Wells.'

'Thank you, Mr Potter, it's very kind of you. Do call me Stella.'

He smiled and Stella couldn't help but like him immediately for the way his pleasure at her invitation sparkled in his eyes. 'I'll do that,' he said, and then he winked in an avuncular way and she was instantly sold. 'So you must call me John. Very glad to meet you, Stella.' He held out a gloved hand and was careful to shake hers gently. 'Here, let me take all that for you.'

'Oh . . . there's a box of —'

'I'll be careful,' he promised. 'This way. Just hand your ticket to the man over there.' He nodded towards him. 'Morning, George.'

'Hello, Potty. Good morning, Miss. Welcome to Royal Tunbridge Wells.'

'Everyone is so friendly,' she remarked, showing her ticket that he clipped for her.

'Keep that safe now for your return journey.'

She smiled thanks. 'I'm Stella Myles,' she said, guessing it was appropriate to introduce herself to this friendly stranger.

George touched his cap.

'Stella's the new governess for the Ainsworths,' Potter added.

'Oh well, good for you, Miss Stella. You'll never want to leave here now, though,' he warned with warm affection for his town.

'I know I'm going to love it,' she replied, 'but I have family in London so you may see me coming and going, George.'

'So long as you always return and bring your beauty back to Kent, I'll be here to see you safely on and off the train.'

She chuckled. 'What a flirt you are!'

Both men laughed, lifted hands in farewell and John motioned for her to follow him. 'We have to go up these stairs. Here, let me take that extra bag. Do you know much about Tunbridge Wells, Stella?'

'Too little, I'm afraid.'

They emerged onto the main street and she looked left, up the steep hill, enchanted by the elegant little shops that lined it and turned into housing, she presumed.

'This is Mount Pleasant Road,' Potter explained.

'It certainly suits its name,' she said, revolving to take in the clock tower and the pretty façade of the railway station.

He could tell she was keen to get her bearings. 'Well, now, behind us is the Lonsdale Mansions – that's a private hotel. In the distance that's Holy Trinity Church. Here we are,' he said, gesturing to a magnificent silver-grey car. 'I wasn't sure if you'd like the hood down. Women do not like their hairstyles being blown too hard, although it's a perfect day for going topless,' he said with a wink. 'But I took the precaution of keeping the hood on.'

She stared with disbelief that this was all laid on for her. Potter reached for the back door.

'Here, let's get you settled and then I can load —'

'Do you mind very much if I ride in front with you, John? I'm not used to all this special treatment.'

He smiled broadly again. 'Of course. It would be a pleasure.' He opened the front passenger door and soon enough joined her in the cab, pulling on his driving gloves.

'What a splendid car,' Stella said, running a hand across the soft crimson leather.

'She's a beauty, this Daimler. It's been in the family since before the Great War.' He gave a honk to someone passing by, who lifted a hand in salutation, and then he gently eased the car down the hill. 'The Pantiles are over there,' he said, pointing. 'They're tiled colonnades that lead from the chalybeate spring that's situated on this end closest to us. People have been visiting here to dip in the waters since the 1600s, including several royals, and it's why the town boasts that title.'

She could hear the pride in his voice. 'Chalybeate?'

'They're mineral springs with salts of iron and people have long believed they have properties to promote good health.'

She recalled her conversation with Rafe and sharing her secret of the tearooms near a spa. Life was strange. 'Have you tried it?'

He cut her a grin. 'No, even though I've lived in Kent all my life but then I have to tell you that the whole Weald is a healthy region. Not like Londoners – all pasty and grey. Not you, of course, Miss Myles.'

'I must say the air feels clean. I swear I can taste the beach.'

'You can. Brighton is about twenty-seven miles as the crow flies but on certain days that breeze will bring the salty English Channel right to our front door. I know you'd probably like to have a nose around but I think I'd better get you to the house first, so you can settle in.'

The township was already behind them, she noticed, but she had an impression of it spreading over the length of a hill that they were descending down to the colonnades that he spoke of. 'Of course, there's plenty of time to get to know these streets. Is there a good bookshop?'

'Oh, my word, yes, several. And Hall's Bookshop, a wonderful spot for antiquarian books. I'll give you directions. Mr Ainsworth when he's home always finds excuses for me to drop him off in town and have a couple of hours' rummaging at Hall's and he almost always returns with a couple of second-hand books, some quite rare.'

'How long have you worked for the Ainsworths, John?'

He signalled he was turning left out of the High Street by

sticking his arm out of the open window and turning his hand in the air. 'Ooh now, that's a question. Let me see, has to be nearly seventeen years now. We're just leaving the main town now and heading out on the London Road.'

'So you've known the two girls since they were born.'

'Indeed. I used to drive Mrs Ainsworth around when she was pregnant with Miss Georgina.'

'Are you her driver? I mean, Mrs Ainsworth's?'

'I'm at the disposal of the family.'

'I was told that Georgina and I would have the services of a driver. Would that be you, John, or do you have other duties?'

'Very happy to drive for you. Mr Ainsworth specifically put me in charge of your needs and those of Miss Georgina's while you're together. He assures me he will cope without me.' He gave her another wink. 'Mr Ainsworth is away quite a lot, anyway; you probably won't see very much of him.'

'Does he work in London?'

'Yes. He travels for his work too.'

'Oh, how exciting.' She knew she sounded wistful.

'And Kent isn't exciting enough?' At her instantly apologetic look, he waved a hand to calm her. 'I'm only teasing. It's a quiet family. We don't hold many parties and the like – all very peaceful at Harp's End. Just a few charity fundraising events, that sort of thing. Mrs Ainsworth does have some social gatherings that she hosts, but as I say, it's a tranquil life.'

Stella gave him a look of huge relief at his remark.

Again they made a turn, this time away from the traffic on the main highway between London and the south coast, and swinging into a far narrower pass lined by hedgerow.

'You're going to be fine. Fitting in with strangers is never easy, but you'll work it out, I'm sure.'

'How do you find Mr Ainsworth?'

'He's not terribly easy to get to know but you probably won't have to. You'll be more in touch with the girls and Mrs Ainsworth, although I suspect she too will leave you very much to your own plans.'

'I hope I can win the girls' trust.'

'Don't try. Just be yourself and I'm sure they'll be charmed by you.' His words resonated solidly in her mind as being wise. Yes, she shouldn't try too hard and instead let the children respond to her.

He seemed to understand her fears. 'Miss Georgina is at an age where she is beginning to assert herself, and that's to be expected, but dare I say she is beautiful like her mother and knows what she wants. She's a modern woman.'

Despite his conversational tone Stella heard only caution shadowing the innocent words. She remembered Suzanne Farnsworth's breezier warning, and repeated it. 'We were all teenagers at one time.'

'Good for you, Stella.'

Stella reckoned they drove for another ten minutes with hedgerow giving way to open country and scenes that made her think of a living patchwork quilt before it closed in again with high brambles. She could just make out chimneystacks towering above quick glimpses of a hipped roofline.

'Is that Harp's End I spy through the trees?'

'Oh, yes, just moments away now.'

Stella held her breath and they swung around a narrow corner and her world opened up again as they eased out of the shadows of the hedges and into a long driveway.

'Here we are,' Potter said, sounding proud. 'I never get tired of this sight of the house,' he admitted.

Home, Stella thought, regarding the imposing Georgian residence that loomed ahead. Its proportions even to her untrained eye looked perfectly square. 'Four floors.' She thought she'd counted silently and was taken aback when Mr Potter answered.

'Four living levels plus the attic and the basement, of course.'

'It's so grand,' she breathed, taking in the pleasing symmetry and gazing at the charming sash windows that were too numerous to count. Stella briefly wondered who was behind those windows gazing back at her but the mansion, every bit as pretty as the doll's house her sister had fallen in love with on a special visit to Hamleys Toy Shop in London's Regent Street a few years ago, soon distracted her from the thought.

'It was built at the turn of the eighteenth century,' Potter said, as he slowed the car to a crawl up the drive, 'and from what I understand it was considered "quaint" by the standards of the day, and in the language of the day that meant modest; not at all flashy.'

'It looks enormous to me,' she admitted, imagining how much her warm French mother would loathe its bleak grey stone walls. 'I live in a modest Victorian semi-detached house of four bedrooms.'

Potter chuckled. 'And I live in a tiny apartment above the garage.'

Stella shared his smile.

'I'm not sure I can even tell you how many guest rooms we have at Harp's End, Stella, but there are four grand reception rooms, including a ballroom.'

'And all this land around us, I presume?'

'Oh, yes, upwards of forty acres, and there are other landholdings nearby that belong to the family with cottages and farmhouses on them.' He manoeuvred the car gently around the gravel circular drive ringed by beds of spring flowers. They crunched quietly to a halt. 'There you are. Leave everything. We'll have it all brought in for you. Ah, there's Mrs Boyd. She's the housekeeper. She's a spinster but perhaps you know the housekeeper is always called Mrs?' He nodded to where a woman in a long, dark dress awaited her with hands clasped. Potter was already out of the car and moving to Stella's side to open her door.

'I didn't,' she admitted, cutting him a grin. 'Thank you, John. Wish me luck!'

He helped her out of the car. 'You won't need it.' He winked. 'Hello, Mrs Boyd, here we are. I've brought Miss Stella Myles.'

'Hello, Miss Myles,' the woman said. There was a soft Yorkshire lilt in her tone. 'Welcome to Harp's End.' She emerged fully from the portico and descended the flight of stone stairs with a hand out in greeting. 'We've been looking forward to your arrival.'

Stella shook her head and, swallowing, put on her happiest voice. *First impressions*, she heard her father's advice, *account for so much*. 'Oh, it's wonderful to finally be here. Thank you for sending Mr Potter.'

'Are you hungry?'

'Not really. Nervous, perhaps,' she admitted.

Boyd smiled beneath hooded eyes and a tightly tied bun but she had a fine complexion and her tone was friendly. 'Come, there's a fresh pot of tea on and the family is expecting you in the conservatory.'

Stella wasn't sure what was appropriate to say to this so she smiled. 'I'd better not keep them waiting any longer, then.'

'You haven't kept them waiting. It's three o'clock and teatime in the house. Please,' she gestured inside but craned her neck to catch Potter's attention. 'Shall I send someone out, Mr Potter, or can you manage?'

Stella didn't hear his reply but saw Mrs Boyd nod and then turn back. 'Right, follow me, Miss Myles.'

'I'd prefer you call me Stella,' she said.

'All right, then. This way, Stella.' The housekeeper didn't sound terribly sure about the suggestion and didn't offer that she be called anything but Mrs Boyd, but Stella was already entirely distracted by the vastness of the house to let this worry her.

'Good grief,' she muttered. 'How will I ever find my way around?'

'You won't have to. We'll keep you moving in a much smaller triangle, I promise, or you could get lost with all the hallways and nooks and crannies of Harp's End.'

Stella knew Mrs Boyd meant this to sound light-hearted and yet it perhaps unwittingly came across as a warning not to snoop. She let it pass.

'Gosh, that staircase!' she remarked, gazing up, astonished by the fussy, panelled design that swept up through the various floors.

'Magnificent, isn't it? True William and Mary style,' Mrs Boyd remarked, sounding proud. 'The panelling is reminiscent of the staircase on the HMS *Titanic*, and we're assured that the structure remains intact to this day, despite sinking.' She chortled but it didn't resemble amusement to Stella's ears. 'But there is a back stairs passage to quickly reach your rooms.'

'Thank you,' Stella murmured, not sure if she was glad she wouldn't be using the floridly grand staircase to the upper levels, or offended that she wasn't important enough to be invited to do so.

'Ah, here we are,' Mrs Boyd said eagerly, 'just through this hall into Mrs Ainsworth's favourite area of the house.' She led an increasingly nervous Stella into a glass-enclosed room that trapped the sun and thus turned up the temperature from a cool autumn day to a mild afternoon. 'Mrs Ainsworth, I've brought Stella Myles.'

5

Stella watched a slimly built woman turn from where she had been admiring a citrus bush. Stella was struck first by her employer's make-up, which seemed bright for a day at home, her slash of red lipstick clashing against the abundance of lime-green leaves beside her. Cat-shaped eyes the colour of the Wedgwood blue pottery she'd seen displayed in cabinets in one of the rooms they'd passed through blinked and regarded Stella. Red polished fingernails glimmered as a barely burned, lipstick-stained cigarette was put out with a low hiss in a nearby upright ashtray.

'Miss Myles,' a smoky voice welcomed. 'How lovely that you've arrived.'

Stella heard no sincerity in the remark and cut a glance at Boyd before stepping forward, hand outstretched. 'It's a delight to be here, Mrs Ainsworth.'

'Boyd, can you fetch Georgie, please?' She touched her golden, upswept hair that was tidily pinned and regarded Stella's hand. Finally, she shook it.

'Certainly, Mrs Ainsworth,' Boyd said. 'Tea will be ready to pour. Shall I . . .'

'No, I'm sure Stella wouldn't mind.' She looked at Stella as though she were an afterthought. 'Would you?'

She didn't think she was in any position to refuse. 'Not at all,' she answered with as much levity in her voice as she could muster.

'Do you take milk, Mrs Ainsworth?'

'No, thank you, and no sugar either. Just lemon. I thought we should meet here where it's warmer,' Mrs Ainsworth continued, and Stella felt that the temperature had dropped considerably since Beatrice Ainsworth had spoken.

Instead she smiled. 'It's beautiful.' She handed her host a delicate teacup and saucer, recognising with a pang of regret for home the distinctive Limoges pattern from a single tiny jug her mother owned. She wished now she'd asked her mother how she had come by it.

'Yes,' her host remarked, unaware of Stella's pain and her tone hinting at boredom. 'I prefer to use one of the morning rooms but it's fully shaded by an oak at present and I didn't think we needed to light a fire this late in the season; not now the sun is finally showing itself. I always think it's akin to surrender to light fires once the daffodils are out, don't you?'

'Er, yes,' Stella agreed, thinking about her brother and sister shivering only a week or two earlier, wearing one thick jumper over another in an attempt to stay warm because Stella wasn't certain of paying the fuel bills.

'Do sit,' Mrs Ainsworth said, gesturing at a cane chair with an upholstered cushion next to an enormous fern. Stella couldn't help but touch it. 'I'm told that one was discovered on the other side of the world – that faraway place called Australia, I think – when a relative went adventuring in the previous century. He brought it home and somehow it has survived.'

'It's incredible. I didn't know they could grow this big.'

Her hostess seated herself languidly in another of the cane chairs and shrugged to show she really didn't care one way or another. 'Called the King Fern, apparently, but you'd have to ask my husband about that. He's the naturalist in the family.'

'Really?'

Mrs Ainsworth looked around, still giving Stella the impression that even breathing was boring. She waved her manicured hand. 'Yes, all of this is his work.'

'I think it's magnificent.'

'Do you?' The feline stare fixed upon her. 'Tell me about yourself, Miss Myles.' She sat back.

Stella was perched on the edge of her chair and took a deep breath. She gave her new employer a potted history, keeping it simple, and while not lying she didn't offer up anything beyond the bare facts, mainly about her education and work experience.

'. . . very glad to teach Grace piano, and although —'

'I was told your parents killed themselves,' Mrs Ainsworth interrupted.

Stella felt the statement hit her like shards of glass, as though one of the large windowpanes in the conservatory had shattered and been hurled down upon her. She couldn't reply immediately and stared helplessly with incomprehension at her employer.

'The agency mentioned it,' the woman qualified. 'I feel we should raise this and ensure that you are completely over the grief.' An attempt to smile kindly failed.

Stella struggled through her shock at not only the callousness but the casualness of the enquiry. She needed to draw on all her control not to bristle openly. 'No, Mrs Ainsworth, I cannot lie. I am certainly not over it and doubt I ever shall be. But I am no danger to myself or anyone else, least of all your daughters.' She was relieved her tone was polite and entirely under her control despite the raw pain still thrumming through her.

'It's just that I prefer to be open about such things.'

Such things? Stella thought, as the woman in front of her carelessly waved her hand in reference to two people she loved.

Stella cleared her throat softly. 'Yes, indeed, honesty is always preferable,' she muttered. Her anger was now as cold as her parents' grave. She mustered an assuring smile. 'And I want you to feel confident that I've come here looking forward to this role.'

'Is that so?' For the first time since they'd met, Stella thought Beatrice Ainsworth sounded genuine.

She nodded. 'From the moment I took the train this morning I felt different.'

'Oh? In what way?' Mrs Ainsworth wasn't watching her; her voice sounded suddenly distant and she was staring slightly unfocused at the tray of afternoon teacakes left untouched by both women.

'Because I was leaving London, I suppose.'

'How sad. I love London. I'd live there if my husband would agree to it.'

'Well, I know my decision was the right one. I hope you feel as certain as I do, Mrs Ainsworth?'

'I had little to do with it. Miss Farnsworth from the agency obviously does. You come incredibly well recommended.'

Stella murmured thanks but her companion wasn't listening.

'Frankly I can't imagine any woman wanting to leave London. And choosing this . . .' Her words trailed off as she heard a familiar voice. 'Ah, here comes Georgina. You'll adore her, as I do.'

Stella's gaze fixed on the doorway and suddenly a petite blonde arrived in an outfit that – to Stella's judgement – looked overly dressy for daywear at home. She also wore a slash of red lipstick. Mrs Boyd remained just inside the doorway.

'Mummy, I thought we were going into Brighton this afternoon and now look at the time!' It wasn't a question, not even so much a statement; more like an accusation. She didn't even cast a glance towards Stella, who had risen to greet her.

'Did I forget to mention we couldn't, Georgie? Sorry, darling. Georgie, this is Stella Myles.'

A cool, appraising gaze, not unlike her mother's but not from nearly as such striking eyes, turned her way.

'Hello,' she said, and it sounded vaguely like a dismissal.

'Hello, Georgina.'

The girl looked at Stella's offered hand as though she wasn't sure what to do with it. She shook it grudgingly and immediately turned back to her mother. 'So Brighton's off?'

'I'm afraid so, darling. Your father insisted we be here today to greet Miss Myles.'

'Call me Stella, please,' she insisted, but they ignored her.

'That's all very well but I don't see Daddy here. What's he doing today, roaming the Weald looking for cuckoo droppings or sketching the petals of some unknown and rare species of daisy?'

'Georgie,' her mother admonished without any heat, glancing now at Stella. 'No need for that.'

'You think it all the time, Mummy. At least I'm prepared to say it. Where is he?'

'I don't know, darling. He said he'd be gone for a few days. You know how he is.'

'I do. He gets to roam the country without being accountable to anyone, meanwhile you promised me Brighton today for shopping and now I hear I'm stuck here and it's such a nice afternoon.'

Stella watched this snappy and revealing conversation between mother and daughter with a sense of growing dread.

'Well, enough said, Georgina. Your father insisted we greet Miss Myles . . . Stella,' she corrected. 'She's to be your new companion and educator.'

Stella blinked. She didn't mind the change of title in the least but it was obvious Mrs Ainsworth was carefully navigating her introduction.

'Remember we said we wanted you to improve your linguistic skills and appreciation of art?'

'I remember *Daddy* saying that,' she said in a pouty tone.

'Well, darling, we'd both like you to be able to converse across a range of subjects, from art to politics, especially if you're to join us properly for the Season in a year or so. We want you as a stand-out.'

'Mummy, I could be dead by then,' her daughter groaned, dramatising the statement further by lifting her eyes heavenward. 'These are holidays, for pity's sake.' She flounced into a chair. 'And the tea is likely cold now,' she complained at Mrs Boyd, who arrived unflappable from where she had been hovering.

'I'll send a fresh tray up,' she said and took this as her chance to withdraw. Stella wished she could tag along with her.

'All the more reason, Georgie. Now, don't be unreasonable. Queen Charlotte's Ball costs a small fortune and you will make us proud when you're presented. I want you fluent in French and —'

'I am fluent!'

Stella couldn't resist and asked her a question in deliberately conversational French. 'What is your opinion of the monster that is reportedly swimming around in the deeps of a loch in Scotland?' Stella was well aware that it was not the same, conservative language taught in ladies' colleges in England.

Georgina Ainsworth stared back at her, somehow managing to look flummoxed and yet at the same time enraged. 'What did you say?'

Stella calmly repeated the question.

'I heard the words you spoke. I wanted to know what you actually *meant*.'

'Surely you know, darling. It sounded very French to me.'

Stella's gaze was locked on the narrowed, unremarkable blue eyes of her pupil. She knew she shouldn't be enjoying this feeling of power but the girl was already loathsome, in her opinion, and she wondered how she was going to get through a day, let alone months, with this child trapped in a woman's body. 'It was a question,' she replied in English, and she explained it as though for Beatrice's benefit when in fact it was clearly for her daughter's.

'That was not the French I know. I understood only some of it,' Georgie snapped.

'And that's why I'm here, Georgina,' she replied, now deliberately loading her tone with interest and encouragement. She had to try! 'I am going to teach you how to hold your own in French no matter who is talking to you. If you work with me, I can promise that no one will be able to whisper behind your back in colloquial French even if you were presented at a coming-out ball in Paris.'

'Bravo, Miss Myles!' Mrs Ainsworth's eyes sparkled. 'Now, that's what I had hoped to hear. Ah, here's a fresh tea.'

She really was quite beautiful, Stella thought.

The conversation stretched to other studies of Georgina's and Stella realised both women found her twice as interesting the moment she began talking about life in the department store. She even made them laugh but in a derisive manner when Stella began discussing the curious habits of some of the wealthier, more eccentric customers.

'Oh, do tell us her name, Stella. That's priceless.'

She shook her head, smiling. 'No, I was taught from my first day at Bourne & Hollingsworth that discretion was not simply a gracious act but part of the strict code of conduct for all members of the personal shopping staff.'

Before the women could press her further they were interrupted by the arrival of another, much younger, Ainsworth girl.

'Hello, Mummy,' the girl said, genuinely affectionate in the way she hugged her mother. 'Hello, Georgie. You look beautiful.'

'Hello, Podge. How were dance lessons? Didn't kill anyone by falling on them?'

'We're learning how to do an arabesque,' the youngster replied, lisping slightly on the word, and as though she hadn't heard the insult. She smiled shyly at Stella. 'Miss Bellamy took turns holding our legs so we could stretch out properly like this.' Grace made a clumsy attempt to balance on one leg while extending and pointing one arm and the other leg.

'Needs some work,' Georgie said with a smirk.

Grace was unperturbed, almost falling over as she tried to regain her balance. 'Hello,' she said, dark eyes sparkling as her gaze fell on Stella. 'Are you my new music teacher?'

Stella couldn't help but smile back warmly at the round-faced child and was struck immediately by how she seemed not to resemble her older sister. 'I am,' she replied. 'And you must be Grace,' she said, helplessly reminded of Carys. 'I love your tutu.'

'Miss Bellamy let us go early because she had a headache and we were allowed to come home in our ballet clothes,' Grace explained to her mother. She looked worried she may be told off.

'Go change, darling. You smell, too . . . of sweaty little girls and sugar. Have you been eating cake again?'

Grace nodded, grinning widely to make her plump cheeks dimple deliciously. 'There were fairy cakes afterwards because Miss Bellamy said she wanted them to . . . to . . . um, inspire us,' she said, stumbling over the word and lisping on it also. 'She said she wants us to learn to dance as light and sweet as her fairy cakes taste.'

'Eat many more of those, Podge, and your tutu will stretch beyond all recognition. You don't want to be the chubbiest ballet-dancing Ainsworth ever, do you?'

Stella frowned at the mounting series of barbs aimed by the elder sister, while the younger showed no sign of offence. Either she was used to it or her awareness was not registering it. She watched, intrigued also as Beatrice Ainsworth flinched away slightly from the second hug her youngest lavished on her.

'Boyd, have Miss Hailsham give Grace a bath, would you?'

'Yes, Madam. Is Mr Ainsworth eating with you tonight?'

'I really couldn't say. Set a place as always.'

'Of course.' She turned to Stella. 'Miss Myles, would you like me to send a tray up tonight? I'm imagining you will likely be tired, and want to get settled in.'

'Er, yes . . . yes, that would be most agreeable, thank you.' She looked back at the Ainsworths but the elder was beginning to stand, as though their meeting was now over and Georgina was already returning to the main subject concerning her.

'So, Brighton tomorrow, Mummy?'

'Yes, why not,' her mother replied, running a hand across her forehead as though a migraine might be edging forward and sounding as though the whole business of juggling a conversation with both daughters, housekeeper and new tutor was taxing; that it was clearly time to drift away and find a divan to collapse upon. 'Stella, I'm sure you could use a free day to acquaint yourself with the surrounds, unpack, get organised.'

Stella wanted to say she could be unpacked in under five minutes. Instead she lifted a shoulder and said, 'An hour tomorrow morning is fine with me.'

She felt Georgina's shooting glare like a blow. 'I'm on holiday, Mummy. I'm not getting up with the birds for French lessons and especially as I want to get going early to Brighton. Tell Potter eleven is perfect.'

Stella gave her employer a quizzical look. Was the mother really going to allow herself to be trampled over? Beatrice looked resigned but Stella leaped in just before Georgina's mother could relent. 'Mrs Ainsworth, if you didn't need me to begin lessons immediately, then I have to wonder why I am here in advance? I could have stayed longer with my young siblings.' Stella knew this was not her employer's problem but once again her mouth had spilled her thoughts faster than she could censor herself. Her irritation now danced between them. 'Given that I'm here and delighted to begin work with Georgina tomorrow as arranged by the agency, then with all due respect I think we should commence lessons.'

Beatrice looked to Georgina. 'Your father did say that he wanted to see you doing something productive in these holidays. It's why he suggested it.'

'Mr Ainsworth suggested it?' Stella remarked.

'Yes, Dougie leaves these things usually to me but he seemed especially determined that the girls don't "squander" their mid-term break, as he put it.'

'Mummy, please! Daddy's not even around to know.'

Stella was not going to let Georgina win this debate outright because she sensed this early battle of wills had to be a compromise at the very least, if not a triumph for herself against what seemed to her now to be a student so indulged she would have nothing but problems with her if she didn't stamp some authority. 'Georgina, how about we agree that if your mother wishes for you to go shopping in Brighton tomorrow morning that you and I plan to have our first lesson in the afternoon . . . could that work more easily?'

Georgina was now trapped, Stella thought. Anything but agreement would be churlish, perhaps deliberately hostile.

'Ah, there you are, darling. That sounds like it could be a happy arrangement,' her mother agreed. 'Let's not argue. I want your father to be happy with us for once.'

Happy with us. Stella would think on that later. 'That's settled, then,' she said, not giving the youngest woman in the room the opportunity to have her say. 'So, I shall see you at, let's say, three o'clock. Where is best, Mrs Ainsworth? I mean, for our study times?'

'Mrs Boyd is taking care of all that. Check with her.'

'Well, thank you again for the tea. It's lovely to meet you both.' Stella extended a hand to Mrs Ainsworth who shook it distractedly. She turned to Georgina and smiled warmly. 'See you tomorrow. We can set up our program for the rest of the holidays after tomorrow's lesson.'

Georgina could barely disguise her scowl as she gave Stella a slit-eyed gaze that could have been taken as anything from loathing to threat. Stella didn't care. She'd anticipated a difficult student and if this first meet was anything to judge Georgina Ainsworth by, then she was living up to that expectation. Grace would be entirely different, she suspected.

'I'll see Grace in the morning,' she said to them as she departed. 'Good afternoon.'

Neither woman responded but Stella was sure Georgina's sharp stare was raking her back.

6

Mrs Boyd escorted Stella via the back stairs to the third level of the house.

'This will be your suite of rooms,' she said, standing at the entrance. 'I hope you're very comfortable here.'

Stella gaped at the high-ceilinged room with its two tall picture windows. She crossed the threshold to see it was painted in a cool soft green with dazzling geometric wallpaper on one section of the wall behind her bed that echoed the colour. 'All of this?'

Mrs Boyd smiled, as if satisfied by the response. She entered the room, spoke in a sighing tone. 'This is one of our smaller guest suites.'

'I would have been more than comfortable in an attic room, Mrs Boyd,' she assured, feeling helplessly out of place in such elegance.

'Oh, dear me, no, Miss Myles. The entire top floor is off bounds to all staff,' Mrs Boyd replied, looking suddenly horror-struck by Stella's suggestion. 'Mr Ainsworth has his private rooms up there. You will have no reason to reach them and there is a locked door anyway, you may have noticed?' She looked over her shoulder towards the hallway and Stella nodded. It was the right response again for the older woman smiled benignly and returned to her more breezy voice. 'The family redecorated all the guest rooms about two years ago now. This one has been painted in a colour that Mrs

Ainsworth had mixed to her precise specifications that she calls *eau de nil*.'

'It's very beautiful. Mrs Ainsworth has exquisite taste.'

'She does. You will see it on display throughout Harp's End.'

'And Mr Ainsworth?'

The housekeeper gave her a look that was halfway between mind-your-own-business and sympathy for her ignorance that she might ask such a question. 'Mr Ainsworth does not get involved in the décor of the house, or the running of the household.'

'Really? Mrs Ainsworth has just informed me that it was her husband who hired me.'

'Perhaps. I wouldn't know about that,' Mrs Boyd replied, barely missing a beat at being caught out. She gestured with a brief wave. 'Your bathroom is through there. Towels are replaced every three days. And you have a small dressing room just through there,' she said with another light wave. 'We do laundry once a week – if you wouldn't mind putting your clothes for washing in that bag and for ironing in that one.' She pointed. 'Leave them outside on a Sunday evening for Monday washing day. I think everything else you'll work out for yourself easily enough. Oh, and if you're cold, I can have a fire made up but we're all pretty hardy here in Kent, Miss Myles, and we probably won't light fires from hereon until the end of September. It's the cusp of summer, after all.' Stella gave a weak smile. 'You'll find the coverlet and eiderdown more than sufficient for this time of year but there are extra blankets in the cupboard over here.'

'I shall be fine, thank you.'

'Breakfast for staff is served at six-thirty, although you are very welcome to come down at seven-thirty if that is easier?'

'No, no . . . I shall be there when the rest of the group has breakfast. How many staff are there?'

'Depending on the time of year and whether we have any formal houseguests, it could swell to a dozen but we are usually around eight of us permanent staff, nine now with you. We have breakfast in the main parlour and you can access that via the staff stairs. No need to move through the main house. In fact, if you don't mind, Miss Myles, unless you're with a member of the family, it is probably advisable to access the house, your room, the parlour and so on, via these stairs we've used just now. If you take a walk around this evening, you'll see where they come out into a side entrance via one of the boot rooms.'

'Of course,' Stella murmured, the notion of hired help fixing firmly into place in her mind; her education and striving towards a career at an abrupt halt while she acted as servant to a family. Another gripe to lay at her parents' dead feet . . .

'Shall I send your dinner tray up at six-thirty?'

Stella looked back, unsure. 'Whatever is easiest for you,' she offered. 'I may go out for a walk so please don't do anything special on my account.'

'I'm sure Mrs Bristow can do a cold spread if that's all right? Then you can please yourself. I'll have it set up over here,' she gestured.

'Dinner in the evening . . . what do I . . .'

'You will join us in the parlour for dinner. It's served promptly at six because the family eats at half-past seven. Your luncheon will be available at noon; something simple – usually a sandwich or piece of pie – again in the parlour. The family is served at half-past midday in the front salon at this time of year, if it is taking a meal at home. Afternoon tea is in the conservatory if you're with either of the girls. If not, please always take your meals/drinks in the parlour.'

Stella was getting the idea loud and clear. 'Thank you. In terms of lessons, where am I holding those with Georgina?'

'We have a room chosen on the next level down. I shall show you tomorrow. It is plenty big enough for lessons. Have you arranged a time yet?'

'Yes, Georgina and I are meeting at three and hopefully Grace and I can begin tomorrow morning.'

Mrs Boyd blinked as she thought about this. 'Miss Grace's horse riding lesson is at nine. Is mid-morning all right?'

'Perfect.'

'Until tomorrow, Miss Myles . . .' At Stella's enquiring stare she corrected herself. 'Until tomorrow, *Stella*. If you need anything —'

'I know . . . the back stairs to the parlour.'

'Indeed. I hope you sleep soundly.'

After the housekeeper had left, Stella took a slow tour of her room that felt almost as large as all bedrooms combined from her home in London. She opened one of the windows to let in some air and was delighted to see that her room overlooked the moors which stretched out behind the house for as far as she could see. It appeared windswept and so thoroughly lonely that she fancied it could almost be virgin grass that no human footstep had fallen upon. As she toyed with this thought, she caught the flash of a figure cresting one of the hillocks so briefly it was almost as if he was from her imagination because he was gone again so quickly. She squinted, straining to see if he might appear again – it was definitely a man – but after a full minute of near enough holding her breath, no person broke cover. There was something comforting in the realisation that those hillsides were not as deserted as she'd first thought and while today was perhaps not the best time, she planned to take long, head-clearing strolls across those grasses as often as she could.

Stella stretched the unpacking to take fifteen minutes, carefully hanging up the garments she'd brought. The rest would arrive in a day or two, she was sure. Two trunks of items were being picked up from her house – mainly books. The three she'd carried with her she now put on a shelf over her desk. A photograph of Carys and Rory she placed on the bedside table with her small alarm clock that had been her mother's; she had bought it new a few years back because she liked the enamelled green exterior. It was a Waterbury Thrift, made in America and sold through the department store. Stella had got it on a special staff discount for her mother. She wound it up carefully, making sure her watch and the clock matched times, for she was sure Mrs Boyd brooked no delays for parlour meals.

Her mother's clock told her it was past four. Despite a yawn she decided she should clamber into some sturdy shoes and go for that walk. 'Blow out some cobwebs,' she muttered.

Stella left her room, closing the door but not locking it, although it did have a key; she remembered that a tray was going to be left for her. As she entered the stairwell of the back passage she noticed the door that accessed the attic rooms. She listened against it. No sound. And for no reason she could explain, Stella twisted the door handle and discovered it was secured, as Mrs Boyd had warned. She presumed Ainsworth reached his private room, as Mrs Boyd had referred to it, via the main area of the house. She shrugged. It felt secretive. Stella told herself it was none of her business and she should focus on the next four weeks and getting back to seeing her family at the end of it. She soon found the small corridor at the bottom of the stairs that would take her either into the boot room or into the parlour.

She decided to face the staff tomorrow morning rather than now and as cowardly as it felt, she tiptoed into where she found John Potter pulling off his wellington boots and hanging up his waterproof coat.

'Hello again,' he said. 'Settling in?'

'Trying to. I thought I should get my bearings and take a walk.'

'Don't go too far. There's some rain coming. I'd stick to the flat if I were you.'

'Really, rain?'

He tapped his nose. 'Have you got a pair of gumboots?'

'Not with me,' she admitted.

He looked around and selected a small pair. 'These should fit. Hardly fashionable but you're in Kent now, Stella. You don't want to get dirt all over your nice shoes.' She looked down at her brogues. Her father had polished them; it was one of the last jobs he'd done before he'd swallowed the pills. Her parents had both left the house so neat and tidy, every possible chore done, including polishing every pair of shoes for their children.

'No, I don't,' she answered, taking a breath to keep that sudden wash of emotion from spilling.

'Get yourself into these. I'll pick you up a pair in Tunbridge Wells tomorrow. What size are you?'

'These are perfect.'

'Those belong to Hilly – she's our housemaid. I'll get you a size five, then. You might as well take this waxed coat as well. The one you're wearing won't be any use if you get caught in a downpour but this hood will save you. It's Hilly's too.'

'You're very kind. Hilly won't mind?'

'Not at all. Got to make you feel welcome, don't we? Can't be easy.' He looked at her in a way that made Stella suddenly aware that Mrs Ainsworth was not the only person who knew of the tragedy in her family.

She left, trying not to give the impression of fleeing. Stella took Potter's advice, however, and didn't go far, never even making it up onto the hills behind the house as she'd intended. Instead she stuck to the driveway that led her to a path cutting away and skirting the property through fields. She clambered over a stile and admired the rich soil of Kent before fringing some pasture where contented cows watched her carefully with large liquid eyes as they chewed. The lowering sun turned the late afternoon decidedly cold and she was glad of the gumboots that were now quite grubby from her efforts.

She toyed with the idea of climbing up the hill to get a look at the house and her windows but when the first teardrop of rain splashed on her arm she changed her mind and pulled up the hood of the wax jacket. John Potter certainly knew his Kent climate. Even so, she was surprised to see the low grey clouds that had gathered like silent sentinels overhead and it felt like they were now driving her back from the moors and inside.

Stella wondered about the man she'd seen and where he may have been headed, especially if he was striding over the forty acres of Harp's End land. By the time she was at the back door again and stamping off the mud she'd gathered, rinsing Hilly's boots at the tap nearby, she'd forgotten about him. Stella glanced at her watch, amazed how time had slipped by her. It was almost six and her belly was telling her she hadn't eaten anything other than sweets since her breakfast this morning in London.

Home felt so distant now. She hurriedly pulled off the damp jacket and hung it back up, easing off the boots as quietly as she could and then picking up her own shoes and overcoat from where she'd left them. Stella avoided meeting any of the staff by skipping back up the stairs. She could hear their voices, though, as they gathered for their evening meal but then even that sound disappeared as she ascended quickly to her floor.

Once again she paused at the locked door to the attic rooms; she didn't need to listen at the door because this time Stella was sure she could distantly hear someone humming to himself.

7

Grace's small chubby fingers were struggling to navigate a reverse octave scale from C down to middle C on the piano.

'I just can't make this finger,' she bemoaned, waggling her middle finger at Stella, 'cross over my thumb.'

Stella was seated next to her. 'Yes, I agree, it would be so much easier if we all had eight fingers,' she said in a dry tone. Grace giggled and it was a lovely sound that reminded her of her young ones at home.

'You look sad, Stella.' Grace frowned in the open way of a child. 'Are you?'

She found her charge's lisp so delightful she gave the girl a hug. 'No, not at all; you just remind me of my baby sister. She's beautiful too and laughs just like you.'

'You think I'm beautiful?'

'Of course you are.'

'Mummy and Georgie say I'm fat and that I'll never be able to enjoy the Season if I keep eating. I like food though, Stella. I'm always hungry.'

Stella took Grace's hands and covered them with her own. 'Grace, I've been given your holiday schedule and anyone would be hungry with what is planned for you. You've got ballet, horse riding, lacrosse, tennis, ballroom dance, deportment classes, piano lessons, French lessons . . . gosh, I felt famished just reading it.'

Grace laughed delightedly.

'You're young and healthy and I promise you, you are going to be a dazzling young woman in ten years.'

Grace smiled shyly. 'Daddy says I am a princess and that a prince will come along one day to marry me.'

She hugged the little girl who she was now certain made do without a lot of hugs. 'Your father is a wise man. I think that's exactly what's going to happen. You won't need to curtsey at the Debutantes' Ball in London because you'll be too busy with the queue of handsome men who desperately want to hear you play the piano, or ride alongside them or dance with them. As for these octaves, I can assure you that it was practice and a lot of growing up that allowed me to stretch between these two Cs. Look!'

Gracie gasped. She counted. '. . . nine . . . ten.'

They both laughed at her wonder that Stella could span her long fingers between so many keys.

'As to the scale, Gracie, it's a matter of dexterity. Your fingers have to keep practising. It's a strange new sensation for them. Look, can you do this?' Stella did the cross-my-fingers action.

'Oh, yes. We do that all the time in school when we're playing.'

'Vainites!' Stella exclaimed delightedly as a childhood memory of how to call a truce or back out of a contest bubbled up.

'Yes,' Gracie agreed. 'I try not to call vainites.'

'Because you're brave and that's a special quality to have,' Stella said, hoping the greater truth of what she was saying might somehow resonate in the young mind of her pupil whom she was sure was passively bullied by both her sister and mother. Perhaps her father was her reliable hero, although it seemed he was rarely around.

As if Gracie could read her thoughts, she smiled. 'Daddy says I'm brave too.'

'Does he? Dads are very special people,' she said, feeling

another memory pushing through. She pushed it back and returned to their original topic. 'So I think if we practise some scales each day through the holidays, you will notice a big difference.'

Without being asked Gracie began again with the piano keys, Stella nodding slowly beside her as the girl negotiated each note. At the note F, when Gracie needed to cross over her thumb and hit note E with her middle finger, Stella began to whisper 'vainites'. She saw her student grin and over the course of a dozen attempts she finally began to make the crossover. When Gracie achieved a clean run of eight notes, they both leaped up and clapped.

Mrs Boyd arrived to dampen the celebration. She blinked to see Stella arm in arm with Gracie, waltzing around the piano room, giggling.

'Er, Miss Myles, forgive me intruding.'

'You're not,' she said, calming her breathing and cutting Gracie a wide-eyed smirk.

Grace performed a fast pirouette, spinning on one foot. 'I did the scale, Mrs Boyd. My fingers crossed over.'

The housekeeper stared, unmoved. 'I see. Well done, Miss Gracie. But I shall have to ask you to keep the noise of your celebrations down.'

'Oh,' Stella said, feeling instantly awkward. 'Are we disturbing you?'

'Not me, Miss Myles. Mr Ainsworth is in the solar. He has very good hearing plus these old places have ways of carrying their secrets to other floors.' She gestured at the fireplace, clearly expecting Stella to understand. 'I'd rather not wait for him to complain.'

'Daddy's home?' Gracie exclaimed.

'Yesterday, early evening, your father arrived back unexpectedly.'

As Gracie rushed to gather up her music book, Mrs Boyd held a hand out.

'Er, I don't think he wishes to be disturbed.' She threw Stella an earnest look.

'Grace, if your father's working, how about you see him this afternoon?'

'I haven't seen him for days and days.'

Mrs Boyd's urging look had deepened.

'I thought you might like a game outside after working so hard this morning,' Stella offered.

The girl turned to her, looking torn.

Stella pressed that advantage. 'I was thinking about hopscotch. Can't imagine you can beat me. My sister Carys can't.'

'I'll bet I can,' Gracie countered, the defiance of challenge sparkling in her dark eyes.

'All right. If you can beat me, you can choose what we do tomorrow morning for our lesson.'

'Not French?'

'Some French, but your choice otherwise.'

'Then I choose a walk on the hills behind the house. I'm never allowed to go alone.'

'Nor will you be, Miss Grace,' Mrs Boyd interjected, unable to help herself.

'Mrs Boyd is quite right,' Stella said.

Gracie looked baffled. 'Well, I want to walk up there like my father does. You'll have to take me.'

'That's a deal, then,' Stella said, offering to shake hands on it, but her young companion made a cross over her heart instead.

'No, you have to swear it properly.'

'I swear. Cross my heart,' Stella promised, making the identical sign over her chest. 'Come on, let's grab our coats and we'll play some hopscotch.' She cast a glance towards the housekeeper whose gratitude was etched on her expression.

'How was your meal last night, Miss Myles?'

'Lovely, thank you. The flask of cocoa was a delicious treat.'

Mrs Boyd smiled. 'I'm glad. Lunch at half-past twelve, Miss Gracie?'

'I want to share mine with Stella, please.'

'Very good,' Mrs Boyd said, closing the door, but not before Stella had caught the look of surprise.

Gracie led her to one of the many courtyards, this time into a walled garden whose perfumed flowers had scented the air well ahead of their arrival. She was delighted to note it also offered the long pathway Grace had promised.

'Is this what you mean?' her companion asked.

'Perfect,' Stella replied, brandishing the chalk. 'All right, I'll draw it up. You find us two stones of about this size,' she said, putting thumb and forefinger together in a small circle.

She busied herself drawing up the hopscotch boxes and listened to Gracie's enthusiastic chatter.

'This is Daddy's and my favourite garden. He made it for me.'

Stella straightened. 'Really? It's so beautiful, Gracie. What are those? Their perfume is heavenly.' She pointed at a row of multiheaded white flowers.

'I can't pronounce it. Daddy says he thinks it was named after Georgie.'

Stella looked back at the youngster quizzically. Grace kept chatting. 'There is a person with that name in an old story. It begins with N, I think. Narsis . . . or something.'

'Narcissus?' Stella offered, dampening her instant desire to chuckle. 'One of the Greek myths.'

'That's it!' Grace replied, delightedly holding up some pebbles. 'Are these what you want?'

Stella nodded, smiling to herself. So Mr Ainsworth thinks his eldest daughter is self-absorbed! In fact, that was quite a modest way to describe a narcissist, she decided, as Gracie arrived to drop a stone in her palm.

'What's my flower, Stella?' she said.

'You? Hmm. I think you would be a daffodil. Look at them,' she said, nodding towards the colourful drift in one corner of the garden. 'They're so cheerful and happy. They're like sunshine.'

'I'm like that?'

'You certainly are.'

'Then I wish there was a story about me and daffodils.'

'Oh, but there's a marvellous poem.'

'Will you tell me it?'

Stella grinned. 'I'll teach you it.' She opened her hand. 'That's cunning, Gracie. Let me see yours,' she said, regarding the roundish pebble rolling in her palm.

Her companion opened her hand and at least looked sheepish about the flatter stone it contained. They both knew Grace's stone would land and likely stay put, while Stella's would most probably roll. 'You're going to do very well in life, Gracie, and you are giving yourself every good chance to beat me. But I'm good, I warn you.'

Grace flung herself at Stella for an unexpected and affectionate hug. Stella looked up as she twirled the girl around and could swear she saw someone staring at them from one of the top floor windows. The net curtain twitched back though so fast she wasn't sure if the person was male or female.

'Have you played this before?'

'At school, only once.'

'All right, I'll go first. So, you throw your stone gently to land on the first square.' Stella rolled her pebble. 'And then you jump over that square to land both feet into squares two and three.'

'I remember this,' Grace said, sounding delighted. 'Let me try.'

'All right, but you have to do a pirouette on square ten. We might as well practise your ballet while we're about it.'

Gracie bent with laughter.

'I'm not joking,' Stella warned, grinning roguishly.

'And you have to teach me the poem.'

'Off you go, then.'

Gracie began her turn and Stella began to recite. '*I wandered lonely as a cloud, That floats on high o'er vales and hills, When all at once I saw a crowd, A host of golden daffodils.*'

Gracie was pirouetting and even Stella began to laugh aloud now.

'*Beside the lake, beneath the trees, Fluttering and dancing in the breeze. Continuous as the stars that shine, And twinkle on the milky way, they stretched in never-ending line, Along the margin of the bay.*'

Grace held up her collected stone. 'Did it!'

'Well done, you.'

'Will you teach me how to say that? It sounded so pretty.'

And so a happy hour slipped by with Grace leaping and pirouetting and Stella encouraging her, praising her, teaching her the poem until Grace was no longer concentrating on where her feet needed to be but was easily reciting the first verse as she hopped along. Stella looked impressed.

'Bravo! That's perfect. You're such a fast learner, Grace. I think we should get you some lunch now.'

'Will you eat with me? I'm all alone; Mummy and Georgie have gone into Brighton.'

'How about you? Do you like Brighton?' Stella wondered as she gathered up the chalk and Grace's cardigan.

'I like the pier and I like fish and chips on the beach and after playing in the sea I like getting warm again with a cup of tea at the seafront kiosk. They even let us take a tray down onto the pebbles. The souvenir shops sell sweets in the shape of shingle and huge sticks of pink rock. I like the concerts too in the park and there's a paddling pool, which was fun when I was really small but I think I'm too grown up for that now that I'm no longer scared of the deep end. Oh, and I love going to the aquarium and seeing all the fish too, even though it smells funny. And there's a little train that runs along the seafront and —'

'That all sounds marvellous. You and your mother must have fun when you go.'

'Oh, I haven't done any of that with Mummy,' Grace corrected, skipping alongside. 'I do those things with Daddy. Mummy and Georgie say that I get in the way. That's why I couldn't go today. Georgie said I'd just be a nuisance.'

Stella felt her heart break a little for the youngster but reminded herself that Grace was not Carys; she must not get too emotionally attached and it was also not her place to judge. Even so, she let the girl take her hand as they walked back to the main house.

'So we can eat together?'

'Yes, I'll have lunch with you, Gracie,' she murmured.

As it turned out, Grace chose to take her meal with the rest of the staff on duty and was clearly a favourite with them – which came as no surprise to Stella, who was now finally introduced to some of the others.

John Potter kindly introduced her. 'This is our cook, Mrs Beecham – but we all call her Mrs B; our housemaid, Hilly, who seems to dodge brilliantly between cleaning and helping Mrs B; while Mary here shoulders most of the domestic duties for the household . . . laundry and the like; Miss Hailsham assists with additional, more personal housekeeping duties for Georgina and Grace; Pete – he looks after the gardens with a team of helpers, and George Roper manages the property – general maintenance and so on. And of course you know Mrs Boyd and then there's me. I do odd jobs as well as drive. We used to have a footman but when Samuel married,

I don't think Mr Ainsworth felt like breaking in a stranger and so we just all seemed to absorb his duties and we manage.'

'It's lovely to finally meet you all,' she said, giving them her warmest smile.

'I didn't think you'd want to eat with us, Miss Myles. I'd made up a tray,' Mrs Beecham said, looking around at the setting. 'Hilly, fetch some cutlery, please.'

'Oh, I'm very happy to share your table. Um, do call me Stella.'

'I do prefer to keep it more formal, Miss Myles,' Mrs Boyd chipped in. 'Stops any confusion.'

Before Stella could respond, Grace bustled back in, having washed her hands, and Stella began to see that the sunny personality of the youngest member of the house had an infectious quality that she hadn't misread. With Gracie's arrival, the slight feeling of tension that had built during her introduction seemed to dissipate.

Grace's effervescent conversation soon had everyone chuckling, although Stella had a new sense of isolation with a question whispering through her thoughts about how she was going to fit into this household – while everyone was saying the right words about being welcome, she was feeling anything but, both above and below stairs. She tempered her bleak thoughts with the rationalisation that it was only day one, of course, as a cottage pie was scooped out and plonked onto each plate and handed around.

'Bread and butter?' John Potter offered. They were more like slabs than slices of white bread, slathered with gleaming lumps of creamy butter. 'Looks like Mrs B forgot to take the butter out of the cold room.' He gave her a friendly wink.

Carrots and peas, cooked until their colours had dulled, looked back at her in a lacklustre bed of the brown sludge of stewed meat that oozed from beneath a thick roof of mashed potato. Nevertheless, she would be lying if she didn't admit it was tasty enough and she was grateful for a hot meal on a cool midday that was such a treat by comparison to her usual bread and dripping, or potted meat sandwiches and a flask of tea. Stella ate modestly, sipping at the glass of milk placed above her plate and listened to the chatter around her.

A jug was passed around to refresh her glass as the phone jangled in the corridor behind them. Mrs Boyd left to answer it.

'Oh, no more for me. I've had plenty,' she demurred to Pete the gardener, keen to top up her milk. 'It's delicious, though, like no other milk I've ever drunk before.'

'That's because you come from London, Miss Myles,' he said. 'Nothing fresh in London – not the way we know it, anyway. Our Daphne gave us this milk just a few hours ago. Aren't I right, Mrs B?'

'Oh, yes, indeed,' the cook assured. 'She's a good milker, is Daphne. Best in Kent.'

A short discussion between the staff ensued about whether Daphne's milk was better in early or late spring that confounded Stella by its intensity but, even so, she found it all enlightening.

When there was a break in the chatter Stella dabbed her mouth with her napkin. 'Well, thank you all very much. Grace, I believe you've swapped your riding lesson to this afternoon, if I'm not mistaken. And your mother is taking you?' She glanced towards Potter, who didn't seem to react. 'Um, I must prepare for lessons this afternoon with Georgina. So, if you'll all excuse me . . . thank you so much, Mrs B, for the lovely luncheon.'

'Ah, Miss Myles,' Mrs Boyd said, returning to the table. 'I must inform you that Mrs Ainsworth and Miss Georgina have been held up in Brighton.'

Stella blinked.

'Miss Georgina asked me to let you know that she will not be available for a lesson this afternoon.'

'What about my riding lesson . . . with Mummy?'

'Miss Grace, I'm afraid your mother has asked me to postpone that now also. I shall rearrange it for next week.'

'Would you like me to handle that, Mrs Boyd, seeing as my afternoon is now open?' Stella hadn't intended for her tone to sound so cutting, but it had sharpened up at the sight of Grace's shoulders dropping.

'No, that won't be necessary, Miss Myles. It's a simple telephone call. Miss Grace, you are welcome to play with the doll's house. We can open up the playroom for you?'

Stella could feel her young student's disappointment rippling through her as if it were her own. 'Grace, perhaps we can continue our lessons. We can go for a walk as I promised and practise some French, if you would like?'

Grace managed to nod and smile, although Stella realised that this was definitely a second-best option to horse riding. It was only later when they had begun a slow ascent of the hill behind the house that she understood Grace's disappointment was not about the horse riding so much as not having that special time with her mother.

'I like to show Mummy how well I can ride and watch her clap and be proud of me.'

'I know. And I'm very sure that she too is unhappy to be missing watching you ride today,' she offered, hating that she was put in the position of protecting Beatrice Ainsworth despite the selfishness. 'There is probably a very good reason that they're late,' she added, hearing the hollowness in her voice.

'I don't think so,' Grace sighed, bending down to pick a daisy. 'It happens quite a lot. I get used to it.'

'I'm sorry, Grace. But we're both a bit lonely so we can cheer each other up.'

'Tell me about your brother and sister, Stella.'

'My sister's name is Carys. *Ma soeur s'appelle* Carys . . . Right, you try it in French.'

Grace skipped ahead and echoed in a singsong voice. '*Masseur* . . .'

'*Ma soeur* . . .' Stella helped.

'*Ma soeur s'appelle* Georgina.'

'Good! Now let's just try it a less conversational way. My brother is called Rory. *Mon frère s'appelle* Rory.'

'I don't have a brother. What is father? Oh yes, I remember. *Père?*'

'*Oui, bien. D'Accord.* My father's name is . . .' Stella resisted saying it in the past tense. '*Mon père est Evan et ma mère s'appelle Didi.*'

'Didi,' she giggled.

'My father's pet name for Dianne.'

'Didi. Oh, that's pretty,' Grace admitted. The daisy chain she'd been making as they slowly climbed the hill was growing.

'She was pretty too.' She knew she was talking to herself and shook herself from memories. 'Your turn. The name of my father . . .'

'Er . . . *Mon père* . . .'

'*Bien . . . continue* . . .' she encouraged.

'He has lots of them, though,' Grace complained and Stella could believe it, remembering her conversation with Rafe about members of these gentrified families.

'Have a go using your mother, then.'

They crested the hill, their lone voices sprawling across a verdant, undulating landscape that Stella gathered had once been ancient woodland. From their vantage she could see farms and villages scattered in the distance. Smudged areas of heath and colourful patches of woods ebbed and flowed around the hamlets, pathways cutting in and around the hills with streams Stella imagined were fast-flowing and icy cold. Their breath steamed but neither of them was especially cold after their hike.

Stella sighed. 'Oh, this is idyllic.'

'I'm not allowed up here.'

'Why ever not?' she asked, fear suddenly trilling through her in case she was breaking a house rule.

'Mummy says it's not terribly ladylike to go scrambling, as she calls it, and Georgie says it turns me into a little urchin.'

Stella toned down her instinctive response. 'Well, my opinion is that there is absolutely no harm in healthy outdoor activity like this. And because you're with me and because we are practising French, it definitely constitutes a lesson.' Stella sat down and leaned back on her elbows. 'I have to just enjoy the scene for a few moments, Grace. I haven't seen countryside like this since I was just a bit older than you.'

Grace arrived to place her daisy chain around Stella's neck.

'Oh, I love it, thank you. But what about you?'

'I can see buttercups over there,' she said, pointing diagonally behind Stella. 'I'll make a buttercup chain.'

'Don't go too far.'

'I won't.'

'I have to hear you. So either sing or recite something loudly.'

Grace laughed. 'But not in French.'

'Practise your Wordsworth, then. "*I wandered lonely as a cloud . . .*" Go on.'

Stella grinned as she inhaled a lungful of the freshest air she had breathed in years. She listened to the youngster reciting the poem with flawless recall and wondered why the women in the child's life weren't in love with this sparkling little girl as she already was.

'And again,' she called. Grace recited it cheerfully, even louder.

Grace was plucking buttercups, looking pleased with herself that she knew the poem so well already. She didn't see the man steal up over the rise. His footfall was as silent as the skylark that Grace had just spotted in her nest in the heath. She craned her neck and wondered how many eggs the little bird was protecting and thought about tiptoeing closer.

'I wouldn't, if I were you,' the man said softly.

Grace turned, startled, to regard a tall man with a flop of dark hair that he now dragged back from his face to reveal a wide grin.

'Daddy,' she breathed and leaped up to fling herself at him, buttercups scattering like golden stars.

He caught her, chuckling quietly. 'Hello, Skipper. Nice to see you up here.'

'I've missed you,' she said, hugging his waist.

'I came in yesterday.'

'I know, and Mrs Boyd wouldn't let me visit you today. She's so stern. You look very brown.'

'Yes, I did a lot of walking.'

'While you were working?'

He grinned. 'I had some time off.'

'Where were you? Mummy couldn't tell me.'

'I was on the Continent, down south.' That didn't mean much to Grace. 'It's always warm there. How is your mother?'

'She's shopping with Georgie.'

'Of course she is. Did I just hear you reciting William Wordsworth?'

Grace grinned. 'Yes, Stella's teaching me it because she thinks I'm like a daffodil.'

'Mrs Boyd mentioned Stella had arrived. How are you getting on with her?'

'Daddy, she's lovely. Come on, come and meet her.'

They both hushed as they heard another voice.

'Grace? Gracie, I can't hear you.'

'I'm coming!' Grace called over the hill.

Her father hesitated. 'Maybe I shouldn't . . .'

'Oh, come on, Daddy. You're going to love her too.'

Stella called out to Grace, relieved when she heard the girl respond and then turned back for one last look at the valley below, convinced she would be returning here as often as she could. She stood on tiptoe and stretched, smiling as she heard Grace arriving and to make her laugh she decided to do a pirouette.

'Look, Grace,' she said, spinning slowly on her toes and exaggerating the stance on uneven ground, 'you can teach me ballet while we practise our French.' She stopped dead, horrified to see a man standing beside Grace. They were both grinning at her not-so-graceful attempt at being a ballerina in her galoshes. Her mouth opened but closed again in shock when a double jolt of alarm slammed through her. She knew him, felt the sound of his name form at her lips but she couldn't say it; his suddenly anxious look of denial forbade her.

Grace rescued her. 'Stella, this is my father.'

Father? She hesitated, not knowing what to say or how much to reveal.

'Hello, Stella,' he said, the mellow voice so familiar because it had been echoing through her mind since the night he'd kissed her gloved hand. He took off a baggy, plaid cap he was wearing. 'Forgive me for interrupting you. I'm Douglas Ainsworth.'

'Mr Ainsworth,' she managed to squeeze out and it was obvious this had to appear to the child watching them as their first meeting. Stella gathered her wits together and cleared her throat. 'I'm sorry. You startled me. Um, it's lovely to meet you. I've heard so much about you from Grace.'

'I was taking some air and heard a voice I knew reciting Wordsworth. That's a first. I gather I must thank you for that.'

Her gaze narrowed slightly. 'And apparently I must thank you for the role I now play in Grace's life. Mrs Ainsworth assured me that you were instrumental in hiring me.'

The man she knew as Rafe gave a small smile. 'I merely encouraged my wife to speak with an agent that a mutual acquaintance calls friend. I was told she specialises in this sort of placement. I'm glad she brought you to our family, Stella. Grace certainly adores you,' he said, stroking his daughter's head in such a gentle and affectionate way, it made Stella's heart feel as though it had leaped higher in her chest. Yes, Grace hadn't misled her; it was clear that she was as adored by her father as she was essentially ignored by her mother. 'And you've only been here a day,' he added. Ainsworth gestured down the hill towards the house. 'Shall we? Come on Skipper, you lead the way. I'd race you down if I thought I could win,' he added, giving her a tickle and laughing as his daughter shrieked and took off, running happily downhill. 'Not too fast,' he called to her back. He smiled at Stella. 'She's like a hare across these hills – so sure-footed.'

Stella felt she had no choice but to fall into step. Grace decided she would run down the hill waving her arms.

'I call her Skipper because she reminds me of a butterfly that calls Kent home.'

'Butterfly? How so?'

'You've met Georgina?'

She nodded.

'I suspect you've likely worked out already that Georgina's beauty is skin deep.'

Stella regarded him and was sure the fact she didn't bluster in denial told him plenty.

'Whereas this girl,' he nodded at the joyful Grace, 'is beautiful at her core, but she is still the caterpillar and one day she will emerge from the chrysalis of babyhood to be a striking young woman,

I have no doubt. I intend she doesn't lose that warm, generous, bright soul, though, as she . . . um . . . pupates.'

Stella winced at the horrible image that conjured in her mind.

He laughed. 'Well, through her metamorphosis into womanhood, should I say?'

'Much nicer,' she admitted and wondered why he hadn't taken the same approach with his eldest daughter. 'Is that why I'm here? Why you secretly but deliberately set me up for a role in your house?'

He looked down and his expression was one of slight injury, which reassured her that he wasn't entirely cynical. 'The choice was always yours, Stella. But I admit I hoped you would come to Harp's End.'

'And I must admit now to feeling manipulated.'

'I would prefer that you don't feel that way, of course, but I can understand why.' His stride was long and assured on the unpredictable terrain; she felt she was taking two steps to each one of his and she dared not take her eyes from the earth for fear of twisting an ankle. 'I'm hopeful you can see this arrangement is good for all concerned. I trust you are happy with the financial arrangement?'

It was Stella's turn to look away as she stomped alongside him, carefully putting a shoulder-width's distance between them. 'It's extremely generous,' she admitted. 'And six months is not so long.'

'You'll be home for Christmas.'

'That's my plan,' and she could hear the wistfulness in her tone. 'Oh!' she suddenly yelped.

Stella tripped but his arm shot out with a lightning-fast response to prevent her falling. She felt his hand beneath the soft part of her upper arm like a scald. It was her mind playing its tricks but even so her response was entirely physical and the warmth spread rapidly through her and against her wishes.

'Are you all right?' he checked.

'Yes,' she replied with an embarrassed half smile. 'I'm sorry for being so clumsy.'

'You'll get used to the landscape and you'll be able to run like Grace downhill before you know it.'

Stella looked at him squarely for the first time today, permitting her glance to linger on his. He was still holding her and she eased herself free. 'Best not,' she murmured, unsure of what she even meant by such a remark. Mercifully he didn't pursue it. Perhaps he too held a lingering memory of the soft kiss of her glove.

'So no one at home calls you Rafe?'

He shook his head and she was transfixed by his unrelenting gaze that seemed to suggest he wasn't feeling even remotely awkward about standing here on the hill behind the house and clearly visible from its back windows. 'Where's that feisty girl I met in the dance hall? The one who couldn't give a damn about what anyone saw or thought?'

She was convinced he could read her mind in that moment, and even gave a crooked grin. 'Oh, I was angry that night and you suffered for it.'

'I didn't suffer. I enjoyed it.'

Stella gave a short gust of a mirthless laugh. She let out her breath. 'You're my employer now. I can't behave with the cavalier attitude of that night.'

He gave a grin of such innocence that Stella could swear she had just glimpsed Rafe Ainsworth, the boy, of what must be over three decades ago. The grin ducked beneath all her defences and bobbed up inside to knock on the door of her heart. He looked ridiculously handsome in his baggy plus fours and tweed jacket and waistcoat. Once again his tie was loosened and his collar open – it seemed to be a trend for him and Stella recalled the inverted triangle of browned skin she'd noticed on their first meeting. He was equally tanned now.

'You've obviously been away somewhere a lot sunnier than the British south coast,' she said, desperate to shift his attention from her.

He nodded, didn't offer a response, and Stella realised she hadn't asked a question so he likely didn't feel obliged. She remembered now his secretive way.

'And you've become rather thin,' he noted.

She ignored the remark. 'So all of this is yours?' she said, sweeping a hand. 'You kept that very quiet.'

'It didn't come up in the brief time we met. I'm not in the habit of talking about it.'

'Is this your family home?'

'It is. How do you find my wife?'

Stella regarded him carefully, wondering what it was he wanted her to say. 'I found her typical of the women I have met from the society she was raised in.'

He laughed. 'What a brilliantly evasive answer. Walk and explain to me.'

'Nothing to explain, really. She's cool, distracted, essentially uninterested in me. Actually, that's not entirely true. She was very quick to leap onto the suicide of my parents.'

He cut her a sharp glance. 'I had to mention it to Suzanne. And it was obviously her duty to lay out the facts to a client.' He frowned. 'I also can't blame her for wanting to know more. Most would, especially as you're in charge of her children.'

'Of course I understand. I just don't get how she couldn't imagine such stringent questioning might be cruel under the circumstances. I had barely caught my breath from arriving. She might have left it to another time when we were alone, when I was more at ease in my new surrounds, maybe after I'd met and got to know the children a little longer. She might also have been more tactful in her interrogation.'

He nodded. 'All of that and more. I'm afraid my wife's subtlety only comes to the fore for more cunning reasons.' At Stella's quizzical look he continued. 'Watch your step, it's quite slippery here.' He pointed slightly ahead. 'What I mean is, she's a genius at the sarcastic understatement but she can be like a blunt instrument when she doesn't care.'

'So I am right. She's not in the slightest interested; finds me dull . . .'

'That's not such a bad thing, though, is it Stella?'

'You mean I shouldn't be insulted?'

'That's exactly what I mean. I prefer not to be noticed, don't you?'

She looked at him, grasping now what he was driving at and had to smile back. 'Yes, I suppose it is if you needed to be clandestine.'

Grace had doubled back. 'Mummy's just arrived home with Georgie. I can hear their voices.'

Stella felt her adult companion's demeanour shift slightly. A prickle of tension now surrounded them. 'Then I shall see you later on, Grace,' she offered, filling the pause. 'Thank you for working so hard today. We'll do some more verses of that poem tomorrow.' She turned to Ainsworth. 'Thank you for walking us down.' She smiled politely for Grace's benefit.

'Why don't you join us for dinner tonight?' he suddenly said.

'Oh, yes, you must!' Grace urged with excitement.

Stella immediately began to step back from them. She even raised a hand slightly. 'I don't think that would be appropriate or necessary. The family is clearly being reunited after your absence, Mr Ainsworth, and I think —'

'But I am inviting you, Stella. As head of this house and your employer I think it is most appropriate that you join our family for dinner. We would all like to get to know you better. It will be good for the girls and for my wife to share your company socially.'

Grace was dancing around them, begging her to say yes but the little girl's pleas were fading to background noise as Stella was sure she heard him murmur, 'I want you to be there.' Or did she make that up, believing them able to communicate without speaking? The invisible connection was both unnerving and reassuring at the same time. She felt momentarily flustered at his intense stare that willed her to agree.

She glanced at the time. It was nearly five. Georgina had missed her lesson by two hours and Stella was convinced it was deliberate.

'What do you say?' he pressed.

'Er, well, I can hardly refuse my employer's wishes, can I?' He shook his head, not allowing her to squirm away from his gaze. 'If Mrs Ainsworth is agreeable, then yes, of course.'

'Beatrice will be fine. We eat at half-past seven. Grace will fetch you if you're a minute late,' he said. 'Come on, Skipper. Let's go say hello to the family.' He held out a hand. 'It's good to see you here,' he said and Stella shook his hand once, sensitive to the soft squeeze he gave it. 'We'll look forward to this evening.'

Stella nodded and watched them walk away. Grace held her father's hand but looked behind and grinned delightedly as Stella gave her a conspiratorial wave as they disappeared around the corner of the house, their shoes crunching on the gravel.

Stella dropped her shoulders and blew out a silent breath. 'What have you got yourself into, Stella?' she murmured softly.

8

Berlin – May 1933

Joseph Altmann was absently humming to himself and looked up from his desk at the buzz from his telephone switchboard with a soft expression of exasperation before he returned his attention to the file of papers. He finished signing his name to a letter typed in triplicate. The carbon copies were attached and he took his time initialling those before he flicked the switch on his intercom. 'Yes, Felda?' he said, aware she could surely hear the soft irritation in his voice.

'I'm sorry to interrupt you, Herr Altmann.'

'Mmm, what is it?'

'There's a visitor here to see you.'

He frowned. 'There are no appointments in my diary, are there?'

The rustle of pages being turned confirmed what he already knew. 'No, Sir. You asked me to keep today clear for your monthly reports.'

'In which case I would be most obliged if you would please have this visitor make an appointment and I shall see him when —'

'It's not a gentleman, Sir.'

He baulked at the interruption but was sufficiently surprised not to take offence. 'A woman? Who is it, Felda?'

'It's a Mrs Bergheimer.'

He paused, ran the name through his mind, searching for

familiarity. He came up wanting. 'I don't know a Mrs Bergheimer. Where is she?'

'I've asked her to take a seat in the anteroom, Sir.'

'And what does she wish to see me about?'

'I'm sorry, but she seems reluctant to discuss it with me. She insists you know her.'

'The only Bergheimer I can recall is a young teacher at my daughter's primary school and I haven't seen him in many years. To my knowledge he wasn't married.'

'What shall you have me do?'

Joseph sighed, stared at the pile of letters still to be read, considered, signed, initialled. And then there were other files full of tasks demanding his time. He'd planned a long day of reporting and this tedious interruption would throw off his concentration.

'Herr Altmann?'

'Yes, yes, very well. I shall be out shortly.' He heard the phone click before he let out a vexed breath through his nose. He screwed the lid back onto his fountain pen and although he would normally put the 22-carat gold-nibbed pen into his breast pocket – a treasured gift from his brother – he defiantly left it on the heavy glass penholder to reassure himself that he would only be absent for a minute or two. He stood, briefly admiring the honey stripes in the wood grain of his French Art Deco Macassar desk that he'd brought in from home, a gift from his wealthy wife for his new role within the Reich office as a senior administrator. That was a proud day for his family with the announcement of his appointment.

Joseph began rolling down his shirtsleeves, becoming more irritated by each tick of his desk clock – another gift from his wife and children – as it reminded him of precious work minutes ebbing away. He glanced at the photograph of his family and smiled.

'Back soon, darlings,' he said, enjoying his frequent eccentricity of speaking to the photo of four – his beautiful Brigitte or Gitte, as he affectionately called her, and their two sparkling blonde daughters on the cusp of their teenage years who resembled their mother, plus the new, unexpected gift of a son, after fifteen years of happy marriage. He looked at his boy, dark and small, cradled in Gitte's arms, and felt the rush of warmth for new life and for the loves of his life. No man could be happier, he often thought, or as blessed.

That photo encompassed everyone he loved bar one. There was a man he loved too . . . the brother he so rarely saw, but they'd shared enough in their childhood that the memories ran strong and vivid in his mind whenever he needed to recall and indulge them.

Altmann walked to the coat stand thinking about his dear brother. He fetched his jacket, which he carefully put on before he moved to the mirror hanging on the wall of his spacious office that was made darker by its wood panelling. He checked his hair was still combed in place, stroked a knuckle against both sides of his lustrous moustache for neatness before he straightened his waistcoat, took off his glasses and placed them in his jacket pocket. Well, his brother may have got the best of his family's looks but Joseph knew he was perfectly handsome in his own way, especially with his oddly lightish-green eyes that people so often remarked upon. How else would he have fought off all those suitors for Brigitte von Krosig's hand in marriage, if he hadn't been an attractive enough fellow? They were a good-looking couple, no doubt about it, and her family name with its impeccable connections and his bright mind made them formidable.

With a final, indignant tug at his tie knot, he murmured, 'Right, Mrs Bergheimer, whomever you are, this had better be good,' and strode to the door.

He emerged to walk past Felda, who smiled and nodded towards the waiting room. He could see through a glass partition that his guest had her back to him. She was clearly not young and so he immediately relaxed and understood now why Felda had seemed uninterested in his visitor. He moved down the row of typists that he personally kept busy five days a week.

'Good morning, ladies,' he said, smiling at each. They cast warm smiles of salutation back. Their day began at eight-thirty but his routine meant his morning had begun an hour earlier as it did each working day and so they hadn't seen him until now. 'New hairdo, Romy? Very nice indeed.'

Romy giggled before glancing up at Felda and her expression straightened, her gaze instantly shifting back to her typewriter. He enjoyed flirting gently with the girls in the typing pool; he didn't have the knack of his brother who was one of those men to make a woman's heart flutter just by entering a room, but he knew he was charming enough. He could wish to be taller but then he'd been wishing that since childhood and given that his adored Gitte had not once complained about his stature or appeal, he rarely felt inadequate about it.

These rambling thoughts led him into the doorway of the waiting room.

'Mrs Bergheimer?' he asked, and she jumped as if stung. 'Forgive me,' he appealed, 'I did not mean to startle you.'

The lady swung around. She was far older than he'd guessed, adjusting that estimate to her mid-fifties. He noted bulging, heavy-lidded eyes that were dark above the slightly hollowed cheeks that sat high on her oval face. The thick underlip reminded him of someone but the notion he reached for seemed to flick away as he became distracted, taking in her clean, simple attire. She was dressed neatly but not with any sign of wealth that would be anticipated for visitors to Joseph Altmann's office. If she were thirty and dressed richly, preferably wearing a wedding band, Felda would have been flitting around like an annoying gnat trying to discover everything she could. But this dowdy, middle-aged woman held little potential for gossip, presumably.

Joseph frowned. 'I'm so sorry, I can't recall us meeting,' he tried politely.

Gitte accused him of having a memory like a Venus flytrap; that every fact he heard or discovered were like poor insects, caught in his mind forever. It was true. His recall was yet to be rivalled and for someone working hard to wrestle this new bureaucracy into shape, it was a helpful skill to be learned across all departments; a reason the interior ministry valued his service. Chancellor Hitler himself had commended his work via his Interior Minister, Wilhelm Frick. And Altmann knew that Frick liked him – no doubt because they were fellow philologists, who had turned to Law.

'I'm the one to apologise,' she said softly, casting an anxious glance over her shoulder. He looked through the glass to where she watched and then back to her, his frown deepening at her curious remark. 'I lied to your secretary,' she explained.

He gave a rapid blink, perplexed. 'Why would you do that, Mrs Bergheimer?'

'I need to talk to you, Herr Altman, Sir.'

'We are talking,' he observed dryly. It wasn't fair to take this approach but he did not like being cornered in this way. 'Mrs Bergheimer, I am a civil servant of transparency. I have no secrets but you are making me feel as though I must somehow protect your visit; become part of whatever ruse this is.'

'It is no ruse, Sir. I beg your indulgence.' Her lip quivered. She appeared frightened.

'Are you all right, Madam? Can I fetch —?'

'No, please!'

Now he was the one who looked startled.

'I'm sorry, Herr Altmann,' she hurried to assure. 'I wish to talk with you in private.'

'I see. About what, may I ask? If it's connected with housing or —'

'It's nothing to do with State government, Sir. It's personal.'

'Madam, please, I have not met you before so I cannot imagine that you and I share anything of a personal nature. Now, really, you must forgive me, but —'

She took his hand, squeezing it so hard he winced. He looked around, both alarmed and annoyed now. He wanted this desperate woman gone but he couldn't catch anyone's attention. Felda was no longer at her desk. Her back was to him, at the filing cabinets.

'I have something important to give you.'

'Oh, yes?' he said, twisting his arm away in irritation. 'What could that be?'

'Notes,' she muttered.

'Notes,' he repeated with exasperation and she put a finger to her mouth to hush him. Joseph's lips thinned. 'Now, look here, Mrs —' he began.

'They're written by him.'

He looked at her with annoyance, only barely covered by the obvious question in his expression.

'Hitler,' she added in a whisper, and stood. 'You need to read them to know the truth.' She moved even closer, pointing a twisted finger that had seen hard work for all of its life at his chest. 'You're a Jew. You will be as scared as we are.'

Joseph Altmann felt his day of reporting unravel at the same speed that his gut seemed to tangle in a twist of fear.

'Let my son in when he visits you,' she said, her anxiety suddenly infectious. 'You will remember him. He is a teacher at your children's old school. He will bring you the notes.'

Gitte paused at her embroidery and looked on with a smile in her pale eyes as she watched her husband cuddle their son. She tucked a wayward strand of her hair that Joseph described as 'curls of trapped sunlight' back behind her ear and sighed.

'You both look so peaceful, my love,' she remarked. 'I admit he's not so placid through the day.'

'He appears a most content baby because he has a wonderful mother.' His wife kissed the air in his direction and he grinned. 'So lovely when the house sleeps and it's just you and me awake.'

'Yes,' she agreed, her shoulders drooping slightly as she returned to her cross-stitch. 'What did we used to do with all that time we had to ourselves?'

'We made babies,' he replied dryly and loved her laugh. 'Shall we make another tonight?'

Her eyes lifted and there was mischief smiling in them now. 'Maybe not another child, my darling, but that shouldn't ever get in the way of your affections.'

Joseph lifted an eyebrow. 'Let's put this dear boy into his cot, then, my love, so we can climb into ours.'

Gitte chuckled and put down her sewing, realising that there would be little more achieved with her needle and thread this evening. 'Here, let me take him.' She stood, moved to his armchair and lifted the sleeping infant. 'He's like a miniature of you, Joseph. This is what you must surely have looked like in your mother's arms.'

'I wish I could remember her,' he said, standing to kiss her cheek and then bending to kiss the forehead of his son. 'But I was lucky to be blessed with another woman who made me feel loved, gave me a family. He's fortunate that he'll have you, my darling, all through his life until he's so old he'll need spectacles to see your beautiful face.'

'Oh, go on with you, you old charmer,' his wife said, giving him a push. 'Check that fire before you come up.'

The sound of their front doorbell startled their sleeping son, who flinched awake, letting out a soft wail. They shared a look of pained annoyance.

'Who can that be at this time?' Gitte admonished, looking down again to soothe her child with soft noises.

Joseph glanced at his watch on the end of the fob he pulled from his waistcoat. 'Someone with no manners, clearly,' he grumbled. 'It's nearing nine.'

The boy was moaning and Gitte gave her husband a glance of gentle misery. 'I'd better get him quietened with a feed.'

'And I shall go chase away this caller because we're on a promise, right?'

She giggled. 'I promise. Give me half an hour.'

He watched his wife leave their sitting room and he reached to put on his jacket, glad now that he hadn't changed into comfortable clothes this evening. It had been another long day at the office and the girls had launched at him as he'd come home, demanding he play with them, and then dinnertime came and went, then reading with his daughters . . . hours had flown.

This time there was an insistent knock at the front door. Joseph decided the visitor must be deaf if he hadn't heard clearly that the bell had sounded.

'All right, all right, I'm coming,' he called, wondering at fate's wit that this was the one night their housekeeper had to herself. She had gone out with friends and wouldn't be back until ten. 'Typical,' he muttered to himself.

Joseph flicked on the porch light and saw the silhouette of a person immediately shift. 'Who is this?' he called, taking precaution not to open his front door yet. A dog barked distantly.

'Herr Altmann?' said a hesitant voice.

'Yes? Who is this please?'

'It's Bergheimer, Herr Altmann, Sir. Er, your children's former teacher.'

Joseph paused with the door chain. It had been six days since the unsettling visit from the middle-aged woman at his office, long enough to convince himself she was deranged and he'd hear no more about it. It felt as though a ball of ice had suddenly frozen hard in the pit of his belly. He took a deep breath and opened the door, recognising the younger man instantly despite the grey flecks in his beard and the new haunted look behind those wire-framed spectacles.

'Herr Bergheimer,' he said, 'what time do you call this?'

'I need to speak with you, Herr Altmann, Sir.'

'So your mother informed.' It sounded like an accusation and precisely how he meant it to sound.

The man looked down. 'May I come in, please?'

'I suppose you'd better, although I was just heading upstairs with my wife and infant son. I planned to turn in early.'

'I shan't keep you long, Sir.'

'Leave your hat, Bergheimer,' he said, nodding at the stand nearby, trying to disguise the anxiety that the man's worried expression and the memory of his mother's intensity provoked. He led the way back into the sitting room. 'Can I pour you a brandy or something to warm you? I'm afraid the fire is dying.'

'I'm fine, Sir, thank you,' the man said in a flat voice, following him into the room.

'Take a seat,' Joseph gestured, closing the door quietly. 'Now, what is this all about? I haven't seen you in years and suddenly your mother turns up at my office unannounced. It's most unusual, Bergheimer, and may I say, disconcerting.'

'You are a powerful, senior man in government now, Herr Altmann.'

'All the more reason I'm frankly annoyed,' he admitted. 'Look, is it money? If you —'

The man looked aghast. He stood abruptly. 'Herr Altmann, this is nothing to do with money. We are not a family with many assets but we are nonetheless a proud family. My father died two years ago but we manage as best we can.'

'I'm sorry,' Joseph conceded. 'That was insensitive of me. Sit . . . it's David, isn't it?'

His guest nodded glumly.

'Why did you send your mother to me?'

'We were being cautious. We felt she was . . . well, less conspicuous than myself. An older woman, she can slip beneath people's notice more easily.'

'But why? What is this about?' His exasperation was not well concealed.

Bergheimer actually looked around the chamber as if hidden eyes might be observing. Joseph watched in astonishment and only just held his tongue. He waited as the man reached beneath his coat into a jacket pocket and withdrew two creased pages that looked as though they'd been crushed before being pressed out flat again.

'What is this?' he said, more out of something to say and relieve the tension because presumably these were the notes that Mrs Bergheimer had referred to.

'Herr Altmann, there is no recording equipment in your house, is there?' his guest suddenly whispered.

'Good heavens, man. Get on with it!' he snapped.

But Bergheimer looked terrified just to be touching the pages. 'Are you familiar with our Chancellor's handwriting?'

'What sort of a question is —'

'Answer me, Sir,' the man demanded, although his voice was even and remained low.

Joseph drew a deep, silent breath. 'Of course I am,' he scowled.

Bergheimer held out the two crumpled pages. 'Would you recognise this as his handwriting?'

Joseph leaned in, not wishing to touch the scruffy pages. Heavy black ink scrawled in an almost illegible tiny hand, including the instantly recognisable affectation that the German Chancellor had adopted of an unnecessary vertical bar on certain letters.

'This could be a forgery,' he denounced before he'd read any of the content.

'It could be but it was retrieved by my mother from the wastepaper bin in Adolf Hitler's office a fortnight ago. She is a cleaner at the government offices in the Reich chancellery. My mother is one of the trusted few permitted to clean and tidy Herr Hitler's monstrously large office, as she puts it.'

'Your mother thieved papers from the Chancellor's office?' Joseph said in a hissed whisper. He watched Bergheimer swallow. 'Do you have any idea of the penalty for such theft?'

The man licked his lips. 'Read it, Herr Altmann.'

Joseph batted the pages away. 'I don't wish to. I want no part of this.'

Bergheimer stood and, visibly trembling, waved the pages at his senior. 'I have thought of nothing else since I read these notes. My mother said she was waiting outside on instructions from his staff for the Chancellor to leave before she was permitted to enter his office. The assistant who entered with her first checked that his desk was clear. Neither of them noted these pages screwed up and tossed carelessly that had missed the bin, remaining hidden behind it until my mother began to clean. She brought them home more as a souvenir to say she had some of the handwriting of the leader of our nation – for posterity, you might say.'

Joseph blinked, his mouth dry, tongue feeling thick and far too warm but unable to swallow as the man continued.

'She showed it to me for amusement. She couldn't read it, Herr Altmann, but I could. You must also read it.'

'I will not!' Joseph snapped. 'Get out, Bergheimer, before I call the police and have you arrested.'

Bergheimer nodded. 'I'll leave. But you're a fellow Jew. You must act. I don't know anyone else of your seniority or influence. Your wife's —'

'I said get out. If you so much as mention my wife or my family again, I shall not be responsible for the consequences of what happens to you. Now you have a mother to take care of, David, and out of respect for her age and for the fact you were one of my daughter's favourite teachers, I am going to ask you once again to leave and never again make contact. Do you understand? I will denounce you.'

'I understand, Herr Altmann, Sir.' He turned to leave. 'Please, I shall see myself out.' Bergheimer moved quickly, hurrying to the sitting-room door, turning briefly. 'I am sorry for the trouble.'

'Go,' Joseph said wearily, his mind already reaching towards a calming cognac. He would pour himself a big slug and take it upstairs where his wife's willing, soothing arms awaited. She would take all this nonsense away with her kisses and tender touch.

He heard the front door close and duly walked into the hallway to lock up, suddenly fearful that Bergheimer might have a sudden change of heart. He bolted the door, checked it twice and then shifted to look out of the glass panel just to be sure that his unwanted guest had gone. There was no one on the stairs up to the porch or on the pavement outside handily flooded with light from the street lamp. His front gate was shut, Bergheimer had disappeared from his life and he sighed with relief.

'Joseph?' He swung around and the sight of his wife in a daring negligee at the top of the stairs instantly helped his mood. 'Is everything all right?'

'It is now, my love, especially glimpsing you through that skimpy lace.'

She laughed throatily. 'If you keep me waiting much longer, I'll be asleep.'

'Nightcap?'

'Why not,' she said with a glinting smile. 'Hurry.'

He blew her a kiss as she lifted the hem of her flimsy gown and disappeared off the landing into their bedchamber. Joseph stretched and heard a satisfying click. With an anticipation of beckoning pleasure, he turned back to the sitting room to pour the drinks and check the fire before he would switch off the downstairs lights but was halted in these steps by the sight of David Bergheimer's hat on the credenza.

Joseph helplessly felt a pang of regret at the younger man's wasted journey and the bad feeling that now existed between them. He lifted the hat to place it on the hat stand's hook; maybe Bergheimer would call back for it. If so, he would see to it that only Frau Muller dealt with him – she would send him packing. But as he lifted the hat onto the hook he was disturbed to see revealed the crumpled pages of the notes that Bergheimer had brought. They had been deliberately secreted, the hat intentionally left behind to hide the notes. No wonder the man hurried away from the sitting room.

'Damn you, Bergheimer,' he cursed.

Even as late as when he'd poured two glasses of best French cognac into their Czechoslovakian crystal glasses that had been a wedding gift, Joseph fully intended to throw the pages into the dying embers, where they would turn to ash and float up the chimney so that he never had to confront the stolen contents again.

But over that nip of amber liquid, the fumes hovering about him and with a curiosity that was stronger than his resolve or the flames, he read the small, looped writing and knew as the sweetness of the cognac turned bitter in his throat that his life would never be the same again.

9
Kent – May 1933

Stella was standing in her nearly empty wardrobe in Kent, wishing now that she had brought her black dress with her that so easily doubled for dinner wear. Her main luggage was yet to be delivered and she stared, embarrassed, at the two outfits hanging before her. She was certain a family such as the Ainsworths would dress for their evening meal, but she had nothing suitable.

She breathed loudly through her nose and it came out as a deep sigh. Stella reached for a navy afternoon dress which had bell sleeves from the elbow with a floaty navy and white polka-dot chiffon overlay and a small soft waterfall bow to one side of the collar. It was starkly simple despite the touch of whimsy and yet she'd loved it on sight in the department store for its effortless prettiness. The dress was sewn in sleek panels that were supposed to hug her hips narrowly but she could feel the room in the dress now. Never mind, she was eating three proper meals daily suddenly and had no doubt she'd fill it neatly again. She had brought this dress as an afterthought, having originally planned to mix and match the couple of day dresses, two cardigans, skirt and two blouses she'd been able to pack easily. Amongst her peers Stella knew she was considered well attired but she could only imagine the range and choice that Beatrice Ainsworth could select from. She dismissed any further pondering on the subject as being wasted energy.

She had bathed quickly, and having stood at the wardrobe for what must have been several minutes of indecision, clambered into fresh underwear and the navy dress. No, it was not as snug as it used to be, and Stella realised as she closed the door to regard herself in the long mirror that she had dropped more weight without being aware of it.

He'd noticed, though. She shook her head. Rafe was here and Rafe was her new boss; the man she'd been secretly thinking on in her private moments, mostly not admitting how disappointed she had become at the notion that after such a fleeting encounter she would likely never see him again. And yet while she'd been pining he'd been plotting, pulling strings behind her like a puppeteer . . . He'd wanted to help her – had made that clear that evening – but she'd treated his offer too casually . . . with disdain, almost. But he'd been true to his word. And Stella couldn't deny the difference his help would make to her family but especially to her life, enabling her to shake off the dark burdens that had pressed upon her shoulders in London.

Nevertheless, was she always going to feel as awkward as she did now? As she regarded her reflection, Stella finally allowed herself to admit that she felt as though she was being coerced into keeping a secret. He hadn't said anything but then he didn't have to; she'd picked up on all of his silent signals that he didn't want anyone to know they had met previously. What if his wife found out? How ugly would that look if it were proved Stella had lied? She lifted and dropped her shoulders with irritation. He had made her angry on their first meeting and here he was doing it again on their second.

Even so, he had seemed to understand her from that first awkward five minutes together. In the taxi to her house, though, it had felt as though they were removed from the reality of their worlds and that somehow in the dark of the vehicle while London streamed beside them they had created a world within a world that belonged to them. They had both been honest with each other, hadn't they? Or had they? Stella smiled. He hadn't directly lied but it was now clear that she hadn't asked the right questions. She knew better now.

She had no doubt there had been a special connection between them that she had felt for no other person. She'd dated men; she'd kissed enough to not feel too much like the yearning spinsters of novels, and also slept with one, disappointing though it had been.

If she were honest, Rafe's brief kiss of her gloved hand had been infinitely more arousing than Harry Farmer's dinner at the Falcon pub in Clapham and his subsequent fumbling, anxious weight atop her in a darkened hotel room afterwards. She shuddered now to remember it and awkwardly tucked a curl of hair behind her ear as she admitted to herself that the ride with Rafe, their shoulders and thighs touching, provoked a tense, even romantic, air that was so lacking in Room 6 that night with Harry.

Stella's gaze raised itself to meet the eyes staring back in the reflection and guilt was mirrored in their blueness. She knew she had to lose any aspirations she may have romanced about in her daydreams. There was no future to it and nothing but pain for her if she allowed herself to imagine anything but the obvious – that he was in London, living out of his club most weeks, and likely charming every pretty young woman he met. She was surely one of a line. And he was married with two daughters! Stella set her shoulders and straightened. *Grow up*, she mouthed at her image and walked to the bathroom.

She combed through her dark hair, wondering now whether she should have washed it again. But it was still glossy and the soft finger wave curls were holding their shape perfectly. She wouldn't need it trimmed for a while. She pinched her cheeks and smudged a hint of a light rose lipstick on, careful to blot the colour back from her lips. Her father had always detested her wearing make-up but working in the store meant she had to keep up with fashions and when Didi had approved her light touch with the cosmetics, Evan

Myles had shrugged and let it go. She was no longer that employee, though, and it didn't feel right to wear too much colour as a governess – or tutor, as Mrs Ainsworth preferred to refer to her as.

She gave herself a final check over, twisting both ways to ensure she had no loose threads or marks on her dress. Stella dabbed a tiny spot of perfume at her neck from her mother's bottle of Arpège by Lanvin and felt her reassuring presence as she checked her watch.

It was two minutes to seven. She didn't want to be late but not overly eager to intrude on the family evening either. She hurried now, quickly closed the door behind her and took the back stairs at a steady clip to get down the levels, while trying not to make too much of a clatter. She emerged into one of the lobbies and nearly bumped into Hilly.

'Whoops a daisy, sorry,' she said, stepping back just in time. 'Hello, Hilly.'

'Good evening, Miss Stella,' Hilly said, using the more formal language of above stairs that Stella instantly noted had been absent during luncheon.

'I . . . er, I've been invited to eat with the family tonight,' she said, words falling out as she tried to gauge the mood of her colleague.

'So we've been told. I am just about to set another place.' A smile was forced and Hilly glanced at her tray. 'They're in the winter drawing room.'

When Stella looked at her blankly, the maid, who was not a lot younger than her, gestured with a nod. 'That door, Miss Stella. Enjoy your evening.'

Stella was left to watch Hilly disappear into a room she could only imagine must be the winter dining room. She felt as though she'd been silently, invisibly slapped by her fellow workmates who only hours earlier had thawed and made her feel welcome; even Mrs Boyd had sounded chatty. Now suddenly she felt on the outer. She took a breath to steady her nerves and walked towards the door Hilly had indicated.

Winter drawing room, she mocked in her mind but without allowing herself to hesitate, she knocked.

Her knock was answered by Grace in a fresh set of clothes and her face gleaming as though a flannel had fiercely scrubbed away the day's fun.

'Stella,' she gasped, genuine delight in her voice as she swung open the door and turned to the others. 'Stella's here.'

Stella stepped inside and the family looked up from what appeared to her a still-life snapshot. Beatrice Ainsworth, attired immaculately in a velvet green dress, was seated straight-backed in an armchair with a crystal glass of what was likely a gin and tonic if the half slice of lemon was an indication. Seated opposite, or rather draped opposite, still appearing thoroughly bored with her life, was Georgina, holding a small crystal glass. She wore a frock as liquid in shape and just as dark as the sherry she was presumably sipping on. But Stella's gaze was helplessly drawn to Rafe, staring at her from where he stood by the grand white marble fireplace that was streaked through with grey and forming the perfect backdrop to show off his tall, fine figure enclosed in a dark suit. Surprisingly, a fire was lit, but she felt only the heat of her host's gaze and she sensed once again that he was using it to communicate to her that their first meeting was no one else's business.

He was less formally dressed than for his night in London. Nevertheless he looked as dashing. Tonight he was out of his practical plus fours and attired for dinner in a suit of midnight blue, without waistcoat, but cut with the new fashion of a double-breasted jacket and turn-down collar rather than the detachable, stiff version. There was no denying that Rafe Ainsworth was a paragon of fashion. He was wearing glasses, though. Small, round and horn-rimmed, they gave him a professorial air that made Stella want to smile.

'H-hello again, Stella,' he stammered. 'I'm glad you could join us.'

She blinked. She'd not heard him stammer before. 'Er, thank you all for inviting me,' she said.

'It was Dougie's idea, I have to admit,' Beatrice said, although Stella heard: *We didn't want you but he did.*

Georgina sighed. 'Yes, we're not used to having servants eat with us.'

'Stella isn't a servant, is she, Daddy?' Grace asked from where she toured the perimeter of the drawing room with her tumbler of what looked to be lemon barley water.

'She is, actually, but you're too dim to understand because you've played hopscotch today and think you're now best friends,' Georgina cut back. Stella held her breath in surprise, realising the young woman obviously felt she was in safe enough company to display her ugly behaviour.

'Well,' Stella said, achieving a benign smile she was proud of. 'I don't feel like a servant to anyone, to be honest. I do, however, see myself as one of your staff and if you'd rather I —'

'Nonsense,' Rafe said in a mild, almost frightened tone. 'Manners, Georgie.' He looked back at Stella. 'You are most welcome and my invitation is genuine. I think it's a fine opportunity for us all to make you feel more at home here at Harp's End. Don't you agree, Bee dear?'

'Whatever you want, Dougie. Have a seat, Stella. What would you like to drink?'

'Er, I'm happy with a sherry, thank you.'

'Dougie, would you —'

'Yes, I'm onto it,' Rafe said, pushing the spectacles further up his nose.

Stella closed her open-mouthed study of his oddly taciturn way. She looked away, taking in the brocades and velvets that dominated this room while trying to make sense of his manner as he dropped the crystal stopper of the sherry decanter onto the silver tray, making his wife jump with alarm.

'Sorry, everyone,' he murmured with a sheepish expression as Grace giggled and Georgina glared at her father with disdain.

'Gosh, Dad, you're such a berk,' Georgie remarked, rolling her eyes.

Stella couldn't imagine how the effortlessly suave ways of the man she'd met in the dance hall, who glided down hills in a long, sure stride, was the same slightly bumbling person holding out a glass of sherry to her now.

'Stella,' he offered, not meeting her gaze, she noted.

'Thank you,' she murmured and took the glass.

'Well, chin-chin, everyone,' he said and moved back to the fireplace. Only now as everyone tipped their glasses did she see him fix her again with a penetrating gaze. It cut past his curious glasses to make her feel as though she were the only person in the room.

'I must say, Doug, it's nice to see you out of your hill walking gear. You do look so fine in an evening suit,' Beatrice said.

'Especially against Mummy's Aubusson rug,' Grace said in the background, now playing with her doll and a ball of wool. Her father cast her a grin and even Stella smiled inwardly at the unintentionally dry statement.

Georgie soon cooled the fun. 'Mummy, perhaps you should just let Dad remain tweedy and boffinish. If you're going to dress him like this, people have an expectation.'

Her mother looked surprised. 'Darling, dress your father? I wouldn't presume. He goes to his tailor at Savile Row and miraculously manages to look dashing like this when I agree he can often appear dishevelled. Thank heavens for Gieves & Hawkes, I say.'

'Dishevelled?' Georgina slid her gaze back to her father, who was wearing the most innocent of expressions. 'You look like a tramp a lot of the time, especially out there on the bloody Weald.'

'Don't curse, darling. It's vulgar,' Beatrice said.

Beatrice's admonishment was as limp as a damp day, Stella thought, and it seemed to her as though everything that rolled off the teenager's tongue was designed to shock. Stella was appalled at Georgina's harsh words towards her father, who simply chuckled as though hearing a silent joke that only he shared. She took immediate offence to the young woman's cutting manner and deliberately changed the subject.

'You were missed today for lessons, Georgina,' she said.

'Mrs Boyd said she'd passed on the message,' her student replied, without even looking at her.

'That's not the point, though, is it?' Stella pressed as she smiled kindly, recalling this was her smile she reserved for difficult customers at the store. 'Your parents have employed me to help you with your education. I'm not sure that putting shopping first is the best way to go about improving your French.' She glanced briefly at Rafe, whom she could swear winked at her.

'Oh, this is so tiresome,' Georgina said, putting down her glass a little too loudly.

'Georgina . . .' her father began.

'No, Daddy, you don't know what day it is most of the time while you go chasing your butterflies and stalking odd birds and . . . and . . . painting your silly watercolours. But this is *my* holiday and I don't really want to be cooped up inside with Stella and her colloquial French. There, that's the truth,' she snarled, swinging her shoulder-length hair and standing up.

Stella was waiting for Georgina Ainsworth to stamp her foot too. 'Mrs Ainsworth, if we've made arrangements for lessons, then unless there is an emergency, it is polite at the very least for Georgina to turn up for them.' She was surprised how commanding she sounded and dared not look towards Rafe, although she could feel his gaze on her. 'I would love a free day to roam the gorgeous Kent countryside but you are paying me very well to teach your daughters and I want to make sure that I fulfill your expectations. I can't of course if the student goes shopping instead.' She watched Beatrice flutter her eyelids as if deeply wearied of the topic. Stella turned to Georgina. 'No more excuses please, Georgina; I will leave your timetable with Mrs Boyd and a copy with your mother and perhaps there need be no further misunderstandings.'

'Y-yes, let's see to that, Bee,' Rafe stammered, reaching for a Scotch that Stella only noticed now. She also noticed him put it to his lips but not taste it. 'I think that's fair enough.'

'Oh, do shut up, Daddy. You're not helping,' Georgie whined. 'Mummy, are you really going to allow a stranger to boss us around?'

Beatrice Ainsworth gave a pained glance to her husband but he was moving away to play cat's cradle with his youngest daughter and it was written on Beatrice's face that she understood she was going to have to sort it out. 'Georgie, do stop complaining, or I'll get one of my headaches. Now, darling, it is fair that you attend lessons because we're paying for them. You told me that your lesson had been postponed until tomorrow so we could stay on in Brighton. I had no idea you'd telephoned Mrs Boyd. Is that the call you made when we were having tea at the Grand?'

Stella shifted her glance to the daughter again, delighted that Georgina had been caught out, but keeping her expression neutral.

Georgina cut her tutor a look of pure loathing.

'Nine-thirty sharp we begin tomorrow and we'll be done by eleven. You'll soon see I am not trying to make your life difficult, Georgina,' Stella tried again.

'But you are!' the girl snapped and ran to the door, leaving the room filled with tension. 'I'll take my meal upstairs. Gracie, tell Mrs Boyd, will you?' She flounced out but only after throwing a scowl at her mother. 'You're no help, Mummy!' And then she was gone. The carpeted stairs mercifully dulled her footsteps although they did hear a distant door slam.

'Why is Georgie always so mean?' Grace wondered, taking her father's hand.

'She's a teenager,' he replied, looking sideways towards Stella, who caught his glance. She didn't believe his rationale either.

'Heavens, that girl is so dramatic. I think I might have been like that when I was younger,' Beatrice admitted with a chuckle. She swallowed the gin and tonic. 'Are we having another gimlet? More lemon this time, darling.'

'Will do.'

Distantly a phone rang. Stella remembered seeing it in the main hall.

'Oh, who can that be?'

'It's always for Daddy,' Grace chirruped from somewhere behind one of the curtains where she had been humming to herself.

With Rafe watching her from behind his wife, Stella couldn't help but notice that now he had the freedom to take off his glasses and smile softly at her. And suddenly there he was, the Rafe she had met in London – calm, confident, suave. She couldn't reconcile the bumbling Dougie Ainsworth with the sure-footed, confident man who was now reaching for the soda syphon.

'I apologise for our daughter's behaviour, Stella. She won't be late again for your lesson,' he said.

Beatrice looked up. 'Grace, go and check on your sister and see if she can't be persuaded to join us for dinner.'

Stella wanted to tell them to let Georgina stew but she held her tongue and sipped her sherry and tried not to blush at the way Rafe's gaze was heating her in places she'd prefer him not to. He sprayed the soda and Beatrice shrieked as a sharp squirt of fizzing water drenched her back. Grace convulsed into helpless laughter and Rafe was around the armchair like a springing cat.

'Oh, my dear. I am so, so sorry,' he said, earnestly. 'I thought I was pointing the spout the right way, but I—'

Beatrice looked horror-struck and vaguely catatonic with an open mouth as the cold water seeped uncomfortably through her velvet dress. Mrs Boyd, who had presumably heard the scream, had barged in and was trying to work out what had occurred.

Stella helped out. 'Er, Mrs Ainsworth was accidentally sprayed by the soda; I'm afraid she's very damp,' she offered.

Mrs Boyd immediately moved to her mistress and helped her to stand up. Beatrice was squirming and squalling while Stella tried to suppress her amusement.

'I'm so sorry, darling,' Rafe bleated.

'Oh, do be quiet, Doug,' she complained. 'You're only making it worse. Grace! Stop your laughing and go speak with your sister!'

Stella cut a glance towards the instantly quietened Grace and the girl scampered off.

'Let's get you out of these wet clothes, Mrs Ainsworth.' Mrs Boyd offered an arm to her employer as though she were an invalid. 'Miss Myles?'

'Yes?' Stella stood and looked at the housekeeper.

'That was a Miss Farnsworth calling,' Boyd said sternly, almost as an accusation. 'I told her you were with the family and she said she will call tomorrow if she can, probably quite late, though.'

'Thank you.' Stella watched the two women walk to the door, unsure of what to do next. 'Mrs Ainsworth . . . ?'

Beatrice waved a hand. 'Amuse yourselves. I shall be back in ten minutes.'

The door was closed behind them and Stella turned slowly now to fix her other employer with an accusatory stare. She said nothing immediately, taking a few moments to gauge his mood as he stood warming himself by the fire and she sensed his sheepishness.

'You did that on purpose,' she finally breathed, still filled with astonishment.

'For good reason.'

'Good reason? You deliberately sprayed your wife —'

He gave her a soft look of exasperation, pushing at the air before him and she immediately dropped her voice.

'Why?'

'I needed a chance to talk with you alone.' Rafe's voice was now so low she had to sit forward to hear him speaking just above the gentle crackle of the fire.

'Bloody hell,' she gasped in a whisper and this amused him hugely.

'A woman who swears properly. That's refreshing around here.'

'I've good reason. What was that all about?'

'Stella, I wanted to thank you for keeping mum about our original meeting,' he said.

'You didn't have to go to such lengths.'

He nodded as though he wanted to explain more but something prevented him from doing so. 'Even so, I appreciate your discretion.'

'Presumably you have good reason for you and I to be seen as meeting for the first time today?'

'I do. However, while it is not my intention to put you into any difficult position, it couldn't be avoided. You will have to trust me on this.'

'But why should your wife mind if —'

'Stella, my wife is . . .' He shook his head. 'She is extremely protective of whatever it is that she prizes.'

'I'm not sure I understand you, Mr Ainsworth.'

'Rafe,' he murmured.

'In a dance hall, you're Rafe . . . even in the taxi afterwards. But not here. Not even by your own admission are you Rafe here. Why is that?'

'I told you I have —'

'Three names, yes,' she hissed under her breath. 'But why would you share with me your preferred name that the women of your childhood used but you don't share it with the women of your adult life?'

He looked back at her with a pained expression that was so poignant in that moment that she shook her head. 'I'm sorry. You do not have to answer that. It truly is none of my business.'

'You did make it your business, though.'

Stella blushed, remembering how demanding she had been that first night. 'But I have new perspective now,' she countered, and they glanced at the door, perhaps both thinking of the women behind it. 'You are no longer a stranger from a dance hall whom I didn't expect to meet again. You are Mr Ainsworth, my employer, and I'm grateful for this short-term contract and would do nothing to jeopardise it, or how your family regards you.' She lifted a shoulder as if to say that nothing more needed to be said. 'However, what you do when you are away from your family is indeed your own affair and I don't plan on making it my concern, so you can continue to count on my discretion.' The way he was looking at her was making her cheeks burn warmer than they should on this cool evening and deep in her heart she knew she was trying to convince herself of her indifference. 'What I'm trying to say is that you appear to have a private side that is unknown to the people you love, and it is no intention of mine to add any awkwardness to those . . . um . . . secrets.' That last word was spoken cautiously as it sounded sinister but contrary to her expectation, all she got from him was a burst of soft amusement.

'Thank you, Stella.'

She bristled. 'I didn't imagine what I said was amusing?'

'You're very hooked on the notion that I have an alternate life to hide from my family.'

'Well, if I've read you wrong, then I apologise. Mr Ainsworth, maybe it's best under the circumstances if I don't share the family meal this evening. Really, it's not —'

'Nonsense! Why?'

Stella let out a slow breath. 'Because I feel uncomfortable.'

'I'm sorry. Is that all my fault?'

'You keep apologising. There's no need . . . really.' She hesitated but Stella felt determined to make him understand and not laugh at her. 'But you shouldn't have to do what you did simply to have a quiet word with me. That alone makes me feel as though we are engaged in something clandestine, when all of this has come about because of a chance encounter.'

'I keep apologising because my family makes it necessary. My wife treats you with indifference while our youngest is the opposite and already so in love with you she could wish you were her big sister. Meanwhile Georgina is unforgivably discourteous and I will have Beatrice speak to her about her poor manners towards you.'

'I'm not sure that's wise; she detests me enough already.'

'No, I loathe her attitude to people, while her high opinion of herself and her own standing needs adjustment.'

Stella gave a sad half smile and nodded silently to signal that she couldn't deny his sentiments.

He made a fist and pressed it silently but firmly on the mantelpiece to show his quiet disgust. 'Her mother protects her, unfortunately. Georgina has been allowed to ride roughshod over people all of her life. She has been indulged so thoroughly that I fear there is no way back for her other than the harsh way with some sort of violent awakening. Boarding school, for instance. I've discussed a finishing school in Switzerland in the hope that her departure will remove the tension from the household that

Georgina can provoke with a snap of her fingers. You witnessed her fine skills tonight.'

'Maybe that's a sound idea. I hear those schools can be firm with their charges.'

He nodded. 'They get away with very little under the keen eyes of the mistresses, most of them older spinsters with an axe to grind about temperament and behaviour . . . and hemlines of the young women of today.'

'Too much ankle?' Stella grinned.

Rafe pursed his lips in a comical pantomime of a high-born lady of the Victorian age.

Stella chuckled as quietly as she could. 'Oh gosh, you'd make a great Lady Bracknell.'

'What do you mean? I already have,' he said, affecting an injured tone. 'I was Lady Augusta Bracknell in the school's production of *The Importance of Being Earnest*. Not a single poor review, either; an agent actually asked afterwards if I would like representation.'

'Oh, yes . . . you'd make a fine actor,' she offered dryly. Again she saw the boyish Rafe break through from the amusement and sparkle that erupted in his eyes at the memory. 'How old were you?'

'Twelve. Seriously, I think I was only given the role because my voice broke early.'

Stella laughed. 'I'm trying to imagine you mincing about on stage in a silk crinoline.'

'My father was horrified at my bustle but I swear they could hear my mother's laughter all the way to the green room. Oh, how I loved her laugh . . .' He looked instantly melancholy, his gaze focused on more than two decades back.

Stella realised they'd got far off the point. 'Anyway, your girls are so different.' She shook her head. 'But if it's any comfort, I imagine that life will help her grow up, when Georgina starts to live beyond the umbrella of her mother's protection.'

He gave a soft snort as he returned to the present. 'You're so careful with your words, Stella.'

'I can hardly afford not to be so.'

'And yet I gather from Grace that you've been challenging Georgina?'

She nodded. 'I intend to, every day, but in private. I think the error was mine tonight in speaking out in front of her parents. The problem is I'm too honest.'

He raised an eyebrow. 'No,' he assured, his tone filled with irony.

She grinned. 'My directness can get me into hot water sometimes but I'm not very good at hinting. I'd rather just be plain.'

'You're anything but plain, Stella,' he mused and the softness in the way he looked at her was unnerving.

Stella hurried on because the mood of the conversation was now feeling similar to the mood of the taxi. 'I don't think you should talk like that.'

'Like what?' he said, stepping close enough that she could smell the woody, spicy scent of his shaving soap.

'You should not be so familiar.'

'I am merely stating a fact that no one can deny. You are beautiful, Stella, and you achieve that without an ounce of affectation . . . you dress modestly, you wear none of the ghastly cosmetic palaver that other women plaster on and yet your skin glows and your lips are —'

'Stop! Please, this is not appropriate.'

'I appreciate beauty in art, in nature, in women. I am merely saying you are not plain.'

'And you've made your point. You made it without tripping, fumbling, stammering or even wearing glasses. As I say, you confound me.'

'Good. I should hate to be predictable.'

Stella forced herself to breathe evenly as Rafe felt to her as though he was filling the room with his presence and she was beginning to suffocate from the bright awareness of her attraction to him.

'And I was simply trying to impress that Georgina was not just appallingly rude today but she has managed to make me feel like some sort of interloper accepting wages and board when I can't perform my job. I get the impression that Mrs Ainsworth finds the debating interminably draining and I suspect it is easier to give in to Georgina's demands than to fight her.'

'Quite.'

'Anyway, I suspect I shall feel like Lady Bracknell by the end of this contract, for all the lecturing I'm sure I shall be giving Georgina. It would be far easier if one of her parents could speak with her so that I can stop being the wicked witch in her life.'

'You want me to have that discussion with Georgina,' he said, his tone flat.

'Well, clearly your wife will not.'

'I doubt I am the right person.'

'You're the perfect person.'

'Why?'

'Because you're her father!'

It struck Stella that her words shredded his controlled façade and for an instant she was able to look behind the suave demeanour to where the real man hid. In that heartbeat she glimpsed anger and loneliness.

'I'm not —' he began.

But whatever he was about to growl back at her was swallowed as the door opened and Beatrice re-entered, talking over her shoulder.

'. . . remove hers, Mrs Boyd.' She looked back into the room. 'Georgina isn't coming down. She's going to eat in her room.

Heavens, it feels maudlin in here. What have you two been up to?'

Stella noticed that Rafe had collected his raw emotions together; his expression had rearranged itself to its former affable and open calm that looked eager to please. His glasses were even being carefully returned, as was his slight stammer – all achieved within the few sentences his wife had muttered.

'Er, I was telling Mr Ainsworth that I was suffering a pang of homesickness today.'

'Really? That's rather bleak, given you've barely arrived,' his wife said, coming to stand by the fire. She linked her arm in his as if to say she'd forgiven him his clumsiness and Stella had to admit they made a gloriously handsome couple.

'Darling, I'm so sorry about earlier, are you feeling much better?' he soothed, tapping her hand.

'I am feeling dry, Dougie. Are you going to fix me that drink?'

'Yes, of course,' he said, 'But I'd advise you all to stand clear of this,' he joked, reaching for the syphon.

The chameleon that she now knew him to be was back in its polite husband skin and yet she'd seen him 'naked' just moments earlier, and the passion in his enraged look at her words was unmistakable but also irresistible. She could feel that passion still; it was like an invisible finger reaching in to place itself on her heart as if choosing her.

'I don't think we need to keep referring to the suicides in Stella's past,' Beatrice said so casually that Stella shuddered and yet she sensed Beatrice's intrigue; there had been no need to mention her parents.

'It wasn't Mr Ainsworth's fault,' Stella said. 'I brought up the homesickness because I was explaining that I think I have a bit of headache tonight.'

'Dear me, that's no good,' Beatrice said as if she'd just told Mrs Boyd to throw an extra log on the fire.

'Yes, and I was asking him if you'd all excuse me tonight. The pain has become more determined.'

'Oh, pity,' Beatrice said in a tone devoid of all empathy. 'Another evening, perhaps?'

'Thank you for understanding,' Stella said, standing. She refused him eye contact but could feel a wave of his disappointment and regret lapping at the edge of her senses. 'Thank you for inviting me, Mrs Ainsworth.'

'Goodnight, Stella,' Beatrice said, turning to take the glass that her husband had brought to her. 'Doug, darling, you'd better tell Mrs Boyd that it's another two places to be removed as I suspect Grace will now lose all interest in dinner with us. You seem to be the new object of desire in our daughter's life, Stella.'

Stella had no idea how to respond to such a statement. 'I'll see Grace after her riding lesson and after Georgina's lesson. I hope that's suitable?'

'I shall see that Georgina attends all of her lessons from now on or she'll answer to me,' Rafe said, his normally mild tone suddenly mousey.

Even Beatrice chuckled. 'You, darling?'

Stella was so fascinated by the way she could now see Rafe shifting between personalities that her gaze lingered on him.

Beatrice cleared her throat. 'Stella?'

'Er, sorry, I was just thinking I could probably work out a proper timetable tonight.'

'But you have a headache,' Rafe said.

She recovered quickly as his glare urged. 'Yes, I'm hoping it won't hang around for too long.'

'I could have Hilly bring up some aspirin,' Beatrice offered.

'I have some with me, Mrs Ainsworth. I shall be fine. Thank you again.'

'As you wish,' Beatrice said, clearly bored with the topic. She sat down and reached for her husband's hand. 'Looks like it's a romantic dinner for two.'

Rafe cut his wife a half-hearted smile. 'I'll go and let Mrs Boyd know. Here, let me walk you out, Stella.'

Outside the door he sighed. 'You won't be able to avoid all of us all of the time,' he murmured.

'Not all. Just you. Good night, Mr Ainsworth.'

10

Stella arrived with an armful of books onto the landing and followed the explicit directions that had been delivered with her breakfast tray. She found the room called the nursery on the floor beneath hers at twenty minutes to nine precisely and Mrs Boyd was waiting for her.

'Ah, Miss Myles, good morning. Thank you for your punctuality.'

'I appreciate your meeting me.'

Mrs Boyd was holding a ring of keys. She began to select one. 'How was breakfast?'

'Thank you for sending up a tray. It was perfect, although I did say that I'm happy to take my breakfast with the staff.'

'Not necessary. You have duties here in the main part of the house with changeable schedules and we wouldn't want to disrupt your flexibility,' she said in a meaningless excuse that made it clear Stella was not so welcome below stairs.

Stella was surprised how much it hurt but remembered her manners and moved to small talk. 'It's certainly quiet here.'

'Indeed, here is near silent,' Mrs Boyd said, holding up a key triumphantly. 'This one hasn't been used in a while. Yes, only Miss Grace is on this side.' She nodded towards a door at the end of the corridor where they stood. 'She's gone for a riding lesson this morning. Miss Georgina and her parents have their rooms on this level in the east wing.' Stella's heart sank a little deeper for her youngest charge, who appeared to be both physically and emotionally cut off from her family. 'You'll have no need to go to the east wing.'

Was that a warning?

Mrs Boyd finally jiggled the lock into submission and they heard it shift.

'Here we are, the nursery,' she said in triumph, pushing open the door, like stage curtains.

Stella was expecting something prissy, with frills and bows – certainly white with soft pastel touches. She was surprised to be led into a room that was painted a rich sage green with all the woodwork picked out in a soft parchment colour. High shelves were lined with what appeared to be an eclectic collection of memorabilia, from leather footballs to hockey sticks to jars of marbles. Books that couldn't find a place in the huge bookcase that claimed one entire wall gathered dust in colourful towers nearby. Sketches and watercolours of varying adeptness and of everything from birds and lizards to landscapes hung on the remaining walls in a motley of unmatched frames. Huge, colourful moths or iridescent beetles were framed beneath glass and there were bell jars of preserved creatures she wasn't even sure about . . . they all appeared vaguely reptilian. School ties, caps and scarves twisted around odd hooks as though they'd been flung from the door and had found a comfortable home by chance, to remain for decades. A marvellous series of colourful kites hung on the walls as well as grainy school photographs and smiling family groups and of clearly much-beloved dogs who claimed their own silver frame. It was too much to take in at once. Brightness flooded in from the tall, oblong windows that had soft white voile curtains to diffuse the sharpness of morning to a deliciously mellow light that added to the tender ambience of the room. She spun around, realising that she was the one giving gentle gasps of delight.

'Forgive me. It's a lovely space,' she murmured, turning back to the housekeeper. 'I didn't expect it to be so charming when you called it the nursery.'

'It's Mr Ainsworth's name for it. I've never known it referred to as anything else.'

Stella was moving towards the windows.

The housekeeper straightened a heavy shell acting as a paperweight on the large banker's desk in the middle of the room. 'We put this desk in here so that you and Miss Georgina could study facing each other rather than side by side. There's paper, ink, pencils, rubbers, blotting paper, sharpeners . . .' She stopped opening drawers and reeling off the obvious. 'Yes, I think all the Ainsworth children down the years spent their infancy in this room. Mr Ainsworth has forbidden us to move any of the memorabilia – dusting it all is fraught because he's so precious about the items here – and yet he insisted this was the room to be used by you for study. I can't imagine why, with all this clutter.'

Stella frowned, wondering if yet another invisible, silent message was being communicated.

'So Mr Ainsworth spent his early childhood days in here too.'

'Oh, yes, indeed,' Mrs Boyd sniffed. 'I might just open a window.' She struggled with a window as she had with the door's lock. It was as though the room didn't wish to permit the present into its chamber of secrets and memories. Mrs Boyd, however, gave a hefty shove with her shoulder, and with a firm grunt the window finally surrendered, sighing open as though expelling the breath in the room it had held tightly for decades.

'There we are. That's much better. Now you and Miss Georgina can't fall asleep.'

'No threat of that, I'm afraid, on French verbs.'

'Well, I shall leave you to it. Apparently we're to send up some hot cocoa for Miss Georgina. Would you like a small pot too?'

'Oh, I don't think that's necessary, Mrs Boyd. Georgina will have only recently finished breakfast, surely? I think she can forgo her cocoa for an hour or two so we remain undisturbed.'

'Um, she has specifically ordered it. And —'

'Well, I'm her tutor and her senior, so forgive me but I'd rather you didn't send up anything as I suspect it will only be disruptive to Georgina's concentration. She is more than welcome to have cocoa served directly afterwards at eleven sharp when the tutorial ends.' Stella smiled firmly as Mrs Boyd blinked in consternation. She put her books onto the desk and began sorting through them in the hope it gave just the right polite air of dismissal. 'Thank you again. This is a perfectly conducive space for Georgina to knuckle down to the study her parents expect.' She lifted her gaze and fixed Mrs Boyd, surely an accomplice of the two Ainsworth women, to show she was not to be undermined.

'As you wish, Miss Myles.'

'Thank you.' She followed the housekeeper to the door, smiling indulgently as she closed it on the woman. *Is every day going to be a battle of wills?* she wondered.

Her mind flipped to Georgina and the trial ahead of her today with this hostile teenager. She thought about how her father had reacted yesterday to the suggestion that he speak with his daughter about her lack of respect. Stella hadn't understood his unfinished response that was nevertheless delivered with repressed anger.

'She's not —' he'd begun.

Not what? Stella had wondered. Not worth it? Not happy? Not going to listen to me? Stella shuddered inwardly, imagining how uncomfortable her household would have been if she had ever dared to mock or bait her father in that manner.

She glanced at her watch. Six minutes to go. Georgina had better not be late . . .

Stella began a slow tour of the room, gazing at the old photos, charmed by the obvious snapshots of Rafe as a boy, which all depicted him either in what looked to be a desert or running seemingly wild on the wilderness of what was presumably the Weald. The pictures of him surrounded by sand dunes were intriguing, especially those with his face half covered by linens in the Bedouin style. There was another lad of similar age, she guessed, but smaller in stature, who was also in a lot of the Arabian-looking photos. Apart from sharing dark hair, they didn't look at all alike but clearly they were close. Cousins, maybe? She squinted, he looked European; eastern Mediterranean, perhaps?

Meanwhile Rafe looked tanned and relaxed in the images on foreign soil; his crinkled eyes suggested he was always smiling, completely at ease in his surrounds, whether he was perched on a camel or peeping out from a makeshift tent that was more of an awning to Stella's mind. She wished she could see the colours of the desert . . . Stella imagined the deep gold of the sands and the richness of the camel rugs and carpets within the tent she could just see. What was he doing in the desert as a child? Where was this?

She spied a family photo in what looked to be a large white villa, except they were in some sort of enclosed courtyard. Date palms bent from pots, a fountain nearby spouted water with crystalline droplets sparkling as they caught the sunlight, and in the background, a man in all white wearing a fez blurred behind the family as he crossed the lens, unaware that he'd entered the photograph. Rafe in shorts and crisp white shirt was presumably leaning against his mother, a dark beauty, his elbow crooked on her shoulder while her arm draped affectionately across his bare legs. Her other hand was moving towards her mouth as though trying to cover her own amusement. Stella's gaze shifted to the little girl who was likely his sister, sitting on her father's lap; she was caught in a moment of explosive laughter and looking at Rafe as though he'd just said something witty. The father wore a genial expression, indulging his happy family. Stella smiled helplessly. It was a moment of pure joy and she felt a burst of envy; she understood that feeling but didn't have it captured on film as Rafe had. She would have to rely on her memory.

Stella's attention was caught by another photo; the same two boys, another couple of male adults, neither of whom she recognised from other photos. They were seated at a table outside some sort of street-side café and in the grainy photo she could make out men smoking in the dim background on bubble pipes. There was another man standing nearby, his hand placed on the young Rafe's shoulder. This man possessed a luxurious greying moustache that curled dramatically into whorled points and had on a lead – rather outrageously, Stella thought – a peacock. The bird did not have its tail fanned but it too comically appeared to be looking directly into the camera. Embroidered on its owner's shirt she could just make out an extravagantly sewn letter 'M'.

The boys were grinning, holding up glasses of what looked like lemonade, and the vignettes of Rafe's seemingly happy childhood made her feel somehow sad for him that his life now felt controlled by his circumstances. She tried to imagine where this photo was taken, searching for clues in the image.

The door swung open, startling Stella, and Georgina blew in. She brought her usually sulky air into the calm of the Green Room as Stella had absently begun referring to it.

Georgina affected a melodramatic cough. 'Heavens! Why here? This ghastly old room hasn't been opened in centuries and yet I'm forced to breathe its dust and filth.'

'Morning,' Stella said brightly, determined not to taint a new beginning. 'You look lovely today,' she added, noting the long-line narrow skirt in a tiny dogtooth weave. Large buttons did up on the side and there was no pull on any of them – Georgie certainly cut a neat figure but Stella noticed her lack of height meant the skirt made her appear shorter still. Nevertheless, Stella would kill to wear it and couldn't help but admire the way Georgina had teamed it with a soft frilled white blouse and a tiny red belt. 'Did you sleep well?'

Georgina looked at her from murky blue eyes. 'Would you care if I hadn't?'

So this is how it was going to be, Stella thought with a pang of disappointment. 'Not really, no.'

Georgina smirked. 'You may be poor but at least you're honest.'

'Poor?' she asked mildly, opening one of her books and gesturing at the seat opposite.

Her student flounced into the chair. 'If you had money, why would you want to be a servant?'

'I have a terrific job actually, Georgina. But I'm taking a sabbatical. Shall we have this conversation in French?'

Georgina ignored the question. 'That's right, your parents killed themselves, didn't they? How perfectly horrid of them. Did you find them or maybe your younger sister did? Was there blood or did they do it neatly with pills and liquor? But then their tongues would have been swollen and blue, I'm sure. How ghastly. Your brother and sister must have been traumatised . . . how can they ever get to sleep at night in the same house where their parents committed suicide?'

Not a word of French had been offered in the teenager's cruel and sour rant. How Stella kept from leaning across the banker's desk and slapping her student she did not know. She forced her rage down, and made a promise to herself in that moment that nothing Georgina Ainsworth ever said would affect her again. 'Georgina, I am not going to discuss my personal life with a child, least of all a student of mine.' She moved into simple, conservative French. 'Shall we proceed?'

'I hate this room,' Georgie sneered in French.

Stella responded in French as though it was simply a conversation. 'You seem to hate everything.'

'I know I hate you most of all, with my father a close second,' Georgina said in English. 'I wish he'd just go away on one of his jaunts and never return. Then we could fire you and I could be rid of both of you.'

Stella helplessly moved back into English despite her best intentions. It was obvious the horrid youngster would not understand the nuances of this unsettling discussion if she continued in French. 'Georgina, that sounds so vicious. Should I be speaking to your mother about your wishes?'

'What? That I wish my father were dead?'

Stella gasped. 'You don't mean that.'

'What would you know? You know nothing, Servant Stella. Actually, that's not quite true, is it? You do know about something I'd love to know about because your father's dead. You must feel so free.'

Trills of anger raced through Stella's body, flushing at her neck where she felt the heat of fury gathering in spite of her attempt to mask her response. Her voice did not betray her, though. 'I asked you not to discuss my private life.'

'I don't see why I can't. You get to poke around in my private life.'

'I have done no such thing,' she snapped, knowing she was being drawn into the girl's deliberate trap and yet helplessly against her better judgement she was participating.

'Of course you have. Just because your life is so dull and poor, you are making sure mine is the same.'

'Georgina, your parents hired me,' Stella appealed. 'I didn't ask to come here.'

The teenager shrugged. 'Exactly. So I wish he would just disappear and then my mother would have to agree to let you go and I would celebrate and get on with my life.'

'You have so much growing up to do,' Stella cautioned. 'Shall we continue?' she said briskly with a feigned smile. Faking it helped, surprisingly. 'Let's write down some verbs and then we can use them in our conversation.' She pulled the inkpot closer and reached for the pen, dipped the nib into it and began writing in French on a sheet of paper.

For a moment all that lingered between the two was the tension of their parried words and the sound of her nib scratching on the paper.

'You have no idea of my life or my plans. Socially you are nowhere near my level and financially you obviously need my money.'

Stella sighed. 'You don't pay me.'

'I wouldn't even if I could. What my father sees in you is a mystery, although if he were a different man I could imagine. He could be paying you for other services because you're pretty enough in a common sort of way.'

Stella tried not to break the nib with the pressure of her gathering wrath. She studiously wrote on, forcing herself to breathe low and long to beat the rising drumbeat of rage.

Georgina sighed, and began undoing her pearl earrings. 'These are pinching.' She placed them on the desk.

Stella pulled the ink closer still and dipped again, deliberately not looking at Georgina but the girl's scathing remarks burned in her mind and, without warning, the words escaped and she helplessly bit back. 'I told Mrs Boyd not to bother with the cocoa.' Now she did look up. 'We don't need the interruption.'

Georgina's eyes narrowed. She leaned forward slowly and deliberately to knock over the inkpot. Stella was quick to move but wasn't fast enough and the royal blue liquid rushed across the desk and splattered over Georgina's beautiful skirt.

'Oh, dear!' Georgina's insincere tone sickened Stella but she dashed around the table all the same, dreading the mess. 'Now, look at my skirt,' her student said, sounding anything but dismayed.

More for the sake of the skirt that Stella had just admired so deeply, she made an effort and leaped up with a sheet of blotting paper. Wordless with fury, she dabbed uselessly at the spreading stain that was greedily crawling across the worsted skirt and privately she deeply lamented that she'd provoked Georgie into this petulant display. She mourned the garment that she suspected would never recover from the ink damage.

Georgina sat patiently, no doubt enjoying Stella crouching at her knees. 'It's no good, Stella,' she said, her tone pitching a disgustingly fake virtue. 'Perfectly ruined, I'm afraid. I'm so clumsy – I must take after my clodhopping father.'

'He's not a clodhopper,' she answered in her quiet despair, realising a heartbeat too late that her defence was dangerous.

'How would you know? You only met him yesterday.'

'Er . . . that's right. But he seemed entirely at home and well balanced on the moors when Grace and I ran into him.'

'The way you defend him is admirable. I hope you don't fancy him because I should warn you, there's something between my mother and father that no one else can touch. Don't ask me why,' Georgina said, her tone dripping with cunning, 'but my mother who had the looks and money to have absolutely anyone she wanted in life opted for the booby prize. My father is handsome enough but he's a buffoon, Stella. He is a constant embarrassment and a drag in my life.'

Stella straightened. 'And you're a little beast in his, I'm sure,' she murmured, unable to help her simmering disgust spilling over.

Georgina smiled. It seemed she'd heard. 'Oh, I can't wait to tell Mummy what you just called me. Now, if you'll excuse me, I shall go change. I have something to discuss with my parents.' The teenager stopped at the door and threw back a smile. 'Not sure how long I'll be. I may even have to bathe again as I do believe the ink has stained my legs. Maybe it's best if we rearrange for tomorrow.'

Stella couldn't hold in her disdain a moment longer. 'No, don't rush back,' she said. 'I shall see you tomorrow, Georgina. I'll rearrange a double lesson.'

'Maybe not, Stella. You may even be packing your bags tonight, if I have anything to do with it.'

'Close the door behind you, please.'

It was slammed shut. Stella walked to the window, her chest rising in deep, angry breaths as she stared out at the hills, determined not to cry although she watched the landscape through the blur of treacherous watering eyes. It felt peaceful out there and the silent stillness helped to calm her ragged breathing. She was finally able to blot away the threatened tears with a swipe of her fingers.

She wondered if Rafe was roaming the countryside again this morning. She'd heard him moving around upstairs late last night. She hadn't slept well – her mind racing with thoughts of Carys perhaps crying herself to sleep and Rory desperately trying not to. But those thoughts entwined all too sinuously with snippets of her evening, particularly Rafe winking at her. She was still struggling to drift off when she'd heard the boards creaking above her. She hadn't meant to derive satisfaction from it, but the realisation that the romantic dinner his wife had mentioned perhaps hadn't turned out as romantically as she'd hoped was quietly pleasing.

Stella hadn't left the nursery. It had been a pleasant time exploring all of the family memorabilia, particularly the photographs of Rafe as a boy. Time had seemed to move fast, though, for suddenly her next class was imminent.

'Stella!' It was Grace bursting in. 'Hello – I'm not late, am I?'

Stella smiled at the rosy cheeks of her youngest pupil, their colour heightened from her riding lesson and her dash up the stairs, still in her jodphurs.

'Mummy said I'm a disgrace to come to lessons dressed like this but I said you wouldn't mind.'

'Not in the slightest! It's lovely to see you.'

'Are we learning more of the daffodils poem?'

'If you wish.'

'I do. I want to learn it all.'

The hour with Grace passed easily and swiftly. Her eagerness to learn and to focus was in direct contrast to that of her sister. While Grace had her head bent, working on writing out some sentences in French, Stella had a chance to study her. She had elements of her mother – the beautifully shaped eyes – and despite her still-podgy build that Stella was sure would fall away in her teens, she could see that Grace possessed her mother's languid manner when engaged.

'Which teams do you play in at school?'

Grace kept writing but still answered. 'I'm the youngest to play in the A team of tennis, and I'm the main substitute for the lacrosse team. Oh yes, I'm second base for rounders but our Games teacher thinks my bowling is coming on so she's going to try me out this year in that position as we're fielding two school teams I think. I'm in the under twelve swimming team and in winter I think I'll make the hockey team . . . I hope so, I want to captain us in hockey one day.'

'Your father was good at sport like you.'

'My daddy is good at everything.'

'Except spraying soda,' Stella replied and Grace began to laugh delightedly.

Grace mimicked Beatrice's shriek. 'Oh, do shut up, Doug!' and now Stella joined in the laughter. This only encouraged the youngster to leap up. 'And now look what you've done to my Aubusson rug!'

Neither of them saw or heard the door open and only realised someone was standing there when a throat was cleared with obvious intent to catch their attention.

Stella turned and her expression dropped instantly as the temperature plummeted around her to see Beatrice Ainsworth. She stood in a heartbeat. 'Mrs Ainsworth.'

Her employer regarded her as Stella imagined a cat might patiently await its prey. It was an unblinking stare of ice-blue malevolence.

'Were we making too much noise?'

'I was just leaving my room and I could hear the hilarity. I couldn't imagine what was so terribly entertaining about French verbs . . . so I came this way down the hall. Now I discover what is so funny.' She looked away from Stella to her child but Stella flinched to see how vicious her expression was. 'Grace, you have disappointed me. I will be cancelling your riding lessons forthwith for the rest of the holidays.'

Grace's expression crumpled but she didn't cry. 'I'm sorry, Mummy.'

'Fresh clothes have been laid out. I'm perfectly sure you smell after being with the horses and dancing around in here instead of getting on with what I have paid for you to do.' She glanced at her wristwatch in irritation. 'Ah, I see your lesson time – if we can call it a lesson – is almost done. Let's leave it at that, shall we? Hurry along, Grace. Miss Hailsham has drawn a bath for you. Don't make a mess, please. I do not expect to see you for the rest of the day. You may stay in your room. Meals will be served there. Don't let me hear another peep from you until tomorrow morning. And even then I'm not sure I want to look at you.'

Stella felt the horror of the cruel words settle on Grace's shoulders and her private response was equally passionate but she had to physically clamp her mouth shut.

Grace cast Stella a look of deep apology. She too could sense trouble.

'Thank you, Stella,' she lisped just above a whisper.

'You worked hard, Grace,' she said firmly, knowing it made no difference but feeling stronger for saying it. 'I'll mark your page this afternoon. Hope to see you tomorrow.'

The child scurried away but her mother was in no hurry to leave.

Stella approached. 'Mrs Ainsworth, I'm so sorry. We were —'

'Stella, I was greeted not long ago by Georgie with a formal complaint against you. It's not one I can ignore, I'm afraid, especially given what I've just witnessed.'

'I can explain,' she said, trying not to let it sound like a bleat, but given the suddenly leaden atmosphere, it sounded worse – like she was begging.

'I'm sure you can. Just as you want to explain you were not ridiculing me in the presence of my young child just now.'

She held her tongue, Rafe's warning about his wife's cunning echoing in her racing thoughts.

'Nothing to say for yourself?' Beatrice goaded.

'Yes, I would like to explain, if you'd permit me.'

'Fine. I shall see you downstairs in my salon in fifteen minutes. Be prompt, I have a busy day.' She swung around and left, a waft of her luscious rose and jasmine French perfume polluting the pleasantly musty, boyish smell of the Green Room. Stella recognised it immediately as Jean Patou's Joy and sighed that Beatrice didn't deserve to wear a fragrance of that name.

11

Mrs Boyd was on hand to show her to Beatrice's salon, which was in a part of the house she hadn't stepped into previously. It felt lonely, their footsteps echoing down the uncarpeted corridors, and somehow this area felt more imposing for the lack of light.

'Cold down this way,' she remarked in a weak attempt to make conversation with the housekeeper as she trailed alongside, listening to Mrs Boyd's heels click on the parquetry.

'It's the western side. The sun takes a while to find its way in over here,' she replied and Stella suspected Mrs Boyd had been apprised of the situation, hence her curtness.

She moved on. 'Um, Mrs Boyd, I have Georgina's earrings that she removed because they were pinching her lobes. She accidentally left them behind on the writing desk in the nursery this morning. Should I give them to you to return?'

'You may like to return them yourself. They're waiting for you,' she added and knocked on a door where she'd paused.

They?

'Come,' called Beatrice's voice from the other side.

Stella didn't have a chance to ask more but presumed the loathsome Georgina would be smirking on the other side too. Mrs Boyd obliged by opening the door and nodding that Stella should proceed. She breathed deeply and silently to calm herself and stepped inside. Stella didn't hear the door close behind her but seated behind a strikingly modern, highly polished oval desk was Beatrice Ainsworth. The entire room was a statement of good taste in Stella's opinion and the single sweeping glance she could afford gave her an impression of muted colours of greys and creams with bold accents of black and silver in stripes or geometric patterns on cushions. The Macassar desk was the centrepiece, though, and she'd seen a similar piece in the furniture department of her store. It attracted a price tag so high most customers she recalled gasped upon hearing it. All in all, the chamber possessed a sharp, crisp look that was entirely in keeping with the era's latest décor and far more modern than the rest of Harp's End. There was no doubt this was Beatrice Ainsworth's private domain.

Equally crisp-looking in a sombre grey three-piece was Rafe Ainsworth, unhappily standing by a window and glaring out. Stella hadn't expected Rafe but she showed no surprise at his presence. Georgina, as expected, was in tow standing beside her seated mother, still wearing her ink-stained clothes. Stella felt another pang of misery for the skirt and now could anticipate Georgina's tale of woe. The script was already written.

'Would you like a seat, Stella?' Beatrice began.

'Not really. I feel extremely uncomfortable so I might as well remain standing.' The defiance, though hollow, stirred her courage. She noticed Rafe turn away from the window to regard the scene as the two sides faced off.

'As you wish,' Beatrice countered but Stella had already looked away.

'Good morning, Mr Ainsworth.'

'Stella,' he said softly in greeting, looking momentarily surprised to be addressed so directly.

'Let's not beat around the bush,' Beatrice launched in, wresting back the room's attention. 'Georgina tells me you insulted her this morning.'

Stella returned her gaze to Beatrice but not before sweeping a glance at the smirking daughter. She said nothing, though, forcing Beatrice to continue.

'Have you no comment? Earlier you gave the impression that you might have plenty to say.'

'I do, although I'm not sure any more that it matters.'

'Why not?'

'Because, Mrs Ainsworth, I believe you have already made up your mind and I'm here simply as a formality.'

'That's rather presumptuous.'

'I apologise for any offence given. I'm just trying to make it easier and not fight it.'

'Did you or did you not call my daughter a beast?'

All right, let's do this, Stella decided and straightened. 'I did. I murmured it to myself because she had behaved abominably during her lesson. She insulted her father repeatedly in my presence, which I found both indiscreet and uncomfortable, given that Mr Ainsworth employs me. She refused to partake in the work I'd set; she ignored the fact that I had prepared carefully for yesterday's and today's lesson, sneering at your investment. Finally in a last-ditch bid to be excused from her tutorial, she deliberately leaned across the desk and knocked the inkpot over. I might add she sneered to my face over this and then excused herself without my permission.'

'Mummy, I surely couldn't be expected to sit there with ink soaking through to my skin,' Georgina remarked with feigned shock.

'Hardly,' Beatrice agreed. 'And that darling skirt of yours I brought back from Paris earlier this year is now completely ruined.'

'I know. I'm devastated,' Georgie moaned.

Beastly liar, Stella thought, enjoying repeating the insult silently. 'Surely I am not responsible for the state of Georgina's skirt?' she wondered.

'I think you are!' Georgie snapped. 'This was a special gift from Mummy and you've spoiled it as far as I'm concerned.'

'But you knocked the pot over,' Stella countered, frowning.

'Because you were haranguing me. You made me nervous.'

Stella couldn't help the gust of disdain she gave. '"Haranguing"? That's a great word, Georgina. And if you'd stuck at it you could have learned how to offer the same sentiment in French.' It was condescending but she couldn't help herself and suddenly no longer cared for the ungracious, manipulative youth she was supposed to be polite to. 'I'm sorry, Mr and Mrs Ainsworth, I really wanted to make this job work – I felt privileged to be offered it – but Georgina is lying to your faces and if anything, she should be punished for today's debacle.'

'Gosh, Mummy, she's the beast, not me! I was simply reaching for a sheet of paper,' Georgina said, adding a tremulous note to her claim.

'Mrs Ainsworth,' Stella said, affecting a tone of reason, 'perhaps Georgina would like to explain to you both how exactly she managed to tip an inkwell towards herself if reaching for paper. If anything, the accident Georgina is describing would send the ink my way. No, I'm sorry, I cannot tolerate the lie. She did it deliberately. She flicked the pot in her own direction to cause a disruption that would allow her to leave the lesson directly after I'd mentioned to her that I had cancelled the cocoa she'd ordered so as to avoid any disruption to our lesson. And, I might add, the paper was on the far side of the desk to my right and nowhere near where Georgina was reaching. If you'd like to check with Mrs Boyd, she'll confirm that as she placed the paper on the desk.'

Georgina gave a look so hostile that if Stella had been one ounce weaker than she felt right now, she was sure she would flee the room. 'And I can't find my earrings either, Mummy. You know the ones you gave me for my sixteenth?'

Stella was well ahead of the minx with the silver tongue.

'They're right here, Georgina.' She dipped into her pocket and retrieved them.

'How convenient!' the girl sneered.

'Not at all. I offered them to Mrs Boyd to return to you a little earlier but she suggested I bring them here to the meeting.' Stella leaned forward and placed the pearl earrings on the desk where they gleamed, fat and accusingly, tempting Georgina to try a final parry over them. She hesitated so Stella took the advantage. 'They're very beautiful and you should not remove them in case someone less honest than I should happen upon them. If you care to, please check with your housekeeper that I am recalling only the truth. And if you wish, Mrs Ainsworth, you may like to double-check my references at Bourne & Hollingsworth. I have never been known to tell lies; it is not in my nature to be anything but truthful . . . and, just as it has now, this level of honesty can get me into trouble.'

'None of this excuses the fact that you insulted my daughter.'

'No, that is true.' Stella shifted her attention back to her daughter and fixed her with a steady gaze to prove her sincerity. 'Georgina, I'm appalled that I lost my composure with you today. I apologise unreservedly for accusing you of being beastly for calling your father a constant embarrassment and a drag in your life. And saying that you wished him dead.' She glanced at Rafe, then to his wife, who looked thunderstruck. 'I apologise to all of you for repeating that but you are forcing me to defend myself. I found Georgina's remarks to be insensitive especially as I have recently lost my father and would give anything to have him still in my life.'

She hadn't meant to open her heart but the words and the powerful emotion they travelled on were out of her mouth before she could close it on them. And now they were free and resonating around the trio of Ainsworths.

Rafe cleared his throat, Beatrice had the grace to look at least slightly sympathetic and only Georgina kept her mask in place without so much as a flicker of acknowledgement that Stella's situation might well have led her to take offence at her careless and sulky criticism.

'Well,' Beatrice said into the awkward silence. 'Of course that does throw a different light on the situation.' Her daughter glared at her. 'Georgie, did you really say those things about your father?'

'Mummy, she is exaggerating ridiculously.' Stella's gaze narrowed as she wondered whether there was no end to this girl's ability to tap dance her way out of situations. 'We all tease Daddy, don't we?'

Beatrice regarded Stella, waiting for her to jump in and deny Georgina's claim, perhaps even accuse her of lying in order to dilute how vicious she had truly been. Stella desperately wanted to; hated the notion that Georgie might get away with her scandalous behaviour. Nevertheless her sensibilities told her it was gracious to remain silent now. She returned Beatrice's look with an unblinking gaze and an unspoken message passed between them as though Beatrice understood that Stella had been truthful with them. She gave a tiny, almost imperceptible nod and with that gesture Stella no longer cared now whether they fired her or not. The fact that Mrs Ainsworth seemed to believe her side of the story felt like exoneration.

Georgina had turned her attention to her father by now and was oozing all the charm she could muster in his direction.

'. . . against you, Dad, you know that!' She giggled for his benefit and Stella felt ill.

'Thank you, Stella,' Beatrice said and her daughter went quiet. 'It seems to me no matter what occurred this morning that you and Georgie are finding it difficult to work together.'

'I am more than happy to help Georgina as I was employed to do.'

Georgina sighed. 'I'm sorry. After today I think I will find it awkward and uncomfortable. You see she's called me a beast and now she's really calling me a liar to your faces. I don't think I want to learn from Stella.'

'Not sure you ever did, though, Georgina,' Stella defended.

'It's no secret that I think I should be allowed my holiday freedom, yes. But I find you difficult to work with, Stella. You're prickly and you have a high opinion of yourself and frankly, it's intolerable.'

Stella wanted to laugh in her face and accuse her of needing to look in the mirror. Instead she looked down. 'I'm very sorry to hear that.' It was neither an admission nor a denial but she could almost sense Rafe cheering silently at her diplomacy.

'And then there's the business of you encouraging Grace to mimic me,' Beatrice launched at Stella.

'I really didn't encourage her, Mrs Ainsworth, and I am genuinely sorry for any offence Grace gave. Truly, I think it was meant affectionately.'

'Oh, how so, Stella? Do educate me on this aspect of parenting I'm clearly lacking in.'

Stella felt herself blush at the barb but she pushed on regardless. 'Well, I've watched Grace poke gentle fun at her father in a similar manner – I think she's an alert, mature girl with a dry sense of humour that is a compliment to you both. I'd be lying if I didn't admit to making similar affectionate fun at the expense of my parents. There was nothing cruel intended by Grace.'

'I see. So while you can see the fondness of Grace for her father, for example, when gently mocking, you cannot see the same affection in Georgie's remarks.'

Bravo, Beatrice, Stella thought. Cunning. 'No,' she replied. Beatrice waited and Stella felt obliged. 'Because Georgina's body language, tone, her whole disparaging manner was about giving offence, while Grace in her mimicry was doing so in a joyful way that was humour-filled and in a tone of genuine affection. You were there, Mrs Ainsworth, and perhaps if I hadn't been you may have found Grace's performance charming. There was no cruel mockery meant.'

It was a far longer explanation than she'd intended and she was not surprised to note that Beatrice was suddenly looking bored of the confrontation and either in need of her first gin of the day, or certainly to be rid of them all from her salon.

'What do you think, Doug? You're very quiet over there and this really is all about you.'

All eyes turned towards the man of the house who visibly quailed beneath the scrutiny. 'Er . . . really dear, I'd rather not —'

'Yes, but I insist. It's not fair that I have to be the ogre all the time and reach all the tough decisions. There is no easy way out of this. Georgie feels slighted and clearly isn't going to get the best out of Stella's tutoring, while I can understand now that Stella's comment in the light of her explanation seemed understandable, albeit unnecessary.'

This is going to be interesting, Stella thought, adopting a careless attitude now. Whatever Rafe said she believed it really was all up to Beatrice and what she wanted. Was she to be bullied by Georgina or was she going to stand up for what Stella suspected the woman knew to be the reality of this morning's confrontation? She looked at him, fascinated as he dithered, hands in pockets one moment, then the next pushing his glasses higher up on the bridge of his nose. He'd perfected his character and was able to move, it seemed, near invisibly around his family, only reminding them of his presence with deliberate antics of clumsiness.

'I . . . er, well, Bee, I do agree with your summation of the situation.'

'That's not terribly helpful, though, darling. Help me to reach a decision.'

'How's this, then? Why don't you and Georgie head up to London for a few days?' Georgina gasped with pure elation erupting into her expression and Stella felt a surge of angry disappointment with Rafe. She'd expected so much more of him.

'How does that help, Doug?' his wife said, sounding softly exasperated. 'The problem is still here.'

'Yes, but we can let Georgina blow off some youthful steam and you can get a chance to rest up, have some fun in the city. How about Claridge's?'

'Oh, Daddy, the Ritz please, please, please! Claridge's is too stuffy and it's being renovated still I'm sure,' Georgina gushed.

Stella had to close her eyes momentarily to prevent her disgust bubbling up and showing itself in her expression. Georgina really was sickeningly spoilt but she'd thought it was just by her mother; now she began to believe her father was part of the problem too.

'Go on, Bee. You need a rest, I think, and a chance for some fun in the big smoke with your friends.'

'Well, you do know how I hate to be trapped here in Kent and I can't recall the last time I had a few days free to myself in London.'

'Take a week.'

What about Grace? Stella wondered. *What about me?*

'Take a week, dear Bee. You and Georgie go bonkers in the shops, enjoy the Ritz and spoil yourselves.'

'Oh, Daddy, you're a brick,' Georgie crooned, rushing to hug him. Stella blinked with deeper disgust at the girl who had claimed she despised her father only an hour or so earlier. She looked down, waiting for the inevitable blade of doom to fall.

'Stella . . .' Beatrice began in a tone that told her it was time to pack her bags.

'Yes?' she replied, resigned.

'Er, Bee, I haven't finished,' Rafe continued, his voice charmingly apologetic for interrupting her.

'What is it, darling?'

'Well,' he hesitated, frowning. Rafe pushed the glasses up his nose further in another heartbeat of delay. He frowned deeper still. 'Um, while I agreed with you that the situation between Georgina and Stella now feels awkward and perhaps even untenable – although thank you, Stella, for taking the generous attitude that you can put this unhappy business behind you and continue to teach Georgina. . . .' He looked momentarily confused as though he'd lost his original thought.

'Yes, Doug?' his wife glared, almost looking as though she wanted to leap up and snap her fingers before his face to liven him up.

'Er, where was I? Um, that's right. While I agreed with you . . .' Both wife and daughter gave dramatic sighs of impatience as he repeated his opening gambit. '. . . what I prefer to suggest is that we design a new role for Stella,' he said, and as his glasses slipped this time Stella noticed that he didn't adjust them and everyone could see his dark eyes simmering clearly now with their intent.

'Really?' his wife's expression clouded with query.

'Yes.' No hesitation now, Stella noted. 'I want Stella to keep teaching Grace, you see. I think Stella is very good for our child.'

'Well, Stella hardly wants to sit around here all week with the odd lesson for Grace. She'll be back at school shortly and then Stella will find herself twiddling her thumbs until the end of the day.'

'Exactly. So I have decided that Stella is going to work for me for the hours that she's not with Grace.'

Stella knew her mouth had opened with shock but the expression on the two Ainsworth women's faces were priceless for the confusion they showed.

'What do you mean?'

'Well, dear, I'm sure I'm speaking English. It's not hard to understand, is it?' The edge of sarcasm was not lost on his wife whose gaze narrowed. Stella was certain she was not used to Rafe pushing through Dougie. He strode towards the door as though he had little more to say and Stella imagined neither his wife nor daughter could surely miss how confidently he moved without a single trip or knocking anything over. At the door he did pause, turning around. 'Stella will from today work for me when she is not tutoring Grace. I will draw up a new schedule. Neither Mrs Boyd nor Georgina has reason to work alongside Stella again. Now you two go off and have fun in London – I'll make the hotel bookings and have Mr Potter ready for you this afternoon.' He glanced at his watch. 'Shall we say a four o'clock getaway? You can be in London by six and at dinner for eight. I'll book a table at the Ritz for tonight as well.' The women were speechless. Stella swung around and eyed him. 'Ah, Stella,' he said, grinning, and there was a wolfish quality to his expression now that she had seen on their first evening but not since. He hid in his sheep's clothing very well at home, she could tell. 'My manners escaped me. Of course this is all dependent on whether you wish to remain at Harp's End. I hope you do. I think Grace will blossom beneath your tutoring and I want her French wildly improved over the next couple of months.'

Beatrice suddenly appeared determined not to be left out of any conversation that involved her daughter, even if she did seem careless around Grace. 'What's so important about the summer?'

'Well, dear, we shall be going abroad.'

'What?'

'Yes, I was going to discuss it with you tonight over dinner but I can't be in two places at once and you shall be in London. So now's as good a time as any I suppose. I've decided we are going on a voyage.'

'All of us, Daddy?' Georgina gasped, as if she dared not even ask the question for fear of being wrong.

'Yes, Georgie, all of us. So my advice to you and your mother is to go shopping for a summer wardrobe because where we're going it will be hot the whole time.'

Georgie actually screamed, alarming everyone. Stella swung back to regard the teenager who was making her mother shrink back at her hysterical delight. 'A cruise . . . is that what you mean?'

'Yes, we're heading east.'

'How far east?' Beatrice asked, dismayed.

'We'll sail to the Levant, Bee. Doesn't that excite you to see the sights of the Middle East?'

'No, Doug, it does not.'

'Oh, Mummy, don't be a bore, we shall be on a ship. Ship's officers, captain's dinners; it's going to be so glamorous, right, Daddy?'

'So glamorous it will hurt,' he confirmed and Georgina missed the undertow of sarcasm he managed to bury in the words. 'Don't worry, Bee, I won't expect you to take to shore anywhere.'

'Whatever for now? Are you on one of your mad jaunts for butterflies or birds or whatever the hell it is you seek? I'm not going all the way to Arabia in order for you to paint some desert wren.'

'You know the desert calls every now and then,' he reminded as if they'd had this conversation before.

She nodded wearily. 'Oh, why now, Doug? It's all too sudden.'

'Come on, be a sport. Look, even Georgie's happy at the news. The girls will need a month off school. I can't imagine that's going to be a problem for you, Georgina.' The teenager was hugging herself. She rushed towards her father and planted a kiss on his cheek.

'I love you, Daddy. Ooh, all those handsome sailors in uniform. I hope we'll dine each evening with the officers in full dress uniform.' She looked over her shoulder, barely noticing Stella. 'Mummy, I'm off to pack for London. We're going to need a lot of evening garb for the cruise. My mind's in such a whirl. I'm not even sure the linens will be in the salons yet for our daywear. Gosh!' She hauled open the door and rushed off, leaving her father with a sheepish grin.

He shrugged. 'Sorry, Bee. I should have discussed it quietly.'

'Really, Dougie, you did that deliberately. Now you've completely backed me into a corner. How can I possibly say no now? Georgie will loathe me. What a madcap idea this is. I think I shall hate it.'

'You won't, my dear. Just sail there and back, enjoy the good food, good company and don't trouble yourself with what I'll be doing and don't even bother getting off in any of the ports. You'll barely notice me gone. Now, I'll put Stella to work immediately if she's to be any use to me. Don't trouble yourself; as I say, I'll work out the new schedule for Grace's tutoring.'

'As you wish, Doug; you seem to have it all worked out.'

Stella cleared her throat. 'Um, I don't wish for there to be any difficulty because of me.'

Rafe looked at her directly. 'Will you work for me, Stella?'

Although it was phrased as a question, she didn't think she was being given an option. 'I will, Mr Ainsworth. You said cataloguing? I have some experience with filing and inventories.'

'I know, that's why you're a perfect assistant for me.' He smiled at them both. 'That's settled, then. We start tomorrow morning. I'll have Mrs Boyd show you to my studio.'

She nodded and looked at the thunderous expression of his wife. 'If you'll excuse me, Mrs Ainsworth?'

'Do as you wish. It seems I have no say whatsoever any more in this house.'

'Thank you, Stella,' he murmured. 'If you'll excuse us, I think my wife and I have things to discuss.'

'Of course,' she blushed and fled through the still open door.

Before it closed behind her she heard Beatrice's dismayed voice.

'Dougie, I've never heard you so forceful before. You didn't even consult me on this.'

The door closed, the voices behind it were muffled to a hush and then disappeared as Stella hurried to the back stairs, needing to reach her room and some quiet to make sense of what had just occurred.

12

Stella had spent the rest of the day in her room, deliberately staying invisible to the family while it adjusted to Rafe's unexpected series of decisions. She distracted herself by knuckling down to craft a long letter to her aunt and uncle. She enclosed an affectionate letter for Carys as well with a flower she had pressed from the Harp's End garden, which she knew her sister would likely keep under her pillow until it crumbled. For beloved Rory she sketched a picture of her walking over the Weald in Kent. She drew it as a day with a beaming sun in the top right corner but with a rainbow on the opposite side simply because Rory liked rainbows; she also depicted a large house of many windows at the bottom of the tall hill – he'd guess this was symbolic of where she was living. There was no perspective but it wouldn't matter to her young brother. She could imagine him putting it up on his wall immediately. She drew lots of kisses in a bubble from the girl on a crest of the hill who bore the best likeness to herself that she could achieve, with a ponytail of black hair, arms outstretched. She was just about to fold up the picture when she heard a soft tap at the door.

Stella realised she hadn't stretched in a couple of hours and her right leg that had been tucked up under her was now sparkling with sensation at blood flowing normally again. She hobbled, wincing, to the door and opened it expecting to see Grace or Hilly. Instead she was met by the grin of Rafe Ainsworth.

'Sorry, you look startled,' he said, and then his grin faded. 'What's wrong?'

She grimaced. 'Ouch! Pins and needles, I'm afraid. I've been writing long letters to home.'

'Ah, best to walk those out or you won't know whether to laugh or cry in a moment,' he offered in a dry tone. Rafe glanced at the drawing she held and without asking permission he reached for it. She didn't resist as he took it.

'It's for my brother,' she qualified, embarrassed that he was studying something so intimate. 'He prefers pictures to letters.'

He nodded, pondering silently. Finally he looked up, his head tipped to one side. 'You look as though you are running and singing and blowing him kisses all at once on a sunny/rainy day. It's really rather clever and I love its naïveté. It's the innocence of childhood and thus it's perfect for your little brother.'

'Mmm, yes, Rory will understand it.'

'He'll love it. I would, if someone drew something like that for me that oozes so much fondness.'

Stella felt the heat treacherously climb to her cheeks. 'I miss them all.'

'I'm sure you do. And by your being here you are doing the very best you can for your family at this time.'

She nodded. 'Thank you, I don't mean to sound like I'm complaining at all – you've been kind.' She turned away to walk out the discomfort in her leg but she wasn't sure if by that gesture of stepping back into her room it was an invitation or not. This was dangerous new territory for her. 'I'm sorry about today. I feel like I'm a walking catastrophe around your family.'

Either he hadn't read her move as an invitation or he was being especially discreet because he hadn't shifted from the doorway when she turned to face him again, although she looked anywhere but at him. Everything about his presence, filling the entrance to her bedroom with his handsome frame and that reticent yet slightly mocking manner of his was unnerving. And even as she thought this she realised that his sardonic way with her was gentle, employed merely to tease. 'Grace wouldn't agree with that; neither would I. So that means fifty per cent of us are very happy with your being here.'

'It's the other half that's more vocal, though.'

'The other half is gone.'

She met his gaze. 'Already?'

He nodded. 'It's nearing four-thirty, Stella.'

She blinked and looked at her watch. 'Surely not. No wonder I have pins and needles.'

'Anyway, Grace and I would like it if you joined us for dinner this evening.'

'Perhaps that's not such a wise idea, Mr Ainsworth,' she said carefully.

'I don't see why not. Last night's dinner was perfectly acceptable for everyone. I'm simply rescheduling.'

She watched him, saying nothing.

'Grace was banished to her room today, I understand?'

She sighed. 'My fault again.'

'I doubt that. Her mother can be vicious.'

'I've noticed.'

'Listen, Stella, you've been cooped up here for hours. You need to stretch and I was heading out for a walk. Would you care to join me?'

Now she genuinely hesitated in fear and he could read her thoughts.

'It's just a walk. Up the hill. Get some fresh air into your lungs. Learn to master those wellington boots. You could practise your pirouetting.'

She grinned helplessly at his charm that came effortlessly when he was Rafe.

'Is Grace coming?' she asked hopefully.

'I've checked but Mrs Boyd can be extremely bossy and has decided that Miss Hailsham is to give Grace a bath and apparently when it involves washing her hair it seems to take on an epic scale . . . industrial-size soap and all that.'

Stella chuckled. 'Poor Grace.'

'I would save her if I could but Mrs Boyd needs to wield her power somewhere and it's Grace who suffers because she can't wield it over me . . . or you.'

'Oh, I don't know about that. She makes me feel privileged to even be past the threshold of Harp's End yet as the same time as unimportant within its walls as she possibly can.'

'Yes, but that was when you essentially worked for my wife, who gives Mrs Boyd reigning supremacy over the household and its staff, but now you work for me and you come under my protection.'

She smiled wider. 'All right, then.'

'Is that a yes?'

She nodded.

'Grab a jacket, it's cooling rapidly. Actually, I'll find a jacket for you. I'll meet you in the walled garden where you played hopscotch with Grace.'

He left her wondering how he knew where she had played with Grace but within minutes she was scurrying across the gravel with a sense of excitement she tried desperately to banish but couldn't.

He was waiting for her. 'Ah, there you are. Here,' he said, holding out a brown, waxy cape.

It looked new. 'This isn't Hilly's.'

'No, it was quicker to take my wife's riding cape.'

Stella held it midair, unhappy about even holding it. 'Oh, I couldn't.'

'Put it on, Stella. It's brand new. I gave it to Beatrice years ago and she has never had cause to wear it. Not once, I promise. It's yours now. You need some sort of waxy coat for here. My wife would likely thank you for relieving her of the guilt of having it gone from her wardrobe where it has hung uselessly for years.'

Reluctantly she took the long cape, loving it instantly, but she forced herself to refuse ownership. 'I shall borrow it and then return it to you. I do not wish to keep your wife's coat.'

'You see it as charity?' he laughed gently, taking it from her again and holding it out so he could put it over her shoulders. She eased her arms through the conveniently flapped holes. He spun her around like a child and did up the buttons quickly and she obediently stood still, privately relishing his attention.

'Not charity. Just not appropriate.'

'Shall we go?'

She nodded. 'Where?'

'I want to show you something.' He led her out of the side gate.

She fell in step and they walked silently down a track edged by tall hedgerow. They were instantly swallowed up by vegetation and the track began to ascend the hill. Stella felt immediately comfortable in their quiet and it was only when the way became steep that she made a sound.

'Phew! This is harder going,' she admitted.

He grinned. 'Worth it, though. Trust me.' He reached out his hand and without questioning herself or his motives again, she placed herself in his grip and he gently hauled her up. He beamed her a look of pleasure. His help made the going easier and although she was puffing by the time they reached the crest, and her body was warmed through from the effort, it had been far less of a struggle with his strong hand to hold.

'Now, look back,' he said.

Stella turned and was rewarded by a glorious view over the patchwork of Kent's fertile farmland. She could see the steeples of several churches and hamlets surrounded by the verdant pastures.

'Oh, Rafe, it's beautiful.'

'I'm glad you think so. This was my favourite walk as a boy whenever I got home from boarding school. I used to kiss my mother, hug the staff and nearly rip off my school uniform for civvies so I could run up here.'

'Run?'

He laughed, sounding boyish and carefree. 'I could in those days. Me and Pirate.'

'I'm presuming Pirate was a dog – the black-and-white one?'

'Yes, how on earth do you know that?' he asked, sounding impressed.

'I saw photos in the nursery today.'

Rafe shrugged. 'He was my very best friend. I called him Pirate because of that black fur around one side of his face.'

'Suited him. He looked like he was grinning out from the photos.'

'That was Pirate's permanent expression. He was a great and loyal fellow, lived until he was fourteen and when he could no longer climb this hill he'd sit down there by the gate, waiting for my return.'

'Don't, you'll make me cry,' she warned with a gentle smile.

'He loved us all but he was my dog. I miss him still.'

'Why don't you have a dog now?'

'Beatrice doesn't care for animals,' he said, his tone instantly losing the soft warmth that had laced it just seconds previously.

'May I ask you something personal?'

'I'm sure I can guess what it is.'

'Is that a yes?'

Rafe cut her a brief smile. 'The answer is I had no choice, Stella.'

'We all have choices. Why did you choose Beatrice when you both seem so . . .' She didn't want to say it.

'Poorly matched?'

Stella nodded, her expression sympathetic.

Rafe sighed. 'Well, there's a long version but the shorter one is that she became pregnant.'

'Ah, Georgina.'

'Yes,' he said, sitting down as though just saying her name punched the wind out of him. 'A mistake, I was told.'

'I was a mistake but no one regretted me. You sound regretful.'

'What do you mean?' he asked, eyes narrowing and glancing sideways at her.

She lifted a shoulder. 'You didn't have to sleep with her. You didn't have to ignore the obvious precautions . . .'

He said nothing for a few heartbeats and Stella was sure she had overstepped her mark.

'H-here I go again, apologising,' she stammered.

'I was trapped by someone who wanted something so badly she was prepared to go to some lengths to achieve it.'

Stella waited, but Rafe didn't elaborate. A flash of anger sparked in his gaze and it was then that Stella felt the truth of her vague suspicion settling into place. Caught by surprise by the sudden realisation that she'd hit on what was likely a family secret, Stella wasn't quick enough to stop the words that came: 'Georgina is not your child.' It wasn't a question but the naked statement prompted him to look away into the distance.

'Is it so obvious to you?'

Now it felt shocking to have her suspicion confirmed but this time she wrestled back control and buried her dismay beneath a deliberately schooled, even expression. 'I told you, I've developed a knack for assessing people. I couldn't match up Georgina with Grace in any way and yet I can match Georgina's personality to her mother and I can match Grace with you easily enough . . . well, with Rafe, anyway, not so much with Dougie.'

She smiled but he didn't, just nodded and stared out in contemplative silence. Stella felt obliged to continue. 'Grace echoes her mother's beautiful eyes. Georgina doesn't especially look like any of the three of you, certainly reveals none of your manner, but it was an impression I had; I haven't reached this decision because I notice you treat Georgina any differently to Grace. In fact, if pressed, I would say you are amazingly tolerant of Georgina's barbs.'

He turned away from the breathtaking vista to face her properly. 'That's because I have allowed myself to feel sorry for her. Her upbringing is not her fault, nor is who her true father is. You can understand that better than most, I suspect.'

'Yes, I can. I think I admire you then in the same way I have admired the man who raised me as his daughter.'

'Thank you. As to Georgina, she hates me but she doesn't know why. I can't even tell yet whether she knows just how much she loathes me but maybe at some level she senses we are not family. I agree it's obvious Grace is from Beatrice and myself and perhaps it's this understanding in the dark corner of her mind that Georgina rebels against.'

She nodded. It was subtle but made sense to her. 'Why all the pretence? Monty, Douglas, Rafe? You've told me about your names but I don't understand the different personalities.'

'Yes, you do Stella, because you understand me.' He was staring at her in a way that made her feel highly aware of their physical nearness and how all it would take was for one of them to step forward to —

She swallowed. 'Do I? I find you incredibly complex, to be honest.'

He smiled. 'No, you don't. What you find complicated is how I fit in here, but you get me, Stella. It's why we're friends.'

'Are we friends?'

He leaned forward and she did not lean back. Although she'd

hesitantly imagined it somewhere in that primal part of her brain, when the kiss came it was more tender than she could possibly have dreamed it. His lips caressed hers rather than pressed against them and in the fleeting seconds that it lasted Stella wondered dizzily if she was imagining the tip of his tongue tracing her mouth as though sketching his own outline and leaving his personal mark. And the touch was so soft it was as though the wings of the butterflies he studied were at work.

When he pulled back with a gentle smile Stella felt as though she'd climbed the hill again for the sense of breathlessness and how urgently her heart was hammering.

'Yes, we are friends,' he answered, and in that very private space where she was close enough to make out the flecks of bronze in what she had thought were deep brown irises, she saw a fire that shone back at her.

Stella sat back, watching him, barely realising she had placed her fingers against her lips. She didn't want to talk, didn't want to lose the moment, or the sensation of his mouth against hers. She needed to slow her heartbeat, needed to understand the implications of what had just occurred.

'I can't apologise for that. I've been wanting to kiss you since the night I first saw you glowering at everyone in the dance hall.'

Her eyes watered and she wasn't sure why. It was connected with what a romantic yet lonely figure he cut; the fact that she'd glimpsed his childhood, the less-than-happy adult life and indeed the double life he seemed to be leading. And the worst of it was that she wanted him to hold her again.

'Which of you just kissed me?' she said, airing a thought aloud although it was only just above a murmur.

'All of me,' he replied with a hint of a wry grin. 'I thought you'd be angry.'

'But you took the chance anyway.'

'I'm a risk taker.'

'If that's true, then it wasn't Monty who kissed me. And Douglas is a family man, so he wouldn't risk his family name. No, it was the secretive Rafe . . . and only Rafe who took that risk.'

He grinned sadly as if disappointed in himself. 'I suppose so. You're not upset?'

She shook her head slowly. 'What is appalling is not that you are committing adultery with me but because I welcome it and I'm glad you kissed me. I should hate myself . . .'

She turned away but he moved quickly to grab her shoulder and spin her around. 'Please don't hate yourself.'

Stella sighed. 'That's my point, I should but I don't. I get no sense of a love existing between you and Beatrice. I feel no guilt. If anything, I am angry that I am so easily fond of you and I barely know you and yet you have both known each other for seventeen years at least and she barely knows you.'

'Again, that is my fault, not Bee's.'

'Then why, Rafe? Why?' she pleaded. 'What are you keeping secret from her? Why does she have such a hold on you? Is it Grace?'

He looked momentarily lost, then glanced at his watch. 'Let's walk. We shall have to be back shortly.'

She nodded unhappily but allowed him to help her back to her feet.

'Do you think anyone saw?'

'No,' he gusted. 'I can assure you that as open as this all feels, we are hidden from the house.'

'Speaking from experience, no doubt.'

'I've never brought anyone up here. Not even Grace. And I sometimes think that Grace is my best friend.'

'It shows. You are lovely together.'

Rafe sighed. 'I'm a terrible father and as a husband I think I fail on all counts.'

She said nothing for a few moments as they began a slow descent.

'Why does being Doug help?'

'I can hide behind him. Beatrice controls him. He amuses Grace and he doesn't threaten Georgina.'

'Why must you hide?'

'Oh, Stella,' he shook his head. 'That's the hardest question to answer.'

'Why?'

'And that's the next one,' he laughed.

'What have you to hide from me?'

'Nothing, I hope. You are with the real me and it feels exhilarating.' He began to lead her down the steepest part of the hill and she noticed they were following a similar path back.

'Rafe?'

He paused to look at her.

'Are we still hidden?'

'From the house, you mean?'

She nodded.

'Yes, the view is obscured by those trees.'

Moving purely on instinct, she didn't allow herself a moment to consider. Stella reached for him and he responded unguardedly, as though it was the most natural response, holding her tightly as she buried her face into his chest and reached around his back.

'Why do I feel so safe in the circle of your arms?' she murmured, sounding mournful.

He stroked her hair and she closed her eyes, revelling in the sensations that his touch brought. 'Perhaps because you've been coping with a lot of grief and pressure; it's always reassuring to be held.'

'No, this is a different sort of safety. I'm in control of my emotions – or at least I thought I was, until now. You're not playing with my heart, are you, Rafe?'

He kissed her head.

'Playing? No,' he said, in a broken tone. 'This wasn't meant to happen. I thought I was strong enough.'

She looked up, torn by the inclination not to be owned by anyone, warring with an equally strong inclination to belong only to him. 'I'm like one of your butterflies, aren't I? You've collected me, you keep me close, you want to look at me and admire me, but you want to put me away again.' She searched his sad expression. 'But, Rafe, I'm not dead and pinned to a board. I'm real. I have feelings.'

'I know, I know. I should never have brought you here. It was selfish and yet I believed I could help your situation to change quickly. I wanted to make that happen.' He leaned back so he could cup her face. 'I thought I could keep you at arm's length.'

'Yet here I am *in* your arms.'

He bent his head towards her and kissed her again. This time his lips were more insistent and she opened up to his desire and returned it. No one had kissed her this deeply before. Stella sensed in this moment that Rafe may well have had many lovers – may indeed still have women beyond his family life . . . but none were permitted this glimpse into his depths, to feel his emotion pouring into her, buffeting against her heart. She held him harder, felt his arousal and trembled against it, wishing with every ounce of herself that their lives were not as complicated as they were.

It was Stella who pulled away, blushing, lips swollen. 'That's a frightening feeling.'

'Well, I've been accused of a lot in my time but never frightening.' He waited, amusement shining in his gaze.

'Is it just me?'

A shadow passed over his expression. 'I've thought of no one else since I danced with you that evening. There's something about you, Stella, which haunts me. I thought if I went away, I could forget you quickly. I didn't, your image only etched itself more strongly in my thoughts. I came home and tried to immerse myself in family but you've seen the results of that. Finding a way to bring you here felt as inevitable as the sun coming up each morning.' He sighed deeply. 'I had no idea, of course, of how you felt. But you're right. I've treated you like a butterfly. But you're a beautiful, desirable one, Stella, and if anyone's pinned down, it's me. I'm the one trapped. I'm trapped by family and duty and now I've ensnared myself deeper by opening us both up to pain.'

'Where do you expect this might go?'

He shook his head. 'I didn't expect anything from you.'

'Except a kiss?'

He gave a smile of hopelessness. 'Not even that.'

Stella looked back down the hill. 'We'd better get back.'

'I wish we could run away together.'

She smiled sadly. 'Do you?'

'I do. But Grace and dinner are waiting.'

'And we both agree that Mrs Boyd is scary.'

They shared a sympathetic, sorrowful smile and continued walking.

He surprised her by halting to show his exasperation. 'Her manner is strange and controlling but Bee loves me, Stella.'

'Is the feeling mutual?'

'No. It never has been. I was tricked into marrying her because she told me that Georgina was my child.'

'And then along came Grace, of course.'

'My wife and her family managed to convince me that a second child – entirely our own – would patch up a relationship that we all knew was broken from the start.'

'You don't have to explain. You and Beatrice met and were together when I was Grace's age, after all.'

'I need you to know this, though.'

'Why? It doesn't change anything for us.'

He shrugged heavily. 'I have a desire to start being truthful with someone as if I'm not careful my entire adult life will be based on lies.' Rafe frowned as if surprised by his own admission. 'Until you danced with me, it didn't seem to matter that I have been moving through the years as if trying to get them behind me as fast as I can.'

'Oh, Rafe, that's an awful thing to say . . .'

'It's honest, though, and I'm not used to confronting my own truth. At the start of this year if I'd been told I was dying of some hideous disease, I really don't believe I'd have been as upset as the next man.'

'So what do you want to tell me?'

'That I had a fling with Beatrice Templeton on leave from the war; my mind was utterly scrambled and I defy anyone to be thinking rationally in such a short space of time away from the Front; it felt like paradise should. I'd been mildly injured and hospitalised briefly and she was one of the women volunteering in the ward where I was being treated.' He began to pace in a short line, turning his back on her to take a few angry steps before swinging around to pace back. 'I convalesced at home for barely more than a fortnight and she visited regularly, undeterred that I had not invited her to my home or into my life. Beatrice seemed determined to offer her help to nurse me back to the best of health. I turned down her offer to live in. I asked her not to visit but she seemed incapable of accepting that I just wanted to be alone. She is an attractive woman, even more striking now, I might add, than she was then but not used to men unaffected by her presence.' He stopped walking, and instead raked a hand of exasperation through his hair.

'You didn't turn down the opportunity to sleep with her, though,' Stella said pointedly and at his glower, she sighed. 'I'm sorry, it was a long time ago and I shouldn't judge.'

'I slept with Bee on the night before I returned to France in 1916. I want to say she made me do it but that sounds pathetic.

I realise of course I had a choice but she did have a way of making me feel guilty. She still uses that stick against me.' He reached for her arm. 'Listen, Stella, everyone took their solace where they could back then. You were only little when war broke out – I'm not sure you understand how it was. There was no certainty anywhere and I didn't believe – not for a moment – that I would return whole, let alone survive the war.'

'Well, my father went to war and he didn't take his solace anywhere but in his wife's bed.'

'Frankly, you wouldn't know if he had slept with every farm girl from Dover to Paris.'

She glared at him.

'Now I'm sorry.' He grinned. 'Life was uncertain but at least your father had a wife, a woman he loved. I wasn't even twenty-one in 1916 and Bee was older.'

Stella could not have guessed that about them.

'And far more conniving that I could imagine a woman to be.'

'Because she was already pregnant, you mean?'

'Yes. And if that had been all it was, I believe I could have ruthlessly walked away from her by the time Georgina was seven and already showing the signs of the indulged, selfish adult she would become. But Beatrice had fallen in love with me – there's no ruse there, I'm sure of it. Beatrice's love is so committed it's almost sinister.' Rafe looked even deeper into Stella's face to reinforce his claim. 'She has told me on various occasions that she will kill herself if I ever leave her. Can you begin to imagine what a burden that is?'

Stella felt a thrill of shock at his confession but it made her thoughts flee to her parents, almost relieved to discover they were not the only people in the world who loved to distraction. 'Yes, I think I can. I suspect my mother felt the same way about my father.'

He looked at her with such remorse that she reached for and

squeezed his hand. 'Go on, tell me so I understand your situation properly.'

They began to walk again, slowly.

'She wouldn't hear of me leaving. I offered her everything. Stella, I can't tell you how ugly it became. She even threatened to kill Grace in her sleep if I walked out on our marriage.'

Stella gasped.

'That's what I'm up against. I admit to loving Grace from the day I first held her tiny hand and gazed into her chubby face. She reminded me of my sister and I wanted to be Grace's protector; needed to be there for her. I didn't want her mother to have such influence that Grace might turn out like Georgina. And so I stayed and I played my part, mainly to be around my daughter but also to hang onto Harp's End.' He swept the lock of dark hair that had blown across his parting and flopped forward.

They'd nearly reached the side gate into the walled garden. 'What does that mean? Why was Harp's End part of the bargain?'

His voice dropped even lower. 'I was persuaded – mostly blackmailed – that I should "do the right thing" by Bee. You see, Stella, Bee's family is loaded and she came to our marriage with such an enormous endowment that it meant I could keep Harp's End at a time when it looked as though estate taxes from death duties would make it impossible for me to do anything but carve up the family home and sell it off in chunks, maybe hang onto just the house or a few of the cottages. I simply couldn't hack it up but by the same token I also couldn't face selling it as a whole to some opportunist; give up my birthright . . . I could have just walked away, I suppose, but I did have a child and my wife was cluey enough to dangle the fact that her money could retain Harp's End. That juicy carrot and her spicy threats wore me down. As I say, her so-called love is twisted. She is, dare I say, obsessed with us being together. She has been ever since she met me in the hospital as "Captain Montgomery

Douglas Ainsworth" as I was known in the military. She liked my middle name and from that young age I've been Dougie to her, and I've allowed that bumbling persona that began when I was injured to simply grow up around our marriage to the point where no one in London knows Doug Ainsworth. I encourage most to call me Monty. It's just easier.'

'More to hide behind, you mean. And she likes Dougie – why? It doesn't make sense as she's so strong.'

'No, but that's the point. Dougie still seems a bit helpless; she gets to control him, boss him around.'

'And even fewer know Rafe.'

'Only one person alive really knows him. There's one other who knows the real me but we are so rarely together . . .' His words tailed off.

'And what would you have me do with this secret?'

'Keep it. Let it remain something precious only we share.'

'Is that all we shall share?' She hated herself for sounding needy.

Suddenly, they heard someone calling 'Mr Ainsworth!' repeatedly.

'That's Potter.' Rafe frowned. 'Over here! The side gate!'

'Mr Ainsworth?' Potter burst through the gate faster than they'd imagined he could. They parted as if burning embers had just landed on their hands. 'Sir?'

'Mr Potter? Is everything all right?'

'Miss Stella,' Potter said, lifting his cap. The poor man looked terrified.

'It's your daughter, Sir.'

'Grace?' They said it together and immediately Rafe began to run.

His stride lengthened as Potter yelled after him. 'She's had a fall, Sir.'

Stella grabbed Potter's arm and they both trotted after Rafe, who had begun to put distance between him and them as he dodged around the gravel paths of the walled garden. 'What's happened?' Stella asked.

'I don't know, to be honest. Mrs Boyd sent me to fetch Mr Ainsworth. We knew you were out walking on the Weald.'

'Right, I'm going to hurry ahead. I suspect I'll be needed.'

'You go on,' he wheezed.

Stella ran into the house and didn't bother with salutations, hurrying past the parlour and up the back stairs into the main part of the house. She overtook Hilly on the carpeted flight, leaping up the stairs two at a time until she was on the landing of the nursery and dashing down the hallway. She could hear voices, which led her to Grace's room. She burst through the doorway to find the adults – Mrs Boyd, Miss Hailsham and Rafe – bent over the bed.

Mrs Boyd was shaking a prone, seemingly unconscious Grace.

'Come on now, Miss Grace,' she was saying.

'Stop that please!' Stella ordered, her training from the department store kicking in. 'Everyone step back.'

Stella shoved herself past a grey-faced Rafe. She glanced at the other woman, young and terrified. 'Miss Hailsham?'

'Yes? What should I do?'

'I want you to call the hospital immediately. How close is it?' Everyone was looking at the unconscious child, lost in their collective shock. 'Mr Ainsworth! How far away is the hospital?'

He looked stung by Stella's tone. 'Three miles.'

'Right, get the car started. It's quicker for us to take her. Please – go now. I'll stay with her, I promise.' She glanced around. 'Miss Hailsham, what the hell are you waiting for?' The woman leaped away from the bed and fled, following Rafe out of the room. 'Mrs Boyd?'

'Yes?' the housekeeper looked up, sounding tame for the first time since Stella had met her.

'I need smelling salts immediately.'

'Yes, of course.'

Hilly arrived. 'Hilly, go and fetch the sal volatile. It's quicker if you go into Mrs Ainsworth's room. It's in the top right-hand drawer of her dressing table,' Mrs Boyd instructed.

'Run, Hilly!' Stella commanded.

She was now alone with Mrs Boyd. 'What happened?'

'Slipped on the bathroom tiles, hit her head.'

Stella raised the girl's legs off the bed and held them above the mattress. 'Do this for me, Mrs Boyd, please.'

The housekeeper immediately obliged as Stella moved to take Grace's tiny wrist.

'She's got a strong pulse and she's breathing so her air passages aren't restricted but let's turn her on her side to be sure. I presume she's in a dressing-gown because she'd just got out of the bath?' she said, smoothing back the child's slightly damp hair.

Mrs Boyd nodded. She too had turned ashen. 'What shall I tell her mother?'

'It was an accident. Grace will be fine – just reassure Mrs Ainsworth so she doesn't panic like everyone else around here. Over here, Hilly, please,' she said to the maid who hurried back into the room. 'You can put her feet down now, Mrs Boyd. Best you go make the phone call.'

Grace was shifted onto her side.

Stella took the tiny crystal bottle with its silver stopper from Hilly; even in her hurry she had time to think that Beatrice managed to make even smelling salts appear elegant. She opened it and gave a gentle sniff from a distance. In spite of her caution the ammonia made her head snap back. 'Hmm, very fresh.' She held the small bottle well beneath Grace's nostrils and soon enough the little girl coughed and spluttered back to life, pushing at Stella's hand.

'There you are, dear Grace,' she murmured gently.

Grace's eyelids batted open but only a slit and she looked frightened. 'What happened, Stella?' she lisped.

Stella smiled for her, grateful that her student's wits were intact. 'I think you slipped over, darling. Does anything hurt?'

Grace nodded. 'My arm. My head.'

'Which arm, this one?'

Grace nodded. 'A lot.'

Its alignment looked odd and swelling had begun. Stella suspected a break but didn't want to add more alarm. 'I won't touch it, I promise. Your head. Is it hurting because it feels like you bumped it, or is it feeling blurry?'

'Both,' Grace replied and her eyes watered.

'Grace, I think we should go to the hospital and have a doctor just check you over.' As she said this, Rafe returned.

'Gracie,' he breathed and was suddenly kneeling down beside her. He took her uninjured hand and kissed it. 'Oh, Skipper, you worried me.'

Stella could smell his fear; even though it was a cool afternoon, he was perspiring and it was the scent of things woody as though his exertions had warmed up his shaving cologne. She suddenly wanted to kiss him again as she watched him stroke his child's head with his long fingers and whisper something that made the little girl grin shyly in spite of the pain.

'The car's ready. Come on, Skip, I'm going to carry you down the stairs.'

'Be careful,' Stella whispered for his hearing. 'I think her arm is broken and she may have concussion.'

He gave her a soft look of despair. 'Can you come with us?'

She nodded.

'Mrs Boyd?'

'Yes, Sir?'

'Phone my wife immediately. She should probably come home.'

'Miss Myles told me to do that and I've already phoned, Sir. Shall I ask Mr Potter to leave now for London?'

'No, the train is probably quicker. Have him pick them up from Tunbridge Wells Station.'

She nodded and stood like a guard at the door as they moved carefully with Grace. Mrs Boyd followed them down the stairs and again acted as sentinel until she saw them seated in the back of the car.

'Oh, Miss Myles, you're going too?'

'Yes, I've asked her to accompany me. Grace won't be parted from Stella,' Rafe lied, to throw the curious housekeeper off. 'Now, drive on, Potter – Pembury, I'm presuming. Close the window, please.'

13

John Potter rolled the car on the gravel and headed around the great circular drive, reaching backwards to close off the glass window between the back and the front of the car.

'Is that wise?'

'It's normal, Stella.'

'Is it normal to have staff in the back of the car with you?'

He gave her a sidelong look of reproach. 'These are unusual circumstances, you'd agree.'

'Tongues will wag.'

'Let them.' He pushed his hair back. 'Bloody hell!'

She flinched. 'Grace will be all right, I promise.' Stella wanted to reassure him by touching his hand, instead she moved as close as she dared by stroking the little girl's forehead. She seemed to be dozing.

'How can you promise that? Have you seen the egg on the back of her head?'

'Yes. It does look tender.'

'I've seen those sorts of injuries kill grown men.'

'This is not a war zone,' she admonished softly. 'Even so, we should not let her sleep.'

They roused Grace, who stirred and mumbled at them.

'Don't sleep, Grace, darling. Why don't you recite your daffodils poem for your father?'

Grace began muttering her poem and they shared an indulgent smile.

'We're not going to the hospital, by the way,' Rafe said. 'It's all at sixes and sevens there because there's a new one being built. And I don't need any attention being focused on us.'

She frowned, his rationale was odd, but now she was concerned for Grace. 'So where are we going?'

'To our family doctor. Hawkin will know what to do.'

'Your wife is going to blame me.'

'I don't see how,' he replied tonelessly, looking out as they began to snake through a valley cutting through the Weald in an area of steep-sided slope.

Stella made a soft clicking sound. 'Men. You can be so naïve sometimes. Beatrice doesn't like that I've shaken her off. And don't think I didn't catch her murderous expression earlier today when you ingeniously brought me back into your employ and entirely under your control. Now she has yet more reason to consider me a threat to her family.'

He didn't answer because they were emerging into a hamlet, rounding a large village green with a sign that read 'Copingcrouch Green' with an enormous horse chestnut tree dominating proudly.

'Looks like a Turner painting, doesn't it?' he murmured.

Grace had fallen quiet again, her eyes opening and then looking heavy as she once more fought her doziness.

Stella didn't answer, looking instead to the south side of the big expanse of the green and where the brass on an 'Autombile Association' sign on the Camden Arms Hotel glinted in the last gasp of the sun.

'Penny for your thoughts,' he said, turning.

Stella blinked. 'I was just thinking – ridiculously, of course – what a romantic village this is, out of the way, and . . .' She shook her head.

'Perfect for a rendezvous?' he muttered.

'No, I . . . just . . . wish my life were normal.'

'You're the most normal person I know.'

'Then I meant, I wish my life had more freedom.'

He smiled sadly. 'I'll see what I can do.'

'Rafe,' she whispered, glancing at Potter who was busily signalling a turn. 'I can't be the other woman.'

He didn't look at her, turning towards the window. 'You already are.'

'I don't want to feel this guilty but I don't ever want to stop holding you.'

'We are guilty. But it's my fault, not yours.'

Potter was pulling into a long driveway of a large Victorian-style house. He crunched the handbrake, turned around and flipped back the connecting window. 'Here we are, Sir. Shall I help you carry Miss Grace?'

'No. I need you to head back to the house because my wife is going to need picking up from the station shortly. Check with Mrs Boyd. Stella, would you please go and get the doctor? I'll bring Grace.'

Within minutes they were in Dr Hawkin's rooms and he was frowning and tutting around Grace. Stella stood by the door, feeling redundant, but trying not to be distracted by the series of college certificates or fine paintings adorning the walls as well as various photographs. Hawkin with a pipe in his mouth and standing with jolly-looking people adopted a far more avuncular air for the camera than he did in his office where he stared into Grace's eyes with his thin beamed torch.

He straightened and looked at her. 'You're Grace's nanny, are you?'

'Er . . .'

Rafe explained Stella's role. 'Miss Hailsham is Grace's nanny.'

'I see, well, it might have been better to have brought this Miss Hailsham who was with her when Grace fell? I mean just so I could ask questions, get the full picture, you see?'

Again Stella felt stumped for the right answer but she couldn't let Rafe speak for her again. 'I suppose I'm here because I helped revive her, Dr Hawkin, and Grace was determined I come with her.' Rafe stole a glance at her at the smooth lie. 'Miss Hailsham was really too upset to be much help,' she added.

'I see. Well, you were wise to bring her to me. Concussion can be subtle; the symptoms can look like all sorts of other minor ailments, from headache to feeling a bit nauseous. But it can also lead to amnesia, ringing of the ears, delayed responses and far more serious consequences.'

Rafe nodded. 'What's our next step?'

'Where's Beatrice?' Hawkin queried.

Stella could tell from the doctor's familiarity that they all seemed to know each other well.

'On her way back from London now.'

'Right, well, Grace is to be kept quiet. No running around, no horse riding or sports. She is to be watched. Any signs of slurred speech or unnatural drowsiness, vomiting or acting as though she's in some sort of infernal fog must be addressed immediately. Don't wait because it could mean there's pressure building in her head – straight to hospital and call me too.'

'All right. That bump?'

'It's going to be very sore and she could feel sick. No hair brushing or shampooing. She'll need 24-hour watching – can you arrange that?'

'I can do that, Dr Hawkin,' Stella offered. 'I have a current St John's Ambulance Certificate in first aid.'

'Excellent. Well, Miss Myles, your job is simply to observe and any worsening of any symptoms – even marginally – just pull the trigger and make her parents bring their child to the hospital.'

'I'll do that.'

'Right. She's probably going to be teary and potentially irritable but nothing that a bowl of ice-cream couldn't help with. As for the studies you were brought on to assist with, there'll be none of that for a while. I would cancel any holiday tutoring, Ainsworth; young Grace is going to need peace and calm days. This could take a week to settle down and another week or two to heal fully,' he said. 'Children are amazingly resilient but I think lessons are out of the question in this instance.'

Rafe shared another glance over the shoulder of the doctor, this time looking as dismayed as she also felt.

Hawkin gave them a ride home in his car as he was en route to some house calls in their district. This time Grace sat curled up in Stella's arms while her father listened to the amiable chatter of the doctor. Stella watched Rafe's profile, the square line of his jaw grinding as he politely paid attention to Hawkin's opinion about the West Indian cricket team that was touring from this month.

'. . . and of course Sussex is playing Cambridge next month – that will be interesting.' Hawkin said, taking a puff on his pipe.

'Yes,' Rafe answered and Stella thought he sounded so far away that she wondered how his body remained upright in the car.

'Here we are, old man,' Hawkin finally said, his wheels grinding gently on the gravel of the Harp's End drive. 'Good luck with Beatrice.'

Rafe returned to the present she noted as he smiled weakly. 'Thanks, Howard.'

It was another confrontation – broken only by the memory of a kiss that needed no words either side of it – and here they were again.

The simmering anger was identical to this morning, all of it emanating from Beatrice, and Stella's only sense of relief was that the smirking Georgina was surprisingly absent.

They were clustered in Grace's bedroom, a large and, Stella thought, draughty chamber, but it reminded her of the nursery with its eclectic clutter that was displayed on every surface. She could see that beneath the shells and pebbles, the teddy bears and finger puppets, the drawings and jars of crayons, necklaces of dried flowers and a crude tea set made of clay with a child's fingerprints dried into the terracotta, that Beatrice had once hoped Grace would be a girl of the magazine-style stereotype. Whatever image her mother had planned for, with her candy-floss pink-striped room, satin bows, pink toile furnishings and cream enamelled iron bed with flounced white muslin so it looked as though Grace slept in a cloud, her child possessed Rafe's curiosity and love of the outdoors. And as much as Stella could tell that Grace enjoyed ballet, she suspected she far preferred horse riding, boisterous sport and running wild on the Weald if given the chance, to anything her mother had in mind for her.

Right now the child looked small and pale, sleeping in that cloud of a bed, and her mother's face was equally pale with lips marshalled into an unhappy line of disapproval.

'I suppose you were on the wretched Weald, were you, Doug?'

'I was,' he said and Stella looked up in surprise that he didn't stammer as she'd come to expect around his wife. He wasn't even wearing his glasses, which she didn't think Beatrice had noticed yet either.

'Typical! And where were you, Stella?'

'She was with me, Bee,' he answered for her. His glance towards the pinch-faced housekeeper standing near the door told Stella that Mrs Boyd had likely already told Beatrice everything she knew.

'I see.'

'Do you? Thank you, Mrs Boyd. We'll call if we need you.' The housekeeper opened her mouth to say something but Rafe cut her off by speaking first. 'Close the door, please, behind you.' Mrs Boyd had no alternative but to leave though not before she gave Stella a look of deep disapproval.

'Bee, Stella is not employed to bathe our child or even babysit her. She is here to tutor – that is all. This accident occurred under the paid watch of Miss Hailsham, whom you have personally appointed.'

'Why are you speaking to me like this when you can see how upset I am?'

'Forgive me, Bee. It is not my intention to upset. I note Georgina wasn't upset enough to return home.'

Stella watched Beatrice's hackles rise fully now. 'Why don't you try and force home a teenager who has, only hours earlier, been given some freedom in London?'

'You are her mother, Bee. And she's not an adult yet. You just order her home.'

Beatrice shook her head with closed eyes. 'You don't understand, Doug.'

He sighed as though he did understand but Stella could tell he wasn't going to have that argument now. Besides, it had been his idea to send them to London. She suddenly felt horribly guilty. Until now she hadn't but it was as though an invisible hand had reached into the room, its insistent finger now tapping her on the shoulder as if to say that she was the reason he'd sent the Ainsworth women away, she was the reason he was defending himself, she was the reason Mrs Boyd had been banished. Was she the reason that Grace was now lying hurt?

'Miss Hailsham left the bathroom, Grace slipped and here we now are. No one is to blame, Bee, but as her mother I would like to think that you are not angry so much as relieved that our child is going to be fine.'

Stella stepped back surreptitiously, hating to share this tense, intimate conversation, and found the shadows. She stood like a sentinel, holding her breath, determined not to interrupt.

'Of course I am. But, Doug, you know how I struggle with Grace. She's like a mad puppy, always cavorting around and getting into mischief. I can't stand the way she's always humming odd tunes as you do. What's worse, she's added numbers or coordinates or something to them now. I have no idea what she's thinking. Georgie wasn't like that.'

'Grace is a normal nine-year-old.' Stella watched his mouth flatten in a way she was coming to recognise as a giveaway sign of his controlling irritation. 'Actually, I suspect she's probably more intelligent and curious than the average nine-year-old, but what would I know?'

'What would you know about anything in this household?' she snapped. He blinked and Beatrice stood her ground. 'I do everything for Harp's End,' she continued. 'You're barely here, always secretly rushing off somewhere. To be honest, I don't even know what you do. I tell people you work in the city but I'm also sure I tell everyone something different . . . he's in finance, he's a developer, he's good with money, he's doing special projects with the government. You see, Dougie, you keep me at arm's length about your secretive life and yet you have the audacity to take me to task over the care of our children.'

'I didn't know that was what I was doing,' he replied calmly. 'But let's both be clear that I would never take you to task over the care of Georgina – in that you are unblemished for you take exceptional care of her. So much care, in fact, that you're afraid to confront her about much at all. Her behaviour this morning towards Stella was difficult to stomach but you let it go anyway.'

Stella wished he hadn't steered his wife's wrath towards the shadows.

'Georgina's attitude is fast becoming intolerable but you do not wish me to interfere. However, with regard to Grace, I think your mothering does come up wanting.'

Beatrice gasped, her expression filled with injury but also guilt.

'Miss Hailsham is not equipped and never was to look after the needs of Grace. But she's pretty and I realise that being around beautiful people is important to you.'

'And you, darling,' Beatrice countered, casting a sharp glance Stella's way.

'You are well aware that Suzanne Farnsworth chose our tutor.'

'Do I? How come I never saw a shortlist? How come you did all the organisation with Suzanne?'

His expression didn't flicker. 'Because Basil Peach is my acquaintance and Suzanne is known to him, as you are also well aware.'

'I've had Basil for dinner on several occasions. Heavens – didn't we only have him over last spring trying to matchmake for him over cocktails?'

'Your point?'

'My point is that I am more than simply familiar with Basil Peach, and I am just as capable of contacting one of his associates to organise my children's tutor.'

'I don't see what you're getting at, Bee,' he baited, and Stella wished he wouldn't.

'Normally you wouldn't go near any domestic arrangements but where Stella is concerned you seem almost mother-hennish in your protection for her.'

'I think I should leave,' Stella said. She was suddenly standing between the snipers and it was about to get painful for her.

'Stay right where you are, Miss Myles,' Beatrice said in a tone so commanding that Stella felt she had no choice but to remain rigidly where she stood.

'So what's your point?' Rafe continued. Stella silently begged that he stop baiting his wife.

'My point is this,' she returned fast and stinging like a whip crack. 'From the moment Stella walked into our lives, you've changed.'

He actually laughed. 'You speak as though Stella has been with us for months and yet she's been in our midst for about forty-eight hours.'

'And we've had problems for all of them.'

'None of Stella's making.'

Beatrice nodded slowly but biting her lip as though sensing she was onto something. 'She's upset Georgie, which in turn upsets me. Now we have Grace injured, Mrs Boyd is put out – none of the staff knows how to be around her.'

He gave a soft snort. 'What does that mean?'

'Well, either she's staff or not. If she's staff, then she should act accordingly, not appear for dinner with the family.'

'That was a personal invitation from me.'

'Which brings me to my point.'

'Well, ring the bells for that!'

'Doug! Whatever's got into you? You're behaving so strangely I hardly know you.' Stella could tell Beatrice was genuinely thrown off her normally impeccable balance by his new tone. 'Shall I put your behaviour down to having Stella around as well? Georgie seems to think you have an unnatural interest in our tutor.'

'Why am I not surprised, Bee? Georgie stirs trouble wherever she goes. If she can see a pathway to causing other people discomfort, she will almost certainly walk down it. You realise she does this for sport, mostly.'

Beatrice straightened, looking fearsome. 'I cannot believe you speak about your own daughter like that.'

'Oh, Bee, let's not dance around the truth and play this charade any longer. Georgina is not my daughter, never has been, not even when you've pretended that a stepfather is allowed to advise his child or raise her in a way that he considers appropriate. Georgina is learning none of life's lessons other than how to manipulate every situation to suit her agenda. Congratulations, Bee, she's turning into you and presumably whomever her real father is. And frankly, I'm glad no Ainsworth blood runs through her veins – my family would be ashamed, as you should be.'

Beatrice appeared so thunderstruck for a couple of heartbeats that Stella was sure they could hear her own heartbeat drumming loudly and echoing around the room. She turned to Stella with a look of poisonous intent. 'Leave us!' she commanded.

Stella fled, not daring to cast a glance his way. She closed the door silently, leaning back against it on the other side and shutting her eyes with dismay as she had just hours ago in the nursery. She moved to the stairwell but still could hear their muffled voices.

'I cannot believe you've just openly spoken of a secret that was ours, Doug.' Beatrice sounded genuinely shocked.

'We can't go on like this, Bee. We're ships in the night.'

'What are you talking about, Doug? I love you.' It sounded so clinical to Stella.

'Love?' The gust of amusement sounded full of pain. 'Your idea of love is ownership by any means.'

'You've not complained before. You've been quite happy to take my family's money.'

'And this is your typical position, Bee. It's all about threat, it always has been. I'm beginning to care less and less, though.'

'I can see that. You're different. What's happened, Doug? Last night you were normal.'

'Was I? Perhaps last night I feared discovery . . .' Stella heard him stop abruptly and she swallowed hard.

'Discovery? What are you talking about?'

'I don't know any more,' he murmured and Stella had to strain to hear him. 'I want to be honest, but . . .'

'Doug, you're not making sense. I know you love Grace, I know you're worried, I also know you seem distracted about something. Is it work?'

He sighed. 'I suppose so.'

'Where are your glasses?'

'They're . . . they're here, Bee,' he said, and Stella looked down in disappointment. Rafe was gone; Douglas was back.

His wife leveraged that return. 'Darling, I trust Hawkin. He's not worried; neither should you be. Grace will be fine – she's such a rough and tumble child, nothing hurts her.'

'That's where you're wrong, Bee,' he countered but he had fallen back into his alter ego; Stella could hear the return of his mild tone . . . all the fight had left him. He had been on the brink of saying something that he knew he couldn't retract or step away from. What else was he hiding?

'Grace has a gentle soul,' he continued, 'a perceptive one. She can be hurt by the least slight. She . . . she seeks your approval.' He sighed.

'I'll try harder with Grace, darling, I promise. And with you. Let's get some time together – just us. We can go up to the Lakes – I know you'd enjoy that.'

'But you wouldn't.'

'No . . . Or how about the Isle of Wight, then, or the Isle of Skye, if you really must, darling?'

She heard him laugh hopelessly again. 'Don't be ridiculous, Bee. The first gust of wind that blew your hairdo askew would make you furious.'

'Well, I'm begging you, Dougie, not to do anything rash, all right? We've been a good team all these years.' She gave a rueful titter. 'Heavens, all our friends envy us our closeness. And they envy me my handsome husband,' she added in a slightly more provocative voice. 'Don't ruin it now. Surely you don't want Georgina to spend her Deb Season knowing everyone is whispering about her parents? That won't do, and Dougie, I don't want to lose you. You may think I don't care, but nothing is ever more immediate in my mind than our remaining together. Sometimes I feel like I don't know you – like a few minutes ago when you felt like such a stranger to me – but I need you, Doug. I don't make it hard for you to go about your mainly absent life, do I?'

'No,' he murmured.

'I wish I knew more —'

'Don't, Bee.'

'All right, darling. I shan't press you. I don't know what came over me. I know there's no one else. I've even agreed to go on this ridiculous cruise to the Levant just to please you.'

Stella heard his sigh. 'Leave Stella alone. She's innocent.'

'I will, Dougie. I was just being a silly, jealous wife but I won't lose you to anyone. You need to know that. I can't.' There was an awkward silence as though a familiar old threat hung around them; Stella realised she was holding her breath, waiting for it to be spoken aloud. It obviously didn't need to be. Beatrice's voice was conciliatory when it came. 'Come on, my love, I'll take the first watch. I'll sit with our daughter and you have a rest for a while.'

Stella heard the creaks of their movement and scampered away, moving as fast as she dared while still being careful to tread lightly in the stairwell when she heard the door open down the hallway from Grace's room. It was Rafe, she was sure, but she couldn't face him. Stella hurried up a floor to her room and closed the door gently, turning the lock, which she'd not done previously.

She backed away and waited, watching the door. Soon enough the soft knock came.

'Stella?'

She held her breath.

'Stella?'

He tapped more insistently. She expected the handle to twist but it remained doggedly still and there were no further taps at the door. Instead she heard his retreat and a minute or so later the soft complaint of floorboards above her as he moved around.

Later, when the house felt still, she tiptoed down to the parlour feeling the grind of hunger. Normally she could ignore it but she realised that in her distraction she hadn't chewed a morsel since her light lunch with Grace more than ten hours earlier. Even a cup of tea would be enough. In the silence of the parlour, still warm from the embers in the range, she pottered around quietly and found bread and cheese to make a small sandwich, which she devoured hungrily. Instead of risking making noise with boiling water and brewing tea, she settled for another cup of Daphne's famous milk and began tiptoeing up the stairs.

She reached the landing that accessed the lobby and was startled by a sudden jangling of the telephone. Stella remembered Suzanne Farnsworth's promise to try and call again late this evening. She quickly put down the milk and hurried to the phone on the sideboard, feeling suddenly responsible for the insistent noise and determined not to be blamed for another headache of Beatrice's. She yanked it up to her ear, about to say 'Ainsworth residence, good evening,' when she heard the mellow voice of Rafe speak first.

'Ainsworth,' he said, crisply.

'It's Basil,' a man replied and she instantly remembered the jovial 'Fruity' from the Berkeley dance hall and Stella felt immediately trapped. Having wrongly assumed the call would be for her, she now felt disinclined to put the phone down and risk a click on the line to signal her presence.

'This is a surprise,' Rafe remarked.

She frowned. It seemed an odd comment for him to make to a friend.

'I know, old chap, but I have no choice but to phone you at home.'

'All right. You'd better tell me what is so pressing that can't wait until our usual rendezvous.'

'Well . . . a canary is leaving the cage.'

Stella's forehead developed a stitch of consternation at the odd turn of conversation. She tightened her grip on the receiver and she still dared not breathe before Rafe spoke again. 'I see. From where?'

'Berlin.'

Her astonishment deepened. *Berlin?*

Rafe sighed. 'Who?'

'Someone we know as Owl.'

Canaries, Owl . . . What was this secret language they were using and why? If it didn't sound so genuinely serious with the mention of Berlin, she might have smiled.

'What has this to do with me?' Rafe demanded.

'Owl will only talk to you.' Basil's voice sounded far less jolly than she recalled.

She heard Rafe's sharp intake of breath. 'I can't imagine why. I've never had anything to do with any connection called Owl. How can he ask for me if he doesn't know me?'

'Oh, he knows the Falcon, all right.'

'Can you be more specific, Fruity?' Rafe growled, surprising Stella with his intensity.

'Let's just say he's an old childhood friend from the East.'

'Joseph?' she heard Rafe reply in a whisper of incredulity.

Stella blinked. *Joseph.* Was that the boy from the photographs who was never far from Rafe?

'He has something for us.'

'You're running my stepbrother?' Rafe continued, now sounding suddenly appalled to her.

'Not really running him, old chap. He's more of a sleeper, really. He's been passed to me in this instance because of the connection to you. I'm just keeping an eye on things.'

'Listen to me now, Fruity. Joseph is a pen-pusher. A mild, gentle desk man the last time I checked. He is no spy. You can't —'

Spy! She stopped herself gasping just in time.

'Nevertheless,' Basil Peach continued, sounding exasperated, 'he insists he has something he needs us to know. The thing is, Monty, we need you to meet with him because he's too far up the line for us to ignore anything he may wish to share.'

'You'll endanger him.'

'He came to us.' She pictured Basil Peach shrugging on his stocky frame.

'How long has this been going on?'

'Two years.'

Stella could feel his shock from two floors above coming down the line of the phone. 'And only now you —'

'Listen, old chap, you know how it is. It's on a need-to-know basis and all that. It wasn't necessary to tell you.'

'But suddenly it is!' he snapped. Stella had never heard him angry and the emotion seemed to bridge the gap in the part of his personality he kept so deeply hidden. As confronting as it was, the passion he spoke with aroused hers. She was sure she was blushing.

Basil was doing his best to soothe. 'I've said we'll arrange the meet.'

She sensed Rafe forcing his wrath down. 'Where?' he asked, his tone as wintry as a February morning. 'Surely not Germany?'

'No, no, although he is playing his cards close to his chest. Refuses to clue us. Said to say "peacock" to you. Means nothing to us – we've checked into it. There's no restaurant or café called that, no hotel linked to it either. Said you'll know.'

'When?' Rafe demanded and Stella suspected he understood

from the cryptic message precisely where the meet would take place.

'A fortnight from today.'

'Can't do it.'

'Why ever not?'

'Because he's talking about Africa!'

'Good grief, man.' Basil blew out his breath audibly. 'Well, then, Africa is where you have to go. He wouldn't request this if it wasn't something important.'

'I'm impressed with your ability to understate.'

'Aren't we Brits meant to be the masters of it?' Basil replied, seemingly unoffended.

'This is not an easy time.'

'Never is, Monty. But you've got your lepidopterist and Kew Gardens cover and I'll have the paperwork drawn up. Africa, you say. Where exactly?'

'I was planning on taking my family on a cruise to Egypt,' Rafe replied, clearly refusing to take his own advice and be specific, plus it sounded like he'd ground his words through gritted teeth. 'Although I'm —'

'Oh, heavens, that's perfect!'

'I was going to say that this other business has to wait. The girls are on holiday, I've been away rather a lot recently as you well know, Beatrice is —'

'Wait?' Basil echoed sarcastically. 'We need this, Monty. You know how it is over there right now. Any information is an aid. I'm sure you've taken a measure even within your own circles that a lot of our people all but openly sympathise with Germany's harsh reparations – in fact, I'd go so far as to suggest that many rather admire Adolf Hitler.'

'Especially as his speech in the German Reichstag was all about maintaining peace in Europe.' The dryness in Rafe's tone and the sad chuckle at the other end gave Stella pause. She'd recalled hearing an extract of that speech of 17 May on the wireless, and now, somewhere distant in her mind, thoughts – not fully formed – niggled on the edge of her consciousness in response to his appeals. The words were non-inflammatory and yet even in her ignorance of politics and the diplomacy of statesmen she had heard that false note, hadn't she? It was as though Hitler mocked the League of Nations that promoted international cooperation to maintain collective security when, as a seemingly strong exponent of peace, the new Chancellor promised that Germany would follow all of the restrictions on weaponry if the other armed nations destroyed their aggressive weapons alongside her.

'. . . and if you believe that you're a fool like all the rest of the liberalists who are being taken in,' she heard Basil say.

She agreed with this sentiment, recalling the tide of anger that swelled whenever she thought of all the men lost to the Great War because of Germany's hostility.

'Of course I don't believe his cunning declarations are anything at all to do with peace; more about putting us on the back foot.'

'Indeed. There's no denying he's rebuilt Germany but while our officials seem to be very friendly with that Austrian-turned-German dictator who talks of only desiring security in the region, few of us in the dark recesses of the ministry trust him or his new Nazi party with anything nearing equality. The fact is, Monty, your friend is too well connected in Berlin for us to ignore anything he wants to share about the Nazi party. We may never get another easy chance to hear what he has to say.' There was a difficult silence before Basil spoke again. 'The cruise with your family is the perfect cover. We'll pay for it, of course, and Kew Gardens can request some special tasks of you. Hide behind that ridiculous moth society you're a member of.'

Rafe ignored the barb. 'You surely can't expect my family to —'

'No danger for them, I assure you; they're passengers like any other. In fact there's not even a need for any of your girls to leave the ship. A voyage to Egypt and the Holy Land is innocent, draws no attention and you are well entrenched at Kew. We need you, old chap. I'll have all the voyage paperwork delivered to your club.' This time Basil barely paused a heartbeat, rushing on to close the conversation before Rafe could put up any further protestation. 'Goodnight, Monty . . . and thank you. King and country and all that.'

The phone line clicked dead. Stella waited until she heard Rafe put his receiver down too before she replaced hers, her mind swarming with tension at what she'd just heard. She needed to piece it together. Grabbing her cup, she hurried upstairs into her room, looking to the ceiling as it creaked angrily above her; he was moving around urgently, Stella could tell. She wished now she hadn't ignored him when he had knocked and called to her earlier. Suddenly she needed to see him again, hold him once more, if just for a moment. A door banged distantly above.

And then the house became silent and she knew in her heart that Rafe had gone.

14

She hadn't slept – not even fitfully – and thus was awake to hear the first trill of the birds. By the time she heard the soft knock she had been dressed for more than two hours. For a wild moment of hope she thought it might be him and if so, she would confess to what she'd heard the previous night and hope for an explanation. Her mind had been running away with her during the dark hours and taken her to clandestine places where her thoughts felt dangerous and frightening. They whispered of old enemies, scores to be settled . . . war. But when Stella pulled the door back it was the dour Mrs Boyd holding a tray. She tucked away her disappointment as she shouldered herself into a cardigan and schooled her expression to one of calm.

'Mrs Boyd, you needn't have —'

'It's all right. I was on my way up anyway,' she said, handing the tray over with a single boiled egg wearing a bright blue woollen egg cosy, two slices of toast with butter whorls on the side, a tiny dish of what looked to be a glistening globule of strawberry jam and a small pot of tea with an even smaller jug of milk and a sugar basin with three cubes. Stella couldn't imagine where the housekeeper might have been going 'on her way' but stayed quiet, covering her confusion with a smile of thanks. 'Mrs Ainsworth would like to talk with you after breakfast,' the housekeeper added. 'Shall we say nine sharp?'

'We shall. How is Grace?'

'Her mother is with her now. Mr Ainsworth kept a vigil through the night from midnight.'

Stella looked startled to hear this.

'Is something wrong, Miss Myles?'

'Er, no, I was feeling badly that I didn't hear anything, offer to help.'

'We didn't need it,' Boyd countered, smiling in an unsuccessful attempt to soften what felt to Stella like ostracism by the Ainsworth women and their minions. 'And Mr Ainsworth is abnormally silent on his feet,' she remarked, frowning.

'So Grace slept well?'

'Soundly, and has woken with a dull headache, which is to be expected. But she seems alert, so we're all feeling a lot happier.'

'Oh, that's such a relief.' Already Grace's fall was fading to an event of less importance. She was safe; in recovery. There were far bigger events to fear now. Her mind was tripping again with alarm. She blinked back to the present moment where the housekeeper was staring at her, nonplussed.

'It is a relief,' Mrs Boyd echoed unnecessarily, her hands crossed neatly in front of her. Why was she lingering? Didn't she know her boss was a spy? Didn't she know he was on a dangerous mission for the government? *Settle, Stella*, an inner voice warned. She cleared her throat.

'Er . . . do you plan to take it in turns for the rest of the day? I am happy to sit with Grace if they —'

Mrs Boyd made a soft tsking sound. 'No need. Between Miss Hailsham, myself and Mrs Ainsworth, we have it all covered.'

'How about her father?' she frowned, recalling Rafe's near despair yesterday and somehow hoping his silent footfall had returned him.

'Mr Ainsworth left for London very early this morning as soon as Mrs Ainsworth relieved him from Miss Grace's bedside.'

The housekeeper's casual confirmation of what her instincts had clued nevertheless hurt, the words feeling like tiny hammers bruising her vulnerability. She showed no sign of this ache in her expression, though. 'I see. Well, I shall meet with Mrs Ainsworth at nine. In her salon?'

'No, she plans to spend an hour or two with her daughter. So perhaps you wouldn't mind meeting in Miss Grace's room.'

'I wouldn't mind at all.'

Stella knocked at Grace's door and heard a muffled voice call, 'Come.'

She opened the door but only got halfway across the threshold. 'Oh!' she said, freezing to see Georgina smirking at her.

'Hello, Stella. I'm gathering lessons are off for my sister.'

'You're home,' she said, instantly wishing she hadn't stated the obvious.

'Well, unless I'm a mirage . . .' Georgina said, rolling her eyes.

'How are you?'

'Not thrilled to be home.'

'When did you arrive?'

'Mummy sent a car late last night.'

Being at the back of the mansion and on such a high level meant Stella heard none of the comings and goings of the family and staff, other than the footsteps of Rafe. She could hear them now echoing in her mind as he packed in haste to leave. Perhaps the same car that brought Georgina home took her father away.

'You look lost, Stella,' Georgina pondered, from where she sat on the bed next to her sleeping sister, head cocked to one side in contemplation.

'It's because of Grace,' she replied, quickly schooling her features to be alert. Rafe was right: Georgina was always on the hunt for mischief. 'May I come in?'

'I don't see why not. My mother is expecting you, isn't she?'

Stella nodded. 'Is she not here?' Again the obvious. She wanted to bite her tongue out.

Georgina smirked. 'She was called away to the phone. Apparently my father wanted to speak rather urgently to her.'

'Where is he?' It was out before she could stop it.

Georgina's attention that had been returning slowly to Grace now snapped back to Stella in blinking surprise, her quizzical expression filled with intrigue. Stella wasn't going to let her have the opening.

'I mean, he said something yesterday about needing to show me some of the systems for his filing.' It sounded convincing enough.

'Really? Well, he's gone to London. Heaven only knows what he does there. Mummy can't tell me. Probably has a woman, or maybe two, given the time he spends away from us. They must be very dull to want him.'

'Georgina!'

'Do I shock you?'

'You disappoint me, especially in front of Grace.'

'Well, you see, Stella, I'm at least sure that Grace *is* asleep.'

She glanced at the little girl, breathing quietly, rhythmically. 'What does that mean?'

Georgina smiled and stood, advancing further towards Stella in an intimidating way. 'It means that you should also be sure that Grace is actually asleep – not just dozing – especially if you're going to be honest in front of her. I might be the gorgeous daughter but I have to admit, the angels made up for Grace's lack in the physical department by making her exceptionally smart with a viciously sharp memory.'

Stella's frowned deepened. 'Whatever are you talking about?'

Beatrice chose this moment to arrive. 'Yes, whatever are you talking about, Georgina?'

'Nothing important, Mummy. Stella and I were just discussing how it must feel to be the other woman in a man's life.'

Stella felt her body turn clammy. No words would come and suddenly she was an observer, unable to participate.

'Other woman? What would you know about being another woman, Georgie darling?'

'Nothing, of course. That's why I was asking Stella if she'd ever been in that situation; her being older and all that. You know, of being someone's mistress . . . what it must feel like to be an adulteress.'

Stella's throat closed to the point where she thought she was going to start gasping for air, like a fish hooked out of its natural watery environment. She struggled to swallow.

'What a ridiculous and curious question, Georgina. Quite rude too. How should Stella know?' her mother admonished with an affectionate chuckle. 'Good morning, Stella,' Beatrice said as she arrived bedside, leaving Stella to wonder whether yesterday's reveal was already forgotten.

'Morning, Mrs Ainsworth,' she choked out, still standing in the middle of the room, hardly daring to make eye contact with Georgina but she knew she must not let this vixen have such control. 'To answer your question, no, Georgina, I wouldn't know about any of that.'

'Really? I would have thought any and every man might be in danger with you around.' She lifted an eyebrow as if they were both aware of a conspiracy and when her mother turned, she grinned sweetly. 'I mean, you're so attractive, who couldn't fail to notice you?'

'Georgina! Be off with you. Thank you for staying with your sister. Now let me have a private talk with Stella, please.'

'I'm going into Brighton, Mummy. Potter is taking me. It's far too boring here – everyone's so maudlin.'

Grace began to stir.

'Bye, Stella,' Georgina added, with a wink. 'Nice chatting.' She departed the room and Stella was left feeling as though a trained boxer had just punched her as hard as he could in her belly.

'You're very quiet, Stella. Are you offended?'

'No . . . er, just a bit shocked by Georgina's line of questioning,' she admitted, finally finding her voice.

'I'm afraid Georgina has men on her mind. She's been seeing a young man – you know, for picnics, meeting for afternoon tea and the like – but I suspect she's more interested in another.' Stella schooled her features to appear interested. 'There's an older fellow, you see,' Beatrice continued in a more gossipy tone. 'Excellent family credentials, who's quite taken by Georgina – and why not, she's quite the catch and undoubtedly setting up to be the belle of the 1934 Season.'

Stella blinked. 'The Season' was so removed from her life and yet she was familiar with its crowd of wealthy families that rented houses or, if they were seriously rich, returned to London residences *en masse* for a chunk of the year to launch the young women in their lives onto the Society scene. It involved everything from attending horse racing to boating competitions but the highlight was the balls. She'd met enough of the folk involved during her days on the department floor to know what a different world they moved in to her. And yet here she was, having a conversation about Georgina being released into a society that prided itself on matching up monied families. She often thought love must be a happy coincidence.

'. . . drives a flashy car, talks himself up. I don't mind. I think a young man should have a healthy ego. Doug won't hear of him taking her out yet. He said both should wait until she's seventeen. Typical father.' She smiled to herself. 'I quite like Reginald. Tons of money – she'd want for nothing and gain a title, no less.'

'Indeed,' Stella murmured, uninterested, her mind racing back over the hidden threat in Georgina's words. *What did she know?*

She watched Beatrice remove a long cigarette from a box of expensive menthols. 'Help me, would you, Stella?' she said, offering a small, square-shaped lighter that looked to be inlaid with some sort of black stone. It was surprisingly heavy when she dropped it into Stella's palm.

Stella flicked the flame. It caught instantly. 'This is rather lovely,' she said to fill the awkward silence.

'From Doug,' Beatrice replied just before she sucked back to drag the flame onto the tip. 'Our first anniversary – I'm quite sentimental about it and I'm not very sentimental about much,' she said. 'Black onyx,' she added as Stella gave it back. The cigarette looked elegant in Beatrice's manicured hand. The smoke didn't drift into her eye either to make her blink or squint, nor did it make her cough. Instead she inhaled slow and deep as the air in Grace's bedroom lost the sharp, medicinal tang of witch hazel that had obviously been daubed on her head and became newly fragranced by the camphor-laced smoke.

'So . . . Stella,' Beatrice began in a tone that sounded suddenly stiff.

'Yes?'

Gone was the languid pose on the bed and the conversational tone. Now Beatrice was straight-backed and focused. 'Yesterday was a difficult day for all of us, I'm sure you'd agree?'

Stella nodded, not daring to break eye contact with the glacial stare that pinned her like prey.

'Good. It was unfortunate you were put into the position of witnessing what should have remained a private conversation.' She raised a hand as Stella opened her mouth to leap in with an apology. 'That was my fault, but I had no idea that my husband was so upset. Doug is usually impervious to the comings and goings of the house.'

'But this was his daughter,' Stella let slip.

Beatrice's lips thinned. 'Yes, and that's my point. I had misjudged how upset he was by Grace's accident. He blames himself, I can tell. Anyway, something was exposed that —'

No, she wasn't prepared to go through it again. Stella jumped in. 'Mrs Ainsworth, I was employed to help improve your daughters' French and appreciation of cultural aspects of life and now I understand that I am to help with filing of information for Mr Ainsworth's work. I'm happy with the work. That's all that interests me. I do not wish to be drawn into any discussion about the family's private affairs.' She could see this brought a relief as Beatrice's shrouded gaze lost some of its storminess. 'And before you feel you must ask, Mrs Ainsworth, whatever I inadvertently shared was never my business and I have no intention of making it so. What I heard I will not be speaking about with the staff or anyone else.'

'I appreciate your discretion, Stella. And I would like to apologise for anything said yesterday that may have given offence.'

'You were both clearly upset, Mrs Ainsworth.'

'Nevertheless, I wish to know for sure.'

Stella took an audible breath. 'No offence was taken,' she lied, but only for his sake.

Her employer's expression rearranged itself away from concern; the brows unstitching themselves as Beatrice's forehead smoothed over and her shoulders relaxed and her gaze lost its hostility. Her slight air of disdain was back as she waved a hand, and a trail of silver smoke followed, as though wafting away the ugly business of yesterday. 'Good. Doug's in London; he just called me a few moments ago from his club. Apparently he's having to bring the voyage he's so determined to share forward.'

'Oh, I see,' she said, the phone call of the previous evening still echoing in her mind. So he was going ahead with the plan of Basil Peach. 'Under the circumstances I completely understand.' She was gabbling. Beatrice was staring at her in bafflement. 'Um, I can head back to London immediately.'

'Why?'

'I won't make it at all difficult, Mrs Ainsworth. I can be gone from here in hours.'

'Stella, stop chittering and allow me to explain. I asked to see you this morning because I had to talk to you about a new schedule. On my husband's instructions I am to have you shown into his attic offices so you can begin your work for him. He has left you a detailed guide to what needs doing urgently. Please don't ask me, I have no idea of his work. I also wanted to discuss an adjusted schedule for Grace, given her new situation. However, suddenly that conversation is academic now the trip is brought forward.'

Yes, you leave soon, she wanted to tell her.

'Apparently we leave in a few days. A few days!' Beatrice exclaimed with as much shock in her tone as though she'd been told the trip was leaving for the moon.

'And much as I don't wish to be travelling right now, I admit that escaping drizzling England feels tempting. Besides, he's not leaving me much of an excuse.'

Stella was waiting for the axe to fall. Something along the lines of: 'Sorry to change the plans; can't be helped; we'll give you a good severance pay and all that.' Her thoughts must have reflected in her expression because Beatrice sighed away her selfish concerns and became more focused on Stella. 'Anyway, Doug has instructed that you are coming with us.'

She gasped, uncertain she'd heard correctly. 'Abroad?' She was aware her tone sounded appalled.

'Yes, Stella.'

'Where to?' It was an instinctive response.

'Oh, heavens. How should I know? Port Said, or something, although Doug is notoriously vague about these things. As you know, he's got it into his head to take us all on a grand voyage and given yesterday's words I feel I should just bear up and go along. Doug says I won't be pressed to do any touring even if he leaps off to do his butterflies and birds and plant stuff. I know he won't be able to resist Morocco . . . Rabat, Tangiers.'

'Why is that?' Her mind was swimming. The 'peacock' rendezvous was in Africa . . .

'His father was some sort of diplomat who roamed that whole region – I've never paid enough attention so don't ask me in what capacity. Mother very beautiful like her son – an artist, I think. Loved the colours of the desert and of the souks.' She sighed. 'They moved around like gypsies . . . what do they call the locals who travel on camels?'

Stella wasn't sure that Beatrice really wanted an answer. 'Bedouin,' she murmured all the same.

Beatrice inhaled deeply again from her cigarette and nodded silently. She blew out, lifting her pointed chin towards the ceiling. 'Probably erected huge and colourful tents too, I'm sure, because the family hated being parted. He speaks of exotic places like Fez and Casablanca – I barely know where those places are. The Levant, do you suppose?'

'North Africa, I believe,' Stella mumbled.

Beatrice tinkled a laugh and noticed Stella's perplexed expression. 'Well, you know your geography.' She smiled a false brightness. 'Anyway, the fact is, my husband seems to prefer biblical destinations than the more run-of-the-mill ones that suits the everyday person, like Paris or Rome.'

Or, Blackpool, or the Isle of Wight, even, Stella thought, betraying no sulkiness in her expression; what would Beatrice know about the everyday person?

'Plus he likes to practise his language skills. Why he can't just sail to France and use his French, or ride the banks of the Danube and speak German is beyond me. No, it has to be far-flung places like Palestine. Somewhere near the Holy Land, is it?'

Stella's thoughts snapped to attention. 'Mr Ainsworth can speak Arabic?'

'Oh, he speaks several languages,' Beatrice replied, taking a final drag, her lips wrinkling in the effort like a prune and then relaxing again with a sigh as she blew out the final drift of smoke. She stubbed the cigarette out on a flat tin ashtray she'd had beside her on Grace's bed. 'I've never taken much interest and only hear him mutter some French when we find ourselves in Paris together. So long as he can order a gin and tonic wherever we happen to be, then I'm impressed.'

Stella frowned, feeling lost.

'Anyway, apparently he now has an even more urgent need of your cataloguing services for this special new job he has for Kew Gardens. So, you're to accompany us, I'm to instruct. Open a window, Stella. If Dougie smells tobacco in Grace's room, he'll bleat at me.'

Stella obliged. 'What about my family?' she asked over her shoulder.

'What about it? You intended to be away from them for a month, anyway. You may be a week or two late returning. I'm sure you can explain. There'll be extra wages, of course.'

Beatrice was consistent with her careless attitude and Stella couldn't bother finding the energy to show her offence.

Beatrice gave a melodramatic sigh. 'This is so typical of my husband. He hasn't even given me a date.'

'It's all rather sudden, isn't it?' She prolonged the enquiry in case Rafe had told his wife more.

'Inconvenient, but that's Doug,' Beatrice said, unhelpfully. Apparently his wife knew less than she. Beatrice glanced at her watch and on cue Mrs Boyd arrived with her set of keys. 'Ah, Boyd, you'll show Stella up to Mr Ainsworth's studio, please.'

'Is it right that I'm to give Miss Myles this key?' Mrs Boyd said, sounding incredulous.

'It's what my husband instructed.'

'Mrs Ainsworth, I —'

'Not now, Boyd. I gave him my word.'

Mrs Boyd's lips tightened as though she had just smelled something especially unpleasant. 'Follow me, Miss Myles.'

Wordlessly, Stella left the room, following the housekeeper. Mrs Boyd's disgust trailed alongside Stella like a passenger on her shoulder as they climbed the stairs to the next level and finally to the locked door outside her room.

'I don't know what this is all about, Miss Myles, really I don't.'

'And I am just following instructions like everyone else,' Stella admitted in a neutral tone.

The door was unlocked briskly, the key wrenched off the large ring. 'And so I'm supposed to give you this.'

'Thank you.'

'Should you lose it —'

'I won't. Thank you, Mrs Boyd.'

'I'll just come up and —'

'That will not be necessary,' she replied, knowing Rafe would not want Boyd of all people even glancing around his personal space. 'You can leave me to my work now.'

The housekeeper's face couldn't have pinched itself more sourly even if she'd just sucked hard on a lemon. 'See you for luncheon, then.'

Stella didn't respond and made a point of locking the door noisily behind her. She allowed herself a small grin as she twisted the key in the lock and listened at the door as the woman stomped away down the stairs.

Stella slipped the key into her pocket and exhaled, only now realising there was another, still more private flight of stairs ahead that felt as though she'd entered a secret cocoon. Her heartbeat had escalated to a persistent percussion she could feel; it was pounding as though sitting high in her throat. It felt like she was under attack from all quarters. What was happening? A few days ago she thought her world could never feel under more pressure as a grieving daughter whose major concern was the responsibility of putting a roof over their heads and food on the table for her young siblings. That suddenly felt wrongly pushed beneath a heavier – no, crushing – responsibility of not only adultery but what seemed to point to state secrets. Even thinking that made her catch her breath. Was Rafe a spy? A government man leading a double . . . perhaps triple life? He had guided her to his lair and whether she was deliberately part of his intrigue, there was no doubting she was now not only helplessly part of his web in what she'd overheard on the telephone but it appeared that he was intently bringing her into his secretive world by allowing her here, into his sanctum.

Fear fluttered through her like a disturbed butterfly as she grasped that she was being helplessly drawn into a world of secrets and espionage. Life was moving quickly and she felt as though she was caught in a hurricane. She climbed the small flight of private stairs that led her up to the attic with a sense of awe; now the fear of only moments ago was being shouldered aside by helpless intrigue as much as desire. She could smell Rafe here. Traces of lavender from his expensive pomade scented the slighty musty, woody atmosphere of this loft room that was alive with the dust motes she'd stirred with her arrival, which now danced in the muted morning light that seeped through the dormer windows. And as she crested the final stair she was struck by how simple and yet elegant this huge room was that must have spanned two or three chambers below.

Even though he wished no one to share his private place, it

nevertheless was painted a soft and welcoming chalky white and like his favourite room downstairs it was crammed with oddities. However, whereas the nursery held his and the family's memorabilia of childhood, this space was all about Rafe's personal items. Here she took in a signed cricket bat, a battered old pith helmet, various photographs, sketches, piles and more dusty piles of books, but it was to his desk that she was drawn, where Stella was sure in this intensely private place she would unlock the secret that was Rafe.

She had already decided in the last few moments to let go of the rising hysteria and to trust him. What else could she do? She was now his accomplice, mistress, soulmate . . .

It was waiting for her as though he knew what she would be thinking. A thick, oblong envelope of heavy stationery with his family crest was leaning against a sculpture of a camel, carved out of a wood with bright whorls and bands of light and dark timber. She couldn't imagine which wood it was but the camel's expression was so lifelike she felt like stroking the statue's bent head.

Carelessly scrawled in black ink across the envelope was her single name. She half expected it not to be sealed but then she knew how carefully he protected his true self. She pulled at the flap and the seal gave up its hold with a tight snap and Stella touched the glue where Rafe's tongue had presumably moistened it. She was annoyed by her vulnerability at the thrill of pleasure that passed through her like a shiver. And her heartbeat seemed to falter at the sight of his handwriting, which curiously appeared on the front of the letter before she could unfold it. She'd anticipated it would be flamboyant but it was neatly penned and spaced in a measured way that made reading the words easy. The only nod to his stylish alter ego, or rather the real Mr Ainsworth, were the tiny hooks and curlicues on the ends of certain letters that seemed to make the overall effect of the handwriting feel artistic rather than workmanlike. *Do not read this in the house. Be patient. Read it in Brighton.*

'Brighton?' she murmured and as she did so there was a knock at the door.

'Miss Myles?'

'Er, yes? Who is it?'

'It's Hilly, Miss Myles. Mrs Ainsworth needs you.'

She closed her eyes with frustration and then quickly opened the letter a fraction.

My dearest Stella, it began and she took a slow, deep breath at how affectionate those three words felt as she read them.

> *I'll be gone by the time you're reading this. I'll bet the mean-spirited Mrs Boyd's expression must have all but collapsed in on itself at the notion of handing you the only other key to the attic room. How do you like my secret space? Not nearly as exciting or intriguing as everyone imagines, I'm sure.*

'Miss Myles?' Another more urgent knock filtered upstairs.

'I'm coming,' she called down, filled with annoyance. She refolded the letter, slipped it back into its crisp envelope and then hid it in a deep pocket of her cardigan. She looked around longingly, wanting to sit here through the day, touch his belongings, get to know the work she was meant to be doing. Instead she stomped back down the stairs and pulled open the door. Hilly flinched on the other side.

'I'm sorry.'

'So am I. Mr Ainsworth wants me to do some tasks for him,' she lied with little effort, driven by the burn to read his words. 'What is the problem?'

The girl shrugged. 'I was asked to fetch you.'

'Is it Grace?' she asked, alarmed.

Hilly frowned. 'I don't think so.'

Her shoulders relaxed. 'Well, I have to collect something from my room first. Give me a moment.' Hilly didn't object and Stella didn't give her time to. She opened and shut her door, slipping inside to hide the envelope in her pillowcase. Quickly, she changed her cardigan to something lighter simply to prove that she had done something on the other side of the door that she now opened and locked shut with a key. As they walked, she attached Rafe's study key to her door key and dropped it into a pocket. She felt the keys chinking together comfortably and the world, just in that moment, felt right . . . as though their lips were touching.

She was led straight back to Grace's room, hoping Hilly's assessment was still correct that the little girl hadn't taken a turn for the worse.

She hurried in. 'Is everything all right, Mrs Ainsworth?'

'Ah, Stella, sorry to interrupt you,' Beatrice said, standing from her child's bed and waving a wearied hand to anyone in close proximity. 'I am headed up to London because I do have to make sure about wardrobe needs; no man understands, least of all my man.' Stella frowned, unable to detect any matter of great urgency. Beatrice continued talking. 'However, I failed to mention that Doug has suggested we advance you some money so you can get yourself some outfits.'

She had been dragged downstairs for this? 'But I don't need any new outfits, Mrs Ainsworth.'

'You most certainly do. You can't possibly take a voyage to the tropics and not have linens and cottons. So far I've noted only woollens and sensible winter clothes. It just won't do. Anyway, take your pick: London, Brighton or Eastbourne are your best options. I suggest you take a train in today, stay over if you wish. We shall pay for your accommodation. Let Mrs Boyd know your requirements.'

Stella stared back, baffled, and her glance moved to Grace, who was mumbling yet seemingly asleep. She hoped they had permission from the doctor to whisk her off abroad.

'Anyway, hurry up and make your decision about where you're headed. I shall no doubt see you on the docks at Tilbury.'

It occurred to her that if she sent a telegram ahead, Aunt Dilys might be able to bring the children down to London overnight. 'Do you think if I chose London I might have a chance to see my family?'

'I doubt it, Stella, so now do buck up, please. I'm sure we can arrange for you to call to wish them farewell.'

Stella shook her head mutely to answer that there was no phone at her aunt's place.

'Oh, well, it's only a few weeks, for heaven's sake!' She sounded so heartless that Stella didn't bother responding. 'Right, I have to go,' she continued, barely looking again at her child although she was certainly doing her best to say the right things. 'Can you sit with Grace, Stella, until Miss Hailsham arrives, please? She seems to be stirring every now and then to mutter but almost immediately drifting off again. I don't know what's best for her. The doctor did say rest so I'm letting nature decide. I suspect she'll wake properly soon but I have to go.' She glanced at her watch. 'She's due any minute and Mrs Boyd has her duties.' Beatrice reached for a cape dangling over a chair.

'Yes, of course, I'll stay with Grace,' Stella replied, her tone dull. 'You carry on – I know you have a lot to organise.'

Beatrice glided out of the room, wearing a short soot-black woollen cape to match her dress giving her the appearance of a bat leaving. Stella sat forlornly on the bed and gazed at Grace. If she looked past the sweet chubbiness, she could see Rafe's expression etched in the child's expression in repose. Calm and strong, just a hint of a smile at the corner of her mouth as though harbouring a secret, but there was nothing sly about it – not like Georgina.

What had Georgina meant earlier? The horror of that conversation returned like a stab of pain. She touched Grace, stroking her hair before holding her hand. The girl stirred, eyelids blinking, open halfway.

'Stella?' she lisped.

She was relieved that Grace recognised her immediately. 'Yes, darling girl. How do you feel?'

'Achey.'

'I know. Do you want anything? A drink?'

The child nodded. 'Lucozade? Daddy says it's good for you.'

'It's good for fever when someone doesn't feel like eating.' She wished she could afford it for Carys, who couldn't swallow food when she suffered sore throats with fevers.

'Hmm. I'm hungry too.'

'Water first,' she said, smiling, and reached for the jug and glass beaker. She knew it would be easy to begrudge Grace her wealth and access to anything she needed, including the sparkling glucose drink that always felt like a treat rather than a health aid, but Grace prompted only pleasure in Stella. 'How about I get you some Lucozade as a treat and you can have a tiny glass of it each day.'

Grace nodded and tried to whisper. 'Mrs Boyd keeps some bottles in the butler's pantry. I've seen them.'

Stella grinned. Grace was ever observant. 'Is it your head that hurts?'

'A little.'

'Happy to talk, though?'

'Yes.'

'No French or any lessons for a while,' Stella said, waggling a finger. 'What do you remember about what happened?'

Grace considered this. 'I remember being in the car with you and Daddy.'

'That's excellent,' Stella said, her fear escalating. 'I wouldn't have thought you could remember much at all.'

The girl nodded, full of innocence. 'I have a really good memory. That's why Daddy likes me to help him memorise stuff.'

'What do you mean?'

'I don't know,' Grace replied, yawning. 'He practises his memory with me.'

'Do you mean recall?'

'I don't know.' She yawned again.

'You must rest.'

'He needed me to remember stuff to do with maps. Numbers. We used to make up little songs and he'd get me to sing them around him to help him practise.' She yawned so widely this time she closed her eyes.

Stella frowned, baffled. Beatrice had alluded to this habit too, equally confused, while Rafe had not offered a word of insight but had seemed deeply irritated by the mention. Stella leaned down and laid a soft kiss on the child's head and let go of the thought, even though the conversation he shared with Basil Peach once again erupted in her mind.

'Why are you "the other woman"?' Grace murmured in a drowsy voice. She opened her eyes again and stared at Stella.

Stella could barely breathe.

'Other woman?' she repeated, her voice breaking on the question, pulse instantly racing as though a starter's gun had just gone off in her mind.

Grace nodded. She turned onto her back so she could look at Stella squarely. 'You said you didn't want to be the other woman to Daddy and he said you already were.'

'Er, I'm trying to recall now. Gosh, you have a fine memory. Um . . . what were we talking about? It was all such a blur. We were both so worried about you.' She knew she was gabbling but Grace waited patiently.

'You said you felt guilty. What did that mean?'

Stella's thoughts fled to control the damage. 'Er, that's right . . . I think I was feeling terrible that your Mummy wasn't in the car with your father, and I was talking to you, Grace,' she said. 'I was trying to soothe you, not let you feel badly about Mummy not being with you.'

Grace considered this for a few moments. 'I heard you say that you didn't want to stop holding —'

'Oh my word! You poor child. I didn't say that to your father, Grace,' she said, her chortle sounding strained. 'Good gracious, no, I was talking to you, precious girl.'

She held her breath, watched the child's forehead crease. 'Wasn't I lying in Daddy's lap in the car?'

Stella nodded, giving her best artless smile and hating herself to be ensnared in this lie to someone she loved. 'You were, but I was holding your hand the whole way.'

Grace grinned. 'Thank you, Stella. Daddy told me when he sat next to me last night that you took control and bossed everyone around like a sergeant major . . . even Mrs Boyd had to pay attention to your command.' She giggled, no doubt enjoying the image of that in her mind. 'I wish I'd been awake to see that.'

Again, Stella sighed inwardly with relief that she'd deflected the enquiry. 'If I hadn't been so worried I would have enjoyed it more,' she confided. 'You should have seen Mrs Boyd, one minute holding up your legs, the next yelling at poor Hilly about smelling salts, then marching down the stairs making sure we didn't drop you. Now I think about it, it is quite funny but not at the time.'

'You'll never be scared of her again, Stella,' Grace murmured, looking like she was struggling to stifle another yawn. 'I think I'm asleep,' Grace continued in a thick voice. 'I'll tell Georgie tomorrow.'

At the mention of the sister, Stella's relief dissipated like a curlicue of smoke scattering in a breeze. 'Georgie?'

Grace nodded, eyes closing before turning on her side into a sleeping position. 'When Georgina asked me what you both talked about in the car, I told her but when I asked what you might mean she said she didn't know. But Georgie is always fibbing. Now I can tell her I do know.'

Claws of terror, with fingers of jagged icicles, raked in her fears again, gathering them to settle in the pit of her belly like a wintry pool of anxiety. So that's what Georgie had been probing at . . .

Just making you aware, Stella, that I know something. Don't get too comfortable. He can't protect you.

Stella took a slow, silent breath that seemed to come up from her toes. She watched the rhythmic movement of Grace's chest and the slack expression. The little girl was fully asleep. She moved back a stray lock of dark hair from the child's closed eyes and held no grudge towards the innocent Grace. But it was obvious that her conniving sister was likely right this moment considering and plotting how best to use this information to her best advantage.

Stella shook her head. Should she leave now? Run away . . . or face up to the consequences?

'I'm no coward,' she murmured into the stillness of the room, as though speaking directly at her parents. 'I'll face the repercussions of my actions.'

She jumped at the arrival of Miss Hailsham.

'I can take over now, Stella.'

'She's just fallen asleep, best not to disturb.' Stella moved to the door. 'I have to pack,' she said, knowing the poor woman didn't understand. But then neither did she, especially as she wasn't sure whether she was packing for going on a trip abroad with the wealthy, or heading home and back to the life she knew that was setting itself up to be much poorer than she ever dared fear.

15

She was shifting around her few clothes in a blur, not really packing, not really thinking about abroad or even going home. Her suitcase was on the bed, but nothing had been placed inside. Stella was carefully folding each item but her mind was elsewhere, flying between Rafe, wanting to be with him, wanting to finish the letter he left her but the escalating panic of discovery and wanting to flee was equally urgent. She could read the letter later. Right now all that mattered was packing . . . getting away, time to think – Brighton would give her that distance to reflect and make decisions.

She didn't hear the knock and so jumped as if scalded when the door opened and Mrs Boyd appeared.

'Good grief, Miss Myles. Why didn't you answer?'

It was a fair enough query but Stella was not in the mood. 'Why didn't you take the hint that I clearly don't wish to be disturbed?'

Mrs Boyd's mouth opened in surprise. 'Er . . . forgive me. Are you all right, Miss Myles?'

'Clearly not.'

'Can I help?'

'No, Mrs Boyd. The choice is mine. I just have to reach it.' Stella didn't care that the housekeeper looked perplexed. 'Did you need me for something?'

The housekeeper shook off her confusion. 'Er, Mrs Ainsworth asked me to give you this.' She held out a thick manila envelope.

'What is it?' It reminded her of the letter in the pillowslip. She'd take it with her and read it well away from Harp's End.

'I wasn't informed of the contents. Only that you'd understand.'

'I see. Thank you, Mrs Boyd.' She took the envelope.

'London or Eastbourne?' the housekeeper wondered.

'Brighton, actually. Going to London would only make me feel sad, and I really don't know Eastbourne, whereas I do know my way around Brighton.'

'Oh . . . er . . .'

'Something wrong with that choice?'

'Not at all,' she said, sounding satisfied.

Stella waited while the housekeeper left her before she opened the package, tipping the contents onto the small desk by the window. A brief, scrawled note in a bold, slanting hand was wrapped around money and a train ticket.

> *Stella,*
>
> *I couldn't wait for your decision. I am leaving for London in half an hour. Enclosed is sufficient funds for a return ticket to anywhere you choose in the south. I am including additional money, which is not taken from your wages. Doug and I feel that this sudden trip is our decision and being forced upon you so we will fund your wardrobe. I'm sure we can lend a trunk.*
>
> *B.*

It ended as abruptly as it began with a large, artistic rendition of the letter 'B' with lots of loops drawn firmly in black ink. Stella shifted her glance to the pound notes on the desk, neatly bound in a rubber band, each crisp and new, serial numbers in ascending order.

'I've never carried this much money in my life,' she murmured in a low state of shock as she stared at the top note with its profile of the King emblazoned strongly in sepia. Stella couldn't resist and counted. 'Fifteen,' she breathed, confirming her expectation. The balance to pay on her parents' house was thirty-six pounds. It felt vulgar to finger nearly half of the money it would take to own it, with a view to lavishing it on clothes. It was worth four hard-working weeks of her previous job. She dared not imagine its true value, given that she was not to be taxed on this cash. It was too much. Stella hurriedly sifted eight of the notes and tucked them into the pocket of her suitcase. She could surely kit herself out for the role of governess or secretary on a voyage with that amount.

In no time she was dressed for travelling, had grabbed Rafe's letter and without feeling obliged to let anyone from the family know her whereabouts, she hunted down Mr Potter in the garage.

'Ah, I've been expecting you,' he said, straightening from where he had been testing the inflation of a back tyre on one of the cars. She hadn't realised that there was more than one motor car within the family.

'Expecting me?'

'Yes, Mrs Boyd warned you would likely need a lift to the station.'

'Mrs Boyd is certainly thorough.'

'Ready? You look it.' He gave a kind smile.

'Thank you, Mr Potter . . . er, John,' she added at his raised eyebrow.

'Can't be that bad,' he said, winking. 'Tomorrow it could be raining.'

Stella dug out a smile. 'Sorry. I've got a lot on my mind.'

'Nothing to apologise for, Stella. Here we are,' he said, opening the door of the gleaming black car. 'Or would you prefer the front?'

She knew he watched her glance into the back seat and although he couldn't know she was remembering how her body had aligned itself so easily to Rafe's during the alarm of Grace's accident, she felt the guilt all the same. She remembered it as clearly as she could now construct every aspect of his face, his features as vivid in her mind like a design etched deep in glass. And if she were that distracted, perhaps Mr Potter noted their closeness too. She felt nauseous suddenly.

'Miss Stella?'

'Er . . . I'm sorry?'

'Front or back, sweetheart?"

'Front, thank you, John.'

He nodded and opened the front passenger door. 'Make yourself comfortable.'

She watched him roll down his sleeves, button them, take his jacket from a convenient hook on the outside of the garage, where he also had his hat. He tucked this under his arm and joined her. 'Should be a nice day for shopping.'

'Did Mrs Ainsworth tell you?'

'Yes, indeed. And you must be excited.'

'I'm not sure what I'm feeling,' she admitted and had never expressed a truer sentiment. 'Do you know the times of the trains?'

'We should be able to get you on the 11.16 and if for any reason you miss that, there's another seven minutes later. It takes just a minute or two past an hour to get into Brighton if you catch the first; nearly an additional half hour if you take the next.'

They travelled in a comfortable silence for a few minutes.

'So how are you finding the family, Stella?'

'Early days,' she murmured.

'That's true. It's a real pity about Miss Grace.'

'I have young siblings. They're always falling down and scraping their knees, or tripping and tearing their clothes. Must be a child's rite of passage,' she chuckled, trying to steer him away from talk of Grace.

'Mr Ainsworth was as white as chalk yesterday.'

She breathed deeply to steady her nerves. 'Yes, I noticed. He was very worried.'

'Probably felt responsible, what with you both up on the hillside at the time.' He glanced at her and her treacherous cheeks felt as though they flushed but she didn't flinch.

'What are you saying?'

He lifted a shoulder. 'Nothing. Just . . . well, tongues wag, Stella. I like you very much and so I'm just giving you advice from an older person who sees how less sympathetic minds work.'

Stella turned to face him fully. 'What do you mean?'

He gave a small sigh. 'He's charming, gallant, kind, and at times rather mysterious, Miss Stella. He would be easy for any lovely young lady such as yourself to fall for.'

Stella gasped.

'Please don't upset yourself. I've travelled enough with Mr Ainsworth and the fact that he's my employer aside, I hold a deep, abiding respect for him and his folk.'

'But . . . ?' she queried, trying to smooth the jagged edge away from her tone.

'But he's . . . well, he's a wolf.'

She hadn't expected such a description. 'Are wolves charming and kind?'

'The one in *Little Red Riding Hood* is.'

'And I'm Little Red Riding Hood, I presume?'

'I'm just saying you could be. There are sides to him.'

'But, John, Little Red Riding Hood saw through the disguise to the wolf.'

At this comment he frowned back at her. 'Yes, yes, that's right, but . . .'

'You are not to worry about me. I have Mr Ainsworth's measure and whatever you believe you should caution me about, there is no need.'

'He is not how he seems.'

'Can you speak plainly? No one's listening and I won't tell anyone.'

'Miss Stella, I pick up Mr Ainsworth from London regularly.'

'And . . . ?' Her companion squirmed, looking like he wished he'd never begun this conversation. She knew he shouldn't have and while not happy about it, she was prepared to make him keep squirming. 'Go on.'

'I don't always pick him up from his club.'

She feigned amusement, while feeling suddenly pathetic for allowing herself to be so vulnerable to Rafe's charm. 'I'm sure he can do at his club whatever it is he does elsewhere. John, what happened to discretion?'

His cheeks showed spots of high colour. 'I'm trying to protect you because I like you.'

Stella softened and let him off the hook he was wriggling on. 'And I am deeply grateful for your concern but I want to assure you that Mr Ainsworth has been nothing but entirely honest with me . . . and because I can tell you care I want you alone to know this, John.' He blinked, glanced her way and back at the road. 'I am not falling in love with him,' she lied, and almost believed it herself.

He let out the breath he'd obviously held. 'I'm glad to hear that, Miss Stella. He's a bit of a tomcat when he's in London and his gentle manner at home is like his shield. Forgive me for speaking out of turn but I think you're a fine young woman and you remind me of our Lizbeth who would have been your age.'

'Would have been?'

'She succumbed to tuberculosis. She was just seventeen when she died in that sanitarium, although I learned she died lying outside in the depths of October when most of us are rugged up.'

Stella took a quiet breath.

'"Plenty of fresh air, no matter the season and lots of bed rest" was all the doctors kept saying to us. I spent all my wages on buying lots of good meat for them to cook for her because they say protein is important. We were saving for one of those new-fangled sun lamp things when she passed.' He shook his head in memory. 'My little girl, she just slipped away from us. We weren't allowed to see her for fear of the disease spreading. They just told us she was dead via telegram. It felt like the war all over again, when we lost our son.' He pulled into the station forecourt at Tunbridge Wells.

Stella had barely seen the countryside passing on their journey. 'Oh, John, I'm so sorry. Was Lizbeth your only daughter?'

'Only child left. We loved her so much. My Marge couldn't have any more after those two. Anyway, the day I saw you I was reminded of Lizzie and I guess the father in me felt protective, that's all.'

She squeezed his hand. 'You have nothing to worry about. Mr Ainsworth has been so careful and kind with me. As we're being honest with each other, I find the women in his life far more dangerous.'

He nodded with a look of understanding. 'Miss Georgina has a streak in her, that's for sure. I should tell you that she's in Brighton, Stella. I'd hoped I'd be getting you to Eastbourne as you're best out of her way right now. She was in a vicious mood this morning.'

'I noticed.'

'She talked about you in the car.'

'John, perhaps you shouldn't be telling me this, I —'

'She believes you are having an affair with her father, Stella.'

'What?' she squeaked, not very convincing in her aim for indignation.

'We picked up her friend on the way to Brighton and Miss

Georgina is never terribly discreet about what she discusses in the car. I think she presumes we're all deaf or mute . . . or too frightened to repeat it.'

'You shouldn't be repeating it.'

'Miss Georgina has never been kind to me. But you have in a short time. And I know she is going to make trouble for you and for her parents, by the sounds of what she was saying.'

Despite her desperation to know precisely what he had overhead in that conversation, Stella kept her dignity and remained aloof. 'John, you must forget whatever Georgina spoke about. If she thought she was safe in being overheard, then we must respect that. I do not feel threatened. I have nothing to hide,' she said with so much control she could almost believe in the innocence she claimed. 'Your concern is touching and I know it comes from the right place but you must not worry for me. Thank you for the lift.'

John nodded with acceptance. Stella was able to leave the car, turning to him with a smile she schooled into her expression.

He handed her a newspaper. 'Don't buy a new one, I've already read it. I will meet the evening train that comes in around seven and another at eight. That should give you enough time. If you come in earlier or later, just ring the house and I'll drop down.' He gestured with his chin. 'You'd better hurry, Miss Stella, here comes the Brighton train.'

She looked over her shoulder for the telltale steam and only now above her scrambling thoughts she heard the huff and squeal of the approaching train. 'Thank you for the paper,' was all she could choke out. She tucked it into her bag.

Stella ran to the platform, getting her ticket clipped as she hurried. The look of silent panic would have told others around her she was frantic at the possibility of missing her train. No one could know that she couldn't care less about getting to Brighton.

She hoped to find a lonely carriage and tuck herself away in a corner by a window to examine the horror of what she'd learned about Georgina, but also to read Rafe's letter, burning through the fabric of her pocket as if to scald her into action. She couldn't find a quiet spot and ended up squeezing between two women so didn't dare take out the letter, imagining their bored gazes settling on Rafe's words. She had to content herself with staring out of the window. She wanted to examine the situation of Georgina and what she may reveal but she couldn't bring herself to think on the troubles that potentially lay ahead for her. So Stella let her mind go blank. She found it wandering to the memory of Rafe's kiss.

'Connecting at Eridge,' the ticket inspector interrupted as he moved through her carriage.

The serene scape of open fields helped to distract her and she barely noticed the stops at Crowborough, Buxted and Uckfield that took away some passengers, including her female sentinels, but it had delivered yet more people into her carriage. She'd taken the chance to shift seats next to the window but the carriage was still crowded and she didn't want to share Rafe's letter with all their noise. When the train began clattering through the valley of the River Ouse she became acutely aware of the higher pitched chatter of women, the flapping of newspapers and the coughs and snorts of people around her.

'Oh look, Tommy,' a mother said opposite her, pointing her son's attention to the river after they'd left Isfield. 'Maybe we could get Dad to take you out soon.'

Stella stared absently at the handful of boats and their passengers, mainly fishermen.

'How will he row with only one arm?' Tommy said.

'You can take one of the oars,' his mother replied, casting a glance Stella's way but she pretended she hadn't seen it. 'The war took your father's arm but not his love for life, Tommy.'

Stella could feel the woman wanted to catch her attention,

perhaps open a conversation, but she didn't want to be trapped in small talk. She thought about reading Rafe's letter – itched to do so – but she wanted to be in a quiet space when she did, not surrounded by people coughing, clearing their throats and murmuring around her. As a result her mood darkened further and she reached for John Potter's newspaper from her bag. Stella deftly opened it up, flicking immediately to page three so she could widen the coverage of the paper and hide behind it. She saw the articles, read the words repeatedly but randomly and absorbed nothing.

What was Georgina planning? How was she hoping to gain the most mileage out of what she thought she knew?

The announcement of Barcombe Mills Station she heard distantly and shifted her weight automatically as one man left and another arrived to sit next to her brandishing a fishing rod. Several other enthusiasts were wrestling with rods and baskets, which captured Tommy's attention and his mother finally had someone to talk to.

Stella buried herself further behind her newspaper, actually reading the article this time about the man called Adolf Hitler, the Chancellor in Germany recently turned dictator. The article posed several questions about the failure of German democracy, the lack of worth for the German mark, the nation's huge numbers of unemployed now well past the half-million mark. It spoke of the plight of the poor in that country and simmering bitterness at their loss of territory and colonies as much as Germany's lack of standing in Europe following the Great War. The article explained the gathering hostility that was gaining momentum within Germany against the war reparations and how the humiliation following the Treaty of Versailles was deeply damaging to a once-proud nation. It quoted the German observer, Gareth Jones, from *The Western Mail* in Wales who was a regular visitor to Germany, and a journalist respected by Adolf Hitler. Jones was apparently predicting another war on the horizon and the conversation she had overheard between Rafe and Basil took on a new dimension. She desperately wanted to read his letter but just couldn't face it right now in light of what Mr Potter had said. She was avoiding thinking further about Georgina until she could just calm her anxiety.

Stella looked away from the foreboding in the article to glance out of the window again as the train gathered speed through the rolling chalkland of the South Downs. Surely the world would not go to war again? But if the comments in this story were accurate, then that's precisely where the little man with the strange moustache in Germany was leading his people. And somehow Rafe was part of this. His childhood friend must know something incriminating about Adolf Hitler or why would London be interested?

'It's very troubling, isn't it?' the man next to her said, catching her attention.

She hadn't realised he'd noticed what she'd been reading. Stella nodded, glad now that she hadn't brought out the letter; he may have read that. 'I don't want to believe it.'

He sighed. 'I don't think we can put our heads into the sand.'

'This article is mooting another world war?' she murmured.

He shrugged. 'By all accounts, the German dictator is quite the orator and stirring up a lot of resentment and hostility towards the rest of Europe. I don't think we can count on peace being maintained.'

'Gosh, that's ruined my day,' she lied, knowing it had already been ruined once she discovered Rafe had left Harp's End. It had got steadily worse since.

Her companion nodded. 'Our government is well informed, though.'

'You know that for sure?'

'I work for the government. This is not how I dress every day.' He grinned, his iron-grey beard stretching with his smile. He had a pipe tucked into the corner of his mouth but it remained unlit. He must have seen her notice it. 'My doctor thinks I should stop.' He tapped his chest. 'I cough too much for his liking. My wife prefers I continue.'

She frowned. 'Really?'

'She knows I become a grouch when I don't. It was Barbara's idea that I go through all the motions of getting ready to smoke it and then . . .' He shrugged.

'Not light it?' she offered and he nodded. 'Clever. How is it going?'

'Terrible,' he admitted and they both chuckled softly. 'You mustn't worry.'

She glanced back at the page, her thoughts worrying about Rafe more than herself. 'Britain has barely recovered from the last war.'

He nodded, trying to comfort. 'I promise you we're taking steps. We're making sure we know what the Germans are up to . . . and the Russians.'

'Taking steps? What do you mean?'

'I'm not permitted to talk about it and I don't work in the right section to talk with any authority even if I did. However, I know we've got a network of people watching the German situation very closely.'

'Spies?'

He said nothing but gently tapped his nose.

'Having spies in Germany surely isn't enough,' she whispered.

'Who said Germany?' he replied in a cryptic tone. 'We need to know what's happening in the Polish corridor, for instance; even as far as the Levant.'

Stella wanted to ask more but the loudspeaker crackled and their approach into Brighton was announced, drowning out any opportunity for further conversation, exacerbated by people moving to gather up their belongings and donning coats again.

As their carriage curled closer to their destination, their height from the viaduct gave far-reaching views over the town of Brighton with sparkling glimpses of the sea. Stella was struck by the heart-stilling notion that if war did occur again, then Rafe would almost certainly be in the thick of it once more, testing the luck that had kept him safe through the last horror. She imagined him signing up to do his duty immediately although it sounded like Basil Peach had already coerced him into clandestine work. Rafe was a born adventurer from the little she knew of him, plus he would be able to escape his problems at home – perhaps he'd see war as a way out?

She hated even thinking upon it. The train began to slow into the station just as she saw one of the new-fangled electric trains pulling out of an adjacent platform.

'Brighton Station. All change.'

She tuned out to the repeated announcement.

'Thank you for letting me bore you,' her elder said, lifting his cap to her. 'I'm Donald Perks.'

'You didn't bore me, Mr Perks. In fact your comments have put me into a contemplative mood,' she admitted as he held the door open for her to alight onto platform eight.

He sighed. 'Forgive me, it was not my intention to spoil your day.'

They walked up the platform, side by side. 'No, not at all but you've made me realise there is so much more important going on than shopping for a voyage.'

'Good grief, how wonderful, a voyage? Where are you off to?'

'I'm a companion to two children and their family is taking a trip east.'

'Marvellous. How far east?'

'Egypt, as I understand it.'

'Port Said?' He queried, sounding astonished.

She grinned. 'Yes. Is it really that shocking? Including the Holy Land, so we're sailing the Red Sea. Sounds so biblical. Have you been there?'

'No. I wouldn't hesitate, though. I envy you.'

'Don't, I'd be very happy if it were cancelled, especially now with talk of war.'

'I shouldn't have raised it,' he said, gesturing for her to go first.

Stella handed over her ticket for clipping.

'If it's any consolation, the British have driven out the Turks that were occupying it after the Great War. Now we're more interested in gathering information on what the Germans and Russians are up to in the region.'

'Really?'

'Oh, yes. You've no doubt heard the adage that information is power? Well, Jerusalem is a bit of a focus for us with what is happening in Palestine and the struggles there, but generally the whole region is a target in terms of its strategic importance for shipping, resources, trade routes . . .'

'So, Britain is spying on what the Germans are up to in the Middle East?'

He gave her a look of horror, a finger to his lips as they emerged, jostling with other passengers into the Brighton terminus forecourt. 'Spy is a sinister word. No, we've had our people overseeing local government but places like Transjordan are now states in their own right. It's more a case that we keep our ear to the ground for any shifts in the balance of power, especially in terms of Germany and its new power-hungry leader. Those restless nomadic tribes carry information that we find useful. We keep a presence, that's all.' He shrugged. 'Anyway, Miss —'

'Myles.'

'You've been a most enjoyable companion.'

She grinned, holding out her hand, which he gently shook once.

'Safe travels in the Levant.'

'Thank you, Mr Perks.'

He raised his cap, smiled warmly and strode off down the hill into Brighton. She looked around at the busy forecourt with its mix of horse-drawn cabs moving slowly around the faster, more nimble motorised versions. The older way would be cheaper.

'Western Road?' one of the cabbies called, catching her attention and making a soothing sound to his horses. 'Steady now.'

'Yes, er, that's the main shopping district, isn't it?'

'Indeed it is, Miss. Tuppence, please. You can alight at the clock tower and turn left into East Street for Hanningtons Department Store.'

She paid her coin and clambered up into the carriage, smiling at the four other passengers.

Her thoughts helplessly roamed back to the potential for war. If Rafe worked in London and was connected with governmental departments – as Basil had alluded – wouldn't he then be informed on these new developments in Germany? Why would they walk across the Weald of Kent, collecting butterflies and making daisy chains as if the world was safe and wonderful if war was brewing again? Why would Kew Gardens need his help cataloguing plants of the desert if the government was more concerned with cataloguing insurgency or, more to the point, German infiltration? And Rafe, a linguist of some stature, it seemed? Why didn't he teach his children French, if he was fluent?

Questions bounced around her mind as she barely noticed their rocking motion down the hill.

'Clock tower!' she heard the driver say.

'Oh, that's me. Excuse me.' She tiptoed, careful of treading on her fellow passengers' feet, and a boy riding at the back of the coach hopped down to open the door for her.

'Thank you, Miss. Enjoy your day.'

She smiled at him. 'The driver mentioned Hanningtons?' she said hopefully.

He pointed east. 'Straight down there and on your right. Can't miss it, Miss.'

They both smiled at his pun before he hauled himself back onto the carriage and rapped the top. The horses were clicked on and the vehicle lurched away.

Stella could see the promenade from where she stood and the greyish sea in the distance. The day had turned cool and the sun that had delivered a warmish morning was now clouded over. She shivered, pulled her coat collar up higher and skipped across the road, turning left into the broad and busy East Street. People moved in a flowing stream but she was not daunted. Coming from London meant the Brighton streets were far from threatening and despite the gloomy thought of war pervading in her mind, she was intrigued to see this southern department store that she recalled her customers used to talk about.

The large store was easy to find – not just by its commanding four-storey domination of the eastern end of the street with its high Victorian Gothic style. It even wrapped itself around the corner, which she presumed turned from North into fashionable East Street. The store seemed to be like a magnet, luring flocks of people through its doors.

She entered its darker world with muted lighting and noted the columns that dotted the ground floor around the main counters where impeccably dressed staff served their clients in genteel quiet, peppered with soft gales of laughter. It smelled polite and rich, not nearly so colourful as Bourne & Hollingsworth, but Stella was instantly charmed by its faded grandeur. She overheard a pair of women move by her suggesting they take tea, and given that she'd barely touched her breakfast, a pot of tea sounded irresistible. It was past midday but it was still early enough for hours of shopping ahead. She followed the waft of perfume and fur-collared coats of the well-heeled women up the stairs to the tearooms.

'Just for one, Miss?' the waitress asked in a long black-skirted uniform.

'Yes, please. Is there a window table, by any chance?'

The girl smiled. 'Follow me.'

She was led to a table next to one of the tall windows. 'I'll have a pot of black tea with milk, please.'

'Thank you,' the girl said, scribbling her note but Stella was already looking away out into East Street where the changeable British weather had indeed changed and umbrellas were being dragged out. Suddenly there was a slow-moving dance of black domes beneath her.

So Rafe could speak Arabic, amongst other languages; it made sense, given Beatrice's explanation of his childhood this morning. She wondered how Rafe had sold his wife the idea of a tutor in the first place. Maybe it was a status symbol to have a governess in tow, she decided, as she gazed absently while peeling off gloves. She couldn't wait a moment longer, public place or not; she would read his letter now and hope for some enlightenment.

'Hello, Stella.'

She swung her head back in disbelief at the voice she knew well and was disappointed in herself for yearning to hear it.

Rafe beamed at her. 'Glad I found you.' No words came easily. She stared at his confident smile as he shrugged off his overcoat. 'Warm in here,' he said, ignoring her shocked silence. The waitress arrived with Stella's tea.

'Shall I take your coat, Sir?' she offered as she set the pot down. Stella watched him charm the girl as he handed her his coat and hat. 'And can I get you something?' The innuendo was there, Stella noted with dismay. How did he do that to so many women . . . including her?

'A tea would be perfect. Black with lemon, please.'

The waitress cast her a swift glance that Stella was sure said 'lucky you' and moved away.

'Why are you here?' she asked.

He lifted a shoulder. 'I had some early business in London and had a driver bring me down to Brighton.'

'I don't believe in coincidence.'

He gave a soft smirk that felt like respect when it landed on her. 'Neither do I.'

16

Stella gazed across the table to where Rafe was seated opposite, looking to all intents as comfortable as if they were a couple who had arrived together. There was not a mote of sheepishness in his returning glance.

'So you came looking for me?'

'I discovered you were headed for Brighton today when I rang Harp's End.'

'Do you know that you never answer a question?'

'No.' He laughed. 'There, I just answered one. Now, one for you; have you read my letter?'

She met his gaze, wishing it didn't have such a disarming effect on her. 'Not yet.' He lifted an eyebrow. 'You said I had to read it away from the house.'

'Yes, I did,' he admitted.

Stella knew she should have left it at that, but he made her feel defensive and that she had let him down or snubbed their special connection by delaying opening the envelope. 'If it wasn't Beatrice demanding my time, it was Mrs Boyd, and if not her probably listening at your study door, then Hilly was banging on it just as I began to read it. Then I thought I'd read it on the train but I was surrounded by other people's noises and conversations. And then,' she waved a hand in exasperation, 'I had every intention of reading it over my pot of tea . . .' She only just stopped from glaring at him for interrupting her plan. 'It feels as though everything is conspiring to prevent me reading it. No one is cooperating enough to leave me alone!'

'Not even me,' he remarked with a broad grin that was meant to charm. Stella showed no amusement. The waitress was back with his drink and perhaps it was Stella's soft scowl that suggested she didn't linger. He turned his head slightly to one side. 'It will explain so much.'

'Why don't you explain . . . now?'

'All right, ask me. Ask me anything and I'll answer you fully.'

She fixed him with a stare. There were so many questions to hurl at him. She didn't want to argue or make accusations yet. She would begin with the least important. 'You speak Arabic.'

'Is that a question?'

'Do you speak Arabic?'

'I do.' He sipped, sighing with pleasure at the taste.

'Why didn't you tell me?'

'You didn't ask and it never came up.'

She kept her tone even but firm. 'How does someone like you come to speak Arabic?'

He shrugged. 'Well, Stella, I was born in Tangier and anyone like me who spent an early childhood roaming around the Levant with adventuring parents is going to pick up its language easily.'

She remembered the photographs she had studied and the easy grin of the boy that she sensed still lurked in the man opposite her. Other women glanced around but he appeared oblivious, with his eyes fixed on her, as if she and he were alone in the room.

'Other languages.' At his amusement she quickly adjusted her statement to a question and even though Beatrice had confirmed it, she still needed to hear it from him. 'Do you speak any other languages?' She was avoiding what she wanted to ask, determined to be calm, fully in control when she did confront his alleged womanising in particular.

'Yes,' he answered obediently. 'German, French, of course, and some Spanish. I can swear in Italian and pray in Hebrew when pressed. I could probably even rustle up some polite words in Russian if my life depended on it – not many, though; a thank you, a please, that sort of thing.' He managed to look sheepish as he put his cup down and a hand up in submission at her glowering expression. 'What's wrong, Stella? Yes, I do speak some languages, but before you ask, I don't have time to coach the girls in the same way that a tutor employed for that reason can. Besides, my experience tells me that children will always work harder for an outsider than a parent whom they're too familiar with.'

She blinked. His rationale was more than feasible. 'And still I feel manipulated.' There, she'd begun her strategic attack.

'Well, don't.'

'And so your "not exactly" visit to Brighton somehow brings you to Hanningtons, where if you look around is populated almost exclusively by women. How odd of you to choose here.'

His gaze didn't shift. It only intensified upon her. His tone, however, had a slight note of injury. 'Georgina told me she would need a lift home from Hanningtons too. I offered because I knew I might have a chance to see you.'

'I don't need a lift home. I have a ticket, thank you.'

'What's really bothering you? Why so hostile, Stella?'

'Because Georgina is about to expose us.'

'Expose us?'

She wanted to beat her fists against him for being deliberately obtuse. 'We've talked intimately in front of Grace in the car, we've kissed on the hill —'

'I kissed a frog once.' He shrugged and was about to say more but Stella's short burst of a helpless laugh escaped.

She hadn't wanted to be amused; maybe it was all the nervous energy swirling inside. 'You're not at all worried are you, but I feel helpless!'

'Why helpless?'

'Because you've made me so,' she growled. 'It's a skill of yours. Women are in your thrall.' She expected him to grin in his disarming way. He didn't.

'Firstly, Stella, Georgina wasn't there in the car so whatever she thinks she knows, it's still only supposition. And I assure you, no one saw us on the hillside. As to my supposed skill with women, romantically I'm only interested in one.'

She couldn't help the spreading warmth of pleasure his statement gave her but she refused to let it show. 'Yes, the wrong one.'

'You know about me and Mrs Boyd?'

Her unexpected laughter made her sip of tea go down the wrong way and she was suddenly coughing as well as laughing with an image of the lemon-lipped Mrs Boyd swooning in Rafe's arms. She could see he was enjoying teasing her and in truth, it was helping her to let go of the early fear about Georgina. She was still worried but his presence had a calming effect. People who had looked over at them especially after her small explosion of coughing and laughter had returned to their conversations. Stella tried again after putting down her cup and clearing her throat. 'And it's going to get us both into a lot of trouble if Georgina carries out her threat to expose us. Grace overheard me saying about not wanting to be the other woman, she's talked about it with Georgina and . . .' She looked around, concerned that she may have been heard or that people were watching too closely. They were not, but her shoulders slumped in a sense of defeat.

Rafe appeared unaffected by the news that had felt shattering to her just hours earlier. 'She won't expose us . . . not even with the little she thinks she knows.'

'Why?'

He gave a careless shrug and sat back. 'Georgina is like her mother. She has already grasped the true power of information. She appreciates that it can be used to her advantage. What's to be gained by her claims, and there's always a risk we can wriggle out of it. No, I know Georgina well enough to confidently suggest that her plan will be to leverage what she thinks she has on us.'

'Blackmail?'

He lifted a shoulder. 'An unpleasant word. I think she'd regard it more as compensation.'

Stella sneered. Nevertheless she considered the fact that she may not be exposed and that Georgina might be bribed to stay quiet. She wrapped her hands around her china cup, warming them distractedly. Rafe must have noticed it was empty and without asking poured her tea. 'So what does Georgina want?' she asked.

'I can't answer that. I've never understood her motivations. Georgina knows a lot of people and a lot of her peers like to be seen with her but I'm sure if I asked her to name a single friend – someone she could trust, someone she can count on – I doubt she could.'

'That's dreadful.'

'She's made it that way. Georgina doesn't let people in. I think she feels deeply insecure and I suspect when she finds someone whose love she doesn't question and who stands up to her, she'll learn to trust; not find it so necessary to be on the attack all the time.'

'You don't feel sorry for her?'

'Not in the least. I struggle to like her these days although there was a time I freely gave my love to her, but she has grown into someone I find morbidly dull. In fact, I don't admire anything about her. I've watched her grow up and provided for her so that makes me feel responsible for her, but she's essentially the product of her mother's over-protective, over-indulgent and cool upbringing.'

'That's so harsh, Rafe.' Stella couldn't believe she was defending the two women she least liked.

'Well, Georgina is nearly seventeen. I had lads fighting alongside me in war who were younger, braver, kinder . . .'

'That's unfair.'

He drained his tea and sighed. 'Now who's being harsh?'

'She's not known war, its demands or hardships. She's been raised in wealth, ruthlessly indulged and it's pointless you complaining because you were one of the people who let it happen. You could have been the difference in her life.'

'I'm not her father.'

'Yes, but as far as Georgina knows, you *are* her father and certainly the only one who has been in her life. Your responsibility in taking her on was to fill that role. Instead you've taken a hands-off approach.'

'Her mother wanted it that way. She kept me at a distance.'

'I blame you both for how Georgina is. She has everything and yet she has nothing. She's so empty it's despicable.'

Rafe stared at her and she felt his admiration hug her. 'I love you all stirred up like this.'

'Do you?'

'Yes, it's refreshing.'

'Love me, I mean?' she said, ignoring the compliment. There. The main question. She sounded calm but she wasn't in control. Her stomach felt as though she was riding the Big Dipper again as she had in her teens at Blackpool, screaming alongside her father's groaning laughter.

He looked down, clearly taken by surprise. 'I do.'

'You don't know me.'

'Other way around, I suspect.'

There was no denying that. An awkward pause stretched. She had to tackle his reputation as a rake.

'John Potter warned me you were a wolf.'

He gusted a bright laugh and then gave a low howl and Stella shooshed him, embarrassed.

'You sound proud of the label,' she remarked, her tone huffy.

He reached across to touch her hand but she pulled it away quickly. 'Stella, John Potter barely knows me.'

'He knows that you seduce plenty of women.'

'Does he?'

She nodded, swallowing visibly, feeling small and embarrassed.

His gaze held her until she looked away. 'What do you think, Stella?'

'He's looking out for me?'

'Do you trust him?'

'I have no reason to mistrust him,' she bleated. 'And he is worried that I am falling in love with you.'

'And are you?'

'Yes! Damn you, Rafe. The falling is over. I'm already at the bottom of the chasm!' She began gathering her things.

His large hand found hers again and this time she didn't pull away. 'Stella . . . no, wait, Stella. Please, listen to me. You know I am not what I seem at home . . . agreed?'

'Agreed.'

'What I want Potter to think is what Potter thinks. The truth is not necessarily what he imagines it to be, in the same way that bumbling Douglas Ainsworth is not me.'

She felt her gaze narrow. 'What's to be gained by lying to Mr Potter?'

'Well, if you'd read the letter you might understand, but let me assure you that while I am no saint I am no womaniser either. The fact that I'm happy to let people think otherwise suits me. Frankly, the majority of women bore me, Stella. Beautiful and vacant, or brilliant and lacking in femininity – I've not been lucky to meet anyone who stirred my emotions into the perfect cocktail until I danced with you.'

Fresh warmth was spreading, lower this time. 'What are we going to do?' she whispered, feeling suddenly lost.

'Do you wish you'd never gone to the dance, Stella?'

'Yes.' Then shook her head sadly. 'No.'

He pulled her towards him and she instantly felt less rudderless. 'Come on.' Rafe stood.

'Where are we going?'

'Away from here.'

'What about my wardrobe?'

'I can fix everything. Meet me downstairs. Go to the East Street corner entrance and head right to the seafront. I'll catch up with you.'

'I've no idea where I'm going.'

'Follow the smell of the sea.'

It sounded a welcome idea to leave the stuffy tearooms and the claustrophobic atmosphere of chortling women.

'I'll get the bill,' he said, reaching into his pocket for some coins.

She grabbed her gloves and sped downstairs, barely thanking her waitress, not sure what she was hurrying towards or from. She angled her way to the front of the store via the ground-floor fashion accessories of hosiery, gloves, umbrellas and a crowded perfume counter.

'Excuse me,' she asked a lady counting handkerchiefs. 'I've lost my bearings. Could you tell me the way to East Street, please?'

The woman pointed over her shoulder with a smile. 'Yes, of course, Madam. Just over there is Hanningtons Corner and that fronts onto East Street.'

'Thank you.' She moved purposefully in that direction and was dismayed to spot Georgina trying on a straw hat. She knew Hanningtons was the only place a woman of her means would shop in Brighton, so she shouldn't be surprised to see her. Nevertheless she froze momentarily but then, as if scooped up by invisible angels, she was moving; she could swear she couldn't feel the carpet beneath her feet. Picking up a huge hat to cover her face, she turned her back to Georgina and moved swiftly behind a pillar. She didn't pause, knew she hadn't been spotted and gratefully blended into the slipstream of other hurrying shoppers dipping their heads, pulling up collars and swirling scarves around themselves as they scuttled out of the store with Stella in their midst. With the hat returned, she forced herself to walk at a normal pace until she'd passed through the corner doors and then burst out, scurrying down the street, swallowing cold air, gasping as if choking from the tension of escape. Stella headed right as instructed towards the sea. Still dragging in lungfuls of air she had to lean against a wall because her heart felt as though it was pounding so hard she could sense the throb at her temple.

'Are you all right, Miss?' a young woman asked. She was in the uniform of the tearooms at Hanningtons.

'Yes . . . yes, just a headache,' she lied.

'Why don't you come into the warm and —'

'Thank you, I shall be fine,' she replied with an embarrassed smile. 'The sea air will clear it.' Stella pushed off the wall and pleaded with her feet to keep her moving.

She pulled a silk headscarf out of her bag and wrapped it around her hair, tying a knot under her chin. She hurried down the street, trying to put as much distance between her and the suspicious Georgina as she could.

She glimpsed the seafront ahead; she could hear it now as well as see its vast greyness and that colour wouldn't change, she suspected, because the weather felt to be cooling by the minute. So much for being on the cusp of summer! A wind had picked up and blew harder, cutting past her overcoat and whistling around her ears to make her bend her head to keep her eyes from watering. It nearly blew her back around the corner as she rounded it and this part of the seafront looked almost deserted, save a few hardy souls pushing prams.

She gasped at the temperature drop now that she was exposed and she glanced around for where she might shelter. There was nowhere. Stella looked left and stopped a passer-by.

'Excuse me, please, Sir, where does this lead?' She pointed.

'To the Old Steine.'

'Steine?'

'Bus terminus.' The fellow flicked a cigarette, pulled his collar up and lurched on. He looked like a worker coming off a shift and eager to be home. She couldn't blame him. She followed in his path, heading back towards Hove, wondering whether it mattered if Rafe found her. What did he expect of her? What possible future was there for them? Her instincts told her she should run in the other direction; go straight home to London and send for her belongings from Harp's End and forget the name Rafe Ainsworth and his wretched letter. Forget the soulful, searching gaze that made her feel naked, or the mellow – often sardonic – manner that teased her, or even the smooth voice that rarely raised itself beyond calm and which seemed to make her feel safe. Forget the boy in the photos and the Arabian desert that she wished she could share with him and hear him speak its language. She hardly knew him, anyway – certainly wasn't much the wiser since their first meeting. She knew she must force herself not to recall his touch, the hardness of his body, the softness of his mouth . . . his tongue, his . . . Stella gave a small cry as someone grabbed her and pulled her into a doorway. It was dark and smelled damp but it didn't matter because for all the instinctive warning bells clamouring within, it was Rafe who held her. The voice she thought she could ignore, the gaze she thought she could forget and the mouth she hoped she wouldn't crave made instant mockery of her resolve. Confronted by him, her best intentions melted away.

'Sorry for startling you,' he said softly and cupped her face. 'May I kiss you?'

'If you don't, I'll die.' She loved the bright smile that parted his lips and stretched his cheeks, fired his eyes and changed his brooding presence.

Stella forgot where she was for several heartbeats, lost in his affection, heedless of being seen kissing in a doorway like a . . . The thought made her pull away sharply.

'Rafe, this makes me feel like a —'

He pulled away. 'Don't say it.'

'Why not? It's how I'm behaving. On the open street, no less.'

He stepped back, pulled his coat closed and reached for her hand. 'All right, then. Will you come with me?'

'To where?'

'Somewhere safe, away from prying eyes.'

'Will it make me feel less like a street girl?'

'That's up to you.'

She took his hand, allowed him to lead her. As they walked, he put his arm around her, pulled her tightly to him, and Stella knew they couldn't be physically closer if they tried. And as soon as she thought it, she knew she must adjust that notion . . . they could be closer. Stella walked, no longer allowing herself to think on anything specific. If she did, she knew she might tear herself free and run like a frightened rabbit. Instead, she anchored herself to the safety of his warmth and bulk and cleared her mind of all thought. *It wasn't wrong* . . . With Rafe everything felt safe, everything felt right.

17

It was like moving in a dream state; she was with the single person she wanted to be alongside and suddenly nothing from outside their special bubble of intimacy could intrude. Her awareness of his presence was heightened to being able to pick out the sound of his individual footsteps on the pavement while the colour and sounds of everything else around her appeared to fade. The lonely cry of seagulls swooping on the beaches became distant sound, while even the rhythmic break of the waves on the foamy shore dragging shingle back against the sucking sands became simply a sigh on the edge of her consciousness. She barely saw passers-by smile, or men who lifted their hats in a silent salutation.

Rafe did, though. He was seemingly focused for both of them; nodding, touching his hat in turn, while all she could concentrate on was her escalating heartbeat. She fixed her gaze on the traditionally whitewashed buildings of Brighton to calm the timpani of fear, to anchor herself, but her eye tripped on a large terracotta façade. Where were they? She was walking up some stairs and then he was guiding her through a revolving door. He did all the work. Her job was to put one foot in front of the other, no words exchanged.

There were voices, people smiled at her. She managed to nod but no smile would come. Stella drifted away to look up at massive vaulted white and gold ceilings. She passed a smoking room with club chairs upholstered in soft leather, small Persian rugs. Where was this place?

They were now following the footsteps of a young man in a uniform. 'Would you like to wait for the lift? It's the third floor, Sir.'

'We shall be fine with the stairs. In fact, just give us the key. We have no luggage, as you can see.'

'Er . . . fine, Sir.'

'My friend needs a rest. She's come over a little faint.'

'Can I fetch you —'

'No, she just needs some quiet for a few hours. I'll sit with her and order some tea and sandwiches later, perhaps.'

'Very good, Sir.'

Stella watched some coins change hands.

'Come on, Stella,' Rafe said and they were climbing one of the grandest staircases she could imagine with its sweeping ascent of wide marble stairs over which chandeliers hung from magnificent archways. She could appreciate it and yet felt disconnected from the beauty as though moving in a trance. Stella heard a door close and with its soft click became fully aware that they were alone in a vast chamber. Its series of tall windows opened onto a long balcony that overlooked the promenade to the beach where the breeze over the English Channel was stirring the waves into gentle white caps.

'It smells beautiful in here,' she remarked.

'The Brighton Metropole was built just over forty years ago and has its own perfumier. They use it to scent their rooms,' he said, still by the door. 'Speaking of rooms, this is not the most lavish, I regret.'

'No, that might attract attention,' she murmured to herself.

'It's booked under your name but I can stay a while without raising suspicions.'

Rafe must have seen her shiver because he walked across the vast expanse of carpet to draw the curtains, which immediately darkened the room mutely lit by a single standard lamp. Stella moved away from the windows and the world outside to where a fire danced in the ornate marble fireplace. He arrived silently behind her to help her off with her coat; his had already been cast carelessly across a sofa together with his hat. She followed suit, removing gloves, scarf and hat. It kept her nervous hands occupied and Stella wondered if he felt the same way.

'I went for the ensuite with hot water rather than cold or sea water,' he said. She heard the awkwardness; was relieved by his uncertainty.

'How long do we have?' Stella hated how her simple query sounded vulgar.

'Long enough,' he replied, picking up that hidden question, oddly lacking in his usual adroitness with words. She waited, forcing him to be more accurate. 'I said I'd pick up Georgina at six.' Stella wanted to glance at her watch. He saved her the trouble. 'Nearly four hours.' Now he sounded sheepish.

Long enough, she allowed to echo through her mind. Long enough to tumble into bed, long enough to fall so deeply in love she would be ruined for others, long enough to spoil each other's lives . . . and those who loved them.

'Stella, listen, if you don't —'

'But I do!' she declared, finally emerging from the stupor. 'I just don't trust our wisdom.' She looked up and his expression was filled with sympathy. She could sense the longing that tiptoed across the tightrope that stretched the short distance between them. Her yearning to be in his arms wobbled its way straight back to him. 'I mean . . . there's no going back,' she offered, her words sounding tremulous. 'We can't undo it. We won't be able to change the hurt it may cause to ourselves or, more importantly, to others.'

'I'm impressed you can think of others in this moment when all I want to do is —'

'Then just do it, Rafe,' she whispered, unable to bear the tension any longer. *To hell with others* whipped through her mind. To hell with having to be responsible all the time; to hell with the world beyond this warm room with the wind blowing people's hats off outside and flames dancing joyously inside, burning with the same hot intent that was coursing through her.

At her challenge spangles of desire stirred deeply and began to pulse in time with her heartbeat, except this time the drumming was a throbbing need. He moved nimbly, silently, and pulled her so close Stella lost her breath. She clung to him, losing herself in the delirium of lust within his embrace. Nestling within the absurd loss of control was a curious sense of safety that his arms provided – here she was home, here she was secure, here no one else intruded.

Clothes were being unbuttoned, eased off shoulders and hips to pool at the floor like discarded skins, leaving them with nothing standing between their flesh . . . no longer even her conscience. That had floated from her when he'd unclasped a final layer of her clothing and the cold had urged her nipples erect. His arms had stolen around to hold her, helpless hands reaching to cup her breasts. Guilt tiptoed away to vaporise in the flames, which were now the only sound in the room to accompany their heartbeats that Stella was sure she could hear. She swung around to face him.

The fire's warmth couldn't touch the heat searing in his gaze. 'Stella . . .' he murmured, stepping back slightly, heedless of his hard nakedness, his voice struggling to get past the passion that was clogging in his throat.

'Don't say any more,' she said, hoping it didn't sound too much of a plea. 'Show me.'

He picked her up as easily as she recalled him lifting Grace and she instantly forced herself to banish that memory, or it would allow all those obstacles back into her conscience. She wanted her mind to remain empty, like the wilderness he loved – whether it was desert or the Weald – and where there was only the parched need for each other.

Rafe laid her gently on the coverlet and the cool of the satin pricked her skin to gooseflesh.

'Are you cold?' he whispered and began pulling away the covers until even cooler sheets made her shiver slightly.

She shook her head but it didn't matter. He was suddenly next to her, his body also pounding with obvious desire yet he deliberately held back while he gazed the length of her in the dim light. She could tell he wanted to talk, wanted to prolong this time that perhaps they might never have again. But Stella didn't want any words in the way right now; words often led people to places they didn't want to go. Words might lead Rafe and herself away from this cocoon back to Harp's End, where people who loved him and trusted them both lived. Or perhaps even London, or St Albans, to where those who loved and depended on her waited.

Her thoughts tripped on the vision of the faces of innocents. *This is madness. This is selfish. This is —*

His mouth tenderly closed upon her lips and sealed her doubt. She wanted him. Stella arched her back to reach up and pull Rafe closer, harder to her and he responded eagerly; seemingly all of his tentativeness had fled too. He pulled the sheets up over them as he moved to cover her body with his – it felt like the tent she'd seen him peeping out from as a boy . . . the place she'd wanted to share with him.

All thought blanked as Stella rode her passion to a height she didn't know was possible and where, in the cosmos of a breathless, beautiful ache of desire, she discovered her new sense of belonging, her true home, which was Room 19 of the Metropole, in his arms . . . moving with him to their own rhythm as their selfish pleasure gave her a sense of healing. Rafe was the conjuror working his magical, cleansing affection on her that stripped away all her past grief and replaced it with tender loving. Her excitement escalated further by his sighing relief as pleasure trembled through him and Stella let go then, giving herself completely. She thought she may have whispered his name as they slipped quietly down the gentler slope to the liquid warmth of their entangled bodies.

Stella made a nest in his arms and settled in with a soft sigh. With the back of his fingertips Rafe traced the shape of her neck and shoulder, passing down the length of her ribs to her hip. There his hand rested, releasing her from the ticklish sensation that had made her smile.

'What are you thinking?' he asked softly, kissing her forehead, his lips lingering on her skin.

'That I love you,' she replied, not giving herself even a moment to consider whether to spill this truth.

'Thank heavens for that. I thought you were going to start muttering about who we're hurting.'

She turned to look at him, ensuring he wasn't teasing her. 'No. I've already considered that.'

Rafe propped himself on an elbow. 'And?' He gazed deeply into her eyes and she could tell he was vulnerable.

'I don't care. I hate myself, but . . .' Stella shrugged. 'It's no good hiding behind bluster or empty words. The truth is I simply don't have enough room in my heart for anyone but you.'

'Your brother and sister?'

'It doesn't hurt them. I am providing for them.'

'Grace?'

She paused. Grace was the one person who might suffer in the equation of their adultery. 'Grace is a child. She can't begin to understand what is happening here.'

'She loves her mother.'

'Yes, but I suspect the truth is more that she wants her mother to love her in the same way that her father loves her. The latter fact hasn't changed because of us, and I refuse to be held accountable for whatever lacks in her mother.'

He considered this. 'And speaking of Beatrice . . .'

Stella lifted a shoulder, her lips thinning. 'Beatrice loves you but in an almost sinister way. I can't speak for her but I can tell you that my feelings come from a different place. I can put my hand on my heart and swear this love stems from purity, not for gain . . . not for a husband, not for status, not for wealth, not for any form of acquisition other than your love in return. If we had to live in a hovel and catch rabbits for food, I suspect my feelings for you would sustain me through the challenge.' She grew serious. 'I thought you wanted to avoid crowding all the others into this bed with us?'

He laughed sadly. 'I do, and yet they loom over us, don't they?'

There was no denying it.

'Dear Stella.' He squeezed her hip. 'Trapping rabbits will not be necessary.'

She turned to face him, in a position suddenly to study individual hair stubble in his chin, the soft suggestion of the dimple she sensed from his childhood, the thick, dark flop of hair that had fallen across his forehead, which she tenderly pushed back. 'I was trying to make a point.'

'Which I do understand. However, I don't wish you to become anxious. Things must change.'

'Do you mean in your life?'

'In all our lives.' Rafe sounded wistful.

'What does that mean?'

'I don't know. There are others beyond our family in this bed, Stella.' She frowned, puzzled, waiting for him to elaborate. 'The old enemy in Germany is beginning to gain strength again.'

She blinked. *Germany*. That was a twist in their conversation she hadn't seen coming. 'Adolf Hitler's in our bed?'

'We can jest but he seems to have a plan in mind for Germany and there's nothing shy about it.'

'War?' she whispered, vaguely horrified to be having a second conversation about it in the same day. It was time to come clean with him. 'Rafe, I have to own up to something but you must promise you won't be angry with me.'

'Have you ever heard me angry?'

'I have, actually.'

'Oh, really,' he mocked.

'Last night.'

He made a clicking sound in his palate. 'That wasn't anger with Beatrice; that was years of disappointment and despair. If anything —'

'I'm not talking about that,' she cut in, embarrassed. She wanted to own up quickly. 'I'm talking about later, when you spoke to Basil.'

Rafe's unflappable demeanour slipped and his expression clouded.

'It was an accident. I was expecting a late call from Suzanne Farnsworth, you see.'

He waited.

'After your argument with Beatrice I stayed in my room, too embarrassed I suppose by what I had witnessed to be confronted again. You came to my door and I . . . well, you know what I did. Later, I tiptoed to the parlour to get a snack. I could hear you stomping about upstairs and, well, frankly, I wanted to put some distance between us. I was on my way back to my room when the phone rang in the main hall. It was so loud I thought it would wake the entire household. I remembered Suzanne and dashed to the phone.' She looked anxiously at him but couldn't read his expression.

'But I answered first,' he said.

'I didn't know what to do. I was damned either way.'

The silence lengthened between them like a dark cavern

suddenly opening up. She stroked his cheek. 'Rafe, I would never repeat anything.'

'I know. It's why I can trust you.'

'What do you mean?'

He leaned back and checked his wristwatch. 'I'm sorry, Stella, I have to go.'

'Wait! You can't leave it like this. You're angry with me.'

'I'm not angry with you. I'm glad you overheard. Now read the letter. Like it or not, you're involved now in an effort to prevent a potential war.'

Stella shook her head.

He sat on the side of the bed. She felt suddenly cold . . . hollow. 'The future is uncertain for all of us,' he warned.

'Is that your way of telling me to forget this happened?'

Rafe moved above her to stare even more intently. 'No! It's to tell you *never* to forget this occurred, no matter what happens.'

She was unnerved by the ferocity in his look. 'I shouldn't have been so honest.'

'Stella, it's your honesty I admire most about you.'

'Then be honest with me. Why are we here?'

Rafe sighed, searched her face. 'We're here because I couldn't bear that our moment on the Weald yesterday was the one and only time I'd kiss you.'

'So you did follow me today?'

He nodded. 'I suggested you'd need a wardrobe for our voyage. I suspected my wife would send you here rather than London where she was headed.'

'Rafe, this is real for me. But I can't live as an adulteress. As it is, when we leave the haven of this room I'm going to feel like a mistress . . . or worse.'

He tried to shoosh her, frowning at her sentiments, but she pushed on. 'My mind is made up. You're the one with the decision to make.'

'And you're the one with the power to break my heart,' he admitted.

'I'm going to ask you again. Do you love me?'

He took a long, slow breath. 'To tell you the truth, I'm terrified by how I feel about you.'

'What does that mean?'

He rolled back to lie against her, covered them both with the sheets to keep the chill off. 'I've never felt this way about anyone.'

Stella wanted to scream her relief. Instead she reached up to stroke his face. 'And?'

'I might ruin your life and everyone else I care about in the bargain because of it.'

The joy turned bitter in her throat. 'Why?'

'I'm no good for you, Stella.'

She pushed him away now and sat up, heedless of the cold or her bareness. 'I can't believe you've just said that.'

Rafe clutched her to him, holding her back against his chest, his arm pinning her close.

'I have never loved anyone as I love you and even though we've spent so little time together I feel we know each other. And I sense you already believe that I am dangerous.'

'You're mysterious,' she qualified. 'You have secrets but I am not frightened by you. I know you're a spy of sorts. None of that is my concern.'

'But it might be,' he warned.

'I don't care. I just want you to be in love with me as I am with you.'

'Beatrice has no impact on me. I come and go as I please. She makes few demands other than fidelity.'

Stella's shoulders slumped. 'That's fair.'

'But I have not been faithful to her. Beatrice gets out of our marriage what she set out to gain . . . status, security and the husband she wants. I am discreet in my few dalliances and they are far fewer than I'm sure many might believe, especially Mr Potter.'

'I see. I hate all of them.'

He pulled her back down, smiling, so he could look at her. 'The point I'm making is that I could never be unfaithful to you. The fact that I now have to return to Harp's End and Beatrice sickens me. You've changed my life – I had it all ordered and in place and you've upset everything.'

'*You* brought me to Harp's End, and under false pretences.'

'Because you're a sorceress who has cast a spell over me.'

She smiled in spite of her glumness.

'The thing is, my darling Stella, I don't think I can even bear for Beatrice to touch me now that I have you so completely in my focus. And she will see that. She won't need her vicious daughter to confirm anything. If she gets so much as a whiff of my devotion to you, she'll poison your future. That's why I am dangerous to you.'

She'd listened but heard something else whispering beneath his words. She had spent too long observing people's mannerisms to not notice the guile in the way he avoided her gaze just for a heartbeat.

'You're lying, Rafe. That's not what you meant.'

He stared back at her, shocked. 'Lying? I'm laying out my heart here.'

'But you're still holding back. Something else unnerves you. What are you scared of?'

'I'm scared of losing you.'

'You won't, not if you love me in the whole way I love you.'

'Love isn't always enough, Stella.'

'I don't believe that.'

'You should. Your parents demonstrated that.'

She sucked in a breath and helpless tears welled. 'How can you throw that at me?'

'Because I have to protect you: from Beatrice, from Georgina, from the grief of your parents and the challenges they've left you with. But especially from me. I have to protect you from the pain I might bring.'

'Are you leaving me today?'

'Not if I can help it.'

'You're running me around in circles. I don't understand what you're hinting at but not saying.'

He gave a nod as though drawing a line beneath their conversation. 'We're going on a voyage, Stella, and you have to be strong and distant from me as I must be with you.'

She hesitated. 'Can you?'

'Yes. I have years of experience of being Douglas or Monty. So, I will seem cold. I need to appear entirely disconnected from you to keep my wife's suspicions unstirred.'

'And then what?'

His expression clouded momentarily. 'I need your help but I'm not sure how just yet. If all goes to plan, when we return I shall be leaving my wife. I doubt she'll agree to a divorce so you need to ask yourself whether you are ready to be the other woman.'

Stella opened her mouth to answer.

'Don't be hasty. Reputation is precious. Consider it long and hard before you decide.'

'What's the point in having an unblemished reputation but living as a miserable spinster?'

He smiled and its warmth burned away her anxiety. 'I love you, Stella. I've loved you since the first moment you sneered at me.'

'I did, didn't I?' She grinned. 'But I thought you were drunk and just out for a good time with whichever girl took your fancy.'

'You saw through me, though.'

Stella nodded, not wanting to spoil this moment, especially as her gloom had been chased away. He loved her. Wasn't that all that mattered?

'What about Grace?'

'We shall work it out. Once the pain passes, Beatrice will accept that she cannot stop me seeing my child. Besides, Grace wouldn't stand for it.'

'Watching Beatrice with you . . .'

He waited, questioningly. She lifted a shoulder in slight defeat. They both knew what she was reaching for.

Rafe smoothed back her hair. 'In years gone it has felt easier to stay than fight her because I've had nothing to fight with. I've not felt passionate enough for anyone to upset my world for.'

'Then knowing that will keep me sane for the coming weeks.'

'You will have to forgive me – I'm apologising now for how heartless I might appear.'

'You're forgiven,' she said, not truly understanding but kissing him softly and immediately feeling his stirrings of passion again. 'How long did you say we have?'

'Just long enough to remind you about what you mustn't forget,' he added, pulling her on top of him as they both dissolved into the intimate laughter of lovers beneath the tousled sheets.

18

She clung to him as they walked back down the seafront and she was glad of the brisk wind that chilled, forcing her to bend into it.

'You should have remained at the hotel. You shouldn't be on the front,' he murmured. 'I'm glad you agreed to stay overnight too.'

'What will Beatrice think?'

'Beatrice isn't thinking about you, darling Stella. Besides, she's up in London. All you'll do if you came home is rattle around at Harp's End trying to avoid me and Georgie. And before you ask, I'll speak to Grace if she's more lively. And you'll be seeing her soon enough.'

She nodded. 'I'm looking forward to staying in that grand hotel but I wanted to hold you a little longer,' she reminded, desperately aware that they would have to part in a minute or so. But just for now the seafront was mostly deserted. 'Imagine this could be crowded with holidaymakers tomorrow. They're forecasting a warm summer.'

'Will you be all right?' he said, ignoring her nervous small talk.

She nodded. 'It's easier than going back to Harp's End straight away. Beatrice suggested I stay overnight so you're right, no one's going to miss me.'

Too soon for her they were back at the same corner. 'We go our separate ways here, Stella.'

'There's so much more I want to say to you,' she admitted.

He nodded sadly. 'But we were too busy.' Rafe glanced around and pulled her back into the doorway of a shop that was closed.

'Come on, Stella. Perk up.'

She shook her head. 'Not sure I can.'

'Why?'

'Because there's no happiness in loving you, Rafe. There's only gloom . . . certainly in the immediate future.'

'Don't say that.'

'She won't let you go. I know she won't. You have nothing to offer her that could make her give you up.'

She knew she spoke the truth. It was reflected in his dark expression.

'I could threaten to expose the truth.'

'About Georgina?'

He nodded. 'And that I don't love either of them.'

'You don't want to hurt them. Or Grace.' All the doubt came home to roost as seagulls let rip with their lonely cries above them, as if sensing her despair. 'No, it's all hopeless.'

'Stella, let me get past this voyage we must take. You heard Basil. I have to meet Joseph —'

'You've told me nothing about him.'

'I will.'

'When?'

'When we're next alone.'

She gave him a look that said she couldn't imagine it occurring again. 'He's your stepbrother according to that conversation with Basil Peach.'

'Joseph is my brother. There is no further qualification. We grew up together as family – there's nothing much else to tell and because he's my brother and asking for me, I will go without further query. As soon as I know more, I'll share it.' He paused. 'Stella?' Her lips pursed with frustration and she looked down, shaking her head. He bent to force her to look at him. 'I need your strength and your smile around me.'

'Even if we can't touch?'

'I'll work something out. But at least I can see you, keep you near. The thought of leaving you is unbearable but I also have to keep you at arm's length to protect you.'

She nodded her understanding.

'Don't let me go alone. It may be . . .'

'May be what?' she asked, searching his face at the sadness she glimpsed.

'I was going to say it may be the last time I see Morocco for a while, if war is a reality. I would like you to see it too.'

'There's so much to talk about – I wanted to ask you about your childhood . . .'

'I give you my word we'll have more time to discuss our pasts.'

'I'm more interested in discussing our future.' Her shoulders drooped forlornly.

Now he did shake her gently. 'Stella . . . you do trust me, don't you?'

She looked up, nodding. 'I know that you love me in the best way that you can. And I know that has to be enough for now.'

'I want you to know this. I was meant to find you. You've opened a door for me, Stella. I see a fresh chance, an opportunity for a new life – the sort I always hoped I might enjoy.'

'So that's why I was put on this earth,' she jested, but it made neither of them smile.

'I didn't mean that,' he said, his eager expression clouding.

'I know. I'm being unfair. But Rafe, being your lover will never be enough. I have dreams too. Maybe I am the one who must distance myself; I'm the one who must be cruel and deny you.'

'Don't, Stella, please . . .'

'It hurts to look at you, especially after today. And it's going to ache to watch you going to bed with Beatrice. It will gall to watch your vicious stepdaughter being facile, smothering you with kisses while callously criticising you.'

'Wait! You have said you love me?'

'I do, much as I loathe myself for such weakness.'

'Then prove it.' Rafe pulled at the lapels of her coat, dragging her closer and kissed her deeply, owning her for the length of that kiss. When she pulled away, he said it again. 'Prove it.'

'How?'

'Don't desert me.'

'Let me go back to London. We can talk on your return. You'll have perspective and so will I,' she urged. It sounded so reasonable, despite her churning emotions.

'No!' Someone walked by and they both looked away from each other guiltily. 'No,' he murmured. 'I need your spirit close and even your smile from a distance warms me. I don't want another day without you, Stella, even if we can't touch.'

Against her instincts, Stella nodded. 'I don't know how you hide that romantic soul of yours.'

'Easy. I only reveal it to people I love. So, since the death of my family, that's you and Grace. Don't resist me, Stella.'

'It seems no matter what I say, I can't,' she admitted.

'Good, now kiss me goodbye.'

Stella stood on tiptoe to pour every ounce of herself into her farewell, loving the way he opened his coat to pull her closer to him in yet another cocoon that was theirs alone.

When finally they broke the link he smiled sadly. 'See you at Tilbury – I won't be at Harp's End when you return. When Georgina asks, I shall deny seeing you.'

Stella sighed. 'I can't wait for the day when we no longer deny each other.'

Rafe pecked her cheek. 'I love you – don't ever forget I said that today.'

'Rafe?' He waited for her. 'Why can't you tell me what's in the letter?'

It was his turn to pause. She watched his hesitation, wondering at the myriad reasons he might present. 'Because when we're together, alone, I just want to make love to you.' It was the right one to make her feel safe. 'When I wrote the letter I wasn't distracted and I could tell you what you need to know in a logical way without you leaping in to ask questions you inevitably would. I needed to say everything, explain what is necessary, so you can absorb it quietly in your time, make your own decisions without the distraction of my presence. I'm sorry that it all sounds so cloak and dagger.'

'I have no choice, do I? I trust you, Rafe. Don't let me down. I was meant to shop today. What shall I tell your wife when she grimaces at my inappropriate wardrobe?'

He winked. 'It's all taken care of.' And then he was gone, hurrying away, his footsteps sounding sad and lonely from the doorway where she stood and only now realised her cheeks were damp with tears.

She hurried back to the hotel, keen to read the letter that he assured would explain so much. Once again she was delayed as she heard a knock at the door.

'Delivery, Miss Myles,' someone called.

She opened the door and a young man from concierge was standing laden with parcels, each with the Hanningtons name emblazoned on it.

'Good grief,' she gushed, shocked.

'They've just arrived for you. Shall I put them over here?' he asked, nodding towards an ottoman.

'Er, yes,' she said, embarrassed for keeping him waiting. 'Over there will be fine.' She'd remade the bed and was glad of that now as she noticed him glance across at it. He was the same person who had offered them a ride in the lift. 'I'm feeling much better, by the way. My friend made me promise I'd order some food.'

'I'm glad to hear it,' he replied, and she realised he was likely well trained in diplomacy.

'Oh, wait,' she said, fishing in her purse for a threepence. 'Thank you for bringing these.'

He palmed the bronze coin. 'Happy to, Miss Myles. Enjoy your stay.'

He closed the door quietly and with held breath Stella began to untie the lids on boxes and the string that held together the loose-wrapped parcels.

She gasped as each exquisite garment was revealed. Rafe said he'd organised everything and he hadn't lied. How had he worked so fast in those minutes while she was panicking about Georgina – perhaps she'd lost track of time. She skipped to the cheval mirror to hold up a deliciously flimsy dress with a floral pink and green summery print with a sash of green the same colour as the nursery at Harp's End. It sported a cloudy ruff collar that floated softly over her shoulders to form a small sleeve. Stella twisted full circle delightedly to watch it fall long, drifting to just above her ankles, and she could see it would follow her body's line tightly and show it off. Stella gave a soft squeal of pleasure at its beauty and then another of dismay at the price. But it was one of six new dresses, each more thrilling than the last, with three suitable for evening. One of these was a magnificent black shift of thin velvet that would surely hug every curve. She teared up at his generosity but mostly his fine taste that wouldn't allow her to look in any way out of place on the ship against the strutting women in his life.

She held the soft velvet of the dinner dress to her cheek,

remembering his touch, and wondered at Rafe's remarks. She would keep her promise and travel with the family, going about her duty. But she also promised herself that everything would change on their return. She knew that she could no longer work for the Ainsworths after this voyage and that she'd better start making plans to return to London permanently in six weeks. She was sure even Beatrice would organise a decent severance pay that would tide her little family over until she could ease back into Bourne & Hollingsworth. After that she couldn't predict the future but hoped it included Rafe.

Stella repacked the clothes, barely looking at the hats and belts, although she tried on the three pairs of shoes, two of which made her feel like Cinderella with a perfect fit and the other evening heels that were slightly loose but she didn't mind. Her feet would swell in the heat, surely?

She rang and ordered a tray of food and was told her soup and bread roll would be twenty minutes. After this she rang concierge, thanked the gentleman on the other end for sending up the parcels and arranged for them to be collected tomorrow morning at nine sharp.

'I shall need a taxi at nine-fifteen please. Would that be possible?'

'Certainly, Miss Myles. I'll advise the front desk that you'll be checking out at nine. Is that suitable for you?'

'That's perfect, thank you,' she said.

Silence settled around her. Distantly she fancied she could hear the waves. She'd missed the sunset and lights now merrily lit the promenade. Stella closed the curtains once again, though. It was time to read Rafe's letter. She slipped the sheaves out of the envelope and was surprised how tense she felt at what might be explained within.

She read the opening again that she was sure she knew by heart, even running her finger across it to touch him somehow through the ink.

My dearest Stella . . . She blew out her breath through her nose in soft exasperation and skipped to the new paragraph.

> *I have so much to say to you but time is short, for reasons neither of us have any control over. Now suddenly life is skipping ahead, making demands of me that are hard to explain, but I need to ask if you can trust me. Do you trust me, beautiful girl?*

'Yes,' she murmured and read on.

> *I realise what I'm scrawling in haste will make little sense, which is why I am relying on your trust. We are going on a voyage, as you know. I am insisting that you come along because I am going to need you to help me. As yet I cannot be sure of how events might unfold so I cannot explain the extent of that assistance. Suffice to say your help is in the interests of everyone's wellbeing – and by everyone, I don't mean my family or yours but the whole of Britain's population.*

She blinked with consternation. What on earth could he mean?

> *I have never told you the full truth but I need you to accept that what I am about to involve you in is between you, myself and the British government. I am employed by the Secret Intelligence Service in clandestine activities in areas where, because of my background, I can move more easily than the regular English gentleman. To this end I must travel to Africa to meet with my Berlin-based brother, Joseph, someone I trust implicitly who has information that might affect the security of Britain and her allies.*

Stella was reassured, knowing that when he wrote this he was not aware of the eavesdropping of that phone conversation, and that he was giving her the truth.

> *I don't think of myself as a spy and yet I suppose that's exactly what I am and how I've been operating for many years now. I go where they send me. Sometimes it is a quick rendezvous with other spies to exchange material; other times I simply observe and bring back information. On occasion I go in what they call 'undercover disguise' as the boffin pretending to study birds or butterflies when I'm indeed studying a political situation, or perhaps a particular person.*
>
> *Regarding Joseph, it's very important I'm able to look him in the eye, Stella. We need few words to communicate – a bit like you and I. We just seem to understand one another and I shall know instantly if he is lying, or simply pretending for different reasons. The fact is, I can't ignore him. The contact has not been made directly so I'm not sure if he's in trouble but it sounds as though he believes he is in possession of vital information that our government should know, and it's my job to get that information safely back to London. He refuses to pass it to anyone else.*
>
> *I am asking for your help because I cannot be sure that he or myself will not be watched and our connection is certainly known, so any cover I might rely on could already be compromised.*
>
> *I know you will have a hundred questions and I'm sorry that I can't answer them, which is where the trust comes in, darling Stella.*

Just make sure you are on that ship. If I can, I will try and see you alone . . . if only to see you smile just for me.

Yours, R.

They'd done more than smile now, she thought humourlessly, as she folded back up the letter. Her lack of humour deepened in the silence of her room. Distantly, if she concentrated hard, she could hear the clangour of plates somewhere in the depths of the hotel and possibly the sound was travelling via fireplaces, elevator shafts, even the stairwells. And then even that vague sound was gone, overwhelmed now by a fresh, urgent one that echoed loudly it seemed in her ears and throbbed in her throat as her heart pounded out the escalating fear of understanding that she was now an aide to a spy. What lay ahead for her? For Rafe? What new danger was she moving towards?

Swallowing her fear, she made herself return to the moment and Room 19 where still her life was safe and the scent of Rafe clung to her. Stella glanced at her watch. It was only nearing seven-thirty. She felt physically exhausted but still couldn't sleep because her mind was moving around in what felt like jagged leaps. She paced the room a few times, her mind blank but her emotions somehow comforted by movement. Finally, she forced herself to sit at the room's desk, found its stationery embossed with gold lettering, and began to write to Carys and Rory. She needed to explain why that calendar they were counting down would need to be adjusted but that when she came back it wouldn't be just for a visit. It would be for keeps.

19

The ship had left New York in the last throes of its winter, or so Stella learned from Grace, whose inquisitive way had discovered a wealth of random facts including that this was the RMS *Aquitania*'s first voyage as a cruise vessel, that it was known as 'the ship beautiful', and that it had collided with another in thick fog during the war years.

'Hmm, that's reassuring, Grace,' she remarked as they leaned over the deck railing and Stella sighed with pleasure at the sight of the vast expanse of ocean.

'There are three classes on this ship. Did you know that, Stella?' her charge lisped.

'I do,' she admitted.

'This is first, where the rich people are,' Grace continued unselfconsciously as Stella blinked, glad to be accommodated in second class because the kind of person walking around on deck here reminded her too much of Beatrice and Georgina. 'Why aren't you here with us?'

'Well, Grace, your father employs me. Therefore I am seen as staff. He could have thrown me into tourist class – that's third class to you. Instead, he has kindly given me a wonderful cabin in second class as a special concession and one that I'm extremely comfortable with.'

'You're luckier than me then because I have to share mine with Georgina.'

'Oh, I'm sure you'll manage,' Stella teased.

She had deliberately kept her distance from the family as best she could, although she'd been on hand to help Grace with her packing as neither of the elder people in her life cared enough other than to say Mrs Boyd would take care of it. Mrs Boyd backed off when Stella became involved and Stella was delighted simply to be around her happy charge again who was no longer as fatigued and the dull headaches she mentioned had begun to lessen in frequency. Rafe had kept his promise and not appeared at Harp's End to her knowledge in that final week and true to his word had all but ignored her quayside before boarding ship. It had been up to her to gather all that he needed for his disguise and she had taken her role seriously of assembling his 'kit' for Kew Gardens, from his sample jars to his microscope. She had even tossed in his notebook from a previous visit to Africa and the Levant.

He'd warned her, of course, about his intended aloofness but seeing him again after that intimate farewell in a shop doorway hadn't stopped her heart from drumming faster, or indeed hurting harder to watch him take Beatrice's arm with such easy affection to escort her up the gangway. Only Grace had bothered to take Stella's hand but she'd lagged, told the youngster to go ahead with her sneering sister, as Stella realised she had been likely left to ensure that the ship's purser had the family's expansive series of trunks brought on board, unpacked and stored away.

When she also had been shown to her cabin by a kindly steward, Stella was silently amazed by the grandeur on board, and for a couple of hours as she explored her new home for the forthcoming weeks she put Rafe aside in her thoughts. She sighed in astonishment at this floating hotel that would carry them off to foreign lands in sumptuous splendour. It included its own cinema and theatre and heavy deep-pink velvet curtains with a resplendent golden fringe for the stage. There were tennis decks and garden lounges, swimming pools and writing salons. The second-class public rooms felt like she'd wandered into an enormous stately mansion with a dining room of mahogany Hepplewhite furniture that could have been borrowed from the pages of F Scott Fitzgerald's novel *The Great Gatsby*. She had read it twice now and was convinced it echoed the decadence and boredom of the Ainsworth women, who struck Stella as being as lifeless as the characters who were hot and weary during that summer of 1922 on Long Island.

Days had passed with her dining mainly with Grace, frankly glad to be ignored by the Ainsworths because as much as she wanted to spend time with Rafe, she didn't want to be an observer while Beatrice hung off his arm, or Georgina oozed her fake charm. Then again, he was behaving in the same manner to both of them. What a horrid triangle; what a terrible life for him to live such lies. It soothed her to sleep to know that perhaps she was the reason that his life would change for the better because he would live it openly, honestly and as Rafe Ainsworth. She'd glimpsed him daily from a distance, leaning over the deck, staring out to sea. He never looked down to the decks below; never searched her out, eyes always on the horizon and yet she was convinced he appeared most early evenings to watch the sun set simply to remind her he was there and thinking of her. She sensed he knew she was looking for him as the dying day lit his face with a burnished bronze. And the horizon represented them . . . she the sea, him the sky, meeting as the sun slid away and —

'Shall we play quoits?' Grace said, meandering into her thoughts.

'We already have this morning.' She knew she sounded distracted but they'd been twelve days at sea on this most beautiful of ships that had seduced her mood from glum to borderline cheerful. How could she not be uplifted, as the weather of the Mediterranean had warmed her, the shimmering ultramarine of its waters had brightened her spirits and she was delighted to note that not even

Georgina's regular barbs could puncture her sense of optimism. A future with Rafe in some shape formed the basis of her daydream. She missed him; he'd been absent for two sunsets and she was trying not to read anything too sinister into that.

'How about hopscotch, then?'

'If you'd like.'

Grace tugged her arm. 'You sound far away, Stella.'

She looked at the youngster already glowing healthily from the time she'd spent playing on deck. 'And you sound so busy!' She tweaked Grace's lightly freckled nose and sighed dramatically at how untidy her hair already looked. 'Your mother is going to accuse me of letting you run around this ship looking like an urchin.'

Grace grinned. 'Daddy will tell her not to nag. I heard him saying to Mummy that it was good for me.'

'It is. Now that you mention him . . . gosh, I forget he's on board sometimes,' Stella fibbed. 'I haven't seen your father for a few days,' she continued, trying desperately not to make it sound like a question.

The girl shrugged and began swinging around one of the nearby poles. 'I haven't either. Mummy said he hasn't been on the ship for a day or two.'

'Oh!' Alarm trilled through her. 'Wasn't this supposed to be a family holiday?'

Grace leaned back as she revolved slowly around the pole. 'He got off in Lisbane. At least I think that's what she said.'

'Lisbon. It's the capital of Portugal. Got off?' She tempered her surprised tone. 'I mean, we all did, didn't we, but you're saying he didn't get back on?'

Grace was swinging with her head tilted as far back as she could without toppling, grinning at the cloudless dome of sky above. 'Yes,' she lisped.

'Grace, stop a moment.' The child slowed obediently, and Stella could see she was dizzy. 'Careful, you'll get sick.'

'Like you?'

'Yes, but I just didn't feel well yesterday.'

'Mummy says you should have your sea legs by now after nearly two weeks on the ship.'

'Does she? I'm glad she doesn't feel this way.'

'Are you any better?'

'Much,' she lied, deciding that the sea was not her friend and she would never agree to sail again. The nausea had erupted once more, which was another reason she was out here sucking in sharply fresh air to keep the dull ill feeling at bay. 'So have we just left your father behind?'

Grace was looping slowly again, gradually sliding lower, distracted but not so entirely lost to her amusement that she couldn't answer. 'No, I think he got back on board this morning. I just haven't seen him.'

'I wonder where?' She made it sound as casually innocent a remark as possible.

Grace giggled. 'It sounded like Mummy said Sardine.'

Stella had to smile. 'Sardinia . . . ?'

'Yes, that's it. Where is Palestine? I heard someone say we were going there too.'

'It's known as the Holy Land – you've been to Sunday School, Grace, so you'd know of places called Judah, Jerusalem, Bethlehem, Jericho —'

'Nazareth?' Grace asked, beaming.

Stella smiled. 'Correct.'

'Before or after the Suez Canal?'

'Oh, bravo, Grace. You were paying attention to the cruise lecture. Well, we'll call into Alexandria. Do you remember where that is?'

Grace looked back with a sheepish expression, then frowned and shook her head.

'It's Egypt, where the Pharaohs once ruled.'

'Ooh, the mummies,' Grace said, wide-eyed and intrigued.

'Yes. Alexandria is the port city named after . . .'

'Er, Alexander the Great!'

'Nothing wrong with your memory, Grace. Very beautiful city, I'm told. Then we visit Cairo.'

'The capital city of Eygpt?' Grace offered hopefully.

'Good!' Stella gave a light clap. 'I'm so impressed with you.'

'Will I ride a camel in Cairo?'

'Oh, I hope so. I hope we both shall, all the way to the pyramids, and after that we sail down the amazing Suez Canal, enter the Red Sea and then we shall sail to exotic Aqaba, which, to answer your question, brings us into Jordan, and after that, Palestine. But first we have North Africa. Shall we go through the cities?'

'I'm bored, Stella.'

She laughed. 'Or just honest?'

'Can I get some ice-cream?'

'I don't see why not. You know where to go?' Grace was already leaving her. 'I'll wait here,' she called to the girl's back, knowing she would return in minutes as it was nearing two in the afternoon and ice-creams were usually offered on the deck directly above where she stood now.

Stella sighed again, revelling in the warmth that kissed her bare arms. England had warmed up too, they'd been assured by ship staff and various announcements. It sounded like summer had arrived with passion. She'd tied her hair up and was in a thin frock, one that Beatrice had offered her amongst various other items that she apparently no longer needed or wanted. Her employer had rolled her eyes to learn that she only had a handful of dresses from her Brighton trip and as Stella had lovingly packed her new summer wardrobe into a trunk, Mrs Boyd had arrived, holding coat hangers and another seven or eight outfits.

'They're yours if you want them. Mrs Ainsworth says they're not needed any more,' Boyd assured in her ever-prevailing mood of disapproval.

'Oh, my, thank you.'

'Don't thank me,' the housekeeper had said. 'I think you're very lucky to be given any of this.' She'd waved a hand to encompass the dresses, the room, the lifestyle, presumably – perhaps even the blessing that Stella was permitted to breathe air within such close proximity to the Ainsworths. However, Stella had taken the clothes with good grace, realising it would be churlish not to, and had been delighted by the range. Some were a little loose but nothing that a strategically placed belt couldn't fix.

The one she wore today was a pale-blue sailor dress, made in Paris, according to its label, and looked to be near new with a panel in its front that buttoned up either side of the wide, square collar, trimmed with white. She wore it with flat, off-white brogues that had come with her packages from the spree at Hanningtons. She still wondered how Rafe had organised all that so quickly. The slightly musty smell of the storage of Beatrice's dress had been blown away by today's soft breeze. If not, then the dab of Stella's mother's French perfume had hopefully chased out any stubborn lingering odour.

Someone arrived to stand next to her. She glanced right and her heart dipped. 'Afternoon, Georgina.'

'Hello, Stella. Are you avoiding us?'

'No.' She could be churlish and mention the lack of invitation but good manners took over. 'I'm here to help your father, not teach you girls, and he doesn't need any assistance right now.'

'How's second class?' Georgina wondered.

'Well, your parents have ensured I am accommodated magnificently.' She smiled. 'Thank you for asking.'

She hoped Georgina would tire of the sugary banter but it appeared not. 'You look especially pretty today, Stella.'

'Thank you,' she replied, wondering where this might take them.

'The only reason I spotted you from above was because I recognised it,' she said, glancing up and down at Stella's dress. 'I wore that to the Yacht Race at Cowes a couple of years ago. It's so very summer '31, but how nice that you're happy to wear a hand-me-down.'

'This is yours?' Somehow her voice remained even but the query betrayed her.

'Used to be. Wouldn't be caught dead in it now.'

'Your mother gave it to me. I thought it was new, something she didn't want.'

Georgina shrugged. 'I'm not suggesting you stole it, Stella, although speaking of thieving, we haven't explored our previous conversation yet, have we?'

Fear crawled up her spine now. 'Which conversation is that?'

'The one about you and my father.'

Stella frowned back at Georgina, today dressed immaculately in a pale pink summer skirt and crisp white shirt with rosebuds around the sleeves. She looked so sweet and pretty it offended her to know how Georgina could beguile the unsuspecting.

'About the affair you are having with him,' Georgina said airily with a smile.

'Don't be ridiculous!' Nausea simmered in her belly and began clambering to her throat. 'Forgive me, I don't feel terribly well again.'

'Take a lot of deep breaths,' Georgina replied in a careless tone. 'I'm not ready to let you leave. I want to discuss whether you do harbour feelings for my father that could be regarded as unprofessional.'

'I have nothing to say to you about that.'

'Guilty conscience?'

'No. I simply will not lend any weight to your intention to cause trouble by discussing such a thing.'

'And yet you sound unnerved.' Georgina stretched her arms languidly. 'You do sound guilty to me.'

'Do I? I rather hoped I sounded angry, or perhaps disgusted.'

Georgina chuckled. 'What on earth do you see in him?'

'I don't know why you'd ask me. Instead ask Grace what she sees in her father. Ask your mother what she sees in her husband.'

'But I am asking you, Stella. Grace possesses blind, childish love. My mother is strategic, although I won't deny her affection for him baffles me most of the time.'

'That's because you don't know him. You don't see him for who he is.' It was a mistake from the moment the words flew from her mouth.

Georgina's intrigued expression now dissolved into delight. 'But you do, don't you, Stella? You don't just see him. You can barely take your eyes from him. And you know him intimately, apparently.'

She disguised her shame. 'Only in your bored fantasies, Georgina! Stop fishing for problems that don't exist. I suggest you grow up and start acting like the adult you pretend to be.'

'Or what?'

'Or learn some harsh truths,' she snapped in another mistake. *Who is the adult here, Stella?* the voices in her mind demanded. *Take control!*

Georgina, who had been smirking out at the horizon, swung around. 'Such as what, Stella?' She frowned, anger creeping through, and Stella noted a hint of panic. 'What do you think you know?'

Grace rescued her. 'Look!' she called, arriving excitedly. 'Strawberry, my favourite.'

Her sister pushed her rudely aside. 'Maybe they'll teach you to belly dance in Egypt, Gracie. You've got all the right wobbly bits for it. I asked you a question,' she snarled back at Stella.

Grace glanced at Stella with an injured expression and it was the little girl's burst balloon of cheerfulness that pricked Stella into losing control rather than seizing it.

'Oh, do shut up, Georgina, you hateful creature. Why don't you leave us alone, if you've got nothing pleasant to say to your sister?'

The eldest Ainsworth daughter grinned, triumphant. 'You're so easy, Stella. You too, Fatty. Enjoy your ice-cream – all of it.' She pushed the wafer cornet that held the ice-cream so it blotted against Grace's chin to leave a smear of pink, and grinned unkindly.

'Georgie?' Grace called and her sister turned back with a look of disdain.

'Yes, Podge?'

'I want to push my ice-cream into the middle of your face.'

Georgina tinkled a laugh. 'But that wouldn't be polite, would it?' she taunted.

'You're always so mean to Stella.'

'That's because I hate her but you love her enough for both of us, and do you know something, Grace? Remember what you told me about Daddy and Stella?'

'Georgina!' Stella warned, her breath sharp and shallow.

'No, I don't remember,' Grace replied, puzzled.

'Well, I do. You were mostly unconscious that day, so you're forgiven.'

'I want you to stop making trouble for Stella,' Grace pleaded, the ice-cream melting from the warmth of the Mediterranean sun, pink channels of wet sweetness trickling through the child's fingers.

'Poor Podge. I'll make all the trouble I can. I want horrible Stella gone.'

Stella closed her eyes; this was unbearable. She felt Grace step forward, and opened them to see the youngster suddenly taller against her sister – she hadn't noticed until now that the child had shot up slightly over spring. But it was more than that. There was something far more intelligent and intimidating about the girl than her sister had likely ever grasped.

'In that case I shall tell you something else I heard in my sleep,' Grace said.

'Go on, then,' her sister baited.

'I don't really understand, but I heard Daddy tell Mummy that he isn't your father. They were arguing at my bedside when I was sick. I heard it clearly, though, and so did Stella because she was there too. And maybe that's what Daddy means when he says I am as different to you as chalk and cheese. Mummy says I look like Daddy and Daddy says when I grow up I'll have the best of both of them. You won't.'

'What are you talking about, you little pig!' Georgie shot back, pushing her sister again.

Stella stepped in, her eyes wide with fright at Grace's remarks. 'Stop it, Georgina, right now. You're making a scene.'

'Did you hear what she just said?' Georgina shrilled, staring angrily at Stella. 'What does that look mean? What do you know? What is this rubbish?'

'Georgina, I think you'd better leave. Don't you have a salon appointment?' She glanced at her watch desperately.

'Ask Mummy, Georgie,' Grace pressed. 'Ask her if you're adopted. Is that the right word, Stella?'

'Both of you, enough! Georgina is not adopted, Grace.'

Grace shrugged in an uncharacteristic way. 'Georgie's always mean, especially to you and Daddy. I'm glad you're not my real sister. It's time someone taught you it's not right to be so nasty to everyone.'

'Well, that someone is not you,' Stella urged, spinning the child around and marching her forwards. 'Don't miss your appointment, Georgina, and take no notice of your sister's taunts. I can't say you don't deserve it but I'm sorry it was such a cruel thing she said.' Stella didn't think she needed to be blamed for any more of Georgina's troubles but somehow she sensed Grace's brutal revelation was going to come straight back and bite her.

She gave Grace another gentle shove towards the opposite side of the deck. Stella glanced back at Georgina, who stood by the railing, the sun beginning its low dip behind her but none of its warmth seemed to touch the young woman. Her normally golden hair refused to reflect the softening light, sitting dully around a scowling, uncertain expression. Stella felt a moment of melting sympathy for Georgina but it was young Grace who snapped her from feeling responsible.

'Stella, I'm not sorry for saying that to Georgie.'

They were halfway down a set of deck stairs. 'No, I can tell,' she admitted, lost for how to handle this situation. 'Come on.'

Grace paused at the bottom and turned. 'I know everyone thinks I'm not old enough but I'm not stupid.'

She gave Grace a look of exasperation. 'Beware anyone who should think such a thing.'

'It's as though Georgie forgets that she loves me and uses me to make herself feel better when she's cross.'

Stella put her arm around Grace's shoulders, unable to help a sense of pride in Rafe's daughter. 'You are certainly not stupid, Grace. In fact, I think you're an oracle.'

'What's that?'

'All-knowing,' Stella replied in an arch tone.

Grace grinned. 'An oracle,' she repeated.

'You have a knack for looking at a situation and seeing the truth. And the best bit about you, Grace, is that you like to see the best in people, including your sister . . . even when she's being cruel to you.'

'I think if Georgie could, she'd prefer to be happy. I'm used to her picking on me but I don't like it when she picks on you, Stella . . . or Daddy.'

She nodded. 'Let's wash your hands and then perhaps we can go up to the soda fountain.'

But in her heart she knew it was now only a matter of time before she was called before Beatrice Ainsworth to explain.

The invitation arrived at four sharp.

'I've been asked to deliver this to you, Miss Myles,' the steward beamed. 'You may care to know that it's black tie in the first-class dining room,' he added.

'Thank you,' she said, hesitating for a fraction before she took the white envelope with its crest and Ainsworth name on it.

She expected a curt note from Beatrice to meet in her stateroom but she was thrilled and mostly shocked to see Rafe's handwriting with an invitation to join the family for dinner this evening. Maybe Georgina hadn't gone running to her mother.

Grace was under instructions for an afternoon nap, or 'quiet time', as the doctor had insisted, so Stella was free. Rather than be out and about on the ship and risk another hiss of words with Georgina, she spent her time ensuring she looked immaculate for the evening. She washed her hair, even running a light scented oil through it to prevent any frizziness; she'd found the tiny bottle of perfumed olive oil in Rhodes on their all-day stop and the young woman behind the market stall had shown her what to do. She smelled rosemary in it, along with citrus and other pleasant scents. Stella smoothed it into her dark hair and regarded herself in the mirror appreciating she looked more like her mother than she'd previously realised. People had always said so, but she'd not caught the likeness in herself so strongly as she did now.

She plucked her eyebrows, tidied her cuticles and buffed her nails until they were smooth and shiny. She creamed her arms that would be bare tonight and because she was wearing her black gown, she suddenly decided it needed a swept-up hairdo. Reaching for the phone, she made an appointment for a female attendant to visit her rooms. Within two hours she was buttoned into the magnificent black shift of satin that certainly did hug the curve of her body as she'd imagined it might when she'd first sighted it in the Brighton hotel. Bell-shaped sleeves were trimmed in black velvet and a softly curving cowled neckline of satin was echoed in an exquisitely over-sized tie at the waist. Her hair was pinned up with a tiny velvet bow and, at her helper's urgings, she had even agreed to a little bit of powder, a touch of rouge and a soft pout of lipstick.

'You look beautiful, Miss Myles,' the woman sighed with a smile behind her.

'I look French,' she admitted, recalling pictures of her mother wearing the same bright-red lipstick that Stella had souvenired from her dressing table.

The woman chuckled. 'You do, actually.'

'Oh, wait,' Stella gasped, lighting up. 'My mother's black pearl earrings.' She dug into the small leather box on her dressing table which held the few pieces she possessed. In moments they were both admiring the dainty pearl orbs hanging from her earlobes.

'Perfect!' the woman breathed next to her. 'Every gent will want to dance with you tonight, Miss Myles.'

There's only one I want to dance with, Stella thought. 'Have you been up to the first-class decks?' she asked.

'Of course, yes. You can fit my parents' house into some of the staterooms.'

Stella laughed. 'Gosh, I'm nervous now.'

'Don't be. They're all wizened and wealthy up there. There are only a few gorgeous young ladies. There's the Ainsworth daughter – she's so attractive and every pair of eyes seem to follow her. But you, Miss Myles, you're going to give her a run for her money.'

'Wish me luck,' she said, overly brightly.

'You won't need it. I'll be watching you tonight as I might be on a shift up in the first ballroom.'

Stella smiled genuinely now. 'Thank you so much for helping me.' She tipped the woman generously and checked her watch as the door closed.

Cocktails were at six-thirty. It was already past that time and she was happy to skip that trial of small talk and arrive for dinner at seven-thirty. She picked up one of the notebooks she'd taken from Rafe's study and moved to the final pages to read his most recent entry.

There was an entry about *Thymelicus hamza*, or the Moroccan small skipper butterfly, and the following page gave details on another called the chalkhill blue, with a sketch that included a soft crayon of blue on the insect's abdomen. It was a helpful distraction that absorbed the half hour of time Stella needed to kill but mostly it dampened her rising anxiety of what mood and turn of events awaited her this evening across the Ainsworth dinner table.

20

'Thank you,' she beamed at the steward who pulled open a heavy door leading out onto the deck. Stella had instinctively anticipated a gust of cold wind. Instead the balmy evening of the Mediterranean was breathless, instantly wrapping her in its slightly moist warmth. She was glad she'd pinned her hair up now; apart from its elegance, she would avoid the inevitable frizziness that humid conditions provoked. The nausea had subsided too. She felt cheered as a result and capable of facing Beatrice's questions when they came, as she was sure they would. There would be no scene in a public situation so maybe she would even have the opportunity to explain the truth of today.

'It's so calm. Are we berthed?'

'No, Miss Myles.' She was amazed at how all the staff she met seemed to know her name. 'We've dropped anchor for a couple of hours to take on some supplies and to ensure we have an easy dinner serve tonight.'

'Oh, so we sail on?' She didn't mean to sound disappointed but feeling hungry and well again was uplifting.

He nodded. 'We dock at Rabat by ten tonight.'

She smiled fresh thanks and climbed the outside deck stairs, carefully holding her gown clear of her heels but revelling in the stillness of the evening. Stella arrived at the first-class main entrance and had to work hard to keep her jaw from opening in awe. The glass dome in the ceiling would allow in glorious light by day, but now it glistened and sparkled with the aid of a huge chandelier, whose crystal teardrops gave her a series of sparkling winks as if encouraging her despite the flips and dips her belly had suddenly decided upon. She'd given a lot of thought to today's outburst with Georgina and realised there were no explanations for it; the facts were plain – the adult Ainsworths' indiscretion had led to their youngest child overhearing something about her sister. They were to blame, not the children and certainly not herself. She had not fanned the fire but tried to extinguish it. It all sounded straightforward in her mind and yet despite her bright mood on the deck below she now felt nervous at what awaited, especially why anyone might still be inviting her to join the family for dinner after what had occurred. Why not a private interrogation?

Her footfall was soundless on the thick, richly coloured carpet of the lounge she had to cross. Save ship staff, it was deserted, which only added to its beauty which she could now see for herself was reminiscent of the work of Sir Christopher Wren. Her being alone increased the tension of her arrival, as clearly with cocktails consumed everyone had drifted into the dining room. She had one more room to cross – the magnificent drawing room, resplendent with open fires, mahogany bookcases and another jaw-dropping domed atrium that was even more impressive than the last.

Doors swung back as if cued to move on her arrival.

'Good evening,' the steward said, nodding politely. The steward opposite bowed his head slightly too.

Stella's lips opened now helplessly at the opulence before her. Grace had breathlessly explained at some stage that the first-class dining room stretched for one third of an acre but only now did Stella believe her. 'Er . . . Good evening, thank you.'

'Miss Myles?' said another voice, his tone as rich as the wealthy patrons who were seating themselves across that third of an acre of sumptuous décor. 'Welcome to the dining room,' an older senior man greeted. 'I hope you approve of its Louis XVI styling?' he wondered and she knew he was clueing her. He would be aware that she was coming up from second class and needed all the help she might be gifted.

'It's mesmerising,' she rewarded him.

The maître d', tucked into a black tailed suit, did a tiny click with his highly polished shoes. 'I'm pleased you like it.'

She paused to glance at the deep pinks and rose-coloured painted ceiling of cherubs and garlands that were a foil for the rich mahogany panels of the room and dove-grey painted walls. She took in the arrangement of pilasters and columns, the sea-blue carpet and matching chairs upholstered with that identical colour and inset panels to echo the pink garlands on the ceiling. Glittering lamps added yet more ornamentation and she sighed, turning to smile at him.

'The ceiling is marvellous.'

'The decoration represents the *Triumph of Flora*,' he explained. 'Of course Neptune is never far away,' he jested and she glanced at the large monogram of the ship represented in the dome – two anchors crossed on a trident that symbolised the god of the seas.

'Makes me feel insignificant,' she breathed. 'The colours so vivid.'

'Oh, I doubt that you could ever feel insignificant. You look beautiful, Miss Myles,' he assured, reading her thought that perhaps black was too sombre to be worn amidst all this gaiety. 'May we show you to the table? The Ainsworths are seated.'

'I do hope I haven't kept everyone waiting.'

'Not at all.' He offered a waiter's arm. 'Please. Daniel, if you would show Miss Myles to the Ainsworth table.'

The handsome young man in a white jacket and black waistcoat and trousers beamed her a bright smile and she allowed him to loosely link arms to escort her. Stella forced herself to breathe slowly, felt the sharp glances of older women cutting up from their conversations to fall upon her like splinters of glass, each a tiny slash of envy. Her youth, the slim figure that allowed the velvet gown to drape effortlessly from it, the suggestion of longing within dark beauty that drifted past them, gave no indication of her rising excitement of seeing him again. She had cast her features in calm, a soft smile just hinting, and her gaze fixed beyond anyone in particular so that she didn't meet anyone's eyes to make her falter until her companion began to slow.

'Here we are, Miss Myles,' he warned, moving off the carpet to thread their way around two tables to a slightly smaller one that could seat up to six, where she saw a bespectacled Rafe leaning in to talk to his wife. She couldn't prevent her breath catching in jealousy, had not been prepared for such pain of envy now that he secretly belonged to her. Rafe was right; he was dangerous for her. She had never felt so possessive.

He looked up at her approach, took off his glasses and immediately stood to greet her. His complexion, freshly bronzed, looked healthy against the starched white of his shirt, the sleek fit of his white waistcoat that she suspected followed the latest fashion of being backless together with a contrasting blacker-than-black dinner suit that included a sharply cut tail coat. There was no doubt that together with Beatrice, in a midnight-blue gown with a daringly wide neckline, they were the most trendsetting and stylish couple in that vast room. Stella would not have been surprised to hear that every pair of eyes had turned towards them at this moment; her own included could not tear themselves from Rafe, ridiculously handsome and shooting her a smile that was all the whiter for the tan it beamed out from.

'Good evening, Stella.' The voice she loved smoothed over her as he dipped his head politely. 'I'm glad you could join us.' His gaze looked hungrily across her and she silently drank in his attention like a butterfly lapping at nectar.

'Oh, hello there,' Beatrice said, uncharacteristically informally. Her voice sounded vaguely slurred to Stella.

'Thank you for inviting me, Mrs Ainsworth,' she said, smiling a quick thank you to Daniel who pushed her chair in. He stole away as Beatrice waved newly manicured nails of scarlet in Stella's direction in a gesture that didn't feel welcoming.

'Not I, Stella,' Beatrice confirmed, putting a hand on her husband's arm in a proprietorial way. She noticed Rafe did not look at his wife; his gaze was riveted sombrely on her instead. Instantly dark and angry, he removed his arm from Beatrice's touch. A thin lock of Beatrice's bright hair slipped free from its usually precise updo and dangled like a strand of golden toffee. 'As ever, it is Dougie who likes you to stick close,' she said, her gaze wandering as she absently tucked the wayward hair behind her ear. 'Champagne, waiter!' she called.

Stella glanced again at the simmering Rafe. 'They'll bring it all too soon, my dear,' he ground out.

'Er . . . it's a privilege to be on this level,' Stella tried.

'I'm sure it is for you,' Beatrice drawled, pulling her red lips into a familiar slash.

Stella breathed slowly. 'Where are the girls?'

'They're taking dinner in their room tonight. It's just us,' Beatrice answered, cat eyes flashing at her and Stella saw the threat in them.

'Champagne, for everyone?' a waiter suddenly arriving asked, his mood as bubbly as the bottles being opened with loud pops and accompanying laughter around the large dining room.

'Stella?' Rafe offered.

'Er, yes, thank you.'

Flutes were poured and with their effervescence fizzing far more happily than the atmosphere at their table suggested they should, three glasses were glumly raised.

'Shall we drink to an enjoyable voyage?' Rafe proposed and Stella heard the ironic note in his toast.

Beatrice was onto him. 'No, Doug, I doubt that can happen. I think instead we should drink to keeping promises, shall we?'

He sighed. 'Bee . . .'

Stella swallowed a sip of the French champagne, tasting its tart dryness, wishing she could enjoy the rest but knowing it would taste acidic if she continued without facing Beatrice's wrath. 'I kept my promise, Mrs Ainsworth.'

'Did you, Stella?' Beatrice took a long draught of champagne, nearly emptying her glass. A bead of it remained on the waxy red coating of her lips as she now focused her fury at its target. 'So how come I have a near hysterical teenage daughter, weeping in her cabin, refusing to come out?'

Stella glanced at Rafe. He stared back coldly.

'I can't say we aren't disappointed, Stella,' he offered.

She blinked, confused and annoyed. 'Then why did you ask me to join you for dinner?' she shot back, looking appalled at him.

'Doug had already sent the invitation before the drama erupted,' Beatrice admitted. 'He refused to go back on it.'

'Maybe he should have,' Stella suggested.

'Smoked salmon, for everyone?' Their head waiter was back, his tone full of delight.

'Thank you,' Rafe said as plates with silver cloches were laid down.

The ladies said nothing.

Stella sat back and her waiter placed a gloved hand on the lid of hers. Another waiter reached between Rafe and Beatrice and with a nod to each other the two men lifted the lids with a synchronised flourish.

Rafe and Stella forced out appropriate noises of pleasure.

Beatrice flouted good manners to lean on her elbow and stare into her plate.

'*Bon appétit*,' one of the men said, sounding awkward, and they moved away.

Stella regarded the bright orange of the salmon twisted into soft rose-like shapes around a mound of floppy cream cheese flecked with herbs. Delicate, translucent rings of onion encircled each other while the muddy green of capers studded the plate. Strategically placed, gleaming drops of citrus gel complemented the quarters of lemon, sliced so finely they were malleable enough to be twisted artistically on the plate. 'How beautiful,' she murmured. 'Seems a pity to disturb it.'

'That's how I feel about our daughter, Stella.'

'Mrs Ainsworth, what exactly did Georgina say to you?'

'That you all but confirmed that Douglas is not her real father. She said it was plain in the sneer on your face.'

Stella, who had been reaching for her fish knife and fork, now placed her hands firmly in her lap. 'I did no such thing,' she said quietly and flicked her gaze to Rafe. 'How could you think something so heinous of me?'

'You could have denied it,' Beatrice snarled, her voice lifting.

'Bee, please . . .' Rafe cautioned, looking around at the other diners.

'Mrs Ainsworth, firstly, while I think Georgina should know the truth it is not my place to tell you how to raise your child, so against my own nature, I fibbed and covered Grace's information . . . but I did it for Georgina's sake.'

'You won't blatantly lie for me, is that what you're saying, Stella?'

'Yes. I won't lie to protect you,' she felt obliged to qualify, trying not to emphasise the last word, given that she did fib to protect Beatrice's daughters.

'But you would lie to protect my husband, perhaps?'

Stella blushed at the truth but she pressed on, ignoring the well-laid trap and refusing to topple into it. 'I can remember most precisely how this afternoon's conversation with Georgina transpired. It was Grace who spilled your long-held secret and I did everything any adult could do to defuse the situation. I also had stern words with Grace. Georgina is unaccountably cruel-mouthed to her sister and even in the short time I've been in her company I notice that Grace is aptly named for how she responds to the constant barbs. This was an occasion where Georgina's harsh tongue hurt sufficiently for Grace to reply uncharacteristically viciously. I was as shocked as Georgina at the outburst, I have to admit, and I'm as concerned as you. No one should learn such traumatising news in this manner.'

'I don't understand it,' Beatrice continued as if Stella had not spoken so earnestly. 'Why didn't Grace even mention to me that she'd overheard us talking? You'd think that would be the first thing she'd do, don't you?'

Stella shook her head. 'I promise she didn't mention it to me either, Mrs Ainsworth, or I can assure you I would have taken immediate steps to prevent it being shared. It came out of nowhere but you have to know that Georgina provoked Grace into it.'

'The truth is I don't believe for a moment that Grace was awake or even conscious enough to make sense of anything being spoken above her that evening,' Beatrice said.

'Are you suggesting I shared with Grace what I unhappily had to listen to and then gave you my word I would never repeat?'

'Oh, let's not run around in circles, Stella. That's precisely what I'm suggesting.'

Stella pushed her chair back. 'Then you'd be wrong, Mrs Ainsworth. Please excuse me.'

'Is that it, Stella?' Beatrice sneered. 'Do you think that's the end of this?'

'It's best I leave now. I do not want to upset you further.' She glanced at Rafe for help but it was as though he sat between them as an interested observer. She wanted to shout at him to offer some support.

'Stella, I do think you should leave but not just the first-class dining room. I think you should leave the ship.' Beatrice sat back, eyes glittering with righteousness.

'Pardon me?'

'You heard. I have already made the arrangements.'

'Bee, what are you talking about?' Rafe was finally surprised into action. 'You've had too much to drink and y-you're emotional,' he said, making sure to stammer his pompous words. 'I think we should wait —'

'No, it's sudden, I agree, but you can't talk me out of it, Dougie. Stella will leave the ship tonight in Rabat. As we speak I'm having her clothes packed. Stella, you can gather up the rest of your private belongings and the purser will see you off the gangplank. By all means enjoy Morocco for an evening but *Aquitania* is making arrangements for you to be flown home to London tomorrow.'

'What?' Rafe growled. 'You can't do that, Bee.'

Stella felt her internal alarm beginning to sound like a distant siren, gaining in intensity and dragging the familiar sense of nausea from this morning with it, even though the ship was barely shifting at anchor.

'That's just it, Dougie. I can, and I have,' she slurred and laughed before turning serious again. 'Stella has created nothing but problems in our family since the day she arrived. Frankly Georgina detests her and I can understand why for all sorts of reasons that perhaps a man can't. She's sacked; that's the end of it.' She waved a careless hand again at Stella. 'I'll have some wages sent to you via the agency. Good evening, Stella.'

Rafe placed his napkin on the table in a deliberate move and stood slowly. He took off his glasses and instantly the man she knew and loved was present. He tucked his fake spectacles into his inside pocket. Beatrice followed his actions with an unsteady gaze. 'And where are you off to, darling?'

'If Stella has to leave the ship, I am not going to permit her to be dumped alone in Africa, of all places.' The stammer had disappeared.

'Do you plan to escort her yourself, then, darling?' Her voice was bitter, ringed with malice. She gripped his arm and as Stella watched Beatrice's knuckles whiten, she heard only threat in the question.

'I certainly plan to escort her off the ship, ensure that she is properly catered for, and I shall myself put her on that flight back to Britain.'

'I see. What if I don't agree?'

'Then don't agree. It won't change anything.'

'Doug, I insist —'

'Don't, Bee. Whatever you want to do, do it. I'm past caring about your threats.'

'Doug!' The shock had battled through the liquor it seemed. 'Please . . .'

He unwrapped her fingers from his arm. 'I'll re-board in Tangier. We can talk then. I'll kiss the girls before I leave.'

'Mr Ainsworth,' Stella began but was cut off by his glare. She was aware of diners beginning to notice the disturbance.

'Still here, Stella?' Beatrice said, her tone openly vicious. She reached for Rafe once again.

'I'm leaving, Mrs Ainsworth. I don't wish any further unhappiness.' Beatrice rolled her eyes as if finding her tedious. 'I shall leave a note for Grace.'

'Please, don't bother. I shan't see that she gets it,' Beatrice warned with an artful grin.

'I suggest you go and sleep off the gin and then the champagne, Bee,' Rafe said, this time firmly unfurling himself from his wife's clasp.

'Doug, don't get off the ship . . . or . . .'

'Or what, Bee?'

When she didn't answer he surprised Stella by leaning down and kissing his wife's cheek tenderly. 'Goodbye, Bee.'

To Stella the words sounded like farewell. She didn't wait to hear his wife's response; didn't want to dare believe the flutter of hope in her chest that Rafe was leaving his wife for good tonight, but wished deeply she hadn't been part of the scene. Instead she fled, keeping her gaze on the carpet as she hurried across the length of that interminably long room, taking the maître d' by surprise as she arrived at the doors again.

'Oh, Miss Myles . . . ?'

As a steward opened the door for her the man's words were lost to the polite clangour of the diners' silver cutlery against china as the sound of waves welcomed her back onto the deck. She kept moving until she was as far as she could go. Stella leaned over the rail and allowed tears to fall in a mix of anger and regret until they were silent sobs and then finally, gratefully, no more than sniffs. She was back in control and of the opinion that Beatrice had done her a favour. *Home*, she thought, with a rush of old yearning. She would be back with Rory and Carys within a day or two and she could get her life into a new order.

'Stella?' She swung around, uncaring that her face may be tear-stained but knowing she had to get through this final confrontation. 'I've been looking for you.'

'I'm not sure that was wise, Rafe,' she said, hearing her own weariness and looking away from the impeccably attired body she felt a powerful urge to cling to in that moment.

'I'm afraid it's too late for regrets,' he replied. 'Beatrice wasn't lying. You are leaving the ship tonight.'

'Good,' she admitted. 'I want to.'

'But so am I.'

'I don't need your help.'

'Stella, go and supervise the collection of your belongings. I shall see you at the gangplank in fifteen minutes.'

'Rafe —'

'Do it!' There was that tone again; the one he'd used with Basil when she'd eavesdropped on their conversation. 'I'm sorry,' he quickly followed. 'I have no business ordering you.'

'Given that you no longer employ me, no, you don't,' she murmured.

'Please . . . just do as I ask.'

She nodded, not wishing to prolong the scene. Stella moved but he caught her arm. 'You made every woman pale by comparison tonight, Stella. I wanted to tell you that the moment you arrived. Frankly, I wanted to take you in my arms and kiss you deeply in front of them all.'

His tone, his choice of words, always managed to undermine her best intentions. Instead of walking away as she'd imagined she would, she covered his hand with hers. 'Now, that really would have given Beatrice a reason to get herself blotto.'

He gave her a sad smile. 'Fifteen minutes.'

Stella parted from him and as she lifted her gown to move downstairs she stole a glance back at Rafe to see a man with an expression so haunted she had to look away.

21
Rabat – June 1933

Rafe raised an arm to thank the purser who was watching them from the deck of *Aquitania* as they stood on the dimly lit dock next to her single trunk. A leather travel bag was all he had by his feet, slouched next to his patent dress shoes.

'We must look ridiculous,' she admitted, glancing at their evening formal wear.

'We look perfectly splendid for where we're headed.'

'What are you talking about? I thought the purser said I was to overnight at a hotel. And tomorrow afternoon I'm on the Imperial Airways flight that's coming up from Cape Town.'

'It is, but you won't be on it, Stella.'

Men arrived. 'Ah, thank you,' he said before slipping effortlessly into French. There was no trace of the usual English accent that plagued Britishers when using her mother's tongue. Stella was sure her mother would have sighed to hear him ask the men to carry the luggage and put it in a car that was waiting; he even provided a description of it. Why not a taxi? They were going to a different hotel than the one she had on her paperwork too.

'Coming, Stella?' he asked as the men left with her trunk between them and his bag balanced atop it as if they belonged together, like a couple off on an adventurous trip, travelling light. Seeing that flashing vignette suddenly helped her to make sense of this evening.

'This has been a charade, hasn't it?'

He turned back. 'Pardon?'

She bit her lip, eyes narrowing in thought; there were other pieces of the whole picture beginning to slot into place like an imaginary jigsaw forming itself in her mind. No, she hadn't imagined it. 'Tonight. It was a performance, wasn't it? Just like the night in the ballroom. You pretended to support Beatrice but you were really needing her to fling me off the ship.'

His expression lost its brightness. 'Beatrice made that decision earlier in the evening as she told you. Stella, I may have been putting on an act in the Berkeley ballroom but there was only sincerity between us in the lobby and in the taxi afterwards.'

Her shoulders slumped. 'But tonight was a perfect piece of manoeuvring. You cannot deny it.'

Rafe turned fully back to face her. 'I had to get us both off the ship. I thought you may be happy about it.'

She closed her eyes momentarily. 'You're not even bothering to lie,' she replied. 'Of course I'm happy we're together, but at what cost, Rafe? You've used me as your excuse so that you can be off the ship to rendezvous with Joseph. Somehow you come out of it like a shiny knight, while Beatrice believes I goaded Grace into her horrible revelation, that I took revenge on Georgina, that I'm behind all of her problems . . .' He remained silent and despite feeling like a shrew, Stella pressed on with her thoughts, aloud. 'So you orchestrated this.'

'This?'

She would not let him play a game of words with her this time. 'Rafe, explain about us both having to be off the ship. Would you do that for me?'

'Can we do this in the car?'

'No. We shall do it right here, so I know what I'm really doing on a dock, at night, in Africa, alone with you. Whatever Beatrice had in mind, it wasn't both of us together right here, right now. But it was clearly always your intention. I'd appreciate knowing your plan.'

'All right.' He sighed. 'But we're still being watched – at least walk into the shadows as though we're leaving the port.'

She nodded, refused his arm for fear of it being reported back to Beatrice, and heard the lonely click of her heels on the ground as they pretended to depart. Once inside the darkness of a shelter where sacks of grain were being stored, she rounded on him.

'I have to be in Marrakech,' he spilled.

'And I have to be there as well, instead of going home to my family?'

'I told you, I'm taking you along as a precaution.'

'Really? That's so reassuring – it's also intensely romantic, Rafe. Careful, or you'll make me swoon.'

He sighed. 'Let me just tell the driver we're here and we won't be long.' Rafe gestured for her to sit on one of the piles of sacks.

Rafe disappeared and she leaned rather than sat in the darkness, wondering at the strange turn her life had taken since he'd swaggered up and asked her to dance. She wished she could blame her parents for this too but the decisions had been all hers since that fateful evening at the Berkeley and she could not deny that even their afternoon in Brighton had only happened because she'd permitted it. More than that . . . she'd wanted it to happen and she'd put her needs ahead of any shame for Beatrice . . . or the two girls, or her own family.

By the time he hurried back into the darkness, her mindset had shifted to a bleak sense that she was a disappointment to everyone.

'Sorry,' he urged across the dark. He waited. 'Are you all right, Stella?'

'I don't know how to answer that,' she admitted, giving a mirthless laugh. 'Tell me all of it, Rafe, so I can make some sense of my world – the one you've thrown me into.'

She could see him nod and imagined he did so with that soft look of injury she'd witnessed on their first evening together.

'All right, I shall tell you everything. As you're aware, I travelled around Arabia and the Holy Lands with my parents but I spent a lot of my childhood here in North Africa. One of my closest friends is a Jew. His father was from Prussia, a diplomat and a close friend with my father both working in this region. His mother died from complications during the birth of his brother, who also died not long after. His father blamed himself and Joseph was caught in the midst of it all. My mother took him in and he became the brother I shared everything but blood with.' He sighed sadly. 'Although we fixed that with a blood oath in the desert,' he recalled wistfully.

How she loved his mellow voice.

'Anyway, we were like tearaways,' he continued. 'Joseph was fourteen months older but more reserved than I, so we were a good balance for each other because he used to complain that I was fearless. He said I made him feel braver. We did everything together, but when he was eleven his father took him back to Germany. I lost my soulmate and as adults in the war we fought on different sides. He was my enemy but every day I prayed that he would survive and I know he prayed for me too from an opposite trench.' Rafe sat on a tower of grain sacks and ran a hand through his hair, untidying the neatly slicked style. 'We've only seen each other a few times since but our childhood bond is as strong as ever. We're both terrible correspondents but do our best to write maybe twice a year. He is my brother and far from my enemy.'

'He's Owl?' she whispered.

'Yes. But I didn't know. Sneaky Fruity plays his cards close to his chest. I hate that he's been grooming him and now using him. I should never have told Basil about Joseph. It seems he went behind my back and made contact alone with him. And Joseph wouldn't think twice about being anything but cordial to someone who claims to be a friend of mine.'

'So Joseph has something to share and will share it only with you?'

'That's the size of it.'

'And the peacock?'

He gave a gust of amusement and shook his head. 'There was an old shisha cafe in one of the squares at Marrakech where we both had our first smoke. It was owned by an old rogue, Yassine, who had a pet peacock he used to lead around and it was always at the café. He named it Mustafa; he used to joke with us boys that the peacock ran the café and only allowed the patrons he liked to drink tea and smoke there. Mustafa used to make a terrible racket at times but he seemed to like the pair of us, so Yassine was happy to take our money.'

'So that message was simply code?'

'That's right. Joseph didn't want anyone to know where we would meet. And I can assure you the only reason I've agreed to this is because of his obvious caution. It makes me believe he has something frightening to share.'

'But you initially dismissed it,' she countered.

'Of course I did. I didn't want Fruity or anyone else in the ministry making too big a deal of this. Firstly, they're all like bumbling schoolboys and with Joseph so well connected in Germany, any lack of caution on their part could become a genuine threat to his wellbeing.'

'Gosh, Rafe, how do you keep track of all the intrigues in your life?'

He blew out his breath in a sighing agreement. 'At this point I'm only worrying about my brother. He's not a spy. He's the sort of person who jumps at a loud sound. Heaven knows how he got through the war. The thing is, Stella, if Joseph's anything, he's loyal and loves me. He wouldn't involve me like this. It has to be something he can't entrust to anyone but the one person he knows will neither dismiss it nor leave it to idle.'

'What sort of information can it be?'

He shrugged and then took a slow breath. 'My belief is it has to be connected with the new regime.'

She held her breath and her tongue.

'My instincts suggest this is about consolidation of power in Germany by the new leader. For Joseph to force me to return to Marrakech he's obviously terrified, or why wouldn't he just come to London, or ask me to Germany? No, he has to be bringing something grave to me.'

'Like what?' she wondered, her tone filled with anxiety. She stepped forward, fists unclenching, and it was all he needed as an indication of her thawing. He moved so smoothly she was in his arms before she could protest.

'Destabilising Europe and the balance of power, I suspect,' he said, holding her close.

'Rafe, you're frightening me.'

'Good; then you'll be careful. I'm sorry to drag you into this but because you're not involved it means I can trust you but it also means I can keep you safe. No one will suspect a research assistant that I'm having a torrid affair with.'

She understood now. Stella didn't appreciate the label or even his rationale but anything that kept him secure she accepted. 'You can rely on me. Whatever you need.'

He kissed the top of her head. 'Come on, we have a long drive to Marrakech tonight.'

'When are you meeting Joseph?'

'Not until Sunday afternoon.'

'So what shall we do tomorrow?'

'Oh, I'm sure we can find something to amuse ourselves . . .' One eyebrow lifted and in spite of the ball of fear rolling around the pit of her belly, Stella laughed and couldn't imagine loving him any more than she did in that moment.

22

She woke to the sound of Rafe's humming and the smell of coffee and shifted to watch him on the balcony. He was in his bathrobe and his hair was damp, not even combed. It was the most untidy she'd seem him and his stance looked as relaxed and carefree as that day on the Weald. Stella stretched and he must have heard her soft sigh of pleasure because he swung around.

'At last, sleepyhead.'

'What time is it?'

'Nearing noon . . .'

'What?' She sat up with alarm.

'I jest. It's not yet ten.' She flung a pillow at him as he approached, which he caught deftly. 'Coffee, my lady?'

'Mmm, please.'

'Let me have a fresh pot sent up. Some breakfast?' She shook her head with a lazy grin. 'Not hungry?' he frowned.

'For you, perhaps.'

'Ooh, vixen!' He grinned and flopped onto the bed to kiss her slowly and tenderly.

'Did we . . . ?'

'No, you slept all the way in the car and then yawned and promptly fell asleep as soon as we got into the room.'

She laughed. 'I'm so sorry. And I must be imagining last night. Didn't you check us into separate rooms?'

He dug in his pocket and found a key, holding it up sheepishly. 'I didn't think you'd mind if I was here when you woke up?'

'I don't.' She kissed him again, teasing him with her tongue.

'I don't think I need breakfast either,' he admitted, pulling off his robe.

'What about my coffee?' she enquired in an arch tone.

'I'm afraid I cannot wait,' he gestured downwards and she delighted in how good it felt to laugh so explosively.

They rolled together until he held himself above her.

'What?' Stella wondered gently.

He shook his head. 'I feel like a teenager again.'

'I remember my teens as being awkward.'

'No, I remember that time as being so full of promise, everything to look forward to . . .'

'Every girl a challenge?'

'Of course. However, I admit I've never opened my heart as I have for you.'

She sighed, stroking back his thick hair, and stared at him.

'Don't believe me?' he queried.

'I want to.'

He kissed her, lowering himself so their bodies kissed too. Stella was vaguely aware of the pleasant thought that their limbs and hips seemed to fit seamlessly. It was as though they'd been originally sculpted as a pair of lovers, forever to be awkward with any other partner but each other. And then that notion drifted to the edge of her mind and disintegrated as thought itself disappeared into a blur of agonising and exquisitely escalating pleasure.

The soapy smell of his skin, a sweetly spiced fragrance from his shampoo and the faint taste of rich coffee on his breath enveloped her as his arms extended, pinned hers gently back, and they heard only their own shared music, moving to its rhythm.

'Don't ever leave me, Rafe,' she pleaded.

He opened his eyes above her, pausing in a shared moment of suspended sweetness. 'No matter what, Stella, no one can take away our memories; keep this moment in your mind always and know that there has never been anyone who means what you mean to me.'

It was an oddly emotional claim; she heard a note of wistfulness as though he might never be able to share this closeness again with her. There was a sense that this was their time and they had to make the most of it. Stella searched his gaze, wondering why she felt so suddenly sad, as though this was goodbye, but then he was lowering himself to hold her tightly as the Moroccan spring delivered the fragrance of sweet damascene roses that would forever remind her of him.

Later on the balcony, both now in their bathrobes and freshly showered, Stella took stock of where they were.

'It's beautiful here,' she marvelled, looking out from the balcony towards the encircling mountains. 'There's still snow and yet it's so warm and wonderful.'

He nodded. 'The view from the roof terrace of the Atlas Mountain range is even more spectacular, if you can believe it.'

'I can't,' she admitted, inhaling the heady fragrance of the climbing roses around their balcony.

'The highest peak of the whole range is in the south-western corner of Morocco.'

'I suppose you know every nook and cranny of it,' she teased.

'No, but I travelled with Berbers when I was younger and got to know the foothills where I saw Barbary macaques, even an Atlas bear or two . . . although they may already be extinct.'

She folded into him, putting her arms around his waist, never tiring of the hard, lean feel of his body. 'Is that when you were happiest?'

He weighed her question in his mind, taking his time, his expression growing more serious. 'I don't think I've ever been happier in any moment than I am in this one,' he said, kissing her hand that he was holding against his chest, over his heart. 'You make me feel unencumbered.'

'Odd term,' she admitted, amused.

'It's true. It's the right word. I feel free when I'm with you, Stella. You don't contain me and yet I'm a willing prisoner to your chains. You were well named by your parents. You're like a constellation all of your own, sparkling and beautiful . . . expansive in your thoughts and your attitude; dark and mysterious when you want to be.'

Stella loved his words but laughed. 'You're a terrible tease. Did you mean what you said about us having today to ourselves?'

'Today and all of tonight is ours. No one knows we're here.'

'No guilt?'

'The world we know is not here.' He pointed. 'It's over there somewhere.'

'So where's this?' she wondered, indulging his notion.

'This is Planet Stella. A star that is a long, long way from the life I loathe. Here, no one intrudes. Here we are . . .' He searched for the right word. 'Naked,' he finished, with a grin, which Stella returned. 'But naked in every sense.'

She nodded. 'I like that very much. I want you to always be honest with me, Rafe, no matter how hard it may be.'

'There's nothing hard about being with you, of course other than my —'

Stella stopped his words by covering his mouth with hers. He buried his fingers deeply into her hair and returned her affection with intensity.

As the scent of orange blossom from the nearby groves rode fresh and sparkling bright over the moodier fragrance of the rose blooms, Stella was sure she tasted the intoxicating potency of love in the kiss of Rafe Ainsworth.

When they parted, lips swollen, their gazes locked, she felt she might tear up from the intensity of what had passed unsaid between them and was glad he broke the tension of their kiss by speaking.

'Tonight we'll dance again, Stella.' It made her smile. 'One last dance,' he murmured and before she could respond he kissed her again, pulling her back into the room as he slipped the bathrobe from her shoulders.

Rafe had hired a car and driven her away from the city into the leafy foothills where she could see pomegranates and figs growing wild.

'I'm useless at geography. Isn't this meant to be a desert area?'

Rafe grinned, looking tanned and relaxed in cream trousers with his white shirt open and sleeves rolled up. 'The Sahara does kiss Morocco with the same intensity I enjoy kissing you, Stella, but it's further south.'

'Have you been to the Sahara?'

'Yes. It's an overwhelming place. It feels as though it has its own religion. You feel spiritually dwarfed by its vast emptiness. I've seen sand dunes that had to be nearing six hundred feet and yet that landscape can change in a few heartbeats when the winds come up.'

'I think I'd love to see it.'

'It's dangerous, even for me, and I acknowledge its power. I was fortunate to travel in a caravan with some of its nomadic people when I was a boy.'

'What a life you've led,' she admitted, stroking his cheek. 'Gosh, it's beautiful here too,' she said, 'although hot.'

'Yes, I think we need to get you a hat or a scarf or something or that beautiful skin I love so much is going to sizzle and blister.'

He started the engine and drove on.

'Where are we headed?'

'I'll take you back to the city but we'll avoid the casbah.'

'I'm presuming that if no one knows you're here then you don't have to worry about being seen?'

'I'm not the problem. It's Joseph. I have no idea who may be observing him. He wouldn't know either. So I'm simply being cautious for now and where I'm suggesting you and I go means we won't be anywhere near the medina, where they may be watching.'

Reassured, Stella settled back, enjoying the breeze as he expertly guided them back to the city.

'Feel like a mint tea?'

'Tea? On such a warm day?'

'Trust me, it's extremely refreshing and cooling.'

He led her into the maze of alleys until Stella had lost all sense of direction but was happy to walk alongside Rafe, their arms loosely linked, and she began to imagine that this is what a honeymoon might be like. She was feeling an exciting sense of abandonment, where all responsibility to anyone but themselves was set aside. Deeply selfish, she knew it, but she also knew it was transient; tomorrow loomed and she was determined to ignore its shadow for a few hours longer.

They dodged the relentless path of merchants and their mules, leaping back beneath the canopies at the yell of cart owners as they manoeuvred their wares through the narrow alleys.

She fell deeper in love with his voice as he educated her about the extraordinary scenery around them.

'That mosque – Koutoubia – is from the twelfth century. The majority of the walls would be end thirteenth, very early fourteenth century at the latest.'

'How do you follow this maze?' she declared.

'It has grown a lot even since I was here. Behind all of these walls are homes – some *dars*, some what's known as *riads*.' At her frown he explained. 'Traditional Moorish houses built around a central courtyard – it's open to the sky so it becomes an airy, light-filled dwelling, often exquisitely decorated with *zellij* – mosaic tiles – owned by the wealthier Moroccan families. They have lots of lush plantings to bring cool and shade. The *dars* don't have courtyards, fountains or gardens and lack decoration but their simplicity makes them beautiful.'

'You wouldn't know from these high walls.'

He nodded. 'And every tiny neighbourhood has its own bakery, place of worship, public fountains for ablutions and so on.'

'Everywhere looks the same to me. I don't know how you differentiate.'

'I'm sticking to the walled paths I know and time marches slowly in these narrow alleys.' He spoke in Arabic to a seller who was haranguing them to look at his teapots that were hung all around where they stood. The man backed away good-naturedly. 'The doors are like little landmarks too.'

'The carvings on them are delightful,' she noted.

'Made of cedar,' he said, nodding. 'The Moors kept their clothing in cedar wood because it smells so good,' he added.

'You're a fount of knowledge today,' she teased as a basket full of pomegranates was suddenly thrust at her by a lad with a heartbreakingly sweet smile. She ignored that the basket bled a bloodlike juice, refusing any prophecy in her suddenly superstitious frame of mind. The boy spoke in Arabic but his enquiry sounded polite and he somehow bowed to her while balancing his precarious load.

'Can we buy one at least?' she whispered to Rafe.

He and the boy conversed momentarily, coin was exchanged and she was handed two large smooth-skinned fruit, fat and blushing ripe, just about to burst to reveal their sweet jewels of flesh.

'I've never tasted pomegranate,' she admitted.

'Now you shall,' he promised. He led her on. 'Come on, they've seen us buy something now, we'll be mobbed in a blink.'

Right enough, she could see the beseeching looks of purveyors of flowers to fruit and vegetables she didn't even know the names of, holding out their produce for her inspection. Rafe took her hand and they skipped happily down another laneway and several others that felt identical until he was guiding her beneath the cool awning and dusty darkness of a shop that sold silk.

'Let's find you a scarf,' he grinned.

Scarves fluttered like the wings of butterflies as the shopkeeper, thrilled to have customers, began to show off his wares. He spoke in rapid Arabic and Rafe translated.

'He's telling us these are the colours of nature. The Moors used natural pigments so they got their reds from poppies and pomegranates, blue from the mineral indigo, black from coal.' He nodded at the fellow speaking alongside him, flinging out endless drifts of silken beauties. 'The yellow is achieved by saffron from the Atlas Mountains.'

'Is green from mint leaves?'

He stopped the man, said something and they both laughed. She blinked in consternation.

'We're congratulating you, Stella. The green comes from the mint plant, yes, orange from henna, and so on.'

They emerged and Stella felt like one of the starlets she'd seen in the movies. She was wearing a summer dress not unlike the colour of the damascene roses and she'd chosen a scarf of rich and light greens on a cream background to dramatically team with it. Rafe had draped it around her hair so it covered her shoulders as well and she realised his gift ensured her modesty now respected the culture of the people she was amongst.

'There,' he admired with a smile. 'Now you really are the colours of Morocco . . . roses and mint.'

She wanted to kiss him but wondered at how brazen it might appear. Instead, she whispered her thanks.

'I'll show proper gratitude tonight, paying in kind.'

'Then I need you to understand that it was *very* expensive,' he warned and they lurched out of the shop, effervescing with amusement in their carefree togetherness.

They passed a stall with fresh stalks of mint piled so high that Stella had to stop to admire the small mountain of fuzzy, intensely green leaves with their jagged edges. 'I've never seen so much in one place,' she claimed. 'It's cooling just standing next to this shop.'

Rafe breathed in deeply, closing his eyes momentarily. 'That's the smell of Marrakech for me. Always will be. I grew mint in the garden at Harp's End just so that I could always have this fragrance close.'

She inhaled, exaggerating the gesture. 'And now it will be the same for me too. I promise to plant some at home. But now I have to taste some mint tea,' she admitted.

The café was not far away and in less than a minute they were seated and a man had already heard Rafe's muttered order as waiters pulled out tin chairs against a whitewashed wall.

'Where's the medina from here?' she wondered, dropping her scarf from her head so it billowed its silken folds around her shoulders.

He pointed. 'In that direction. Don't worry, we are a long and complicated path from where the meet is tomorrow.'

The tea arrived; a small silver pot sprouting mint stalks and small, pale-blue glasses with silver handles. The fresh herb countered all other smells around her as the waiter tipped the muddy liquid into their glasses.

'*Shukran.*' Rafe nodded his thanks. 'You can sweeten it if you wish,' he said to her, pointing towards the misshapen lumps of sugar the colour of dark toffee.

She watched him sip without sweetening and followed suit, blowing first at the lip of the glass she held delicately between thumb and middle finger. Instantly Stella liked the taste of the weak green tea with its hum of the fresh grassiness of the mint that left its cool aftertaste. It reinforced their exotic location and she smiled at the man with the monkey on his shoulder who was approaching the handful of Western customers dotted around the café. It would be their turn soon enough, she presumed. 'Are you thinking about it?'

'Hmm?'

'The meeting tomorrow. Is it on your mind?' she pressed.

She noted him trying to cover the truth by looking away. 'Not really.' Rafe shook his head as the monkey owner arrived, said something in Arabic. The man responded and they shared a moment of amusement before the monkey shifted position to sit on the man's head as he walked on. Rafe turned back. 'I presumed you didn't want a photo of yourself with that monkey?' His tone was light but she knew when she was being deflected.

Stella trod softly. 'This time with you is already crammed with precious memories. I don't need to add a monkey to it.'

He gave her a delighted grin and lifted his mint tea in a gesture of cheers. 'Because if you had posed for that photograph, we'd have had every snake charmer and basket weaver for miles following us.'

Stella tapped her nose as if to say she had worked that much out. 'You were saying?' Stella continued. She wouldn't be distracted this time.

'What was I saying?' He frowned.

'That you're not concerned about the meeting. I find that hard to believe.' She waited patiently through the ensuing pause.

He drained his glass and then shrugged, shifting his position as though readying to leave. 'He's my closest, trusted friend apart from you now, Stella. I'm looking forward to seeing him.' His tone had a careless quality to it and Stella heard the lie.

'Rafe . . .'

He cleared his throat and returned his attention to her. 'Shall we?'

'Rafe?'

Amusement dissolved and his expression hardened. 'What do you want me to say? That I'm frightened that he's been followed, that I am fearful for his life, that I think this meeting has the potential to go so very wrong? Is that what you want to hear?'

'Yes, if it's the truth.' She reached to touch his hand lightly, exquisitely aware that a show of affection was inappropriate in public. She withdrew her hand quickly. 'What could go wrong?'

He looked up to the sky with frustration. 'Anything and everything, Stella. He wouldn't know how to shake a tail. Joseph wouldn't even know if he was being followed. He's setting us both up for trouble.'

'Then don't turn up. Rafe, just leave a message and let's go . . . today . . . right now if we must.'

He had begun shaking his head as she spoke and now he turned to regard her with an expression of extreme tenderness. 'I told you, he's my brother. He's frightened. If this were Carys or Rory, would you abandon them . . . leave a message for them?'

She swallowed the rush of words that was rising to fight his negativity but at the mention of her sister and brother she felt all the righteousness that was brimming a heartbeat ago vanish. 'No,' she admitted.

He nodded. 'Let's not spoil today.'

'But Rafe, what if —'

'Life is all about "what ifs" and "if onlys", darling Stella. But we make our decisions based on what we know in the moment. And in this moment all I know is that someone I have loved as kin since childhood needs me and that he wouldn't put me in danger if he could avoid it. Clearly he's unnerved enough to risk it.'

'I don't know what to say,' she said, feeling like she was losing her purchase on him, when only an hour or so ago she had never felt closer to anyone.

'Don't be forlorn, Stella, not today.' He lifted a shoulder and grinned. 'Tomorrow will pan out how it must. Maybe Joseph will arrive alone, we shall have precious time together, he can give me what he came for and we can farewell each other without being observed. Or perhaps it will unfold differently. I never worry about what I can't control, Stella. The spy business is hardly without risk and I didn't come into it without open eyes.'

'No, the worst part is, you like it.'

He watched her for a long moment before he nodded. 'I certainly feel useful, if that's what you mean. As to liking it, no. I like being back in Morocco but frankly I'd prefer to be walking the Weald. I like England and its miserable weather and its colour green. I like hearing my daughter quote Wordsworth, I like watching you pirouette in gumboots, or lying brazenly naked in my bed. I don't like war, Stella, and preventing war is what this is all about. I don't like spying, I like peace, and so if I can be one tiny cog in a machine that maintains peace in the world for the next generation, then I will do what is asked of me, including working as a spy when asked.'

Rafe's gaze had intensified but it felt to Stella as though he was speaking words of love, not fear. Her eyes had welled and now a tear escaped and rolled treacherously down her cheek, chased by another.

'Don't cry, my darling,' he pleaded.

'I'm scared for you. I'm scared of losing you.'

'Stella, I have a creed that has served me well all of my life and that is to focus on what is good about my life and to only concentrate on the present. Right now you are everything that is good about my life and we are here, today, alone and with the freedom to just love one another. That's what I'm keeping my attention on . . . you and how much I love you right now and that dance you've promised me this evening.'

She dipped her head, searching for a handkerchief in her small bag, sniffing back the tears that refused to be stemmed.

'Come on,' he urged. 'Why are we allowing emotion to get the better of us and ruin our day? Let's walk ourselves back into our happy mood.'

Stella dried her eyes and looked around self-consciously. No one seemed to be paying them any undue attention and she squared her shoulders with the knowledge that the situation Rafe was walking into tomorrow was so beyond her control, that nothing she could say or do might change it. He was right. It was easier to ignore tomorrow and worry about making today special – perhaps the only time they may have alone in the foreseeable weeks – maybe months – until he could get his family life sorted and give her a glimpse at the future they hoped to share. The thought of growing old together felt like sunshine in her heart and for the first time she gained a sharper understanding of her parents' terrible pact. Neither wanted to spend a day without each other; they'd grown as old together as they could and for one to go on without his or her closest friend obviously had felt like a far worse torment than losing their lives. The horror of their decision would never leave her, but she was growing closer to forgiveness.

'Ah, there's that smile I love,' he said, hugging her briefly once they had left the tiny square.

'I don't believe I want to see anything more.'

He frowned. 'What do you mean?'

'I want to be where we can be alone, in each other's arms. That's when I feel happiest. That's when I know you're safe.'

'Back to the hotel?'

She nodded.

They walked, without touching or speaking. Stella didn't think they needed to. Soon their skin would touch, their fingers would knit, their tongues would communicate without sound. Stella let the press of people and carts, their animals and the noise of the streets take over. She followed Rafe's figure through the slim, darkened alleyways, enjoying the sound of their lonely footsteps on the cobbles before they emerged into sudden bright sunlight and a host of locals going about their daily chores and business.

He turned around, throwing her a smile. 'All right?'

'It's taking longer than I thought,' she admitted.

'Quick detour. I want to buy you something.'

She shook her head. 'You already have,' she said, touching the silk of her scarf that was back to covering her hair.

He ignored her, grabbing her hand. 'Just here,' he said, and sneaked a kiss against her cheek before he pulled her into a cavernous stall that smelled of spice and florals and was crammed with jars of oil. Baskets of rosebuds and lumps of crystal were dotted around.

'*Salaam*,' Rafe said to the man behind the counter, as he touched his chest.

The shopkeeper beamed from beneath a bushy moustache. 'Good afternoon, Sir,' he said in English.

'Is Mohammed around?' Rafe enquired, switching to English.

The man covered his heart with a hand. 'Sir, I am Youssef. My father died last year.' He muttered an oath in Arabic.

Stella watched Rafe's expression falter. 'I'm sorry to hear that. He was a friend of mine since I was a boy. Always very kind to our family.'

'He was ailing for many years. I am his youngest son.'

'Youssef,' Rafe breathed. 'You were probably just a teenager last time I saw your father.'

'Then you have not been back to Marrakech in a while, Sir,' he said, hands now either side of his bulging belly. 'I have sons of my own now.'

'That's marvellous. Your mother is well?'

'Her health is fragile but she continues to insist we teach her grandchildren English alongside their Arabic and French.'

'Your English is perfect,' Stella said, joining the conversation.

'And you are the most beautiful customer I've had the pleasure to lay eyes on, Miss.'

Rafe laughed. 'You're a chip off the old block, Youssef. This is Stella Myles, a very dear friend of mine.'

Stella privately squirmed but kept her expression even; she understood his caution.

'Then I would be delighted to find a fragrance that is as individual as you are, Miss Stella.'

Rafe turned to her. 'This is a Berber apothecary. Youssef can attend to everything from bunions to toothache – it's our version of a chemist but not an aspirin in sight. His family has also long been a superb blender of essential oils to make fragrances.'

Stella gave Youssef a bright smile and he joined her to shake hands. 'Ah, you already use our famous argan.'

'Argan?'

'In your hair.'

In a self-conscious gesture she touched the dark waves that had fallen free when she'd released them from the scarf. 'How can you know that?'

He tapped his nose. 'I am trained to know it. But do you know how the argan oil is harvested, Miss Stella?'

She shook her head, glancing at Rafe, who was clearly enjoying himself by his grin.

'Argan oil begins with goats eating the nut of the tree. The goats then eject the nut, shall we say.'

Stella's mouth opened with delighted surprise.

'You understand, I see. Our women take the ejected lumps of digested food and crush it. They add water and then it is pressed. That first cold press is used for the cosmetics, including hair oil.'

'Ah,' she said with understanding.

'The second press is a hot press – the paste is warmed and the resulting oil is then used for cooking.'

'How does it smell?' she wondered with a look of dread.

'Just how you say, um, nutty,' he assured with a chuckle.

'There's a final press, isn't there?' Rafe asked.

'Yes, Sir. The third is used as a liniment for the *tedleek* . . . um . . . I have lost the English word for this,' he admitted. He frowned, searching for the word, gesturing rubbing his shoulder.

'Massage,' Rafe explained to Stella.

She nodded, impressed. 'All of those uses from one little nut. Fascinating. Tell me about all your herbals, Youssef,' she said, strolling around the shop.

'This is saffron,' he obliged. 'Tea with saffron is helpful for stiffness of the joints.'

'Roses?' she asked, pointing at the baskets.

'So many uses, it's countless,' he admitted. 'The oil for instance helps with puffy eyes.' He pointed at some orange blossom, smelling sweetly in a huge tray. 'Orange oil, very good for peaceful sleeping; a drop or two in their water and your children will not disturb you,' he said, waggling a finger.

They shared a smile. 'I'll remember that when I have a child,' she promised. 'And this?' she asked, staring at a jar full of black powder.

Youssef rubbed his front teeth with a stubby finger. 'Makes your smile white.'

'No!' she said, filled with disbelief.

His hand flew to cover his heart again. 'I would not lie to you, Miss Stella.' He reached for a small lump of pale stone. 'This is alum. It is a, how you say . . . ?' He gestured rubbing it under his arm.

'A deodorant?' Stella wondered.

Rafe nodded. 'My family used to use it. It's astringent, and also a brilliant styptic so you can stem bleeding. It also makes a good mouthwash . . . altogether, very useful.'

Youssef was nodding, full of approval. 'Also helps with leprosy and gum disease.'

'Gosh!' Stella exclaimed.

Youssef pointed to some small crystals, lifted a few in his hands and offered them to Stella to smell.

'Menthol?' she wondered.

'Crystals of eucalypt,' Rafe replied.

'To keep moths away?' she offered and both men laughed.

'Very good, Miss Stella,' Youssef said, waggling a finger again.

'To chew,' Rafe answered and took a small one. 'A way to achieve sweet breath.'

Stella grinned, her previous glum moment seemed to have passed and she felt light-hearted again, surprised at how her emotions were seesawing these days. 'And these?' she asked, staring at a mound of pebbles of a translucent golden hue.

'Frankincense,' the two men answered together.

'Oh,' she breathed, delighted. 'I've always wondered what it looked like since I was at Sunday School.'

'Sir, I think a sandalwood-based perfume would suit Miss Stella. Come, please, let us find you the perfect oil to dab on your wrists tonight,' Youssef said, turning his attention back to her.

An hour later they drifted back to the hotel, Stella armed with a richly scented fragrance of sandalwood, roses, bergamot and a host of other beautiful smells that formed a concert of harmony that suited her skin and, as Youssef assured her, 'personality' to wear at night.

They spent the afternoon in their room, shutting out the rest of life, and their world now stretched no further than the breadth of their bed. Here Stella found the ultimate comfort wrapped in Rafe's arms and had to hold back the tears again when he looked deep into her gaze and admitted: 'If I died right now, I would die happy because of today.'

She shooshed him, cradled his head near her naked breast, and they slept away the afternoon heat in each other's arms, content in the tingling aftermath of their lovemaking.

'Tonight we dance,' he whispered as they slipped into peaceful sleep.

23

He found her on the balcony as the sun was dipping closer to the snowy caps of the Atlas.

'You left me, wicked wench,' he croaked.

She turned, chuckling. 'You were sleeping so peacefully I didn't want to disturb you.' That much was true but she then felt obliged to follow with a lie to save them both more heartache. 'I only woke about ten minutes ago.' Stella had stirred more than an hour earlier to stare at the man who shared her bed. Rafe was still a relative stranger, she conceded, but consoled herself that she knew as much as she needed to. It mattered only that she had finally found love; a love so fierce that she knew it was akin to bereavement that these coming few hours may be their last together for a long time. With this notion came the memory of her parents and their intense bond and an unexpected stirring of guilt for her anger at them.

With him so tranquil, lost to his dreaming, she had felt alone and that created the space for her fears to fly back like dark shadows. Those she loved and even those she didn't, including Beatrice and Georgina, sat on the imaginary boundary of her mind and nodded. Yes, indeed, she should be scared, they warned. *There is no future with Rafe. Rafe is a lone wolf. Rafe is a dangerous influence. Rafe is in waters deeper than you can imagine. Rafe would never leave Harp's End. Rafe would tear your family apart because your very love for him would force you into a choice.*

Rafe might not survive tomorrow.

That last one came at her like a snarling beast and its shock brought with it a fresh wave of the familiar nausea she thought she had left behind on the rocking ship. But it had found her again on a beautiful late afternoon on the stillness of the land of Marrakech and she'd had to run to the bathroom and retch quietly so she didn't disturb him. Acid liquid had erupted violently to burn her throat and sting her mouth, leaving her prone on the cool of the mosaic floor, panting and frightened. What was happening? Something was stalking her. Was she harbouring a sinister illness, or was her love for Rafe so intense that it had moved beyond that glorious feeling of irrepressible brightness that glowed in every cell and become a physical incarnation of fear? Fear of losing him, fear of abandonment, fear of him returning to the life he loathed but knew, fear of him preferring his strange marriage with Beatrice that gave him freedoms most family men did not experience, fear that the child he loved would ultimately trump her? Fear that she simply wasn't enough?

Finally, after an interminable time, when the breathlessness had ceased and the roiling in her belly had dissipated, she had hauled herself to her feet and placed a damp flannel on her face. The cool worked. She had rinsed her mouth, brushed her tousled hair and pulled on a thin cotton bathrobe to stand in the shade of the balcony to wait for him while she shared the sun's journey towards day's end.

She watched him now, the lie that came so easily floating between them, smirking at her.

He yawned and stretched in his comfortable ignorance and without embarrassment for his lack of any covering. She heard his shoulder click and his contented sigh at the sound. As impossible as she may have thought it a short while ago, Stella felt her body arouse once again at the sight of his nakedness.

'How old are you, anyway? You look so good for it.'

He gave her a look of arch offence. 'You above all should know I am good for it.'

Stella reached for him and pulled him tightly to her. She needed his jaunty humour to carry them through this . . . they simply had to get through another day – less than twenty-four hours, even. By tomorrow noon it would be over and they could make plans for the rest of their lives.

He was still sleepy and buried his head in her shoulder. 'What time is it?' he asked, his voice echoing beneath the canopy of her hair and within the cradle of her shoulder. Stella felt his head shift, knew he would look to the mountains to make up his own mind. 'Must be nearing six,' he decided.

She straightened. 'How do you do that? Is there anything you don't know?'

He grinned back at her. 'Plenty. I don't know how you got this tiny scar, just here,' he said, running a finger beneath her chin. 'I don't know what your middle name is. I don't know how it is that you don't have to say anything yet I can hear your voice in my mind and I feel I know what you're thinking. I also don't know the square root of eighty-three.'

She laughed helplessly, pushing him away but not losing contact with his fingers. She never wanted to lose contact. 'Fool.'

'I envy fools and their innocence,' he admitted and Stella heard the wistful note, understanding what had prompted it.

She threw him a look of sympathy. 'Has Mr Guilt arrived?'

'Knocking at the door but I refuse to answer.'

'Good, ignore him.'

'He'll smash it down, of course.'

'But we'll be gone by then,' she assured, smoothing back the hair that habitually wanted to flop across his forehead. 'We shall climb down off this balcony and run away from all those people making us listen to Mr Guilt.'

He moved fast to kiss her, chuckling at the mental image she'd prompted, but a moment later he looked up from her lips with an earnest expression. 'When this is done, Stella, I want you to run away.'

She squinted at him, focusing squarely on his eyes to gauge the meaning behind his ever-carefully chosen words. 'What about you?' she asked, tiptoeing with equal care.

'With or without me, get away from Harp's End and London. Follow your dream of the café in the spa town.'

She began to deny him but he pressed on.

'Promise me,' he urged.

Again the farewell bells sounded in her mind but she wasn't ready to face reality yet, panting with fear and heartbreak on a bathroom floor. It was only when they were parted that the demons whispered their doubts. When he was awake and moving around her, like now, so full of life and ideas, smiles and affection, she believed in their future.

'Rafe, don't let's talk about what we can't yet see or know. You told me to focus on the now.'

He nodded and turned away but she caught the sad expression before he could rearrange his features into a smile. 'I'm showering. Soon it will be time for cocktails. Answer the door, would you? There's a delivery coming.'

'What is it?' she said to his back as he left her.

'You'll find out,' he replied and within moments was humming in the bathroom, the sound of water splashing noisily.

There was a knock at the door. Stella opened it to find a member of the hotel staff holding a box.

'Madame Stella?'

She nodded.

'*Merci*, *Madame*,' he said, smiling and offering his light load with a small bow.

She took the plain white box. '*Merci, Monsieur*. Oh, pardon . . .' Stella gestured for him to wait. She rifled through Rafe's trouser pocket and found some Moroccan francs. '*Merci*,' she repeated, dropping the coins into his palm. He nodded and left.

Stella checked, seeing the package was addressed to her at this hotel. She blinked, eased the lid from the box and pulled back the white tissue to reveal a magnificent silken fabric of green and ecru. It looked to be a pattern of leaves and stars. Holding her breath, Stella lifted the fabric and it unfurled from its rustle of tissue to reveal itself to be a summer evening gown. She gasped at its simple beauty and the effortless drape of fabric that created its intriguing, yet wholly modest criss-cross neckline whose folds broadened to achieve pretty caps for sleeves.

It was feather-light and figure-hugging.

'Like it?' he asked from where he'd obviously been watching her from the doorway.

She blinked, astonished at how silent he could be. He was towelling his hair but she smiled in a delicious rush of love for the delineated areas of his body that were tanned. His knees to his ankles were bronzed, as were his elbows to fingertips, with a white band where his watch habitually covered. His face and neck glowed and there was the V at the base of his neck where the sun had kissed it long and deep.

'What?' he said. 'Do you hate it?'

She shook her head, overwhelmed suddenly. 'I love it but not as much as I love you.'

'Wear it for me?'

'You've orchestrated all of this. Did you never doubt we'd be here together?'

He looked back at her with a sheepish discomfort.

A silence stretched and it turned awkward. She laid the flimsy sheath of a dress against its tissue.

'What's wrong, Stella?'

'I've always thought of myself as someone in control of herself, and yet you've been pulling all the strings in the background of my life since we met.'

He didn't move as she'd expected but stared at her from the threshold of the bathroom. 'I can't tell you how to feel, Stella. I can only show you how I feel about you, about us. It's true I wanted you here because I may need your help but I wanted to make you happy as well. I wanted us to have time away from everyone and everything we know.'

She gave a grimace of annoyance. 'I hate feeling sorry for myself. It's such wasted energy.'

'So get ready. I'll meet you downstairs in the bar, mint julep at the ready.'

She kissed his shoulder as she moved past him into the bathroom. Tonight she would look like a goddess for him and if it were to be their last evening for the foreseeable future, she would ensure her image and desirability was all he would think of when he left her to return to Beatrice.

She stepped into the lounge that was brimming with drinkers and was aware immediately of appreciative glances. Heads turned and smiles from men drinking together or alone were flashed in her direction. But her attention was drawn to Rafe, whose silhouette she picked out immediately as he stood alone on the verandah. The sun had set but the dying echo of its presence had left the sky in a red blaze around him. She laughed inwardly. For a girl known for her pragmatic nature, how ridiculously fanciful she'd become since meeting him; her life felt a long way from London's Underground, grocery shopping and battling through traffic to get to work each day. That all seemed to belong to a different world now.

The gown billowed gently at her ankles and she was sure she must look as though she were floating across the room. He'd seen her, turned fully and leaned back against the balustrade to watch her approach. The ceiling fans beneath the verandah's ceiling stirred the otherwise breathless evening and she realised they were not alone once she'd stepped out of the lounge and into the evening. But the others didn't matter.

He kissed her hand and then leaned in to kiss her cheek, his eyes glittering darkly in the low light as they turned away to look out across the gardens.

'Nothing to say?' she murmured.

'I'm speechless, that's why,' he replied. 'I don't know which word best describes how you look or how it makes me feel to look upon you. Humbled, I suppose.'

'Another odd word choice,' she jested. 'Why humbled?'

'That you'd choose me.'

She shook her head and considered him, wondering whether to say what was in her mind. She decided she would. 'Rafe, perhaps what I like most about you is that you aren't aware of the effect you have on women. Either that or you are ruthlessly self-effacing.'

He shrugged. 'Most people bore me, Stella. I don't put myself around enough of them to see my reflection . . . if I can put it that way.'

She took his hand, smiling gently at his explanation. 'Well, thank you for the compliment and for the heavenly dress; I really don't know how you do it . . . size me so well, I mean. You could have a well-paid job at Bourne & Hollingsworth any day of the week!'

He gave a low chuckle. 'You and Georgina are a perfect match; I've been buying for her since she was a little girl.' She knew he was right, recalling how well Georgina's sailor's dress had fitted. She banished the annoyance that recollection brought. 'Women's garments are so much more interesting than men's,' he said, flicking at a lapel.

'Shall I put your name forward to the buying team, then?' she offered, laughing as she spoke. 'We can both work and travel together buying beautiful clothes to sell in the department store. What a team we'd make.' Her amusement faltered as something dark ghosted through his expression but he rearranged his grin so fast she couldn't chase down that haunted look. Besides, he was already signalling to a waiter, distracting them both from the notion.

'I promised a mint julep. And I think you must have one. It will match your gown.'

'Both so appropriate for Marrakech,' she remarked. 'The leaf design even looks like mint.'

He grinned, spoke to the waiter and turned to sigh at the scape before them. 'A beautiful night for a beautiful woman.'

'Stop now. I was impressed by you long ago; no need to charm,' she teased gently, linking his fingers in hers.

Rafe shrugged. 'I could wish I'd tried my hand at poetry.'

'Why can't you?'

He gave a snort of disdain.

'Why not? You have years yawning ahead of walking moors and climbing hills.' It was meant to sound light and jaunty but her remark won only a glance of soft wistfulness she couldn't fathom.

'There is some bad news, I'm afraid.'

Stella's expression fell. 'Oh no, what?'

'There's a fellow I know – Wilkinson – also staying at the hotel tonight and he invited himself to join us for dinner.'

Even though her expression reflected disappointment, she felt relief drain through her. She'd expected worse. 'Couldn't you put him off?'

'Did my damnedest,' he admitted, as the waiter arrived with a tray. 'Ah, here we are, lovely it is too, served traditionally in a silver cup.'

Stella beamed as she was handed a cup, so chilled it had frosted over, with a sprig of mint waltzing lazily amongst clinking ice cubes. She smelled the fumes of the spirit base.

'Good southern bourbon served here,' Rafe said, clinking cups. 'Here's to balmy, wonderful nights of lust,' he said with a wicked glint.

Stella paused, before adding, 'To warm and happy days ahead.'

He didn't reply to that but sipped, looking away to the darkening sky with now only a glimmering slash of its glow from moments earlier.

'I know most people marvel at sunsets but I personally prefer the promise that sunrise brings.'

'There you are,' she said, trying to avert the sudden sadness that had crept between them. 'You're already a poet.'

He sighed and pulled her close. 'I'm sorry about dinner.'

'Does he know who I am to you?'

'He didn't ask. A gentleman wouldn't.'

'Good, because I sensed you were embarrassed when we were with Youssef this morning.'

He glanced at her.

'I'm not offended but I suppose the sooner we are honest, the easier it will be.'

He raised his cup again. 'To honesty.'

She sipped, wondering how sincere that toast might be. Stella allowed the potent yet sweet and scented drink to slip down and somehow warm and cool her throat at once. The minted ice was deliciously chilling against the fiery bourbon.

'Good evening,' said an aristocratic voice interrupting them.

'Ah, Wilkinson.' Rafe shook hands with a man a few years older than himself. His voice was terribly posh to Stella but his smile was as warm as the bourbon.

'Hello, my dear,' he said, turning and offering his hand.

'John, let me introduce you to the woman I love. Her name is

Stella Myles. We've only known each other a short time but I feel as though I have been searching for this girl all of my life.'

Stella stared at Rafe, dumbfounded, her mouth still open in disbelief as John Wilkinson shook her hand gently. 'That is quite an introduction, Miss Myles. I'm positively charmed to meet you.'

Rafe gave her a look that asked, *Was that honest enough?* He drained his cup. 'Let's get some champagne, shall we?'

She blinked in consternation, looking away from him. 'Hello, John,' she said, her mind racing as to what had just occurred and why. 'Please, call me Stella. I hear we're dining together this evening.'

'If you'll allow me to bully in on your romantic evening,' he said with a polite nod. 'Given Ainsworth's obvious infatuation, I'm sure you have hundreds to share together yet.'

'I hope so,' she said politely and smiled for him, even though she felt troubled not only by Rafe's mood but his hedging around their future and now his reckless announcement of their relationship. Granted, she'd asked for it. 'I'm starving, actually,' she added, realising they hadn't eaten properly today and what had been in her belly she'd effectively violently emptied earlier. 'Rafe, let's eat, shall we?' she suggested, hoping that food might soak up the flute of champagne he had pilfered from a passing tray and was about to chase the julep down with.

Dinner turned into a sombre affair for Stella. The men discussed Britain's economic woes before inexorably turning to Europe's doldrums and ultimately to Germany hauling itself from the ashes of war in the fist of its new leader.

'Odd-looking fellow, isn't he?' Wilkinson observed.

'Short,' Rafe commented, swallowing a cognac after his fourth champagne. Stella was counting.

'Usually the most aggressive as a result,' their companion added with a grin. He had not kept pace with Rafe's drinks and

Stella noted their fellow diner had remained sober and charming throughout their dinner of roasted chicken that was terribly English but Rafe had ordered some authentically local side dishes; one called couscous that was a Berber specialty. It had arrived in a mound, flanked by whole roasted vegetables and served with chopped mint and lemon.

'Delicious, isn't it?' Wilkinson had winked at her.

'It's so exotic. I've never tasted anything like this before,' she admitted.

In any other circumstance Wilkinson would have made an amusing and enjoyable dinner companion but Rafe's increasing intoxication and his mystifying mood change that had prompted it was worrying her. Music had struck up as most people from the dining room had thinned out to finish their evening next door with the small orchestra. 'Well, dear friends, if you'll excuse me, I think I'll take a quiet smoke of my pipe on my balcony and that will do me nicely for today.' John Wilkinson touched her hand. 'Thank you for a lovely evening, my dear; I'm sure every other man tonight envied me.'

'You can bet they did,' Rafe said without slurring but Stella's irritation was no longer happy to remain tucked neatly out of sight and it took all her effort not to scowl.

'Goodnight, John. I hope we meet again.' She stood to show her intent and feigned a small yawn. 'I shall turn in too.'

'Stella?' Rafe said. 'The night is but young.'

'Night, old chap,' Wilkinson said, tapping Rafe on the shoulder. 'Tonight's on my tab.' He walked away before Rafe could protest, perhaps sensing aggrieved words about to be exchanged.

Rafe lifted a careless hand in farewell but his stormy gaze was riveted on her. 'Where are you going?'

'To bed,' she said, smiling at the waiter who pushed her chair in for her. 'Goodnight, Rafe.'

'Wait!' he called far too loudly.

She was glad there was only one other couple dining – two men, laughing loudly with each other over balloons of brandy. She turned back.

'Rafe. Don't do this.'

'Do what? What am I doing?'

'Making the ruin of our single evening any worse.' She turned away and in her haste and annoyance stupidly took the wrong doors and found herself back out on the verandah. She swung around to find a different way back but he was right there behind her, his voice as soft as his footfall.

'I'm sorry,' he said.

'Why?'

'Why am I sorry? Because I've upset you.'

'Why did you try so hard to upset me, I mean?'

'What have I done?'

'How much more did you plan to drink? Until you were so drunk you couldn't support yourself?' She turned away from him, placed her hands in frustration on the balcony, promising herself no tears. She despised even letting fly with these angry words.

Rafe put his arms either side of her so his hands rested next to hers. 'It takes a lot more liquor to make me lose my faculties, Stella. I admit I am drunk on love, though, and what I can't have.'

'Can't have?' She turned around in the circle of his arms. 'Can't have? I'm yours. What's not to have?' she said, searching his face in the light of the lanterns that had been lit since night had closed in.

A whisper of a breeze stirred a curl of her hair, which he caressed between his fingers with a sad smile. He leaned down and kissed her and it was a heartbreakingly gentle gesture. 'Just the sight of you, especially tonight, is intoxicating. Can we blame that?'

'Why so sad, then?'

'I like Wilkinson but I wanted to bore him into leaving us. I needed you all to myself.'

'You have me, Rafe. And even if we're forced apart, you're right here,' she said, placing her hand over her heart. 'And I will always be right there,' she said, swapping to place it over his.

He covered it with his own. 'Let's dance, Stella. Let's begin tonight again.'

She made a face as though she didn't feel like it.

'Please,' he urged. 'Let's go back to where my love for you began . . . on the dance floor, you in my arms, but frosty at me.' A smile twitched at the corner of her mouth. 'Dance with me?'

'One dance before I take you up to my bed and only because you're a good dancer and those are thin on the ground in London, let alone Marrakech, I suspect.' She fought her way back to find her mood of affection and amusement.

'One last dance,' he said, taking her hand, pulling her away from the railing.

She didn't much care for the sound of those words but refused to remain wintry with him. 'Here?' she said, looking around.

'Why not? I don't want to share our last dance with any observers, not even the orchestra.' He began to move her, light on his feet as always, although she could tell his mood was far from bright. She wished she could approach whatever it was that was dancing between them. Stella wondered whether it was his fear about tomorrow, or was it his fear about all the days stretching beyond that and the recriminations they might contain over betraying his family? 'Stella?' he interrupted.

'Yes?'

'Stop thinking, stop trying to second-guess me. I can almost hear your thoughts. Just close your eyes and dance in my arms.'

And so Stella danced with him, like liquid mercury, cleaving to him but not binding him in a proprietary way. That's where Beatrice went so wrong, she realised in a moment of epiphany as they moved to the sound of a distant waltz that found them from the ballroom.

Beatrice had wanted to own him, control him, in the similar greedy way that a passionate collector might covet an item.

Rafe touched the tiny peephole of flesh in the small opening that the folds of her gown afforded. She smiled for him but he was lost to her, staring at where his finger connected with her skin.

'You will never be loved as I love you,' he murmured.

The temptation to quiz him on this prowled around her but she resisted it. Right now she just wanted to be held and to dance with the man for whom she held a love that could never be equalled.

24

Stella was sure she'd barely slept and yet woke with a start to find she was alone; she sat up, panicked.

'Rafe!'

He dashed in from their verandah, looking concerned, although she noted he was dressed immaculately in a pale suit, his hair combed with precision, clean shaved and skin glowing as though he'd just stepped out of a movie. How had he achieved all of that soundlessly?

'Sorry, I thought you'd gone,' she explained. Her shoulders relaxed and so did his expression. Stella shook her head. 'How did you fit all that into that small holdall?' she said.

'I cheated.' He winked. 'I had a suit sent on.' His voice turned businesslike, as though closing a door on the last two days. They both stood on a new threshold and there was only one direction in which to move. 'Time's against us, Stella.'

The words sounded prophetic, even as she yawned.

'I'll be ready in a blink. Is there some tea?'

'Coffee?' he offered in an apologetic tone.

She rose, padded over from the bed and hugged him, not wanting to confront the issue of today that was nevertheless so tangible that she felt it was standing like a third person in the corner watching them. 'Thank you, yes, please. I'll be quick . . . just like you were last night.'

His grin was sheepish. 'I'll make it up to you, I promise.'

'You'd better,' she warned, not explaining that although his lovemaking had ended uncharacteristically abruptly, she had been content to hear him sigh and drift into a deep sleep.

When she emerged from the bathroom to a pot of coffee, her hair was neatly plaited back, face scrubbed of all trace of make-up. She dressed rapidly in a narrow cream skirt and a shirt, with a tan belt that she'd deliberately planned to wear today. It was neat, simple and forgettable: precisely her intent. Stella did not want to draw undue attention. Even the dark plait would be tucked beneath a hat and she dug out the glasses she'd lifted from a shelf in the nursery at Harp's End. She put them on now and looked at herself in the mirror and blinked at the difference her careful preparations for today had made. She swallowed a few sips of black coffee in the hope of stemming the biliousness that had plagued her since the voyage. When would it end?

'Good grief!' he exclaimed as she swung around.

'So?'

'Where have you gone, my beautiful Stella?'

'Well, I'm guessing you want me to be as invisible as I can be?'

He approached, looking awed and amused at once. 'Are those my glasses?'

She murmured a laugh. 'I've become a thief somewhere over the last few weeks too. Yes, I confess, I found them on a shelf in your study and pocketed them. With plain glass in them, I too can play your sneaky game.'

'You look marvellous. I think you've aged about a decade.'

'This is what you can expect to see in ten years, then,' she warned. And there it was again: that hesitation before the smile.

'Clever you.' He distracted her by swinging her around. 'The plait is hilarious too – I'm surprised you didn't go the whole way and pin it into a tight bun so you can be every inch the librarian.'

'Wouldn't fit under my hat,' she said, retrieving it from the bag. 'Look.' She plonked it on and pulled a face of pursed lips.

He laughed. 'You would make a thoroughly good spy. Your preparations are perfect.' His expression clouded. 'Listen,' he said, taking her hand. 'It all feels amusing but I'm walking you into a serious situation.'

'I know. I'm deliberately taking a light-hearted approach only because I know how tense you are.'

'I wouldn't be if I were alone. Your presence adds a layer of worry I have not experienced previously.'

'So tell me what you want me to do.'

He blew out a deep sigh. 'It's hard to say because I don't know what to expect. However, rather than groom you, I'd prefer you played it by ear as you have played life since I met you. You're good at it, Stella; you have sound instinct for situations and you know how to fade, how to step in, when to act. I trust your judgement. The point is, I need you to understand completely that this is not a game.'

She opened her mouth but he wouldn't let her interrupt.

'No, wait; I need to impress upon you that whatever information Joseph is bringing with him is as dangerous as a loaded gun pointed at your heart. I want to make sure that the gun never has you in its sights.'

'Or yours,' she said, with a warning look.

'Or mine. However, this is between Joseph and me . . . and whomever else is following him, if anyone is following.'

'Will this information be written down or are you going to memorise it?' she wondered aloud.

'Basil Peach believes it will be on paper. So it's truly a loaded gun,' he warned.

'I understand, Rafe. You want me to be ready to take that gun, I suspect.' He stared at her and in that look she saw fresh respect.

'I'm your decoy, aren't I? Also your back-up, I now realise. I've reached the understanding that I am to take the document and its important contents if for any reason you can't.'

He shook himself as if from a trance but Stella knew she'd surprised a man who wasn't used to surprises. 'You take your lead from me and if I say sit here or go there, you do as I ask. None of that fiery spirit is to show. I want you to play the part of the meek researcher.' He took off her spectacles and gave them a shine, placing them gently on her nose again. 'The meek, bespectacled researcher, whose only interest is helping me collate information for a new exhibit that is being sponsored through Kew Gardens for the Linnean Society of London.'

'The Linnean Society?'

'Started in the 1700s, world's oldest biological society and named after Carl Linnaeus.'

She nodded, frowning. 'And he is?'

'A Swedish naturalist interested in all things botanical and zoological, and the word for butterfly collector is lepidopterist, by the way . . . and if you want to sound very smart, the archaic term, coming from the Latin for chrysalis and its normally golden colour, is aurelian.' His forehead creased with concern. 'You see how nervous you've made me, I'm now babbling and I never babble.'

'Unless you're with Beatrice.'

'That's a different sort of babble. I'm entirely in control of that form.' He turned away, hands on hips. She'd not seen this expression before. He was frightened. 'Stella, I've changed my mind. Please stay here.'

'Rafe, calm down. You're going to meet your old friend again and share a few hours. All you have to do is give me a sign and I'll disappear back to the hotel or . . . get me involved as you choose. Welcome7I promise I will follow your lead.' She let go and reached for the small satchel she had also prepared. 'See, now I completely look the part.' She smiled, trying to push confidence into him, knowing she was his problem and yet he needed her there to add another layer to his disguise.

She watched him take a slow breath as though letting that previous fear go before he looked at his wristwatch and then at her, fully resolved to their duty. 'Let's go.'

Despite the warmth and humidity of the climate, Stella couldn't deny that the atmosphere in their room of love had become so brittle that she felt she could snap it.

This will all be over in a few hours, she told herself silently. Stella gave a last glance at the bed and reminded herself that the next time she laid her head down on its pillows, all this frightening business would be behind them. They would return to London and make plans for how to be together. The thought of cold, grimy London brightened her immeasurably and she banished all doubt, stepped forward and linked her arms around his neck, grateful for the small heels.

'Let this kiss be a promise for what we're going to do when we get back into this room,' she said. She kissed him slowly and with as much passion as she could load into the moments of such intense connection that even the sounds of the birds faded, replaced by the whoosh of her pulse.

Rafe stepped back, looking moved. 'You frighten me when you kiss me like that.'

'Why?' She smiled tenderly, her lips still close to his.

'I don't want to let you go.'

'After today I promise you never will. Come on, let's get this over with.'

They walked in silence, a new tension settling in her throat; a lump of worry she couldn't dislodge no matter how much fresh air she sucked in or tried to swallow. She put it down to the familiar nausea that haunted her but knew she was trying to trick herself. The fact is, she was scared, but it was easier to lie. He kept a distance from her, two paces ahead, and his stride had lengthened purposefully so that Stella felt she had to add a hurried skip every few steps to keep up. Her mental image of them made sense, though; today she was his research assistant and no emotional closeness must be detected.

She followed him through narrow streets that felt strangely familiar to her as they all looked the same. She could hear melodic yet curiously tuneless music coming from somewhere. Trance music, Rafe had told her previously, but she couldn't remember what else he'd said about it.

It seemed that suddenly Rafe's fears had leaped from his shoulders onto hers because he appeared fully collected now and focused. He moved with purpose but his lope had fallen into that easy rhythm and she knew he was back in control of his emotions. Her lover – the one who heard poetry in his mind and lived off emotion – had disappeared within and pushing forward was Rafe, the ruthless, cold-hearted spy.

She noticed he ruffled the hair of young children rushing to their local bakery. He smiled at the water sellers, took a moment to wave a friendly *No, thank you* at the fruit merchants who were yelling their wares near their laden baskets. He grinned at the man with the barrow of oranges, still dew-laden and ready to offer up their sweet juice. Despite behaving distantly he was aware of her following and looked behind him from time to time to warn her of mules and carts.

A man offered her teeth-cleaning sticks, while a nut and nougat seller caught her attention; she shook her head at both as young African men sat in an alley hammering out a catchy rhythm on their small drums that halted her. She paused to enjoy their music but Rafe scowled over his shoulder and she hurried on past other musicians, people selling hats, others selling baskets. Women reached out to offer to paint her hands with henna while men with monkeys on their shoulders beckoned.

Stella made every effort to close off her attention to all but Rafe as they entered the medina, an arresting zoo of sound and colour, smells and people moving in all directions. They crossed it quickly but once again her fascination was captured, this time by a snake charmer who sat cross-legged in the middle of the throng. His long white beard was tied into a tiny plait at its end and his scarlet turban failed to hide the white wisps of hair escaping at one edge. Stella felt the rush of helpless alarm, recoiling at the sight of the snake that could kill with a single dose of its venom swaying before its owner. She'd always thought snake charming to be a myth and felt as mesmerised by the scene as the snake appeared to be by the odd music.

Rafe had doubled back, and was now hissing in her ear. 'Stella!'

'How dangerous that is,' she breathed. 'Amazing.'

'Not really,' he remarked, herding her away and forwards.

'Oh, so you can snake charm, can you?' she asked, wishing they could have lingered.

'I guess anyone could if the snake had its mouth sewn shut as that one had. The serpent is helpless; will likely be dead in a few days.'

Stella felt new shock rippling through her.

'It's just entertainment, Stella.'

He gestured down a quiet alleyway. 'It's not far. A couple of minutes now. Stella, it's time you moved entirely into character.'

A new sound assailed them and Rafe tipped his head. 'It's *salat*,' he remarked and moved on as the midday call to prayer was sounded by a reedy voice singing from a minaret in the medina.

She nodded, pulled her hat further down as she felt the wailing voice add fresh tension that knotted in her gut like a pulled thread. They walked without talking or touching as men and boys hurried past them to pause at fountains to wash before prayer.

Keep my man safe, she threw out into the universe and then, as if sloughing off a skin, she shrugged off Stella, his lover, and became Stella Myles, research assistant to Douglas Ainsworth, man of science.

After several minutes of moving in a vacuum, Stella sensed they were entering a new square. This one was almost peaceful by comparison to Marrakech's main marketplace even though people were still busy hawking their wares.

Stella noticed that Rafe's stride turned to a saunter. He swung around.

'Would you care for a tea, Miss Myles?'

She was careful to keep the appropriate distance. 'Only if you're having one, Captain Ainsworth.'

His blink was the only sign of his surprise at the title she'd used. It sounded right to her, though. 'In Morocco, they take mint tea. I grew up here so can attest to its cooling quality.'

'Then I should like to try one, for it is certainly a warm afternoon.'

'Over here, I think.' He pointed. 'These tearooms should do us.'

They ducked into the cool shadow of the awning that reached out from the nondescript building. The café had no name but she knew they'd arrived at Mustafa's because on the wall behind them was a mural depicting a peacock. This was indeed the shisha café where Rafe had, as a boy, tried his first smoke.

The tables were empty, save theirs, although she could smell tobacco coming from the depths of the café. A waft of fresh mint drifted by and its fragrance comforted her, as if assuring that all would be well.

He spoke in Arabic to the man who arrived to serve them. Their discussion seemed to last longer than she considered plausible; she noted that the waiter glanced at her, back at Rafe, then smiled and nodded. Rafe gave him a wad of notes.

'Is everything all right?'

'Stay in character,' he murmured. 'So, tomorrow I have organised for a driver and a guide. We will be travelling into the foothills of the Andes. I really do need to sight the local butterfly of the family *Hesperiidae.*' He leaned back in his chair and fanned himself with his hat.

Stella tipped out the contents from her satchel, opening a notebook and flipping through the pages. To the casual observer her jottings would make perfect sense but Rafe would recognise passages from his own notes that she'd dutifully copied out in different inks, some in pencil, as though written on a different day, in a different mood. Rafe was right – she was cunning enough to make a half decent spy. In another situation she might have enjoyed that thought but increasingly this situation was beginning to feel intense, more dangerous by the moment. Rafe's casual pose had not changed. He was not darting his glance around to pick up potential observers, and he was avoiding her, to make her feel less conspicuous.

'Of course the best place to view butterflies is in the High Atlas.'

She nodded, frowning over the top of her glasses. 'Shall we be going there, Captain Ainsworth?'

Their tea arrived and was set down quickly. He sighed and sat forward as he gestured for her to enjoy.

'Yes, I thought I might try for the end of the week. It will be much cooler up there, so you'll need to wear appropriate layers. Butterflies prefer the cooler climes. We may sight a rosy grizzled, perhaps even the local cardinal.'

'Oh, that would be grand, wouldn't it?' she said, sipping her tea. 'Um, what time is your appointment, Sir?'

'Noon. My guest should be here any moment.'

'Would you like me to move, Captain . . . give you some quiet time together?'

'Not at all. I would like you to meet him. He's someone I have known since we were boys together in Africa.'

'What does your friend do, Sir?'

His mouth twisted into a sort of shrug. 'It's hard to be specific with Joseph. He's an administrator of some kind.'

'So he followed a very different line of work to your academic pursuits,' she remarked, hoping this small talk was on the mark. She smiled politely, realising he'd replied and she'd not heard a word. She was aware of her pulse escalating, could hear it, if she concentrated, pounding behind her ear. She must stay calm. She promised him she could do this. Why was she so nervous? Rafe was looking entirely at peace . . . but then he was a practised spy and she was just a trainee store buyer who dreamed of having her own tearooms in a spa town.

'Oddly, he is the one who looks more the academic,' he finished and smiled. She sensed he saw pride in her performance and offered encouragement . . . and something else. She blinked, lingered for a heartbeat but couldn't read it. He looked away into the square and drank his tea in silence. Stella busied herself reading his notes – pages she'd read many times over the past week or two. She rehearsed in her mind what he'd asked her to remember.

The call by the *muezzin* abruptly ended. It was noon. The men of Marrakech were at their mosques praying, some in the square had unrolled small mats and faced Mecca to pray.

A gentleman, small and slim of stature, wearing pale linens, broke cover from one of the many alleys and walked across her eyeline. She shifted her attention to watch his approach. The gaze from his curiously light eyes scanned the surrounding stalls so he appeared nervous, even from this distance. He took an odd skip every few steps as though wanting to hurry but forcing himself not to. It was Joseph, all right, wearing a look of relief he clearly couldn't help at spotting his friend. Stella watched him smile from beneath a luxuriant, dark moustache and lift an arm in salutation to Rafe. Her lover responded and she knew him well enough now that although he made it look casual enough there was genuine joy in his expression.

'Hello, Joseph,' he called, standing. He sounded choked.

She watched his friend arrive and had to swallow to banish her rising emotion to see these two men wrap each other in a heartfelt hug; two boys from that sweet photo with its romantic, adventuresome backdrop of the desert were reunited. Stella was sure Joseph was weeping, from the way he took off his small round glasses and whipped out a handkerchief to polish the lenses. She noted he dabbed at his eyes, while Rafe hurried to make introductions.

'Er, Joseph,' he cleared his throat, clearly swallowing his emotion too. 'This is Miss Stella Myles. She is my research assistant. Miss Myles, this is Joseph Altmann, my oldest and dearest friend.'

Joseph returned his glasses and blinked behind them. His eyes were an olive green, she noticed, and were part of a series of spare, handsomely assembled features.

'*Enchanté*, Mademoiselle Myles,' he said and nodded over the hand she extended.

'It's a pleasure. What a lovely way you are introduced. That must feel special,' she replied in French.

'We are brothers in all but blood,' Joseph admitted.

Rafe moved them into English, signalling to the waiter for a tea for his guest. He muttered just for their hearing, 'Honesty doesn't help in the spy game, Joseph, but given your candour and at risk of being reckless and especially in the presence of both of you who deserve no lies, you should also know that Stella is not only my lover but she is also the love of my life.' Both Joseph and Stella gaped at him. He shrugged. 'There are only three people alive in the world that I can put my hand over my heart and claim that I love and would die for. Two are seated right here,' he said, smiling softly.

'Why wouldn't I want you both to know of each other's meaning to me?'

Stella looked back at Joseph with a perplexed smile; worried now for the danger of this admission, having been so careful before about staying in character. She didn't think anyone had heard, but even so, why take such a risk? It was as if he wanted someone or something else to take over, to make the decisions for him. She shrugged and fell in with his spirit of honesty. 'I have never fallen for anyone until I met Rafe,' she admitted, unsure of what else to say other than the truth. 'I love him.'

'As do I, so I'm not just enchanted, Miss Myles, I'm honoured to know you. It seems you and I are amongst the very few who have impressed Rafe enough to even know his preferred name, let alone be worthy of his love.'

The same waiter arrived, setting down a fresh glass of tea for Joseph. It was a convenient moment of distraction.

'And is Brigitte as beautiful as I recall?' Rafe enquired.

'Radiant with her new son in her arms.'

'Congratulations again. A son! Well done. You're a better man than I.'

The men laughed conspiratorially. 'No, a real man makes daughters, they say,' Joseph offered generously, 'but he's such a sweet boy, we do dote on him . . . so do the girls.' Then he pulled a face of disgust. 'They dress him up in dolls' clothes! Brigitte finds it amusing. I am personally disturbed but then as they do that to the dog too I have to accept these are the mysterious ways of females.' He looked at Stella and winked.

Helplessly charmed, she wondered if both these men were pressed from the same mould. 'Be assured, it's very normal. I'm told you came here as youngsters,' Stella said, sweeping her gaze behind in a casual gesture in case they were being watched. She couldn't pick up anyone intent on them but it was so fleeting, she desperately wanted to check again but instead returned her attention to Joseph.

'Indeed we did. I'm sure Rafe has told you about the peacock and Yassine laughing in the background as we coughed and hacked our way through our first smoke.'

'Mother was livid with us,' Rafe recalled in a tone of pleasurable wistfulness.

'And Bel was jealous.'

She watched Rafe swallow. 'Furious we did it without her,' he chuckled sadly, glancing at Stella. 'Bel is my sister.'

'I gathered,' she replied gently, realising only now that this was the first time she'd heard his sister's name uttered. *Isabella? Annabelle?* There was plenty to still learn about Rafe but as always it felt as though an invisible but enormous clock ticked loudly around them.

'You can be frank in front of Stella,' Rafe assured with a deep and meaningless chuckle. 'Be calm, Joseph. She knows. Hence her disguise. She has perfect vision and beautiful hair that you can't see and a laugh to light your world.'

Joseph shot a look of sympathy over his glasses at Stella, who wished she could take hers off. 'My world is filled with darkness, it's true,' he said softly over a fresh gust of amusement, designed to fool any watchers. Stella was impressed by both of them, especially Joseph for whom she knew this must be torture. 'I shall not waste time on preambles. I don't believe I was followed but I live in a nation of suspicions and cannot take our safety for granted.' He removed a small book from a leather satchel.

Rafe gasped. 'I'm being flung back a quarter of a century,' he gusted merrily, slapping Joseph on the shoulder. 'I remember this!' he exclaimed, adding in a lower voice: 'You're doing fine. Sip your tea. Just pretend we're catching up on old times.' Rafe took the album, seeming to know what to do. He began feigning soft laughter, pointing and showing photos to both of them. Stella took his lead, cast an expression of deep interest while inside she churned, wondering what was about to happen.

'This is an old photo album that Rafe's wonderful mother – our mother – sent to me for my seventeenth birthday,' Joseph explained to Stella. 'My father had moved us back to Germany and I was so missing my life with the family I loved as my own in Tangier so she filled this little book with memories of childhood. Rafe, I do think my favourite is this one of us in the tent.' He flipped a few pages and sighed, pointing at it. Stella picked up the signal that passed between them as he tapped the particular photo she recognised from the nursery.

Rafe laughed. 'Hell, what were we then? Ten?' He nodded, his expression full of pleasure. 'Got it,' he murmured. He sipped at his now cold mint tea. 'We couldn't have been any older, could we?' He made an obvious shift to show it to Stella. 'Here, look at this,' he offered in a light voice but his words that followed chilled her. 'Remember it, Stella,' he growled in the lowest of whispers.

Joseph glanced at them both. It was as if they'd reached some sort of precipice and they were all peering over the top to dizzying depths below. He grinned with effort but the words didn't match. 'And now let's see if I have indeed made it all the way back to the land I love, the brother I worship, without bringing the devil with me.' His voice shook and his fingers visibly trembled as he reached into his pocket and pulled out a sheet of paper. 'This is why I'm here. You should know that only recently the Chancellor of Germany outlined his new foreign policy that rejects aspects of the Treaty of Versailles.'

The warm day's temperature felt as though it instantly plunged around their table and Stella put down her cold tea as a chill shuddered through her; they were still smiling, nodding amiably, as Rafe acknowledged what his friend was saying. 'Equal armaments,' he said, agreeing that he knew this much.

Joseph shook his head, his smile faltering. 'So much worse, Rafe. The relationship with the Soviet Union will be non-existent soon, I suspect; our ambassador in Moscow told him as much this month. He is feigning moderation to London but his eye is on the Polish border. He is talking about trebling the army, creating dive bomber units.'

'Germany's not permitted to have an aerial capability.'

Joseph shrugged. 'Tell our Chancellor that. I happen to know that pilots are in training. Our decorated world war ace is in his element. Herr Göring and his cronies only last month established an air ministry. A Luftwaffe! Hitler doesn't care about the Treaty or its sanctions. He has every intention to defy them.'

Rafe's expression darkened. 'I can't say I'm shocked.'

'Well, you will be when you read this.' Joseph pushed the sheet forward. 'These are pages from draft notes that I am horrified to admit I have acquired through dishonest means. I am betraying my own people but I have no choice because the Chancellor no longer believes that people of my heritage *are* Germans. From what I can tell, these notes seem to form part of a manifesto he's drafting for Germany. He aspires for purity of the race. Aryan, he calls it.'

'What are you talking about?' Rafe growled, his façade falling away.

Joseph removed his hand from the sheets. 'Read them,' he urged, whipping out his handkerchief again to once more attack his lenses before pushing the spectacles back up his nose nervously. 'His new racial ideology has Jews at the helm of his hate list. I couldn't believe it, dared not, in fact. I've sat on this for weeks but in April a boycott began on Jewish stores, although attacks on our shops began even earlier in March. There are calls to remove Jews from the legal, medical and educational system. I have no doubt now that it's going to happen.'

'Hitler had the Enabling Act passed,' Rafe explained to Stella.

'It means he now rules simply by his own decree and can determine his own laws; no need to pass them through the Reichstag.'

Her throat felt as dry as the sun-bleached awning they sat beneath.

Joseph continued as though Rafe had not spoken. 'It's a steady breakdown in our society. No more kosher slaughtering of animals one month, the next we can't send our children to school if it over-reaches the Jewish "quota". And this month students across Germany burned what they called un-German books in an action against an un-German spirit. If it wasn't true, I'd laugh but I wept to hear that in the order of thirty thousand books were burned in a "cleansing by fire". Jewish intellectualism, whatever that's supposed to mean, is cited as being un-German. People are being brainwashed and the propaganda is rife.'

Stella watched Rafe nod as though he was aware of this particular atrocity. 'I'd heard about the book burning, but I had no idea of the scope of all this racial vilification, Joseph.'

'We've lived with persecution down the centuries and no one wants to tip Europe back into war, my brother, so coming to the rescue of a few persecuted Jews is unlikely to be on the agenda . . . except it's not just Jews, it's everyone that our dictator suddenly believes might speak up against him and his dark regime. Pacifists, socialists, liberalists, intellectuals, poets! They're all on his list of hate. Ever since these came into my possession my perspective on the ministry has changed. I realise now that I've been working for a dictator who is determined to own the minds of his people so there is no more free thought. What previously looked innocent, such as the training of pilots, has taken on a new and sinister aspect. I've heard artists, writers, poets, thinkers – they are all wanting to flee the country. They feel the next step might be the burning of the writers themselves.' Joseph stopped, shaking with the emotion of his fear.

Stella could see his perspiration was nothing to do with the climate and she was privately appalled that they were both being defiantly open about their discussion. If they were so worried about being observed, why were they being so obvious? It seemed Rafe no longer cared about being watched or being cautious. He'd been careful for her presumably but now felt confident; either that or he was taking a fatalistic view, which she could believe given last night's odd behaviour and today's honesty to Joseph. She was feeling as though he was deliberately pushing her away and yet making sure his brother knew that she was the important woman in his life. Why? And what was the charade with the photos? What should she know? Stella sensed with every ounce of perception that the clue she needed was already present even though it was invisible. *Pay attention, Stella*, it demanded. And so she snapped her focus to all the elements before her: photo album, two sheets of paper yet to be unfolded, Rafe outwardly calm and jovial yet there was nothing casual about his seemingly casual gesture, certainly nothing happy in that smile of his. And Joseph was now freely perspiring: frightened, nervous. She wanted to scoop up the sheets of paper, throw them in her satchel and run. They had what they came for – why weren't they moving, escaping potential harm? She opened her notebook again in a desperate attempt to appear distracted, uninvolved. She saw the lines of writing but couldn't read them. It didn't matter. She was acting out the charade.

'Read it, Rafe. Tell me this wasn't worth risking everything for,' Joseph was saying. 'It's in Hitler's handwriting, for heaven's sake. The persecution has already begun but maybe I was deliberately blind to it or too protected from it because of my station. Now . . .'

It felt to Stella as though her throat was closing with anxiety for them and a helpless hushing sound escaped as she tried to stem their words as a mother might to her children. 'Is this wise?' she asked, although it came out in a squeak just as a shadow fell across them.

'Not at all wise,' answered a new voice and its owner's arm

reached between herself and Rafe. He was dressed in a greyish olive linen suit that sat unhappily below receding blond hair and a pale complexion. He was smiling but there was little sincerity in it going by the cold, pale eyes that glared above it. 'I shall take that,' he said, clamping a hand down on the papers that Rafe had just grasped. 'Thank you,' he said in a sarcastic tone, withdrawing the pages.

Stella closed her eyes momentarily, recognising the unmistakable accent of a German speaking English.

'Greetings, Herr Altmann. Why don't you introduce me to your companions?'

Stella was aware of three other men lurking. They'd surely materialised from one of the alleys behind the café. She glanced at Rafe, who appeared unmoved. Had he anticipated this outcome? He seemed suddenly more relaxed for the man's arrival.

'Karl. You of all people,' Joseph said, his tone resigned, as though relieved the terror of discovery was now past.

'Herr Klipfels to you from hereon, Altmann,' the man cautioned.

Joseph nodded, as though now fully accepting the inevitable. 'This is my friend, Douglas Ainsworth.'

'Mr Ainsworth,' Klipfels said. 'English, yes?'

'If you wish,' Rafe said. 'Escaping a cold German spring, Mr Klipfels?'

The German's smile broadened but remained as wintry as his near colourless eyes whose corners didn't so much as crinkle with the stretch of his thin mouth.

'It's just that your pale skin looks a little burned,' Rafe offered, his tone full of generous concern.

'Not yours, though, I notice,' Klipfels replied.

'I grew up here. The Moroccan sun is my friend, the streets of Marrakech a boyhood playground.'

'I was under the impression you grew up in Tangier?'

'Should I know you or have you been busy doing some homework?' Rafe exclaimed, betraying no surprise despite his words. When Klipfels didn't answer, he grinned. 'I did, yes. So my skin is well accustomed.'

'And who is this charming companion?' Klipfels wondered, bored of Rafe's feigned charm.

'As you've done your background checks, I imagine you know that I am carrying out some special work for Kew Gardens. This is my research assistant, Miss Myles.'

'Research?' He laughed. 'Is that what they call a tryst these days? How would you like to have dinner with me tonight instead, Miss Myles . . . later some German-style conviviality, yes?' he asked, stroking her cheek.

With Joseph looking as helpless as a trapped rabbit and Rafe seemingly enjoying the tense banter, Stella felt it was left to her to disrupt proceedings and give her companions a chance to think through their escape. She pushed her chair back and stood. 'How dare you, Sir!'

As she'd guessed he expected her to remain meek because of discovery, her fiery response took him by obvious surprise. He stepped back and Stella filled the space he'd left, taking her chance.

'What are you suggesting?' she snapped in breathy horror.

Klipfels glared at Joseph, then at Rafe, finally returning his unsure gaze to her. 'My sincere apologies, Miss Myles. A wrong presumption.'

'Presumption?' she thundered, finding fear a helpful boost for her rage. 'Are all Germans as poor mannered as you, Herr Klipfels?' She watched him squirm, pushed on, buying more time for the two men still seated. 'Well, your apology is not good enough. I'm deeply offended that you'd humiliate me in front of my employer and his friend I have only just a few moments ago met.'

'And what were you all discussing?' Klipfels asked, trying to wrestle back control of the situation.

'I have no idea,' she said, making sure none of her outrage had left her voice. 'Surely as you arrived you could see I was reading?' She gestured angrily at the notebook on the table.

He ignored it, reached again past the silently seated men and picked up the photo album. The air seemed to still as he did so; Stella wasn't sure why. He flipped through the pages, his expression one of perplexed amusement. He looked up at Stella with query. 'So what is this?'

She shrugged. 'Why don't you ask Mr Ainsworth or Herr Altmann? I am an assistant on her way to our next research location. We stopped for a minted tea,' she pointed, exasperated, 'because Mr Ainsworth had an old acquaintance to meet. As to that you're holding, it was simply a walk down memory lane for two old friends. What on earth is this all about?'

He had haplessly paused on the very photo that Rafe had impressed upon her to remember. Her heart was pounding so loudly now she was worried that Klipfels could see it drumming against her ribcage, preparing to explode from her chest.

'The photos, gentleman?' He turned away from her mercifully.

'Look here, what's it to you, anyway?' Rafe demanded.

'Nothing, Mr Ainsworth,' Klipfels answered, flinging down the album. 'I realise, of course, it is a useless diversion for your meeting. But this,' he said, waving the pages that Joseph had so desperately passed on, 'is none of your business. It's none of your colleagues' business and certainly none of the British ministry's business.'

'Klipfels,' Joseph appealed.

'You, Altmann, are in a lot of trouble. Traitorous trouble.' He gave a tutting sound. 'You're not very good at this espionage work, Joseph; you should have stuck to budgets and reporting. We were friends.'

'I thought we were,' Joseph nodded sadly. 'Our children go to school together, our wives lunch, you and I take brandy of an evening. Indeed, friends.'

'But no longer, Herr Altmann. Not now that you've betrayed that friendship,' Klipfels replied.

'I don't see it that way. Our family's friendship is in jeopardy through no fault of mine. Going by what our Chancellor's new plans are for Germany, it seems he marked us as enemies in his lunatic mind so you and I have no say in it. We are mere puppets.'

Klipfels bristled. 'We may spare your family, if you cooperate, Joseph, and tell us how you acquired these pages.'

'Spare my . . . where are Brigitte and the children?'

'In safe care. She is a good woman, your wife; excellent family. We know she is not to blame.'

'Please, Klipfels, don't take this out on my darling family.'

'Then help me to keep them all safe.'

Stella tasted sourness in her throat at the undisguised threat. It wasn't just fear, she really did feel sick and maybe retching over Klipfels' cream leather shoes was the answer for breaking this awkward deadlock. Instead, in her panic, she bumbled into another diversion of her own inspiration.

'Oh, Captain Ainsworth, there's that charming couple you introduced me to a couple of days ago.'

Everyone, including Klipfels, looked to where Stella was pointing at an elderly man and woman who had wandered arm in arm into the square. They were foreigners; the pale linens gave them away, along with their oversized hats and his walking cane and flouncy kerchief poking out from his outside breast pocket 'Um, let me recall, Mr and Mrs Harpsend, isn't it?' she offered in panic. 'They were fossicking when we found the skipper.' She could barely believe the ridiculous notions she was fabricating.

Klipfels looked understandably baffled.

Rafe in contrast looked amused. He glanced back at her, vague astonishment ghosting before he grinned. 'Oh, yes, poor old Dick and Daisy who were lost, you mean? Of course,' he said, turning back to look at them.

'They're so interested in your work as a lepidopterist,' she gushed. 'Shall I call them?' She didn't wait for his reply but raised a hand and yelled to the couple – perfect strangers – who mercifully heard an English accent and predictably turned towards it. 'Hello again, Dick,' she repeated. They raised their hands, obviously confused, but no English couple would risk being rude, and that's what she counted on.

Instantly the atmosphere surrounding their table changed to urgent.

'I wish you hadn't,' Klipfels warned.

Stella frowned at him. 'Hadn't what? Been polite to people we know? Look, what do you want with us, Sir? I have work to do for Captain Ainsworth.' She reached down, opened the notebook she'd studied and began reeling off details about the Linnean Society of London and the trail of the butterfly they were hunting.

'. . . . drawing of a Moroccan small skipper, *Thymelicus hamza*, but we're looking for *Pyrgus onopordi*, er . . . the rosy grizzled skipper, for the uninformed.' She pressed on, desperately trying to be as dull as she could. 'Any amount of Moroccan meadow browns – hundreds – and graylings, more than I could bear to count, but our task this trip —'

'Do be quiet, Miss Myles,' Klipfels ordered.

'Karl.' It was Joseph who sighed. 'Release Miss Myles. She is here purely by coincidence. I suspect you're making her nervous.'

'Release!' Stella's voice was huffy but the Harpsends were frowning, discussing whether to come over. She knew Klipfels had an eye on them too. Precious seconds ticked by. 'What does that mean? I'm no prisoner to be released!' She looked between the two men. 'What's in those pages?'

It was Rafe's turn. 'Something Herr Klipfels is embarrassed by. Run along, Miss Myles.' The Harpsends seemed to have made a decision and were tottering in their direction. 'Hurry up, Klipfels. Perhaps she can stop them.'

'Take your things and leave, Miss Myles,' Klipfels directed and she could feel Rafe's relief like a sharp gust of wind shoving her away.

'Miss Myles,' Rafe continued, matter-of-factly, 'I shall meet you back at the hotel. It looks like today's excursion into the foot-hills is a lost cause until we sort this business out.'

'What business?' she said, looking between Rafe and Joseph. She didn't want to leave either of them.

'Certainly not yours,' Klipfels urged. 'Gentlemen? Shall we retire to somewhere where we can talk in private?'

'Stella . . . please,' Rafe appealed but without the usual tenderness in his voice. 'It's best you leave. Write up yesterday's notes, especially regarding those fossils we found.' He closed the album, closed her notebook, piled them up and gave them to her, covering her hand with his own, which she felt like a farewell. There was a warning in his gaze that only she could sense.

'What about you, Sir? When shall I see you?'

'This afternoon.'

She knew he lied. They were all liars. All acting out the charade.

'Run along now,' Rafe added, his tone cuttingly off-hand.

'As your employer says,' Klipfels sneered.

She ignored him, eyes only for Rafe. 'And you will be all right . . . Sir?'

'I shall be fine,' he assured. He began to move, Joseph dejectedly doing the same.

'No scenes now,' Klipfels warned, 'or we shall have to have you accompany us, Miss Myles. And I should warn I have other colleagues posted who are carrying pistols. Let's all stay calm and no one gets hurt.'

Rafe shot her a beseeching look of warning.

'I'm sorry, Miss Myles,' Joseph said, his face corpse-grey. She remembered that colour well from her parents. Was he a dead man? Was Rafe? She was torn. Should she shout for help and hope against hope they might all get away, or listen to Rafe now and hope he knew what he was doing? If he'd been in hot water previously he'd clearly got away. He was smart, clever, silver-tongued. He would keep them safe, wouldn't he? Klipfels just wanted the pages. Joseph and Rafe were of no use to them beyond that, surely?

Joseph was muttering another apology.

'Sorry doesn't cover it, Mr Altmann. We had plans,' she said, burying the truth in hollow words, surprised she could still remain in character and not reach for Rafe, scream for help. He wouldn't want that, though. He had likely anticipated that this might happen, hadn't he? Dawning entered her mind in a blindingly sharp manner, as though she'd stepped out of a dark room into bright sunlight. No, he'd *known* it would happen as he'd known that Joseph was no spy; Joseph wouldn't know if he were followed; wouldn't have a clue of the skills of espionage. She had a better training in duplicity through her work on the sales floor than Joseph Altmann did in his senior administrative role, whatever it was. It explained Rafe's odd mood, his getting drunk, it even explained the argument on the ship and his manoeuvrings to give both of them one full day and night of loving together, because he'd known in his heart there would be no more. And he'd anticipated she would be smart enough to get herself away; that he would manipulate the situation to enable it and that she would use her perceptiveness and alertness to live up to his estimation of her. But he'd wanted that precious time alone with her first. In her moment of clarity, she believed it was likely Rafe who had whispered to Grace about Georgina's lineage, reminded her of that argument between himself and Beatrice and words spilled that shouldn't have been uttered in Grace's presence.

All of that risk and hurt because Rafe wanted to hold Stella . . . alone, without prying eyes. His farewell.

One last dance, Stella, his voice echoed in her mind like he was wishing her adieu.

Stella wilted, pain and terror combining to double her up. He was already out of reach. 'Rafe!' she cried to him, but it came out as a whisper.

He looked back, ignoring her suffering. 'And if for any reason I'm held up, do get that stuff to old Fruity, would you? He's waiting for it – you know what a stickler he is for deadlines.'

And then he and Joseph were gone, hurried from her by their German escort as the elderly pair arrived.

'Oh, my dear,' said the woman as Stella crumpled against them. 'Harold, darling, quick, she's swooning.'

When Stella regained her wits, she was in the shadows of the café being fanned by the elderly woman, with her husband and one of the waiters watching on, concerned. Her head snapped back with the eye-wateringly pungent smell of ammonia laced with an astringent top note of lavender.

'There you are, that's better,' her companion said, fanning harder. 'Take this, Harold,' she said, handing off a tiny, clear glass bottle. Her husband stepped forward and obediently took the smelling salts. 'How are you feeling?'

'I'm . . . I'm fine. Did I faint?'

'I think you did, my dear,' her new friend admitted. 'Would you like to use my fan?'

Stella shook her head, everything flooding back now. 'Have they gone?'

The woman blinked. 'Er . . . ?' She looked around at her companions and it was the waiter who answered in French.

'The men have left, Madam,' he confirmed.

Stella moved slowly to stand. 'Did you see the men I was with?'

Harold nodded. 'We did. They were leaving and you called us over.'

Harold's wife, exasperated with his explanation, took over. 'Should we know you, my dear? I'm sorry, perhaps our ageing minds are letting us down but we don't recognise you. You're not the Hampton-Cooper girl, are you?'

Stella felt nervous laughter warbling in her throat, knew her emotions were rising towards hysteria and clamped her mouth shut. She coughed it out instead, shook her head in response, forcing a sense of control about herself. When she felt she could, she answered properly. 'I'm sorry, no. I'm Stella Myles.'

They looked at her blankly, then at each other as if running the family name of Myles through their collective memories.

'You don't know me. Forgive me.' It would make no difference to explain so she fibbed again. 'I mistook you for another couple.'

'Oh,' the woman exclaimed with gentle understanding. 'That's quite all right. Happens all the time.'

'Which direction did they go?' she asked the waiter in French.

'He does not wish you to follow,' he replied, dark eyes fixing her with an implacable stare.

'Tell me.'

'He has paid me not to,' he said.

She was aware of the couple's attention darting back and forth between them. 'I shall double whatever he paid. Triple it!'

He stood unmoved. 'I am not for sale,' he answered.

Her mouth quivered in her sense of helplessness.

'He also paid me to escort you back to the hotel.'

'I don't want you near me.'

'Nevertheless,' the man said, ignoring her. He was older and something in his tone overwhelmed her natural desire to imagine herself hypothetically spitting at his feet, but her combined sorrow and rage was such that she could imagine such a heinous display of poor manners to make her dead parents fidget unhappily in their graves.

'My dear?' the woman asked.

'I'm sorry. I came over so light-headed. I had no idea that I would faint.' She gave the woman a peck. 'You've been so kind, Mrs . . . ?'

'Margaret and Harold Eversham. Card, Harold, dear,' she said, turning to her husband who instantly dug in his waistcoat pocket. She took it and passed it to Stella.

She read it, nodding, taking a slow deep breath to steady herself and her nerves. 'Norfolk,' she said, unsure of what else to say. 'How nice.'

'Beautiful. We live on the Broads. You're most welcome to visit some time.'

'You're very kind.'

'Well, you seem sad, my dear. Norfolk might cheer. Can we do anything for you?'

She shook her head. 'No, this man will guide me to where my friends are. Thank you for being so generous and understanding.'

Harold tweaked his white moustache, mumbled something about it being no trouble at all. His wife squeezed her hand. 'We're staying at the Hotel Gallia . . . it's a fine *riad*, my dear, must have been a rich old merchant's home before it changed over to a guest house. Feel free to look us up there. We're staying for another couple of days before we go to Tangier.'

'Thank you.' Stella set her shoulders and forced a smile. 'I'd better go find my friends,' she said, feigning brightness. 'Thank you again.' She nodded at the waiter.

'I am Zarif,' he said, bowing slightly, hand over heart.

'Thank you, Zarif. Shall we?' she said in English this time.

25
London – June 1933

Stella sat on a bench in Kensington Gardens, not far from the Peter Pan statue, and wished she too could disappear into Neverland. She'd spent some time in the ornamental Italian Gardens that she'd read somewhere had been a grand gift from Prince Albert to his beloved Queen Victoria. It was all a little florid for Stella, with its marble fountain and massive stone urns and statues, and she'd drifted down, following the path of the Long Water that would lead into the Serpentine to find a spot where she could be still and unnoticed for a while. Sitting near Peter with a copse to her back, flowers around her and the waterway in front was ideal. It was only nearing nine-fifteen so the day was young and few people, save those taking the fresh air with infants or workers using the gardens to cut through from Bayswater to Knightsbridge, interrupted her vision with their movement.

The morning was warm, the day promising to be hot, and the emergence of drifts of daisies reminded her that the warmest season spoke of happy moods and laughter – but she would forever associate the feeling of the sun on her skin with a sense of misery.

She'd arrived early for her appointment and had time to contemplate and observe those few Londoners going about their day. She felt every ounce the outsider, amongst the nannies and mothers who emerged through the park gates with their new-fangled large-wheeled stroller prams. Her father had insisted that the cumbersome large perambulator that had been purchased when Stella was born would do just fine for her siblings who came so much later. Inevitably it was she who had struggled to control a baby inside the monstrous vehicle with an eager, often restless toddler at her side when her mother asked her to take the children out for some air. What wouldn't she have done for one of these modern contraptions, where the infant faced out and could see the world rather than staring at the sky or up into their mother's nostrils.

She had sat here now for more than an hour considering the exquisite bronze sculpturing of tiny fairies and squirrels and other furry creatures playing around Peter. Her thoughts had ranged from how life's odd journey had brought her to this place.

It had been a week since she'd arrived home from North Africa. She could not bear to remember returning to that hotel room of love feeling so bereft. She'd paced for several minutes, glad to be rid of hotel staff and even the waiter who seemed to know a lot more about what had occurred than she did. He'd even given her instructions, apparently briefed by Rafe during their hurried discussion in Arabic. It's why she recalled now how Zarif had glanced her way during that conversation. Rafe must have all but accepted that the meeting with Joseph would turn sour. Zarif had escorted her, reminded her to write down every single memory of the twenty minutes or so with Joseph before Klipfels arrived. To find Fruity, to give him everything.

'What do you mean by that?' she had asked.

The waiter had looked back uncomprehendingly. 'You are supposed to understand, Madam,' he had said as politely as he could in French.

But she hadn't understood, not until the journey home on the aeroplane. She'd ripped open the envelope she found waiting for her on the hotel dressing table and knew in her gut, before the contents spilled, that there would be paperwork for only one person. Her instincts served her well. There were no return travel documents for Rafe Ainsworth.

In that hotel room she had crumpled in on herself, coming to rest on the floor in deep, silent sobs of heartbreak, fully appreciating that he'd feared since before they left England that he would never return.

And in the course of the next few hours she'd drifted in and out of her grief, finally emerging into the latter half of the afternoon to realise his note was still crushed in her hand. Of course he could write nothing down that was incriminating – he could tell Zarif nothing that could be repeated to their enemies either – and so she had needed to read between the lines of his affection and regret.

My darling Stella,

If you are reading this, the worst has occurred and we are separated. Poor old Joseph. I had to presume he would be watched because of his position so close to the power brokers. And I had to presume he would be followed on his sudden departure from Berlin even if they were not sure about what he may know. I mustn't dwell and write of my love and admiration for you, for I know as you do read this that time is frighteningly short and you must use the travel documents enclosed and get yourself back to London.

Please do not look for me, do not linger in Morocco for me, do not talk about me to anyone. Be safe and get on that flight back to England. I trust you and that clever, agile mind of yours to work out everything.

Make it all count for something, my darling. Make me even prouder . . . I love you with all of myself; even my shadow that now whispers goodbye to you, Stella, because I will not feel your soft skin again or hear your bright laughter. But wherever I am I cannot miss you because you are here with me, remember? You covered my heart with your hand and promised me you will always be there. And so it is . . . we are bound in spirit and, perhaps, other ways, to keep you in happy company.

She didn't understand that sentence but couldn't dwell to work it out, knowing he was probably feeling uncharacteristically emotional when he wrote the letter.

Go home, Stella, my love. Don't forget to give dear old Fruity all that stuff on the research expedition we assembled for Kew. Anything else of mine, for whatever it's worth, please keep as you see fit and take back.

She could tell how careful he was being in this letter, wanting to say so much more than he was, but urging her to understand. They'd assembled nothing for Kew, so that was a ruse for anyone who happened upon this letter other than herself. So that left his few clothes and the photo album. She would take it all back with her. She needed to think but Stella felt her heart racing with the tension of needing to leave at once, to get away as he was urging her to.

I can never regret asking you to dance but forgive me now for the sorrows I have caused you since. I'm guessing, though, there may be at least one or two happy memories that will remain when the sadness fades.

When you wear green, think of me, mint juleps, minted tea and our hours in Brighton, our day in Marrakech, a waltz in Piccadilly and twenty unforgettable minutes in a London taxi that changed my life. To you alone have I given all my love and that will never change.

R.

Too broken in her mind to do anything but obey and flee to the loving security of family, she had washed her face, gathered up her few belongings, including his shirt that smelled of him, which she wrapped his notebook in. The photo album she tucked into her handbag. The flight to Britain, which should have been a thrilling experience of awe and wonder, felt as though it was happening to everyone else in the narrow metal tube that was roaring them through the skies. Stella was lost to her thoughts, wracking her mind for what he'd tried to communicate to her. The man seated next to her had given up on the small talk when Stella had donned sunglasses and leaned her head against the window. Couldn't he see how red her eyes were? Why did he want to talk about the woman he loved, their new baby, their whole happy life stretching ahead?

With the drone of the aeroplane's engines sounding like drills into her mind, even her miserable thoughts were drowned. It wasn't until she'd noticed her neighbour showing the air hostess a photo of his wife and child that a glimmer opened in her mind like a door from a lit corridor into a dark room. When her neighbour had released his seatbelt to use the bathroom, Stella had hopped up to rummage in the overhead compartment for Joseph's photo album.

With reluctance she opened it to confront smiling pictures of Rafe and his non-blood brother in childhood in happier times. She didn't think Rafe had changed much; he had been a good-looking boy who fulfilled all his handsome promise. She came to her favourite image. There he was grinning from the opening of a tent flap, looking relaxed and as merry as she could imagine him being, surrounded by desert, even a camel obligingly heaving into view in the distance.

Remember this, he had said – no, *hissed* – as he had pointed meaningfully.

Why? What was in the image she had to focus on? Rafe. Sand. Tent. Camel. She shook her head. She'd flicked through all the rest of the photos, pondering each for clues. She'd checked the actual album itself, picking at the corners of the lining, wondering if anything could be beneath. No luck and no point because if something were hidden in such a way, surely Rafe would have clued her. Except he had clued her, hadn't he? *Remember this.* Stella returned to the photograph she could sketch out now if asked because she knew its grainy image so well. Maybe it was the place . . . maybe its location was what Rafe needed her to communicate. But she failed to see how saying out loud 'Moroccan desertscape' was going to help anyone with anything. Perhaps it wasn't Morocco, though – was that the point?

She blinked in consternation, recalling again how deliberately he'd gestured. Rafe had wanted her to do something with this photograph – only this one – and his words about getting the stuff back to old Fruity were not hollow either. Rafe rarely wasted words and certainly not in that urgent situation.

Then it came to her, in a flash. *Was there something on the back of the photo?* She eased it out of its corners and as it came away from the page of black card, so did a page of the flimsiest tissue paper covered in tiny handwriting. Time stilled as Stella carefully unfolded the sheet. It was not his handwriting. It belonged to Joseph, who declared in the briefest preamble that this was a faithful copy that he'd translated into English of the notes made in March 1933 by Adolf Hitler, Chancellor, of his plans for the German Reich. Unless this was the deepest of conspiracies, then Joseph had not lied and Poland was indeed in the German leader's sights, as was a 'cleansing' in his adopted nation. Her neighbour had paused in his return to his seat to remain standing and to talk to the air hostess so Stella kept reading, despite the fear tingling through her that no one but Basil Peach must read these notes after her. Hitler's thoughts were sometimes garbled, often ranging, but it was clear – even to Stella – that the thinking was more than simply inflammatory. The man was looking towards domination in Europe.

So now that whole scene in the café made sense to Stella. Between Rafe and Joseph they'd purposefully handed Klipfels the original, intentionally ensuring if Joseph were followed that his observers would see him handing over those papers. Klipfels had looked at the album but dismissed it in favour of the sheets of paper shiftily withdrawn and given to Rafe. How quickly Rafe had caught onto the unspoken plan that the information was hidden in the album and that the original could be given back – must be given back, in fact – to protect the copy. So simple and yet so cunning. The years had clearly not dulled their ability to think as one, to understand invisible messages, to read signs between each other. They had deliberately given Klipfels a sense of security that he'd got the information before it left German hands, when both Rafe and Joseph had known all along that the duplicated information was to be carried back to England in the photo album, whether that information was delivered by Rafe or by Stella. Masterful!

And so now here she sat with blackbirds busy about their gathering while other birds happily warbled in the sunshine. She watched a youngster rush up to the statue and hug it. Stella smiled, believing that's how she felt about Peter Pan too . . . and about Rafe, who was also something of a boy who had not truly grown up but lived in his own Neverland world. She looked at her watch. Eight minutes. More than sufficient time to get to where she needed to be.

Stella stood, feeling the cold unstretch from her stiff body. Once she fulfilled this task for Rafe maybe she might feel another leash snap that connected them so that the bonds of attachment could loosen just enough for her to escape the tight hold he held on her. She didn't want to leave Rafe behind but knew that to survive this terrible year of her life, she had to lock him away and change her life, go somewhere else. To where she had no proper idea yet . . . only that it was time to leave, time to take care of herself and her children, as she'd come to think of her sister and brother.

She turned and headed towards the great pond that sat before Kensington Palace. They were to meet on the side adjacent to the bandstand. She carried nothing but her handbag, which in turn held her purse, a handkerchief, a powder compact she would not need and a double-sided sheet of handwriting that belonged to a German Jew.

Stella arrived at the enormous pond and scanned the landscape. She wasn't alone but the majority of her companions were ducks and geese making an enjoyable racket. A mother and child were feeding the waterfowl, the child squawking with both fear and delight at the larger, more eager birds.

She checked her watch again. Two minutes. Stella wandered the circumference of the pond, finally coming back to her starting point in line with the bandstand from where she saw a figure hail her.

She recognised Basil Peach immediately by his monocle and rather than wait for him to approach, she covered the distance quickly on flat shoes.

'Hello, again, Miss Myles,' he said and she heard once more the friendly warmth she recalled in this man but also knew it now to be his public tone. She had heard him speak in an entirely different tone to Rafe when he'd forced him to meet Joseph against all of Rafe's instincts.

'Mr Peach,' she said, evenly.

'Thank you for coming.'

'I don't believe I had much choice. We both have something for each other.'

'Indeed.' He smiled. 'Shall we sit?' he offered, gesturing to the chairs that had been stacked beneath the canopy of the bandstand to keep out of the rain. He pulled a couple free. 'I thought it was quieter here than next to the pond. All those ducks make quite a racket, don't they?'

She smiled thinly and sat down. She'd never felt lonelier than in this moment to be surrounded by empty chairs, as if the seats surrounding her were occupied only by ghosts.

'So, Miss Myles, are you well?'

'As well as I can be under the circumstances.'

He had the grace to look down. 'I'm deeply sorry that you became involved. That was not my call, of course. Monty obviously insisted.'

'Had he not, you would not now have what Joseph Altmann brought with him.'

'We had no idea what he was bringing out.' He looked in pain, his brow creasing with worry.

'But you did know it was dangerous for Mr Ainsworth.'

'They were family. He wouldn't have hesitated in any circumstance. My dear, these are not easy times. I have a job to do for our government and I do my best not to get emotionally involved.'

She hated Peach in that moment. If not for Rafe's plea, she would have walked away from this man without wasting another breath on him. He had no idea she'd heard their exchange during that phone call and how he had manipulated Rafe. 'Nevertheless, it was brave.'

He nodded carelessly. 'You have the stuff Altmann brought from Berlin?'

She tapped her bag, only now realising he had no idea of what the pages contained. 'Yes,' she reassured. 'And you have something for me.'

'I do.' He touched the breast pocket of his light raincoat. Stella blinked, not understanding, but he was already talking again. 'It's courageous of you, Miss —'

'Mr Peach,' she interrupted, now hating his jolly, sweet face for sending Rafe away, for causing her a grief that she knew would never leave her. He stopped abruptly, staring at her, slightly alarmed. 'I will not be giving you the papers Rafe has acquired until you give me what I want and it is not kept in your coat pocket!'

He shifted position, looking around. 'Please calm yourself, Miss Myles.'

'Calm? You're asking me to calm down when the man I love is lost to me.'

'Love?' He looked astonished and then almost in the same moment she saw that he understood.

'Dear old Monty.' She glared at him, hearing his patronising tone. 'Forgive me, I can see that it was real for you, Miss Myles.'

'It was real for him too.' She had to believe it.

'Monty only had to look at a woman and she —'

'Don't, Mr Peach. I know you believe you know him, that he is your friend, but you are mistaken.'

He shrugged with repressed smugness.

'Do you know his full name?' she demanded.

'Montgomery Douglas R. Ainsworth. Captain, if I'm not mistaken, and something of a war hero . . . predictably.'

'And you knew him as Monty?'

'It's what he asked me to call him by.'

She nodded. 'That's right, Mr Peach. He was known as Monty by everyone he kept as distant as he could.' As he baulked she pressed on. 'No, you need to understand, you only think you know him. You are a colleague. That's it, Basil . . . or should I call you Fruity?'

'No one calls me Fruity,' he corrected, his cheerfulness gone.

'Oh? I thought that was your name at school.'

'It was. I only share that with a few people.'

'Precisely. You think he's your friend but he shared it with me, chuckled about it – not unkindly, because that wasn't his way.'

'We used to go out often, drinking . . . dancing.'

'Because he felt sorry for you, Mr Peach. I understand you care for your elderly mother, which is a fine thing to do, but he knew you were lonely for company of your own age, particularly female company.'

'Listen here, many's the time old Monty and I got quite filthy together and shared many a secret.'

'Really? Did you know that he never actually drank the gin you thought he was consuming? Did you know that night you met Madge and myself that he was as sober as I am now? He threw most of it on his suit so he smelled drunk.'

He blinked with annoyance. 'No, I didn't know.'

'And the secrets you think he shared . . . Let's go with an obvious one, shall we? Do you know what the R stands for in his name?'

Basil Peach turned red. 'A family name, no doubt.'

She shook her head. 'It belongs to a name that only his sister, his mother, his closest friend, Joseph – a brother to him – and I were privy to.'

'His wife must have known it.'

'Perhaps she does but I doubt very much she was familiar with the short form of it. I only know him by one name, which he told me less than an hour after I met him, Mr Peach. You've been acquainted for years and don't know it, his wife has been married to him for at least seventeen years and calls him Doug.'

'What do you want from me, Miss Myles?'

'Apart from your apology, I want to know where he is.'

'I am genuinely sorry for calling into question how Monty felt about you.'

'Felt?'

He took his monocle out. 'He's dead, Stella.'

She looked back at him with a dull expression. This was not a shock; it was not even a scenario she hadn't anticipated since she'd crumpled to the floor in the Marrakech hotel room. Her heart had known it since he looked back once with such regret between the shoulders of the Germans. Now her mind simply had to catch up and resign herself to the confirmation of what her heart knew.

'I wished to spare you this.'

'Don't spare me. Tell me, and then we can go our separate ways.' Her voice was granite-hard.

He sat straighter and sighed. 'Two bodies were found in a deserted area of the foothills of the Atlas Mountains. Our people have confirmed them to be Ainsworth and Altmann. It had been made to look like a car accident but you and I know better.'

She swallowed. 'Their bodies?'

'Both are buried in Marrakech.'

'Mrs Ainsworth?'

'She was contacted immediately. Knows only of the accident. Certainly doesn't need or indeed, I suspect, want to know any more.'

'How are his daughters?'

'I cannot answer that, Miss Myles. I did visit Beatrice Ainsworth; she was under the impression that I represented the Foreign Office. It was easier that way. I didn't meet the daughters.'

'I see,' she said. Stella unclipped her bag and retrieved an envelope. 'I hope this was worth two men's lives, Mr Peach. Two men whom you sent to their death for this.'

'Monty insisted on working alone. He took risks, refused any assistance. Miss Myles, I—'

'Don't, Mr Peach. I do not require your placation, especially when you head home each evening to the cosy little bedroom you've probably slept in since childhood!'

He cleared his throat, but the fresh bloom of red at his neck told her she'd hit the mark. Good! He needed to feel humiliated if he wouldn't show remorse.

'Have you read it?' He looked at the envelope greedily.

'Yes, of course I have. It is the ramblings of a mad but dangerous man. I trust Britain will act.'

He opened his palm, clearly reluctant to snatch the envelope from her despite his eagerness. She duly placed it in his hand and stood. 'Forewarned is forearmed, they say, Mr Peach. I hope our nation will share this knowledge with her allies and not allow Herr Hitler to follow through with his dream of domination.'

Once again he looked around, fearful of being overheard. 'No one else has seen this?'

'No one. But Mr Peach, it's a copy.'

He looked up in alarm at where she stood.

'A faithful copy made by Herr Altmann. I saw the original, saw the handwriting of the German Chancellor, and will attest to that should I ever be asked.'

'Is that a threat, Miss Myles?'

'Not at all. It's a promise. And as security, I have written down everything I know, including your name, the date and time of this meeting, everything I overheard of the conversation you had with Mr Ainsworth when you forced his hand into going on the cruise to his death, which I suspect you knew might occur.'

His denial died in his throat as she sneered at him.

'It's all locked up in a safe deposit box to be opened upon my death, Mr Peach, so it's in your interests to leave me well alone.'

'Good gracious! What do you think I am?'

'I think you're a snake, Mr Peach,' she accused, smiling at how it suited him. 'Or if that's too metaphorical for you, how's this? I think you hide in the grass like a snake – a cowardly, unimportant little government man who has gallant, brave others do his bidding.

You sent the man I love to his death and you knew he'd go and get exactly what you wanted because you'd involved Joseph whom he loved and simply couldn't permit to walk into danger alone. You knew Joseph was under threat and you did not hesitate to put Mr Ainsworth into the same orbit. In fact, recalling that conversation you bullied him from your safe, warm, hidden bed in the grass of your London office of the Secret Intelligence Service.'

His expression was pinched with affront. 'Someone has to manage the affairs, Miss Myles.'

'Lose that indignant tone, Fruity,' Stella sneered, surprisingly herself at her behaviour, although it felt empowering to strike back at the person she held ultimately responsible for Rafe's sacrifice. 'One day someone might manipulate you into a dangerous situation and I wonder how you will cope? I wonder if you'd walk to your death as calmly and determinedly as the man I love did. He couldn't keep Joseph safe but I now realise he would rather be damned than let Joseph go to his execution alone. And even as he did so he made sure that London received what it needed because he was loyal and he also kept me safe, though I don't know why. I'm lonely, Mr Peach. I'm grief-stricken, and I don't know how to claw my way out of this well of self-pity and loathing, although I suspect today is the first rung of that ladder. The next is to walk away from you and that letter and to work my damnedest never to think on either you or it again.'

Basil struggled but didn't successfully disguise how affronted he was. Spots of colour pinched his cheeks. He withdrew a buff envelope from inside his coat pocket. 'I was asked to give you this.'

She stared at it, not touching it. 'By whom?'

'By the man you loved.'

'Not past tense. I still do love him, Basil.'

His glare softened at the use of his name and the tenderness in her voice. She felt her hate for him drain from her body. It took too much energy to retain her anger. 'I'm so sorry, Stella. I miss him too, if that helps to know. I really did think of him as a friend and although friends don't send each other into danger, we're already fighting a war that most of the country doesn't even know about yet.'

She pointed at his chest. 'Then be one of the brave people who fight for peace. Don't let it happen. You have information now that can at least get people working towards prevention.'

'You make it sound simple.'

'It is, in my mind.'

'He was brave to the last,' he finished, handing her the envelope.

'Have you read what's inside?'

'Of course I have,' he said, and they shared a sad smile at his echo of her words. 'He insisted I organise some matters for him. He came up to London after our phone call on your behalf.'

Stella frowned. 'I didn't know.'

He shrugged. 'Please take it.'

She did so.

'To be frank, I don't know the full extent of what is in there, only that he was making arrangements. It was disgustingly wrong of me to think that Ainsworth was simply providing for you. Given what you've told me, no doubt he has done a lot more than I could imagine and we should put my appalling manners down to the green-eyed monster. You're a beautiful woman, Stella, and Ainsworth was always surrounded by them. I always hoped one might take an interest, you know – one of his cast-offs – but as long as he was in the midst, no one looked my way.'

'Madge looked your way. Did you ever bother to take her out again?'

He looked stunned. 'Madge. Your friend? She was fun.'

'Well, I saw her yesterday and she's not attached to anyone and would like nothing more, I suspect, than to have a constant companion; someone she could rely on and trust . . . someone to love.'

He blushed furiously. 'Really? She was so pretty, I didn't think for a moment she was anything more than a party girl.'

Stella raised her eyes to the sky. 'Madge is working at the millinery counter at Bourne & Hollingsworth. I suggest you drop by. Her day off is Wednesday.'

'I don't deserve your forgiveness,' he admitted.

'No, you don't, which is why I haven't forgiven you, Mr Peach, but I don't wish ill on anyone . . . even you. You and Madge would be good for each other – she takes no prisoners. Don't say I haven't warned you.'

He grinned, despite her warning.

Stella held out a hand. 'I hope you won't take this the wrong way, but I trust we shall never meet again.'

He gave a small cough. 'I understand.'

'Make it count, Basil. Make his life matter.'

Stella walked away before he could answer, striding purposefully down the beautifully straight avenue, rounding the duck pond and heading as quickly as she could towards Lancaster Gate. By the time she left the park she was hurrying beyond a walk, finally breaking into a jog, tears streaming, heedless of people noticing and pausing as she desperately tried to outrun her despair.

EPILOGUE

OCTOBER 1938

The young woman in the starched apron tapped on the door of the tiny office.

'Someone to see you, Stella.'

She looked up from some bookwork. 'Oh, thank you, Sarah.' The girl turned to leave. 'Wait,' Stella called. Sarah halted, looking alarmed. 'Your apron tie is coming loose. Come here, let me fix that.' Stella stood and pulled the ends of the sash. 'Hmm, your uniform is looking a bit worse for wear too, isn't it?'

Sarah looked sheepish. 'I didn't want to ask but I know how much importance you place on how we turn ourselves out for the customers.'

'That's right. We never drop our standards. Indent for a new one. I'll make sure Miss Baker is aware that I've authorised a new uniform.'

'Oh, you're very kind, thank you,' Sarah gushed.

'How's that young man of yours?'

'I'm worried he'll be conscripted.'

She nodded. There was no answer for this, other than an empty placation. Instead she gave her staff member a cheer-up smile. 'Well, we just have to hope it doesn't come to that, Sarah. No one wants another war.'

'That Hitler does.'

The name sent chills through her. Stella had worked hard not to think upon that meeting in Kensington Gardens in five years but she wondered now whether Basil Peach ever did take any action based on the hard-won intelligence that she had smuggled out of Africa. Britain and its allies had granted the Führer, as he was known, the right to annexe Sudetenland, which suggested the warnings had fallen on deaf ears. Uncertain and rocky times certainly felt like they were travelling towards them and Stella hated that she had been living with the fear of this situation since 1933.

She cast a look over her shoulder at the paperwork that would have to wait and walked out to the front of the tearooms, anticipating a supplier wanting to offer wares at a discounted rate to her current one. But the woman waiting for her near the door, clearly feeling awkward, and who raised a nervous hand in salutation, was possibly the very last person in the world Stella imagined would come looking for her. There was a real nip in the air now that warranted the dove-coloured overcoat trimmed luxuriantly with fur at the cuff and collar. Stella's still keen buyer's eye noted expensive leather shoes and an even more costly handbag, that even conservative styling couldn't hide. Golden hair was cut shorter with soft curls emerging from beneath a matching grey-blue, broad-brimmed hat of satin. She looked lovely, relaxed, even tanned. Stella stopped behind the counter, stunned, to take a moment and be sure she wasn't imagining it.

'I can't believe it! Georgina Ainsworth?' she exclaimed in disbelief.

It was a quiet morning, so there were only a few people enjoying a pot of tea, but they all looked up.

The newcomer ignored the scrutiny and, pulling off her tan suede glove, twisted her upraised left hand, grinning. 'It's Mrs Rex Frobisher now,' she said, a diamond solitaire glittering above a gold wedding band.

Stella hurried around the counter and then halted again,

unsure. It was Georgina who moved to gather her up and hug her tight. 'Stella,' she breathed, not letting her go quickly. 'I'm so glad you're here and that I can see you again.'

They stood back from each other and Stella was shocked to discover that she was feeling a pang of bright sentiment. If someone had told her a year ago that she'd be delighted to see this person, she'd have smirked in disbelief. 'Gosh! Look at you, you haven't changed a bit!'

'Oh, I think I have, Stella,' she murmured, her smile faltering. 'But only for the better,' she added. It's why I'm here. I need to . . .' She searched for the right word. Stella sensed that to apologise wasn't enough for her. 'To atone,' she said, and shook her head.

Stella felt happy within to realise she felt nothing but warmth to see a familiar face. This was no time in her life for grudges or regrets. 'What can I get you?'

Georgina looked around. 'A cup of tea, perhaps?' she said in a gently wry tone. 'Only if you can spare the time?'

Stella waved away all protestation. 'Are you alone?'

'Rex figured we'd like some time to ourselves. He went to the library to read the papers. We're on honeymoon.'

'Oh, Georgina! This has made my day. Is Grace up north with you too?'

'No, she's at school but I'll tell you everything about her over that pot of tea,' Georgina replied and Stella heard the hesitancy.

'Let's find somewhere private then. Come with me,' she said, relieved to be welcoming her former nemesis as a friend. Rafe would be proud and she felt a gust of happiness spread like a warm blanket around her shoulders. 'Sarah, be a darling and bring a tray out into the garden, would you?'

'In a jiffy,' she said.

Stella led her guest out through the back of the tearooms and into a conservatory.

'What a lovely place this is, Stella – so much light, and as though the gardens are inside.'

'It reminds me of Harp's End because of the conservatory. I decided it made the perfect gathering place for taking tea and passing time with friends.'

'You've even got a fireplace!' Georgina exclaimed.

'I felt that was lacking in the Harp's End conservatory . . . though I'm channelling Mrs Boyd and trying to hold off lighting it for another week before I give in to winter.' She winked.

'I like the colour palette throughout your tearooms,' Georgina noted.

'*Eau de nil*,' they said together and laughed.

'Come on,' Stella said. 'We have so much to catch up on.' She led her guest down the corridor. 'I live upstairs. That's our office,' she gestured and then walked Georgina through a side door to outside. 'Just around here is my private courtyard, where I can find some sanity, but it's a sunny day despite the cool, so maybe let's head down into the garden. The orchard should be lovely – we can get drunk on the smell of all the apples I can't keep up with. Apple chutney, apple jam, apple paste, even dried apples . . .'

'Apple tea, perhaps?' Georgina offered and grinned, allowing Stella to lead her to where a table and two chairs sat beneath a laden apple tree and looked back upon the house at the back of the tearooms. 'It's lovely. I swear even the little I've seen makes me believe I could live in Harrogate.'

'Spa towns always have a particular atmosphere and Harrogate has a rich history – it's certainly an easy place to call home. Please, do sit,' she said. 'I can't quite believe you're here.'

'Me either,' Georgina admitted. 'I'm only sorry it's taken so long. I've thought about you many times,' she said, no doubt watching Stella's expression frown with surprise, but she pushed on. 'However, the truth is it wasn't until Rex suggested York and

Scotland for our honeymoon that I realised we could easily swing through Harrogate and see you.'

'How did you know where to find me?'

'The letter, the one you sent Mother about five years ago.'

'Ah,' she said, 'that's right, I would have just moved up here. I left the south around mid '33. However, my short time at Harp's End left unfinished business, particularly Grace. Do tell me about her.'

Again she noted Georgina's reluctance. 'My mother was wrong to deny you contact. You can imagine what a traumatic time it was for Mother . . . for all of us.'

'Yes, and that's why I didn't pursue it. I hoped time would heal and permit me to at least be able to write to your sister.'

'I'm so sorry it's all taken so long.'

Stella looked at Georgina with a sense of wonder. 'Is this really the Georgina I knew talking to me? You're apologising?'

'I'm deeply sorry about all of that too.' She laughed. 'I was every inch the little beast you accused me of being. I'm horrified, Stella, when I think back at my behaviour. Amazing what five years of growing up does. I was sent to a finishing school in Switzerland. They were so strict. It didn't matter how much I cried, they wouldn't let me go home. By the time the first holidays came around, though, the strange thing is I didn't want to leave . . . Finally I fitted in: I had some real friends, I wasn't being allowed to get away with my awful behaviour,' she admitted. 'I improved my French,' Georgina threw Stella a glittering smile, 'I met Rex and he changed everything for me. He wasn't chosen by Mother, he wasn't even from our circle of people – he's a farmer! That wouldn't have been my mother's choice at all. Good heavens, I'm a farmer's wife,' she declared and they both laughed. 'Who'd have thought?'

'Marriage suits you,' Stella said. 'So does smiling and being happy. You look so radiant.'

Sarah arrived with a tray of tea implements. She expertly laid it out on the table between them, together with a slice of fruit cake. 'That's Stella's French mother's recipe,' she said in a well-rehearsed line, smiling politely at their guest. 'Is that all, Stella?'

'Perfect. Everyone happy in there?' She nodded back towards the tearooms.

'Calm waters,' Sarah said. 'Peg's headed out to do the midday pick-up.'

'That's fine, thanks.'

Sarah left them in the dappled sunlight. They both watched her leave and Stella sensed she needed to let Georgina approach the topic of Grace in her own way.

'Congratulations. You've clearly built a wonderful life and business.'

Stella shrugged. 'I enjoy my life. I have about a dozen staff and several people help with the baking. We're doing nicely and beginning to make quite a name for Stella's Tearooms around the region. We've been approached to open one in York too, can you believe? I shake my head. But tell me more about you! It's so exciting to have you here.'

'You're being awfully decent. I wasn't sure what sort of welcome to expect. Rex promised me that the passage of time would make things easier between us but I was scared you hated me.'

'Oh, I did. But as you have, I grew up too. You were just a silly twit of a thing, Georgina, so dreadfully indulged it was almost like parental cruelty.'

Georgina exploded into laughter. 'Yes. Mother has much to answer for, although I can't blame her entirely.'

'No. She bears the major share but I blame all the adults around you.' They both looked down immediately as Rafe loomed between them. 'Do you take milk and sugar?' Stella quickly asked, reaching to pour.

'Just a dash of milk would be lovely, thank you. Where are your brother and sister? I hope they're well?'

'They're at school. They should be home after four. They're doing just fine. Rory wants to be a footballer and Carys thinks she may be an actress – well, that's this month's plan anyway.' Stella raised her eyes to the heavens with an ironic grin and Georgina smiled.

'They have ambition. That's great.'

She couldn't bear it a moment longer. 'Please tell me about Grace.'

'I'm sorry that I sound so reluctant, but Grace is not a happy child at the moment.' Georgina shrugged. 'She's a teenager and that rebellious mindset is compounded by the fact she's dreadfully smart, as you no doubt recall . . . but she's also deeply traumatised by losing both her parents.'

'Both?' The teacup stopped before it reached Stella's mouth, her hand frozen with shock. 'What happened?'

'My mother's lungs were pocked with cancer tumours. The physician suggested it was her smoking. They tried surgery twice but she was very ill after the second hospital expedition and truly, Stella, I don't think Mother wanted to fight it. Apparently the disease has been on the rise since the Great War.'

'In men, surely?' Stella remarked, feeling obliged to say something.

Georgina shook her head. 'Her physician told me that so many more women have begun smoking since the war that they are noticing a steep rise in deaths from my mother's complaint. She was never far from a cigarette. Kept her slim, she said, but I think it was to calm her nervous agitation. She had terrible bronchitis as a child, I gather, and her lungs were not strong anyway, so smoking was really a very bad idea – she couldn't walk up a hill, for instance. Another reason my parents didn't connect. You know how my father was always such a great outdoors person. My mother was the antithesis of that.' She sighed. 'How did they ever imagine themselves as a couple, one wonders?'

'I'm so sorry, Georgina. Was she even forty yet?'

'Nearing forty-eight.' Stella felt surprised to hear this but recalled learning that Beatrice was older than Rafe.

'She always looked younger than her years,' Georgina continued, 'but frankly, Stella, she wanted to die. She'd been dying a little each day since . . . well, since that cruise.'

And with those words the five years of distance that Stella had worked so hard to put behind her closed up and she was back in Marrakech watching Rafe leaving her.

'Anyway,' Georgina continued, 'she's been gone now for three months and it's time I sort out things for Harp's End when I get back from my honeymoon. We may not sell it – Grace is against that, so is Rex – but it needs to be cleared out. I came here for several reasons, but one of them is to see if there is anything of my father's that you might like to have . . . I mean, perhaps some of his sketches? You are in a few of them.'

Stella looked back at her guest in deeper shock, unsure of how to respond because there was so much to say, but she couldn't imagine in that moment where to begin.

'I'm . . . I'm really lost here. But as you're asking, there's a wonderful photo of him peering out of a tent that was in the nursery. If the family doesn't want it, I'd be glad to have that – it's the original and has much meaning for me.'

'Consider it yours. It's the least I can do for you.'

'But really, Georgina, I don't need anything from Harp's End.'

There were a few moments of silence between them as Stella added hot water to the teapot, waiting for the topic of Grace to be addressed properly. A bird, smaller than a crow but bigger than most garden birds, landed on the fence to watch them.

'Good grief, that's a large bird,' Georgina remarked.

Stella cocked her head in thought as she handed the cup and saucer to her guest. 'Well, I never; that's a young jackdaw. Do you know, I saw one the day we took over the premises and came out to admire the garden and I haven't seen one that close up since? Look at his glossy feathers in the sun – almost purple they're so black.'

'I've not seen one before.'

'I happen to know a lot about jackdaws.'

'Really? How come?'

Stella's gaze softened at the memory and decided they might as well confront the spirit of the person who swirled around them. 'I discovered they were your father's favourite bird. I have one of his notebooks that I carried to Morocco for him; he wrote at length and with affection about them, especially their intelligence. Interestingly, there's a myth that suggests if a jackdaw appears it is foretelling the arrival of someone into your life.' She smiled. 'And here you are.'

Stella looked back at the dark bird observing them and she had the most fanciful notion that Rafe was there in spirit, watching over them. It felt comforting but she chose not to share this with Georgina. 'As a species they are hilariously attracted to shiny objects and will distract you in order to thieve a silver milk-bottle top. They store up anything that reflects the sun like a horde of treasure and unlike the rook or raven, these little fellows don't eat carrion so I am happy to make them feel most welcome in my garden.' She didn't add that she hoped this one would linger now that she'd had the whimsical thought that it carried the soul of Rafe within it.

It was that thought that made her take full control of the conversation. 'Georgina, let me make this easier for you; do you want to talk about your father?'

Her guest looked down and seemed to gather her courage before she spoke again. 'It's just, I know you were with him before he died. Mother's death has sharpened my resolve to be a better daughter – it's a pity I made this decision so late. Of course, the authorities couldn't explain anything to us about how and why he died in a desert with a German man beside him. Witnesses placed you at the hotel. I was told that an elderly couple helped with enquiries. They said they saw him leave you and that you went back to your hotel with a man from the café, or something. But even so, it's all such a mystery and Mother refused to demand more – she let it all slide, as she let herself slide away from both of her daughters as if we didn't matter much any more, especially since I met Rex, but I do worry about Grace.'

'I'm glad to hear that,' Stella admitted.

'I've always loved her. Even now when she's making herself hard to like. She was always so wretchedly sunny but right now I'd give anything to see her happy again. Anything. She likes Rex because he accepts her exactly how she is, so I'm fortunate in that regard. But she seems to think I'm bossing her around when really all I want to do is make sure she's strong here.' Georgina tapped a finger to her temple. 'I need to know she's healing.'

'I know all about losing parents too young. It's not just the shock of losing people you love but your whole life seems to change in that moment. Everything you've known is thrown in disarray. And she's a teenager – it's a lot to handle at once. You have Rex, you're in love; I'm sure she's feeling lonelier than ever.'

Georgina nodded, frowning as if absorbing this thought deeply. 'And she lost you too. Even though she won't hear of it being sold yet, she couldn't bear to return to Harp's End, demanded to go to boarding school, which to be honest was probably a good decision because she has a lot of support there. She's such an emotional sort of character.' Stella nodded, impressed by Georgina's display of wisdom. She really had grown up fast in these last few years.

'She's a carbon copy of her father,' Georgina continued, 'although I see lots in her that reflects Mother too. She won't have it, of course, as Mother was not terribly affectionate, but Grace is a moody fourteen-year-old now, so you can imagine what that's like.'

'Yes, indeed. I'm experiencing similar trials with my sister. They'll come through it – I mean, look at you!' They shared a sad smile. 'I did write to her a few times. Has she ever mentioned my letters?'

Georgina nodded, looking embarrassed. 'I'm sorry she hasn't responded. She blames you, Stella.'

Stella had to look away and swallow her distress. 'I wondered if that was the case.' The jackdaw still observed them. She cleared her throat. 'I wish I could change that. I'm a firm believer in talking things through . . . if I could see her, perhaps?'

'We can try. She's angry at the world. It stole you, for a start, and she worshipped you; but then it stole her father, and when she discovered the truth of what had occurred between you both, she went into deep shock. She didn't speak for weeks and then only in French for a while.'

Stella looked up, startled.

'She's past all of that now but you know what a chatterbox Grace used to be – that's no longer part of her personality. She's lost that glow that she seemed to shine on everyone. I think time will help Grace see it all in a new light. She needs to forgive you, I suspect, for apparently deserting her, taking away her father, allowing him to die, making her mother so miserable to the point of her wishing away her health. In her angry mind, Grace wraps it all up in the ribbon of Stella.'

Stella moaned. She wrapped her arms around herself and rocked on her chair. 'I must see her. Let her rage at me if she wants, but I know it will be better if she can see me, blame me to my face, ask me whatever she wants. Will you tell her you've visited? Please, Georgina, try and make it possible for me to visit Grace or vice versa. I have to set things right between us.'

Georgina drained her tea, put down the cup and saucer and squeezed Stella's arm. 'I didn't come here to upset you about Grace. I promise I will do my utmost to bring you both together.' Stella's shoulders slumped with relief. 'I also didn't come here to ask you about your relationship with our father. I'm here to make amends for the way *you* were treated and to ask you to teach me about the man I ignored. Losing Mother has forced me to confront how you felt when you lost your parents and we mocked and punished you further at such a time of grief. I'm deeply ashamed, Stella. My parents were far from perfect but without them I feel rudderless and I know the angels are giving me a second chance with Rex. He is strong and steady.' She ran a hand through her hair that fell in soft waves to frame her exquisite face. 'Heaven knows why, but he loves me and I know it to be real because he doesn't let me get away with any of my former bad behaviour. He spoils me in ways my mother wouldn't understand. Rex might take me for a simple picnic as his idea of a treat before he'd buy me a new dress. He sits of an evening and talks to me about anything from . . . oh, I don't know, seashells to politics, and never tires of my opinions, my dreams. He wants me to study again. He encourages me to take up hobbies that don't require me having to buy my fun or friendship. In fact, he has introduced me to so many lovely people that I feel I now have a circle of friends in Hampshire – people who enjoy me, look forward to seeing me and I can count on. I've never had that before. I was such an empty person until Rex and he's filled me up with everything I lacked, especially love, Stella.'

She smiled, understanding completely. 'How long have you known him?'

'We met in Geneva. He was delivering his little sister to the same school I had returned to in order to do a term of volunteer work for. My role was to introduce the new girls into the dorm, help with their homesickness and how to fit in,' she said, breaking into bright laughter at the memory. 'It was love at first sight for me. There I was putting my arms around his weeping baby sister and desperately wanting him to put his arms around me! Of course Mother came to the realisation that Rex is almost everything she had hoped for in terms of my marriage. From a disgustingly wealthy family; eldest son . . . he ticked the most important boxes for her. But in truth he's everything she wouldn't like. Rex is tough – hard, some say – but only in the right ways, I've come to appreciate. He doesn't believe in frittering away money on things that don't matter – I don't know how many times he's said to me that I don't need a new frock for every occasion, and that we only require the minimum of staff. I run my own household and just have some help in every few days to do laundry, look after the grounds. There's a massive family home that's his but he prefers the gatekeeper's lodge – more than big enough, he says, and doesn't cost as much to heat!' She said this affecting a deep voice that made Stella laugh. 'And you know, Stella, I don't care – I need so much less than I ever imagined would be possible for me – because I love him and I love our life. I even cook a meal for him each night, can you imagine?'

Stella shook her head. No, she definitely couldn't imagine that. She reminded herself to remain focused on the pleasure of reconnecting with Georgina rather than lose herself in dark thoughts about Grace that were trilling in her mind.

'And it delights me to plan a dinner that will please him. He seems to enjoy my cooking even when it flops – he can make me laugh about it, want to get it right next time. Now we're married I'm going to try and entertain . . . up at the big house. I shall plan my own menu, supervise the cooking, arrange the flowers myself and . . .' She shrugged.

'Suddenly what to wear becomes the least of your problems?' Stella offered and Georgina let out a gust of laughing agreement. 'So he's shifted your perspective.'

'He has. Now I appreciate what is important because I can actually feel it. I think I was moving through life without any emotional compass. Rex looks at me the way I saw my father looking at you. I understand how he must have felt now. Did he tell you that he wrote to me?' Stella shook her head, privately shocked to hear it but then Rafe was always full of surprises. 'It was a long letter, about ten pages, which I reread from time to time to remind myself. He told me about him and Mother, about him and you, about him and me. He said he needed to explain it to me this way in case he never had the opportunity to tell me to my face. He wrote it on the ship, I gather. Perhaps he knew he'd never return.'

Stella hated to revisit this topic but indulged Georgina's need to uncover truths. 'I have never forgiven myself about how you found out about your parentage.'

'It's their fault, not yours. They hid it. Why? Did they not think I'd discover it eventually?'

Stella shrugged. 'I'm sorry that I can't explain it.'

'Why the secret?' Georgina wondered. Stella could tell she was thinking aloud.

'Shame, perhaps? Your mother was all about appearances. She tolerated plenty so long as life appeared to be perfect and harmonious. I like that you still call him your father, despite what you've learned.'

'He's the only father I've known and I punished him for all the time he was alive.'

'Why, Georgina? I never understood that.'

'I think I knew. Somewhere in the pit of my subconscious I recognised that Grace was his and I wasn't. I don't know how. Call it instinct. When I was little and it was just me as the youngster in the family I worshipped him – although he was so rarely at home and when he was I felt he didn't notice me because my mother just dominated every moment with him. I wanted him just for a while to myself. I was never happier than when he'd let me sit in his lap and he'd read to me, or let me look at his sketches. And then when I was eight along came my sister and I could tell, as young as I was, that he instantly loved her more. As she grew, began to look like him, even show some of his mannerisms that people remarked on, I began to hate them both. They were like a little club of two and I wasn't allowed to join. I looked like Mother and yet I didn't have her shaped eyes or her mannerisms. When I mentioned this, she'd fob me off and as I grew up all that sense of not belonging turned outward I suppose and became vicious. I don't think I enjoyed a single happy day from turning thirteen onwards. I hated both of my parents for a while, then I fixated my despair upon him . . . and Grace, although I had to work at it because they were both so irritatingly easy and pleasant. I just wanted to be part of their club. I sensed the oddity of my father but Mother just seemed to look past it; pretend it wasn't there. I couldn't imagine how he could be so successful in his business dealings and yet be such a stumbling, bumbling character – it didn't add up. Mother liked him weak and his laughably gentle hobbies of bird watching or butterfly spotting. It only made me madder, whereas it just seemed to entertain Grace. Perhaps I sensed it was a ruse.'

Stella now understood why Georgina was here. 'You want me to tell you about the man I knew, don't you?'

She nodded. 'Yes. It's the only way I can let it all go because it's important to get on with my life – a life that can now finally be happy because of Rex. But the shadow of the family and its secrets lingers. I want to set it free. I just need to understand.'

And so Stella began, first by pouring a second cup of tea. She told Georgina everything she could about the character of the man she loved that his daughter so badly wanted to know, including their happy times in Brighton and in Marrakech. It took close to an hour of Stella talking and Georgina barely blinking, listening in rapt attention.

Finally, Stella shrugged, not prepared to share her suffering of his loss, ending her tale in the café with Margaret and Harold coming to her aid. 'That was the last time I saw him.'

'A spy?' Georgina whispered, her tone awed.

'A real chameleon, but then you know that. The man I met in Piccadilly that night you would not recognise as your father. I fell in love with an entirely different Ainsworth to the one you knew. He was effortlessly charming, ridiculously handsome, highly aware of his surrounds and people around him, a fantastic dancer – and he didn't wear spectacles. Did you know, all of those pairs he possessed had clear glass in them?'

Georgina sighed. 'Is that meant to make me feel better?' Her query wasn't asked unkindly.

'No. Just a way of explaining that I was duped too. Nothing shocked me more – apart from losing him – than the day I met him at Harp's End and then helplessly had to join the guile to protect him. It was a burden I neither chose nor wanted. But I loved that stranger I met in London and hated discovering that I was working for his wife, looking after his children. Honestly, Georgina, it was untenable, and I tried to get away but was dragged in further when the need for him to get to Morocco for the government arose. He needed my help, your mother insisted I come . . .' Stella shook her head. 'It was awkward and you were difficult. It was always going to implode. What I didn't know is that he was orchestrating it. He had to get himself off that ship but without your mother – and not for the reason you think; more for her safety and the protection of his family. I now believe that it was he who manipulated poor little Grace into spilling what she heard. I might even be persuaded to believe that he deliberately goaded your mother to have that argument in Grace's bedroom that night so that, even though vaguely conscious, she would soak up what she heard.'

'But why?'

'To get me thrown off the ship too. He used the same trick, don't you see, to get me away from your mother's employ and under his authority. I can see that all so clearly now. So should you. It was cynical but your father was trapped, in a way; he was a patriot and he was putting his country's needs ahead of his own. I have no doubt in my heart that he was a thoroughly good man, but spies have to be cunning, manipulative, shadowy people who live by their wits.'

'Did he tell you he was working for the government?'

'No. That secret I worked out alone; I discovered it by chance on that same evening of Grace's fall. I challenged him on it, he was truthful and then of course he needed my help. He couldn't trust anyone else to smuggle the information back to London.'

'What have they done with the information?'

'Who knows, Georgina? I'm not privy to that. Going by what's happening in Europe, absolutely nothing, I suspect. Our government seems to be appeasing that man in Germany but they've had more than five years' warning of his intent. There are senior people working behind the scenes who have been suspicious of him since he first came to power and what your father and his friend Joseph delivered was simply proof of their collective fears.'

'You think we're going to war?'

Stella nodded sadly. 'I don't think handing over Czechoslovakia to Germany is going to keep his hunger for power sated.' She gave a low sigh. 'But then, what would I, a lady who owns a tearoom, know?'

'You call him Rafe . . . I've never heard that name.'

She explained.

'I really didn't know him at all, did I?'

'But you do now. He so desperately wanted to be a good father to you but you were difficult to love, Georgina. You pushed him away viciously, but you need to know that he genuinely wanted to help you through your difficult period. He ran out of time.' She watched Georgina's eyes water. 'I'm sorry to upset you.'

Georgina pulled a handkerchief from her sleeve and sniffed into it. 'Don't apologise. I deserve to confront all my terrible behaviour and it makes me feel even more generous towards my sister who is growing up through far more difficult circumstances. I must try and remain understanding of her mood swings. Nevertheless, I envy your knowing the darker, more heroic side of him.'

'You mustn't, because look at me . . . he's ruined me for others!' At Georgina's look of pity, she grinned. 'But that's how I want it. I've loved, I know how wonderful it is and I don't want to try and recreate it with anyone else. You've found it with Rex. You know what I'm talking about. Besides, he gave me all of this too,' she said, waving her hand and more. 'He so wanted me to follow my dream to open the tearooms and I couldn't let him down. It was him who found this place and bought it. I only learned about its existence a week or so after returning to Britain and accepting that he died over there.' She lifted a shoulder. 'He had a colleague deliver a letter that explained his hopes for me. I couldn't let him down, especially as he'd given me my future . . .' She stopped before she said more. Was she ready to share it all?

'Please don't think I begrudge you any of this, Stella,' Georgina assured, cutting into her thoughts. 'I have more money than I'll ever need.'

Stella had to laugh at her candour.

'I'm glad he made amends for how our family treated you.' Georgina looked at her watch. 'Speaking of Rex, I can't believe how the time has flown. I need more time with you; there's so much more to talk about.'

She nodded, stood and Georgina followed suit. They walked slowly out of the orchard and up the garden. 'Promise me again that you will remember me to Grace. Please tell her I would love to speak with her, or write to her . . . perhaps I could visit her at her school?'

'Of course I shall. And maybe next time she and I can come together.'

Stella's hopes lifted. 'Next time? I like the sound of that. Please do persuade her to come as well. Talking together, hugging again, it will help us all heal. Where in Hampshire is home for you?'

'A village called Sonning. Grace's school is on the East Sussex coast. But Rex is worried that should war come, we'd be vulnerable. He's talking about sending Grace and myself away, but . . . to where? I don't want to live alone, raise Grace, and raise our child.'

'Child?'

'Um . . . I'm expecting, Stella. I thought we'd get to all of this so much earlier but then Rex said put women together and they'll talk forever and still say it's not enough time.' She smiled brightly. 'I'm just eight weeks, so I'm not telling anyone. We had to take our honeymoon late, you see, because of Mother's passing. She lived long enough to see me married but then we couldn't go off on a romantic holiday as she was dying. Rex was all right to wait for the honeymoon but that didn't mean he waited on everything!' she said, lifting a perfectly shaped eyebrow to make Stella chuckle. 'Now we're going to have a wonderful few weeks driving around England. He wanted to take me to Europe but I prefer to be closer to home. Morning sickness is such a killer.'

Stella nodded. 'I know. Oh, congratulations, Georgina.' She hugged her. 'Listen to me now, why not come here?'

'Pardon?'

'If you need to leave the south, come here. This house is enormous – there are eight bedrooms up there. We use four. Look at the size of this garden: more than enough room for a school of children to play. And perhaps Rex would feel safe having you in Harrogate? Think about it. The offer's there any time for you, for Grace . . . and for your child. Lots of help here too, and together perhaps we can help Grace heal,' she said, taking Georgina's hand

and feeling the wonder of this new connection.

'You were always so generous, thank you for forgiving me. But would you really want a baby around . . . I mean . . . I know you have your brother and sister, but they're growing up. A crying baby is —'

'I would love it. I'm not nearly as removed from infants as you imagine,' she replied with a wry smile.

Georgina frowned, trying to catch her meaning, but she was interrupted by the sound of a young voice approaching where they were standing in the middle of the pathway. A woman emerged from the back door, chasing after a child who looked to be around four years old.

'Oh, hello Peggy.'

'I'm sorry, Stella. We're just home from school but he saw you from the window.'

Georgina watched Stella bend down and open her arms with a look of pure affection. 'Rufe! I was hoping you'd be back in time.' She shook her head at Peggy. 'I wanted him to meet our guest.'

The little boy ran into his mother's embrace, chattering about a painting he had done for her today.

'Ooh, I'm sorry to have kept you waiting, darling,' Stella said, loving the smell of shampoo she could still detect in her child's soft dark hair, but now it was time to meet his stepsister, if that's what Georgina was. 'We shall go and view your painting, darling, but first, would you say hello to Georgina? She's a very special person. Georgina, this is Rufus, my son.'

Young Rufe squinted up at Georgina. 'Hello. Are you a friend of Mummy's?'

'Er . . . yes, I am,' Georgina answered, glancing at Stella with a look of atonement. 'Hello, Rufe,' she breathed. 'What a handsome little boy you are.'

He nodded with a wide grin that reminded Stella, as it always did, of Grace. 'Mummy says I look like Daddy.'

'I think you do too,' Georgina admitted, and Stella heard her fighting back the emotion. 'Just like the photos in the nursery.'

Little Rufe didn't understand, and grabbed his nanny's hand. 'Come on, Peggy, I want to fetch my painting for Mummy.'

Stella threw her a look of gratitude as she moved off with her son before turning back to the stunned Georgina. 'You see, Georgina, he gave me everything . . . not just his love, the roof over my family's head, a business to keep me financially stable, but my whole future. I need no other man but that little one for now growing up behind Rory . . . I shall keep him safe, teach him well, ensure he's loved by his family . . . and greater family,' she said, squeezing Georgina's hand again, 'if you'll help him to be part of your lives.'

'Oh, Stella . . . why didn't you tell us?' Georgina sounded cut.

She shook her head. 'Imagine your mother's response. Apart from the pain it surely would have caused, she would have thought only the worst of me; that I was hoping for some sort of financial support. And you've just finished telling me how you felt about Grace usurping your place in the family; Grace would have hated Rufus for the same reason.' She shrugged. 'She may still do so, although I doubt it somehow.' She took Georgina's arm. 'Please don't be angry with me. Rufus is all I have and need of your father. He, with my beautiful brother and sister, complete me – I'm happy, independent, optimistic. That's more than most might be able to claim.'

'Would you have told me about Rufe?'

'Not without your visit, no, but to be honest, I wanted to tell you the moment I hugged you hello. I've been desperate to share him with his other family but we've been talking nonstop since you arrived, finding the right moment was hard! I'm just glad he got home from school in time.' They laughed. 'I wouldn't have let you go without knowing about him, or seeing a photo of him, though.'

'So our father lives on through your son. New beginnings,' Georgina whispered, tearily.

To new beginnings, Stella echoed in her mind, deciding that this really was the start of a new era in her life.

They hugged, holding the embrace as Stella looked over Georgina's shoulder to where the jackdaw perched. He blinked his near human-looking eye of silvery iris and neat pupil with what Stella took to be approval before the curious bird leaped from the fence and was gone from them.

Dance on, Rafe, she cast to its disappearing outline, feeling that he would return to check on her and their two families coming together. *I'll keep them all safe, I promise.*

ACKNOWLEDGEMENTS

I have an aversion to planning out stories. For the most part I set out with a single character and a dilemma, which expands to capture other people until suddenly there's an adventure of sorts underway. That said, I thought that *The Last Dance* was to be a cosy tale of an illicit love affair in southern England but somewhere along the way it turned into an international spy story involving smuggled secrets and a brewing world war. I don't know whom I have to thank for that but as I usually discover there is a host of people I owe a debt of thanks to for helping me to complete the storytelling journey.

So, my sincere gratitude to VisitBritain for assisting me to piece together the Kent section and for the trip to the new London Transport Museum in Covent Garden – it is a quirky, fun installation for all visitors.

In what now feels like another lifetime I was once a daily commuter between Brighton and London, but my 1979 knowledge was still too recent for my story so Brian Halford from National Rail kindly connected me with Phil Marsh from Cleek Railway Solutions. Phil passionately set about educating me with regard to the south-eastern railway network of England in early 1933. I don't believe there was a single question I posed that Phil didn't have an answer to; he even made it possible for me to sight the rail ticket of the exact journey in the exact month and year I needed. Thank you, Phil – you're a gem.

The reading squad must be thanked and while they see reading early drafts as anything but a chore I am ever grateful to Pip Klimentou, Nigelle-Ann Blaser and Sonya Caddy for their feedback.

To the team at Penguin Australia that has moved beyond the publisher role to become a beloved cheering squad, my love and thanks – especially to you, Ali Watts; also to Saskia Adams, Lou Ryan, Sharlene Vinall and Rhian Davies for having my back – and my thanks also to all at Penguin Random House for your immense care and support.

I must also thank William Wordsworth for penning a poem I have loved since I learned it at school at about the same age that Grace learns it in my story.

Finally, to family – more important than anything else. Thank you for being mine. Fx

BOOK CLUB DISCUSSION NOTES

1. In the opening pages of the novel, Stella whispers to her parents' caskets: 'Love like yours can only end in heartbreak.' Did you think these words foreshadowed any kind of tragedy?

2. In Rafe's attic study Stella finds butterflies pinned to a board. Discuss the symbolism of this in relation to the two main characters.

3. Rafe seems an entirely different man when out on the Weald or in the desert. Discuss the various internal and external settings of the novel, including the cruise ship. What role did these settings play in the story?

4. As a character, did you love Georgina or loathe her?

5. Discuss the differences between Stella's middle-class upbringing and that of the Ainsworth children. Do you admire the Ainsworths, for all their indulgent ways?

6. Was Stella right to follow her heart, given the circumstances and the prevailing mood of the era?

7. Rafe tells Stella: 'I've not been lucky to meet anyone who stirred my emotions into the perfect cocktail until I danced with you.' Discuss the ways in which you think Rafe and Stella are perfect together.

8. Which do you find the single most evocative and memorable scene in this book?

9. Was Rafe's ultimate act 'right' or 'wrong'? Would you have done the same?

10. Do you think this novel had a happy ending or a sad one?

Read on for a sneak peek of

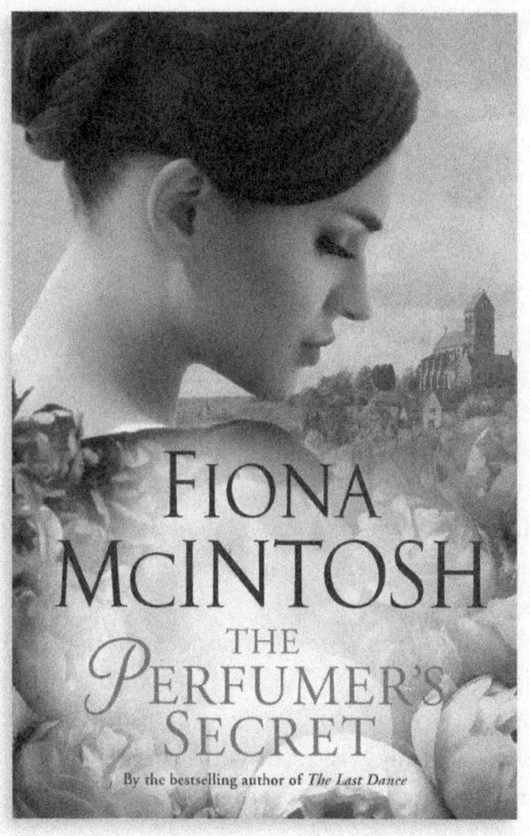

Brought to you by Penguin Books

I

1 AUGUST 1914

I loathed the man I was to marry today.

A hand reached across and covered my wrist; it was hairless with blunt, well-kept fingernails.

'Be still, Fleurette.' I hadn't realised how I was fidgeting. 'Collect yourself,' my brother continued. 'Father would want you composed, representing the family so publicly.' Henri tipped my chin through the veil which, though sheer, likely hid me enough to blur my expression of anguish.

Henri's purposeful mention of our genial father demanded I obey. I was nothing if not dutiful. They say we all make choices in our lives, but I was born into a family who made nearly all of life's choices for me. In their defence I had little to complain about. I was the precious daughter to be cherished and admired like treasure.

I had failed to comprehend until recently, however, that this was not simply a charming notion. I was indeed the family treasure and I could be exchanged like a coin, traded as human currency. I was as helpless as a glinting gold sovereign passed from one hand to another: a bargain made, a transaction secured.

And now with the deal done – and just the ritual required to confirm its existence to everyone else – my angst counted for naught. I made another attempt to take the legal position, my last bastion, the only aspect of this vile union I could attempt to hide behind. The war, it seemed, might be my ally.

'Henri, in the eyes of the law, we shall be unmarried. Without that certificate from the mayor, the priest can't legally wed us.' I spoke the truth.

'Don't start that again, little sister. I can assure you that the mayor and his councillors have far more on their minds than a society wedding. I have personally pressed the point an hour ago and not even our name and its weight – or Aimery's or my threats, I might add – can convince his assistant to interrupt the town's war meetings. Besides, the mayor and his adjoint aren't even in Grasse,' he said, sounding exasperated because he knew I was aware of this last fact.

True. We were supposed to have had our civil ceremony yesterday but with France on a war footing, awaiting declaration, no town hall anywhere in the country would have been inclined to concern itself with legalising a marriage, not even one for an elite pair of families such as ours.

'When is the mayor back?'

He lifted a shoulder helplessly. 'Tomorrow, hopefully. The emergency meeting in Nice at the prefecture will likely close today when declaration of war is surely formalised.'

'Can't anyone else —'

'No,' he snapped. 'It is unbefitting that a lower representative would wish to perform a marriage ceremony today with the nation in such flux – even if he were in a position to or permitted to.' I wanted to leap in and press my point here but Henri was ready for me. 'Now,' he continued, cutting the air with a raised palm. 'Enough. It has been hard enough to convince the priest to go ahead but if he has acquiesced, then I suspect you have no higher authority.'

'I have my moral —'

'Let it be, Fleurette,' he sniped, brushing imaginary lint from his trousers. 'We are toppling into war with Germany! These are hardly usual circumstances. Heaven will forgive you – it's just a formality, and it's not as though we won't be having the civil ceremony.'

'When?'

'The mayor has sent word that he will do his best for us – let's hope tomorrow.' He was flushed pink with simmering anger and I watched him run a finger between his collar and neck, grimacing with displeasure at me. 'Now, neither I nor the De Lasset family will ever forgive you if you get in the way of this important union. We can hardly cancel after months of preparation. This town needs this marriage. Plus our mobilisation orders will be through at any moment – let's at least get the church wedding completed. The civil duties can be sorted quietly. I know it's backwards – *I know* – but I need you to tolerate the discrepancy. If our church can, you can. Please think of everyone else . . . anyone else, in fact, instead of yourself for once.'

The rebuke hurt. I was not selfish but I was angry with our priest for bending the rules of our faith, the laws of our land, simply because the wealthiest families demanded it. No doubt Henri or my equally boorish husband-to-be had coerced the priest – the new window for the apse, perhaps?

'Henri, I will be lying with a man who is not legally my husband,' I bleated.

'Not in the eyes of the law, no, but it shall be fixed. What are you hoping for? That we shall cancel because of a piece of paper?' He glared at me. 'Are you going to disappoint the entire town, all of its people gathered to celebrate what is arguably the most important marriage in recent times, perhaps ever, for Grasse? Two of its elite families, formally unified: it's the dream, Fleurette. Don't spoil this dream, this optimism, given that every able man here is about to march off to do his country's duty.'

'Exactly! How can we be sure of the legal paperwork being achieved without Aimery's presence?'

I suspected he had no ready answer – this was my final flag, my last standing post. I was shocked that he was more than ready for me, though, with a voice filled with disdain.

'The declaration will be chest-beating by Germany. We have to observe our mobilisation duties but I suspect we shall all be making our way back to our homes within a week, perhaps two at worst. It will be short-lived and Aimery will be home, but for now he wants to leave Grasse as a married man, potentially with an heir already seeded, and you are going to ensure you live up to everyone's expectations. That's your duty.'

I closed my eyes in revulsion. Now my body was being spoken about like a field, ready to be turned over and . . . oh, it was too ugly to contemplate.

There was no response to my brother's tirade. I was struck mute; I opened my eyes to stare at my gloved hands and the small mound beneath the glove of my left hand, third finger. The glint of crimson winked at me. It was a half-carat ruby set between curves of old mine-cut and rose-cut diamonds. The result was a ring shaped like an eye . . . and it stared back at me from under the lace with accusation in that red eye. Aimery could not engage me for marriage with an heirloom ring; he had nothing of his mother's and I suspected he would have ignored something of hers even if he had it to give. Instead, this had been designed at enormous expense in Paris, but without my involvement, of course. And so it reflected only Aimery . . . flamboyant, no doubt outrageously expensive, ostentatious in its bright colouring – demanding attention. The shape was odd and I already imbued it with a sinister sense that it would always spy on me. I hated it, but then everything about this marriage carried despair for me.

An odd pain enveloped me in the claustrophobic carriage, sharp and nauseating. It was the height of summer and the flowers in my hand and threaded through my hair might wilt; that was the reason given for us not travelling in an open landau. Churlishly, I decided the real reason was more likely Henri's concern for his hair and the carefully applied pomade. The pain deepened; perhaps I was panicking, like the time I thought Felix had chopped his fingers off with a lavender scythe, or the morning of the June picnic when I fell from my horse and everyone's voices were coming from too far away . . . or the day my mother died, which in itself was beyond my comprehension as an infant, yet as young as I was I recall my father's body sagging like an empty sack of rose petals and not understanding why.

I was not prone to being flighty and in my defence those memories belonged to isolated, intensive events that I could conjure authentically. Today's anxiety didn't feel as though it would pass, or that someone would come along to make it feel better; today was the start of a new life I feared. The desire to shrink from it was sufficiently overwhelming that I felt as though I was trying to tear part of myself free . . . me and myself needed to separate in order to get through what duty now required of me.

I looked away from the stone dwellings of the town as we picked our way through the streets, drawing ever closer to the sound of the single cathedral bell chiming our imminent arrival. My gaze fixed on my hands in my lap, which were finally still. The fingers beneath the pearl-studded silken Chantilly lace were straight, unblemished by any hereditary disease like my father had suffered. I tried to pretend the internal ache was coming from their joints, pathetically I suppose, trying to commune with my dead father in a moment when I had never needed him more.

I privately wished Henri the pain of our father in his own

fingers. Perhaps he sensed the curse pass between us as I remembered the physician's description of Father's arthritis. My recall of any event was so reliable I could watch the scene, hear the words accurately replay in my mind.

'Your joints are building their spurs,' Dr Bertrand had observed, puffing on a pipe as he bent to inspect my father's hands, despite his host's muttered protest. 'They're called Heberden's nodes, if you prefer me to be precise,' he said, frowning. Bluish smoke had escaped his lips and moved like a phantom, stealing around the room, scenting it with top notes of the whiskey I smelled in my father's decanter and the dry leaves I threw on the campfire that my brother and I set the previous winter. I reached hard and could still conjure the taste of tea and a gentle hum of what I thought might be vanilla. Father would have waved a finger in appreciation at my observation.

Ah, those crooked hands; they had taught me everything from how to ride a horse to how to pluck a tiny, delicate flower at dawn without touching the fragile bloom, a necessary ability in our family business. The only skill I could think of in this tense moment in the carriage of misery with Henri was that the only talent my father's hands had not physically taught me was gifted through his blood. I had known even then, as a beribboned child with a black kitten making a nest in my lap while Dr Bertrand mused over my father's arthritic fingers, that my heightened sense of taste and smell was emerging in tandem with my twin brother's equally strong talent.

Our elder brother Henri had known too that, once again, he was different to his siblings. And he could not cheerfully regard this talent we'd acquired as a blessing; even now it sat between us as an invisible presence, taunting him despite its silence. Henri had learned how to ignore it but never to disguise the impact it had on his constant desire to impress our father.

The Delacroix twins had 'the Nose'. The divinely bestowed

gift of olfactory superiority allowed us such a heightened sense of smell we could distinguish aromas beyond the average person. Thus our ability to develop complex fragrances with depth and skill made us gods of our industry. Except I had the misfortune, I suppose, to be born a woman. Had I arrived into any other family, I suspect my prowess would have lain dormant. As it was, only Felix was taken seriously as the upcoming perfumer of the family but I was permitted to contribute my thoughts as a sort of invisible consultant to Felix and my father. It was enough – it had to be, for I had no choice in this. However, more obvious than my passion to use my skills was that the inherent ability had bypassed the heir, and so Henri found creative ways to punish us for this fact. I realise now that most of the time even poor Henri wasn't aware of just how deeply angry he was to lack this highly prized skill.

It was unusual for two such closely related family members to possess the flair that for most felt unattainable. Oh, indeed, recognising bouquets was a skill that could be acquired with a workmanlike diligence. No, what I'm referring to is a sixth sense. An inherent aptitude for deciphering dozens – no, scores – of elemental tastes and smells, even when jumbled together. As a youngster Henri's wrath tried to trip us up; he'd blindfold us, demand we perform like circus animals. What he couldn't realise was that denying us the sight of the source only heightened our proficiency. If he'd paid more attention, he would have recalled that whenever Father smelled a perfume, or even a single flower, he would close his eyes as if to be deliberately blindfolded from any visual cues.

I couldn't touch this exquisite pain I was feeling in my fingers now. I couldn't soothe it, or send it away. I had no idea from where it emanated: my departing soul, I thought, and I knew Felix would scoff at the dramatic notion.

I would give anything for my father's gnarled hands to reach out and hold mine now; he would know what to say, would know how to quell the pain. He would cancel this pantomime and counsel all involved that he wished a happy rather than a dutiful marriage for his only daughter. He had never favoured Aimery for me, wouldn't hear of it when it was first proffered several years back. In fact his horror had matched mine. I'd had a reliable ally until now; why hadn't he stated in his will that I should marry whom I wanted and not have my marriage arranged? My mother, rest her soul, might not agree. She herself had been forced into a union of duty demanded of her aristocratic English family. Fortunately for Flora St John, the man on the other end of that bargain was Arnaud Delacroix. I doubted she could regret her family's agreement, hammered out in Paris, as I understood it, between the two heads of the household, for it had been a wise and – luckily for her – a blessed one. Although no one could have known that, surely, at the time. The agreement would have been made purely on the suitability of his and her families' combined financial clout. I wish I'd known my mother longer than two brief years and could ask her now how it had felt to be sold on.

I gathered from others in the household that she had been a golden-haired beauty with a milky complexion and pale eyes and was treated like a goddess by my father. She roamed my memory more as a line-up of senses. I could recreate her preferred fragrance simply by closing my mind and thinking on it: honeysuckle, jasmine and rose would linger in my thoughts. I could dimly recall the sound of her gentle voice; I could also latch on to a memory of her hugs and kisses, but her physical presence was not easy to conjure. She was like a ghost who drifted through our house in photographs or the portrait in my father's salon; she was real only through her possessions – jewellery, clothes, her ivory comb and hairbrush – but I couldn't miss her because I didn't know her. We lost this fragile woman to complications from her pregnancy when we twins were just over two years old.

My parents' life together was short but I am constantly, almost deliberately, assured by others that it was filled with affection. She had loved him completely, according to our old nurse, who was like a mother to mine and a grandmother to me. She told me how Flora St John had wanted to run down the same church aisle I was approaching in her hurry to become a Delacroix of Grasse. The name counted for so much, not just in the south-west but in all of France and England too, and now I was giving up that fine name for an even more powerful one.

Except I did not want it.

The person who did desire it for me cast a look of smug pleasure my way as we rounded the corner to crest the incline to where my future beckoned. 'I think the whole town has turned out,' he remarked in an airy tone, tapping my hand in a proprietorial way. 'You should feel honoured. Look how happy they all are for you, for us.'

'Father would not approve of your decision,' I said, finding the courage to throw down one final challenge. 'And you know it. It was discussed years ago and he told you then he would not sanction it.'

Henri looked back to the adoring townsfolk, cheering and clapping as we passed. I recognised many of them. I should have been smiling, waving to them. I did neither.

'His last breath was about wishing he'd seen you in your wedding finery.'

'He'd approve of my gown, Henri, but not of the person you're forcing me to wear it for. It's not that he didn't like Aimery; even you must know he behaved oddly around him, as though there was something about him that made Father's hair stand on end. I can be specific, though – I don't like Aimery.'

It was stale debate. Henri did not trouble himself to argue it again. Instead he sighed at me as one might an insolent youngster. 'You will marry Aimery De Lasset today because it is an excellent match for our family.'

'For you,' I whipped back, living up to the label of a petulant child.

'As head of this family I am tasked to make the decisions,' he said in a voice leaden with forced patience. I could tell Henri was schooling himself not to be baited today.

'As eldest by a mere five years,' I said, feeling a pathetic glimmer of victory at qualifying his status, 'you may have the power to make decisions, Henri, but it doesn't capacitate you to make good ones, as you are ably demonstrating today. It's simply an easy one – solves a problem in your mind that doesn't exist in reality. If you would only wait, I would help you to make a brilliant decision on this matter and a prosperous one too. Trust me, Henri, I know my role. This is the wrong choice and definitely the wrong time.'

His irritating smile widened indulgently. 'I'm sorry you feel this way on your wedding day, Fleurette, because frankly I believe twenty-three is an ideal age for marriage. Who knows when you might decide the perfect lifetime partner has walked into your life? No, little sister, we shall not wait for an emotional readiness of your choosing that could be years away and thus miss the chance at this union of our two houses. Between us I think our father indulged you too much; his zealous refusal to consider a marriage between a Delacroix and a De Lasset bordered on fanaticism.'

'Do you think our father was mad, Aimery?'

'Don't be ridiculous. You're twisting my words.'

'In that case, you're saying he possessed a genuine and fundamental objection to our houses joined in blood.'

'I never understood it and he never bothered to explain it. We all know the bitter rivalry of the past but as both fathers got older their blood cooled, plus of course they were both so successful there was no need to keep fighting one another. Until you grew up there was no reason to discuss marriage, and I'll admit I remain perplexed as to why our father didn't feel inclined to pledge you to

De Lasset, if just to keep our perfume empires strong, but he always did indulge you. Nevertheless, he's not here now and he's not the one looking to the future of our family, whereas I am, and I do not share his views. I have no reservations for this union because it makes every bit of sense to me. Furthermore, neither Aimery nor I am prepared to wait any longer. You're in your prime now; you will never look more beautiful, your skin will never glow as much, your body will never feel or move the way it does now.'

My value was now being reduced to the youth of my flesh and I wanted to accuse him of having no knowledge of my prime – or any other potential bride's prime, come to that – but he lectured on, trampling my thoughts.

'Be grateful for your charmed life, Fleurette. You belong to the second-wealthiest family of Grasse and your marriage into the town's richest family is surely a rite of passage; the timing is perfect and you know it ensures strength for the town as well – the whole region, in fact.'

He was so transparent with his manipulation I felt a momentary pity. Henri had always lacked subtlety. It was only I suppose in the last year or two that I'd come to understand Henri so fully, with his odd sense of inferiority. He had so much in his favour simply by being the eldest – that special status of being entitled – but still he envied his siblings, hungered for what we had.

If my father treated us all with what felt like identical affection I suspect my mother held a special and deeply embedded compassion for Henri. I gathered this from the old nursery maid who helped raise us. Henri was Flora's firstborn; the celebrated arrival of a son and heir made him her most beloved. It also helped, I'm sure, that he echoed her family with hair the colour of the sunbaked beaches of our childhood. He must have looked like a little angel as an infant; the grainy photos attested to this. Now, though, that once shiny hair was thinning and looked less like straw and more like wispy gold thread. His hairline had receded to reveal wings of shiny scalp that made his forehead seem a little too large. He compensated with a wiry moustache, ostentatiously curled so its tips flew north. And a newly grown beard offered the added benefit of making him seem older – the air of the patriarch he was aiming for. He trimmed his gingery beard to a point, like an exclamation to end a debate and prove he was, at twenty-seven, virile and capable of growing hair.

Meanwhile, Felix and I were the antithesis of Henri; we were a pair of midnight sentinels to his once angelic gold. Our fluff of infancy darkened quickly and by five we sported the lustrous near-black hair of our father's ancestors and we knew we would turn first moonlight silver before we became white as our predecessors, while Henri continued the march into bland baldness. The dissimilarities continued. Where Henri was slightly built with sloping shoulders hidden by skilled tailoring, our brother was strapping and I too was long-limbed, wide of shoulder, and both of us glowingly healthy to Henri's somewhat wan appearance. He routinely took 'herbal inhalations', gargled with salt, had taken to the waters at Lourdes for several years in an annual pilgrimage . . . anything to keep the feared infection at bay. He sniffed eucalypt and had rubdowns of tonic of menthol as he worried incessantly that he might contract the same disease as our mother. He would often ungraciously claim that she'd bestowed weak lungs upon him. Perhaps if he gave up smoking his expensive cigars from Cuba, it might help . . . but who was I to question our family's head any longer? Soon he would no longer be head of my family. I would belong to another man, another head of household, another controlling son who strived to live up to his ancestors.

Another bully.

The horses drawing our carriage slowed and paced out a wide circle on the cobbles sprawling in front of the cathedral before we finally lurched to a halt. We'd arrived at the place where one half of me would likely give up on life. The other half would bear witness to that surrender but hopefully remain safe, hidden, alive and dreaming of better luck for us both.

'Marriage, family, duty is everything our father stood for,' Henri finished, as though wanting to slam the book shut on any further discussion about the suitability of this marriage.

I insisted on aiming to have the last word, though. 'Well, as you're selling me off like a stud horse, Henri, you really should take into account my fine teeth!' I said, my voice finally breaking as my body felt itself sundered. It seemed as though only a shell now remained inside the carriage, dabbing quickly at her eyes, while the spirit version of me shrank and surely floated outside, finally free, to await on the church steps for the Delacroix bride to emerge from the froth of white inside the closed carriage.

'Do your duty,' Henri urged in a clipped tone. I watched his face betray the sneer that was close to the surface. Henri had no time for girlish tears. 'A wise and solid marriage is the only contribution demanded of you . . . that, and some heirs. You can manage that, surely?'

'Duty?' I heard my voice squeak on the word. 'Henri, we're potentially going to war and you're more troubled by a strategic marriage arrangement and —'

He made a condescending tutting sound. 'Hush now, Fleurette. It is not your place to discuss politics.' I could almost see myself blinking in disgust opposite him. 'Besides' – he smirked – 'this is why young women should not focus on men's business. You may claim otherwise, Fleurette, but you are as emotionally vulnerable as the next girl. Let me remind you of the shared blood that runs in the veins of the German Kaiser and the Russian Tsar. They are hardly going to prolong any bad feeling against each other. War may well be declared . . . yes, words, but it likely won't amount to much fighting.'

I couldn't be bothered arguing otherwise. Henri's tactless hint at the next duty of horror I would be required to perform was suddenly crowding me, smacking in my mind as one might swing at a fly with a swat. He was not a deliberately cruel man but I could almost hear the snapping sound in my thoughts, almost feel the sting of his taunt.

And I replied in a similarly cruel vein, although I was ashamed of myself for stooping this low. '*You* should marry him, Henri. You've always had a fondness for Aimery.'

His glare was ringed by invisible rage. I could feel it wanting to reach out and grab me by the neck as he used to when we were little and he was up against both of us. Because Felix was bigger, stronger, Henri picked on me instead, even if he wanted to fight back against only my brother. I was never a match physically but Felix had schooled me in how to use my wit instead. But I had failed him today. Today my tongue was a blunt instrument, clubbing Henri with the only weapon I had against him.

His secret had always been safe with us. We were brothers and sister. No matter our differences, we shared the name of Delacroix and nothing stood between that and the rest of the world. Except now. Now the brother I had protected was casting me adrift into a new world I did not want . . . not yet.

I was his chattel. In that moment I hated him as much as Aimery and if not for Felix's sympathetic grin from the top of the cathedral stairs as he spotted our arrival, I may have faltered. But the glance from Felix told me to bear up. I looked at the male version of me; we had shared our mother's womb during the same thirty-nine weeks, emerging within a minute of each other. I was born first and took regular delight in reminding him of this. Everything was shared, often our emotions – especially today – and I knew he was losing his best friend in a way that most couldn't understand and everyone would underestimate.

'I will forgive you for that insult, Fleurette, though I'm sure I don't know what you mean by it,' he lied. 'Catherine also would not appreciate your sentiment.'

I might have liked Catherine in any other situation and I would be a welcoming sister to her if she married Henri. However, her family's driving need for her to be a Delacroix at all costs was surely out-muscling her instincts. If only she'd met Aimery first and they could have married, then I wouldn't be facing my trauma; maybe I could blame poor Catherine for this dark pathway I now had to walk?

'Fleurette?' His tone this time was surprisingly gentle.

Yet I responded as if he'd hit me. 'Yes!' I clenched two fists in my lap in a bid to contain my fury. 'I know, Henri, I know . . .' I gave one last sniff. 'Let me gather myself.'

'I want to say something meaningful to you.'

'Don't,' I warned. People were hushing around the carriage, and the coachman was waiting as a footman put down a stool for me to step onto.

Henri held the door closed a few moments longer.

'Make it work, little sister. This is a match unrivalled in our family history . . . or theirs. It is one made in heaven.'

'Or rather one on paper, using arithmetic with a lot of French franc symbols.'

'Fleurette, you are a beautiful, young woman with an intelligence to match. Learn how to use those gifts amongst the others that have been bestowed upon you to get what you want.'

The words drove into me like the chilling blast of the mistral blowing ferociously in November, roaring through my mind, taking with them my haughty resentment and perhaps even the arrogance that I should have the right to choose the man I marry. It was not so for any of my friends. Why should I be different? I was a romantic fool. Felix regularly accused me of wanting to script my life when it would be controlled by seniors, or take its own merry path and would likely throw up obstacles to clamber over, or throw down challenges to fight through. A slit of comprehension opened for me like a shaft of dawn's sunlight breaking over the hills of Grasse.

Henri's revolting choice for me would indeed ensure the success and wealth of ongoing generations. 'Keep it in the family of Grasse' had been one of my father's favourite phrases and no doubt that philosophy was one he had wanted to apply to our unions. I couldn't be selective about when his advice was relevant. It never stopped being relevant. Protecting the industry of Grasse, protecting the family's interests and its ongoing success, was my job too, and part of my job was to marry strategically.

Love was irrelevant – a lucky by-product, if it occurred.

'We have to go, Fleurette,' Henri said, and his tone was even kinder.

The door to the carriage was opened and the sounds of the people who lined the courtyard and some of the narrower alleys that fed into the cathedral square hurried in. Henri stepped out first to applause that turned wild as I emerged to take his hand with as much grace as I could muster.

'You have never looked more gorgeous,' he whispered. 'If I were Aimery, I would consider myself the luckiest man on earth.'

I looked into his earnest expression and saw no guile. Poor Henri. He truly believed this was for the best. In which case, I should do the same. Accept my lot now and get on with it. I could hardly complain that I wanted for much.

I braced, took a slow, deep breath and found a smile for my brother. 'Walk me down the aisle, Henri.'

Women sighed, thrilled at the sight of the first Delacroix bride of the new generation to step out, ready to take her wedding vows at the cathedral of Notre-Dame du Puy. Others, mainly boys, hung from windows, whistling and vying for my attention – a little smile, a sideways glance, perhaps. I gave nothing but hoped they'd all forgive me, imagine me a nervous bride, desperate not to trip or stumble. I began to understand, feeling their collective surge of pleasure. How impossible it must have seemed to my brother and his partner in this transaction, to consider cancellation or postponement.

These might be the last smiles for a long time and although war had yet to be officially declared and we prayed it might still be averted, I think we could all feel its press. This wedding was needed to keep everyone optimistic for the future.

Henri and Aimery had forgone the age-old tradition of the man calling at the house of his bride and then walking with her to the church, gathering a long procession of townsfolk behind them. Henri considered it beneath us and it troubled me that he saw us as different from the townsfolk in anything but privilege. Each of us children had been born and raised in this town and our father had come here from Paris as a boy. We were locals. Perhaps the word Henri didn't utter but heard in his mind was 'peasants'. Either way, I had to forgo what might have been the only fun of the day for me, to walk with the people I loved and perhaps channel their joy into mine. It seemed they'd all proceeded to the church anyway, just without the main couple.

I noted their sense of celebration had not been dampened and they were determined I still follow some of the ritual. Each stair to the cathedral was flanked by two children who belonged to the workers of our fields – I knew each by name. Between each pair they'd stretched a white ribbon. Normally, I would have been required to cut those ribbons intermittently on my journey from my home to the altar, but they seemed happy enough to make me cut the ribbons on the stairs. The first boy, Pierre, son of one of the violet growers, solemnly handed me some tailor's scissors that looked cumbersome in his small hands.

'Mademoiselle Fleurette,' he said, bowing sweetly.

I could hardly refuse. '*Merci*, Pierre,' I whispered, touching his curly head, before I cut his ribbon and the crowd cheered.

I lifted the hem of my gown, which was made of transparent embroidered silk covering the palest ecru satin. The elbow-length, gently ruffled sleeves of sheer Flanders lace had been fashioned from my grandmother's bridal gown. We were a superstitious lot, we Delacroix. The overall colour effect seemed to match the marble of the shallow exterior stairs of the cathedral we were ascending, and I wondered how many happy brides – like my mother – had wanted to run up this short flight towards their intended. I had walked these smoothly worn stairs most Sundays of my life and never dreaded them as I did now. From within the womb of the cathedral's stone walls I could hear the echoing sounds of people restless in their pews – coughs and the drone of men's voices, the light laughter of women – before the organ's soft background hum became louder, turned into official wedding music, and hushed those tones.

The pain had left me. I was no longer whole, though. I genuinely believed in this moment that part of me had escaped and now observed my other. I reminded myself that when Henri let go of my arm, my twin would be standing alongside the groom to keep me strong, get me through the trial of agreeing to be Aimery's wife without shouting my true feelings. Felix had already disappeared into the cathedral, no doubt quieting anyone who hadn't realised I'd arrived at the gateway to misery. I imagined his crooked smile with that glint of mischief in his eye, urging me to be strong.

The thought encouraged me and I turned once, reaching deep to find a glimmer of a smile for the still applauding townsfolk outside. They loved the old families, loved what we did for the town; they especially loved my father for how he looked after everyone who worked for the firm of Delacroix. It didn't matter whether they picked the flowers, worked on the factory floor in the distillation process or drove the carts that would make deliveries – they were all viewed as vital, valuable and worthy of his smile, his care, his kindness at all times.

We were the European chieftains of this industry. We were the royalty of Grasse, beloved old families of France.

We are the Perfumers to the World.

Perhaps it was this thought that warmed up my expression as I turned to lift a hand of appreciation to the townsfolk for their welcome when I helplessly locked on to the searing gaze of Graciela Olivares. She seemed to be standing on a low wall, for her shoulders were easily visible above even the tallest townsfolk. This gave her a clear pathway of sight to burn her fury towards me. I wanted to assure her I was as helpless in this event as a tethered lamb. It had never occurred to me that she wouldn't be Aimery's wife. If only I could explain that the talks between the two heads of household happened in private and were announced without me having any say in the agreement, that my pain matched hers . . . but Henri was dragging me into the shadows of the cathedral porch, where the heat of day and Graciela's fire were instantly chased away by the cool.

I took one long last draught of freedom and on the air I tasted my beloved Grasse, picking out its flavours with ease as though I was pointing to each on a store shelf. They were imprinted on my memory and I could select them as I chose, and yet when they reached me fresh of a morning it was as though I smelled them for the first time.

The sun-coaxed honeyed lusciousness of rose came first, tumbling on the soft thermals rising from the valley to the summit where I stood, soon to take holy vows. I reached for the waft of violet . . . there it was, syrupy and haunting, before it was pushed aside by woody, camphorous rosemary and the earthy yet elegant thyme that was never far away. They were using essential oils we'd distilled months earlier. Right now we were approaching jasmine harvest but the sensual jasmine would come into its own tonight. Even so, more flavours crowded; I wished I could linger to pick out more, but Henri was guiding me into the shadow of the vestibule.

People were clearing throats, glancing around, standing. Children were staring. I couldn't bear to meet the glance of anyone; instead I fixed my gaze on the dark stone of the church walls ahead.

Henri touched my fingertips, which clasped his arm loosely. 'Ready to do battle?' he whispered in the strange language of our mother's tongue.

It seemed timely given what Europe was facing but it was an old jest from childhood and nearly undid me. However, I embraced the affection he'd hoped he could elicit with that question.

'Tally ho,' I whispered, using the familiar yet odd response that none of us children had ever understood.

He grinned and I saw her in him and a fleeting echo of our father's smile. And then we were walking, our steps matched to the solemn music; underfoot I crushed fresh rose petals, dropped by the small child chosen as flower girl for the ceremony. Blanche was the daughter of one of our staff. I wondered if she was imagining her own wedding day. I wished Blanche a happier union as the fragrance of roses once again lifted and cradled me in its familiar scent, which I had known throughout my life. It reassured, and I held myself straighter to the organ's sombre music, which Henri had also chosen.

Eight hundred years of memory and knowledge embraced me. I knew this former cathedral, now simply called our church, almost as well as I knew my own home with its crooked stone pillars soaring to the vault of the gothic ceiling and strengthened by iron girders. Simple, grey marble tiles underfoot echoed its inherent modesty. Cold stone surrounded me and for now suited my heart. I noted some crumbling in the dark grey walls.

'We should contribute some money to restore our church,' I whispered. It was inappropriate – a useless comment – but I needed to have a reason to talk to Henri or I would be forced to acknowledge the beaming audience come to bear witness. Maybe that was the bribe offered to coerce our priest into overlooking the necessary paperwork. He was a sweet, elderly man, no doubt intimidated by both the Delacroix and De Lasset chieftains.

'It's fine,' Henri said, patting my hand as he might an obedient pet. He surely knew what I was thinking.

I shifted my gaze from my hem towards the high windows near the ceiling. It had always intrigued me that all but one of the windows had clear glass. Perhaps Henri was right to leave the cathedral be. The sobriety made that single, richly stained glass window all the more beautiful for its presence.

We were nearly there and I finally had to look ahead to the cluster of men awaiting me: priest, husband-to-be, twin. Felix glanced over his shoulder, flashed me a devil-be-damned grin and whispered something to the man he stood next to. But the groom did not turn; he stood patiently, as he had waited all of his life for me to grow up and be old enough for him to steal me from my family.

Henri and I drew alongside. I stood nearly shoulder to shoulder with Aimery but he would never see me as his equal, never recognise me as my own person; from today my role was to support his every need and, above all, deliver him the heir he now required . . . and perhaps a few as spares.

Only months ago I'd listened to the men talking about war, but the conversation had a distant quality as though even they believed it couldn't ever happen. The news filtering through newspapers and various reports suggested the shared royal blood of Queen Victoria's grandchildren may not be enough to save Europe from dragging itself into all-out war because of the troubles between Austria–Hungary and Serbia.